THE DARKNESS
AND THE DAWN

THOMAS B. COSTAIN

THE
DARKNESS
AND
THE DAWN

A Novel

DOUBLEDAY & COMPANY, INC.

Garden City, New York

With the exception of actual historical personages, the characters are entirely the product of the author's imagination and have no relation to any person in real life.

THE DARKNESS
AND THE DAWN

Book I

CHAPTER I

1

OF ALL the myriad dawns which had broken over the dark Wald this one was the most beautiful, because never before had nature been afforded so much assistance. Three mounted figures occupied the crest of the hill: Macio of the Roymarcks, who had been the handsomest man on the plateau in his day, and his two daughters, both of whom were lovely enough to aid the sun in achieving a moment of transcendence. The morning vapors, which the natives called the rawk, had been dispelled and the long grass looked almost blue. The hills behind them were a rich blending of colors, gray and mauve and purple and even a hint of red. The silence was complete, as it should be at such a moment.

The three riders were not concerned, however, with the beauty about them. They sat their horses in a motionless group, gazing fixedly in the direction of the flat meadows to the east.

"I hear them," exclaimed Laudio, the elder of the two daughters. She was a slender girl, dark and vivid and with the fine eyes of her father.

A faint thud of horses' hoofs sounded in the distance. Macio nodded his head with its rather noble brow and ran his fingers excitedly through his beard, which was turning white. "As soon as Roric passes that clump of trees," he said, "he will give Harthager his head. And then we will be able to judge."

"I see them!" cried Ildico, the younger daughter. Her voice was a light and pleasant treble. Occasionally the dark race which peopled the plateau produced a phenomenon, a daughter with hair like the sun and eyes like the vibrant blue of Lake Balaton at midday. Ildico was one of these. Laudio would rank as a beauty anywhere; save in the company of her younger sister, where she went unnoticed.

After a few moments of intense concentration, Macio sighed

with deep content. "We may put our doubts aside," he said. "Look at the action! He has much of strength and will. I am almost ready to declare that this morning we shall crown a new king of the Roymarck line."

"Ah, Harthy, my sweet Harthy!" breathed Ildico in an ecstatic whisper. The delight she felt caused the tips of her red leather riding shoes to curl up more than even the cobbler had intended.

An interruption occurred at this point. Despite the intensity of Macio's concern in the performance of the two-year-old Harthager, he turned to look in the opposite direction. A second horseman was approaching them, riding at an easy gallop. The head of the family looked back at his daughters with a disturbed and angry air.

"Who can this be, spying on us?" he asked. "I decided to start the test before dawn so that no one would be around. If we have ever had a secret which needs keeping, this is the time. I don't want anyone to know yet how fast the black is."

"Can we signal Roric to stop?" asked Ildico.

"It's too late to do anything."

Roric was already riding across the flatlands at a speed which seemed to increase with each stride. Harthager, a black thunderbolt, was in his full stride. Macio looked at a strange device he carried in the palm of one hand which might have been called the rude forefather of the sandglass. He whistled shrilly. "I can hardly believe it!" he exclaimed.

"It's Ranno of the Finninalders," said Laudio, who had continued to watch the leisurely approach of the other horseman. "I thought it might be and now I recognize the feather in his cap."

"Young Ranno!" cried her father. "I would rather share our secret with anyone else on the plateau than young Ranno. What brings him here at this hour? How did he know we were going to have the test this morning?" A flush of irritation had spread over his handsome features. "Someone must have given it away."

"You are wrong if you think I did," said Laudio. "But I don't see why you are so upset about his coming. He can't do us any harm."

"You think not? It's not only our chance in the races which is at stake. Don't you realize that we are under the thumb of a man who claims everything for himself? If Attila gets wind of the speed of this youngster, he won't wait to take him off our hands."

"Ranno is honorable!" cried Laudio, indignantly.

"Honor does not count when it comes to horses. I have learned that through bitter experience." Macio looked suspiciously at his dark-haired daughter. "Are you sure you did not invite him?"

Laudio stared at him defiantly. "Why do you always suspect me? I have already said I had nothing to do with it. But I am glad he has come. He is paying us a neighborly visit. That's all."

She tapped the flank of her mount with the blue leather of her heel and rode off to meet the visitor. Although she had neither saddle nor bridle, she sat her horse with ease and mastery. It was the proud custom of the people of the plateau to ride bareback and there was not a single bit of equipment among the five of them, Macio and his two lovely daughters, his son on Harthager, and the visitor riding in from the south.

The pounding of the black's hoofs was now like thunder from the hills. Macio looked again at the device in his hand. "It passes all belief. It is a miracle." He scowled back over his shoulder. "What a bad stroke of luck that he is here! He always looks after his own interests. They have always been that way, the Finninalders. Do you think this is just a friendly call, Ildico? At this hour of the morning? Mark my words, young Ranno has heard something."

"Do you think you should express doubts of him before Laudio?" The younger daughter looked unhappy over the situation which had developed. "I am afraid you have hurt her feelings badly."

"I am upset myself."

Harthager was nearing the end of his run and Macio did not raise his eyes from the device. "Another hundred yards and we will know!" he said, in a tense whisper.

"Will it be a new record?" asked the younger daughter, excitedly.

"I can't be sure yet. But I think so. Yes, yes! It is certain now. He will be well ahead."

Ildico clapped her hands exultantly. "Harthager the Third!" she said.

"Yes, Harthager the Third."

Using only his knees, Roric checked the speed of the black two-year-old and brought him up the slope of the hill to reach a stand-still in front of them. He nodded his head at his young sister and grinned broadly.

"How did you like that?" he asked. He was a taller copy of Laudio, slender and handsome and with a poetic darkness about him. "Didn't I predict we would win everything this spring at the Trumping of the Baws? That is exactly what we are going to do." Then he turned to face his father and his manner became anxious and solicitous. "Well? Was the time good, Father? Good enough?"

Macio leaned over his horse's neck to pat his son's shoulder. "Yes, my boy. The time was better than good. It was remarkable."

Roric smiled eagerly. "I thought it was. But I could not be sure."

"I began the count when you turned that clump of trees. There can be no doubt about it. He was well ahead of the record. I was particularly careful because I did not want to deceive myself."

The three exchanged smiles of delight over the result of the test. "I knew he could do it," said Roric. "In spite of what Brynno says, I didn't find him hard to ride, Father."

"Of course not!" cried Ildico, indignantly. "He's as gentle as a lamb."

Macio turned sharply in the direction of his golden-haired daughter. "Have you been disobeying me?"

The girl shook her head. "No, Father. But it has been a great temptation. You haven't been fair to me. Because I am a girl, you tell me I mustn't ride him. But he likes me. I think he likes me better than anyone. As soon as he sees me, he neighs and comes running to me. I am sure I would find him gentle."

Her father snorted indignantly. "You will never find out be-cause you are not to try. If you show any tendency to disobey me, I shall have you locked up." His voice took on an appealing tone. "Ildico, my beloved daughter, can you not see how dangerous it is?"

Laudio and the visitor had reached the crest of the hill by this time. Ranno of the Finninalders tossed one long and muscular leg over the neck of his horse and dropped to the ground. He had arrayed himself in considerable grandeur for this early morning visit: a tall peacock feather in his cap, a riding tunic of a lustrous green, wide trousers of yellow, a belt of gold coins so heavy that they clanked as he moved, shoes of green fretted leather, each fret stamped with the tree and raven of the Finninalders. Roric, who disliked this young neighbor, said to himself: "He has the look of a suitor in his eye. Which of my sisters does he come courting?"

"I offer you my most humble respects, Macio of the Roymarcks," said Ranno, bowing to the head of the family. He then turned to the younger daughter. "And to you, Ildico. You are looking more lovely than ever."

"We bid you welcome," said Macio. "But you come at a very early hour."

"I have had no sleep. Some visitors arrived last night from—from a point not far east. We talked through half of the night about what we may expect since a certain man of great power has planted his sword in the ground again. I then took horse and rode over, feeling that you would be interested in what they told me." He nodded his head and smiled. "It was a fortunate time I selected for my arrival. I have seen something this morning the equal of which I may never see again as long as I live."

The black was showing impatience at the inactivity in which he was being held. Macio leaned over and laid a reassuring hand on his moist withers. He then looked at his visitor. "You think well of him?"

"I thought I had a promising lot this spring," answered Ranno. "But having seen this one perform, I am out of conceit with all of mine. Did you make a count of his time?"

Macio nodded in assent. With a slight pressure of his knee, he brought his mount around until he faced the east. He raised one hand in the air.

"Listen to me, all of you," he said, with an almost fanatical gleam in his eye. "You, Roric, my son. And you, my two daughters. And you also, Ranno of the Finninalders, son of my old friend, who has happened to be here on this great occasion.

"You may think," he went on, "that I am making too much of what has happened before our eyes this morning. But I must say what is in my mind. It is known to all of you that the records of our race have been preserved only by word of mouth. That is why we have so little certain knowledge of our beginnings. We know that we come from the very far east, that at one time we lived within sight of the Snowy Mountains and that we migrated with the seasons. We have always been breeders of fine horses. Even in the days when we held out our arms to the Snowy Mountains on rising, it was so. We strove always to improve the breed. When we were forced to leave our ancestral grounds—for reasons long forgotten—and moved to the west, it was so. When we passed the Valleys of the Korama, of the Upper Volga, of the Urals, it was still so. The breed grew stronger when we sojourned in Sarmatia and later when we settled for many generations in Illyricum. Now we have lived for centuries on this fruitful plateau. We are few in numbers and so we could not hold out against the might of Rome. Today we are a part of the empire of Attila. In spite of our political misfortunes, we have never ceased to strive for supremacy in the breeding of horses."

He paused and looked in turn at each of his listeners. "This morning we have accomplished at last what we have striven for so long: the goal of our ancestors, even when they were harried westward and left their footmarks in unfamiliar sands. I declare to you, after an accurate count of the time, that we have raised in Harthager the fastest horse the world has ever seen."

There was a moment of silence and he then turned to young Ranno. "We have had the honor of raising him and we are proud of it. But in the end he will belong to our people and not to us. And that means, young Ranno, that the secret must be kept close. We do not want him taken away from us. That is what will happen if a whisper of today's test gets out."

The representative of the Finninalders bowed soberly. "You can depend on me to say nothing of what I have seen," he said.

2

What followed was in keeping with certain customs which had been developed over the years in the family of the Roymarcks. Ildico, as the youngest, took the lead. Her hair, showing a slightly reddish tinge under the warm morning sun, streamed out behind her as she set her horse to a triumphant caracoling. Her father had dismounted and walked proudly at the black's head.

"Stand back!" Ildico cried to the handlers and field workers who came running out as soon as they arrived in sight of the horse sheds. "No one is to go in yet except Justo, who will heat the water."

The overseer, who was withered with age, asked in a quaver, "Then we have a new king, Lady Ildico?"

She gave a proud nod and her eyes beamed at him. "Yes, Brynno." Her voice was high-pitched with excitement. "A new king indeed! A great king, an emperor! The fastest we have ever had. My father says he is the fastest of all time. Tell Justo to hurry."

By the time they reached the sheds Justo had placed red-hot stones in the water trough and it was hissing furiously and sending up clouds of steam. Not knowing the custom, Ranno followed the members of the family inside and was unceremoniously ushered out by Ildico.

"I am sorry," she said, giving his arm a shove. "This is for Roymarcks only. Finninalders stay outside." Then she laughed. "It's what we have always done. No one else is allowed to touch the horse or to watch."

Roric and the two sisters dipped pieces of soft cloth (for nothing rough must touch the hide of the new king) in the warm water and proceeded to give the black a rubdown which could only be described as reverent. They hummed an air as they worked, a monotone which repeated itself over and over, with curious quirks and twists. The head of the family intoned words to the air. It might have seemed that he was telling of the great deeds of the Roymarcks but instead he was reciting the story of the fine horses they had raised. He told of a powerful black on which an emperor of Cathay had ridden (until he became frightened and fell off), of a gallant roan which had carried his master across all of Sarmatia in three days, of Harthager the First and a mad gallop he made to Vindobona (which later became a famous city named Vienna) without a single pause to take the word of Roman legions approaching, and who had died of his efforts. At the finish Macio said, with a hint of moisture in his eyes, "The bones of these kings have moldered away and today a new king stands in their stead."

When the glossy coat of the new king had been thoroughly rubbed and dried, and he had been patted and made much of, and a lump of saccharum had been secretly conveyed to him on the palm of Ildico's hand, he was given the smallest kind of a drink of water. Then a basin of oats was placed before him and he began to eat with finicky tremors of his mouth and nostrils.

In the meantime the head of the household had been searching in a chest of extreme age and dilapidation, which looked as though it had originated within sight of the Snowy Mountains also. He emerged with a jeweled headpiece and a pair of ancient combs. While he adjusted the headpiece, his two daughters employed the combs in smoothing out the mane and tiring it with silken tassels.

The toilet of the monarch having been finished, Macio walked to the entrance and threw the door open. He said to the servants who had pressed against it in a state of intense excitement, "You may come in." Ranno followed them into the shed and, giving Ildico the benefit of a wink, he asked, "May a mere Finninalder enter now?"

Macio walked slowly to the other end of the long, dark shed. He took down a silver chain from a section of the wall where mementos of the past were hanging. It was a handsome thing, heavily studded with opals and turquoises and squares of carnelian and sardonyx, and suspended from it was a silver figure of the Roymarck horse with rubies for eyes.

Harthager seemed to sense what was coming. He ceased eating and raised his head high in the air. The head of the family walked close to him and placed the chain around his neck.

"Harthager the Third," he said, with as much solemnity as a bishop anointing a king in a great domed cathedral. "May you be worthy of the Roymarck chain which so many of your forefathers have worn. We expect great things of you. We believe you are destined to be remembered—perhaps for all time."

Then he stepped back and stood in an expectant attitude, listening. The members of his family followed his example, turning their heads toward the door through which they could see a corner of the fenced meadows where all of the Roymarck horses had been collected. There was a long moment of silence. Then from the fields came the single neigh of a horse, a high, triumphant note. Another followed and then, almost instantaneously, the rest joined in.

Macio's face lost the look of doubt which had been settling

over it. He waved an arm in the air. "They know!" he cried. "They know what we have done. And they approve."

Laudio was smiling delightedly but Ildico gave full rein to her emotions. She did not care that tears began to stream down her cheeks when the black monarch pawed at the ground and trumpeted an answer to his fellows in the fields. She put a hand under her brother's arm and leaned her yellow head against his shoulder.

"Look at him, Roric!" she whispered. "See how high he holds his head. See the look in his eyes. He knows he's a king!"

When the excitement had subsided to some extent, Ranno came to Ildico and studied her face with a puzzled frown.

"It's true," he said. "You actually were crying. You seem to take this seriously."

"Of course I take it seriously," said the girl, turning on him, angrily. "It is the most important thing in the world to us. No, not quite that. It is the second most important thing. And let me tell you this, Ranno, I shall always remember this morning as one of the great moments in my life."

The visitor shook his head. "Do you look on me as a friend?" he asked. "An old enough friend to be honest with you? I am very much afraid that you are a fraud, my pretty Ildico. Consider for a moment that uproar from the meadows. Do you really believe it was a—a tribute from the rest of the stock? Latobius and Laburas, hearken to me, and all the other gods!"

Ildico looked at him so fiercely that for a moment he thought she was going to spring at him. He even took an involuntary step backward.

"Of course, I believe it!" she said. "Now I will be honest with *you*. Do you know why you have never been able to raise horses as good as ours? You don't love them and you don't understand them. You don't believe they have strange powers, that they can feel and hear things in the air. It's true. We believe it, all of us, we know it is true."

In spite of her earnestness, Ranno continued to regard her with an amused grin. "Have it your way, then," he said. "I accept the reproof. But I *did* see that ancient overseer of yours leave the shed before this—this touching ceremony began. Of course we should not be skeptical and say that he was going out to the mead-

ows to be there at just the right time; in other words, to make
sure that the uproar began at the exact moment."

"It is not true!" cried Ildico. "I hate you, Ranno of the Finninalders, for saying such things!"

He grew serious at this point. "No, no, not that, Ildico. I will
get down on my knees and beg your pardon. I will accept anything you tell me. But you must not hate me. *That* I could not
bear."

The ceremony over, the company walked slowly out of the
shed. Ildico, beside her father, was aware that the black eyes of
Ranno were still fixed on her with a disturbing intentness. She
said to herself: "Why doesn't he look at Laudio? He must not
behave this way. There will be nothing but unhappiness for all
of us."

3

It was a time of crisis in the kitchen, which constituted with
the long dining hall the largest part of the low red-roofed home
of the Roymarcks. The last smoked shoulder of ham hung from
an otherwise empty rafter. The casks which had held the salted
fish were empty. The supplies of vegetables buried in pits for
winter use were exhausted. It was a difficult thing to feed so many
mouths on dishes made of crushed grain and on eggs and old hens
no longer capable of laying eggs.

Ildico was in the kitchen, discussing what could be done with
a rather meager catch of fresh fish from a nearby stream when
she was summoned to attend her father. It might have been expected that on the death of their mother the older sister, who
seemed most capable in her quiet way, would have assumed
charge of the household. Laudio was of a dreamy disposition, however, and not as practical as her beautiful younger sister; and so
the largest part of the burden had fallen on the decorative shoulders of Ildico.

"Where is the master, Nateel?" she asked, giving her remarkable hair a quick upward twist and binding it in place with a red
ribbon.

"In his room, Lady Ildico."

The life of the household centered in the dining hall and the
kitchen. The rest of the space in the house was given over to tiny

cubicles where the members of the family, the servants, and such guests as might be on hand spent the hours of darkness. They were small, dark, and airless, and the furnishings consisted of pallets of straw and pillows (for feminine use only) of feathers. The room of the master, however, boasted a chair, a bed, and a small tapestry on one wall. He was lying stretched out on the bed when his daughter answered his summons.

"Sit down, my Ildico," he said. "We have things to talk about. I have just said farewell to the young man. He asked me to say that he would have paid his respects to you and Laudio before leaving but that he had a very busy day ahead of him."

"He seems to be a very practical young man," remarked Ildico.

"He is indeed. I will come back to that later." The master of the household seemed unusually grave. "I had a talk with him after breakfast. The news from the Hun court is serious, my child. Attila has decided to make war—against Rome, according to most reports. He is going to raise the largest army the world has ever seen and he will demand from us, from the people of the plateau, all the men and money we can supply."

Ildico felt a sudden contraction of the heart. "Will Roric have to go?" she asked.

Macio gave a somber nod of affirmation. "I am afraid that he will be expected to command the men we send. A score, in all probability. He must have his baptism of fire sooner or later but it wrings my heart to think of him fighting in such a cause. Some men are saying that the time of the twelfth vulture is over and that now Rome must fall. Perhaps they are right. But must the mastery of the world be yielded into the hands of the Hun?"

There was a long pause and then Ildico sighed. "Will we be expected to supply horses?" When her father nodded his head in affirmation, she said, quickly, "But they won't take Harthager!"

It might have seemed that the prospect of losing the new king was as distressing as the certainty that the son of the house would lead a company in the fighting. Macio looked thoroughly unhappy. "How can we tell? They may demand from us everything which runs on four legs. Yes, they may take Harthager."

"Won't they realize that he represents centuries of careful selection and breeding?"

"I doubt if that will mean anything to Attila. He is more likely to say, 'What better ending for a fine horse than to carry one of my men into battle?' I am very much afraid, my child, that we must reconcile ourselves to losing our new king. His reign is going to be a brief one."

"My poor Roric!" said Ildico, her eyes swimming with tears. Then she added, "My poor Harthager!"

As though this were not enough trouble for one day, Macio proceeded then with another explanation. "I am not sure that this will be a complete surprise to you, my small one," he said. "You are very observant and I think you are wise as well. My talk with young Ranno was not limited to the matter of Attila's exactions. He has asked me for your hand in marriage."

"No, no!" cried Ildico. Her father's surmise had been correct. She had been more than half expecting some such announcement but this did nothing to lessen the distress she now felt. "It is Laudio he must ask for, not me. It has always been understood he would ask for Laudio."

"That is true. I discussed the match with old Ranno several times before he died and it was always Laudio then. She was our first daughter and you were no more than a very small and saucy child. But it seems that young Ranno has been thinking it over. It is you he wants. He made that very clear to me this morning."

"I won't marry him, Father!" Ildico spoke with a passionate earnestness. "I won't! He must be brought to his senses. He must be told that he is expected to marry Laudio, that it was so arranged between you and his father."

Macio was surprised at her vehemence. "But, my child," he said, "I cannot dictate to the young man and tell him who he should want as a wife. He is a very determined young man and knows exactly what he wants. What are your objections to him as a husband?"

"I don't like him!" Ildico's eyes, which ordinarily seemed soft and completely feminine, were now filled with a determination the equal of anything her suitor could have produced. "I have never liked him. I think—I actually think, Father, that I hate him!"

Macio was completely at a loss. He stroked his long beard and frowned as he studied her face. "But why this dislike? He seems to me a handsome man. He is managing his lands as well as his father did. He has ambition as well as ability."

"And what more could a girl ask?" Ildico indulged in a short and far from amused laugh. Her eyes had turned as cold as blue jewels and the line of her nicely cleft chin had become a study in self-will and determination. "Don't you know, Father, how generally he is disliked? Roric grew up with him and has always hated him. The son of the Ildeburghs, the boy who was carried off and sold as a slave——"

"And who escaped and is now in the service of Attila," said her father.

"He was a gentle boy, Nicolan of the Ildeburghs. I liked him very much. They say he has become a splendid soldier. He was the same age as Roric and Ranno of the Finninalders. He and Roric were close friends but they could not get along with Ranno. His servants are afraid of him. Make no mistake about Ranno, Father. If the time should ever come when we are free again, Ranno of the Finninalders would try to take your place as leader of our people."

"Now you are indulging in wild speculations. How can you tell what ideas the young man has in his head?"

"Look at him. Watch him. You can read his designs in those calculating eyes of his." Ildico had fallen into a breathlessness of speech in her desire to convince her father. "There is another reason. When that terrible governor was put over us by the Hun——"

When she paused, her father supplied the name. "Vannius?"

"Yes, Vannius. When he seized the Ildeburgh lands and killed the owner, old Ranno came to terms with him and took over the estates. I know you never speak of it but everyone in the plateau knows about it. Everyone knew it was an injustice and he was hated for taking advantage of a friend's misfortune. Young Ranno has shown no intent to right the wrong. He still holds the Ildeburgh lands." She got to her feet and looked down at her father with eyes which blazed. "Do you think I would marry him as long as he holds the lands of that unfortunate family?"

Macio rose in his turn. "You must not fret your pretty head, my Ildico," he said. It was clear he still regarded her as a child and not as a forceful member of the small family circle. "I did not know your feelings were so strong. But I confess I am still puzzled. Does Laudio feel as you do?"

The girl's face clouded over. After a moment she gave her head a shake. "No, Father," she answered. "I am very much afraid that Laudio loves him."

4

Macio was awakened that night by a steady pounding on the gate of the palisade which surrounded the house. He sat up on his bed and listened for a moment. There was not a sound in the house but this did not mean that everyone was sleeping. It was certain that many of the servants had heard and were lying on their pallets in silent terror, their heads tucked under the bed-clothes.

The head of the household, who would have been the head of the little nation of plateau dwellers if they had been strong enough generations before to maintain their independence, had little more stomach for venturing out into the darkness than his people. A stout Christian, he still believed that the night belonged to the Devil, as indeed did all the good priests in the world, all the way up to the great bishop in Rome who was called the pope. When Bustato, the major-domo, had closed all the doors and windows for the night and had bolted them securely on the inside, the master was as willing as the most apprehensive servant or the sulkiest groom to leave the great outdoors to the powers of evil. When the shutters rattled, he was as likely as any of them to say to himself that it was not the wind, that it was the Tailed One, the Flame-spitter, Old Horny (a few of the names they had for the Prince of the Underworld), trying to force his way in.

But there was something insistent about the pounding on the outside gate, a regularity which was human and not to be mistaken for the haphazard efforts of an angry devil to break through barriers before riding off on the wind to find some less careful victim.

Macio got out of his bed. "This must be seen to," he said. He reached in the dark for a winter robe lined with bearskin and slipped it over his shoulders. Outside the door he picked up a bow and pounded with it on a metal shield hanging on the wall. The sound reverberated through the silent household.

"Get up!" he cried, angrily. "There is someone at our door who seeks entrance."

The first to answer the summons was Bustato, the major-domo, looking thoroughly frightened.

"I am sure, Master," he said, "that it is no human hand knocking so loudly. It is the Devil demanding to be let in."

"I will open the gate myself," declared Macio. He glanced around him at the other members of the household who were beginning to gather. Their faces were moist with sleep and every bit of hair they possessed was standing on end with fright. "But you will all go with me."

"Who is it?" he asked, when they reached the gate in the outer palisade.

"It is not the Old One, Macio of the Roymarcks." The voice on the other side of the gate displayed no impatience at having been kept waiting so long.

"Ah, it is you, Father Simon," said Macio. He reached for the bar which kept the gate clamped securely in place. "What brings you to our door at such a late hour? Is there trouble?"

"There is always trouble, my son. But I think that on this occasion my motives are mostly selfish."

The gate swung in and the midnight visitor stepped into the compound with a readiness which demonstrated his desire for some supper and a couch for the balance of the night. It was very dark, there being no stars in the sky, and the low-burning torch, which Macio had taken from a sconce in the dining hall as he came through, gave no clear outline of the visitor's appearance, save that he was small and attired in a priestly robe. A water bottle was swung over one shoulder and he leaned on a pastoral staff.

"I came afoot," said the priest. "I thought it the safer way."

Macio led him into the house. The servants were already scattering with eagerness to finish their sleep. Bustato had closed the gate and was driving the bolt back into place. He struck with great vigor. Fear rode on open gates when night came down and the stars were hidden.

"You are here because of Stecklius," said Macio, when he and his guest had seated themselves in the hall where no one else could hear.

The priest nodded his head. "It is indeed because of Stecklius. He thinks he will win his way back into the good graces of Attila by making a determined effort to wipe out Christianity here."

"We have been hearing rumors about it. Has he any conception how many Christians there are on the plateau? You have been a faithful evangel, Father Simon."

"I doubt if he has a full list. But of that we cannot be sure. It was to warn you that I came. It is quite possible that his first move will be against you and your household." The priest indulged in a deep sigh. "Stecklius has sent me notice that I am to leave or face the consequences. Well, my good friend Macio, I do not intend to leave the plateau country which I have come to love. I have had such orders before and have paid them no heed. But this time I must go into seclusion, I think."

"I am happy to receive you in my house, Father Simon," declared Macio. "You will stay here with me and together we will laugh at Stecklius, that ugliest of all the dwarfs, that thick-skulled Hun."

"There was a hint in the message I had from the worthy Stecklius," said the priest, "that I should be wise enough to return to my own people and so cease from causing dissension and trouble in the realm of the great Attila. It is twenty years since I left the island of Britain and, if I returned now, I would find all my old friends and brethren dead or scattered. It is an odd thing that in the blessed island from which I came we cannot sleep at nights for thinking of all the wicked heathen here in the land of the Alamanni and up north where the Norsemen live. It is so easy to see the evil in other people and never recognize it in ourselves. If I went back I would not be content to try my hand at saving the unregenerate among my own people—where they exist in great numbers, I assure you—but I would soon be caught again with the old desire to be about my Master's work in distant fields. I would come back; and so there is no sense in my going away at all. No, I have lived here so long that I think that now I must remain, even if I have become obnoxious in the sight of Stecklius."

Ildico made her appearance at this moment, carrying a lighted lamp in her hand. Her hair was very much disheveled from sleep.

"I was told Father Simon had come," she said, "and so I had to welcome him, without waiting to attire myself properly."

The priest got to his feet. "I am happy to see you, my daughter. It is a long time since I have been here and our little yellow bird seems to have been growing up in my absence."

Macio addressed his daughter. "Our good friend has come to stay with us. He will be welcome to remain here as long as he can stand our tendency to think more of the welfare of our horses than the comfort of our guests."

"For a few days only," declared the priest, firmly. "As soon as I have made certain necessary arrangements, I shall retire into the sanctuary where I spent so much of my time years ago."

"The cave in Belden Hill?"

The lamp held by Ildico made it possible for them to see that the priest looked very tired. He nodded his head, which, after the fashion of the earliest missionary orders, was shaven in front.

"It is a dry haven I have on the Belden," said the priest, "and it is so well hidden away that I can stay there in peace. Do you think I would bring down the wrath of the Attilas and the Steckliuses on my dear friends by settling myself in their midst? No, it is kindly thought but in a very short time I must be on my way. In the meantime I shall be very happy to stay in that little room behind the hearth about which no one but you has any knowledge."

"And all the servants on the place," said Ildico.

"You know how little we have to fear from them, Father Simon," declared Macio. "You will be at least as safe in our dark hideaway as in the cave on Belden."

"And there is always food here," said Ildico. "I will see that something is prepared for you at once."

Through a suspiciously quiet house, the master conducted his nocturnal visitor to his own room. His groping hand found a particular place in the paneling and pressed down firmly on it. There was a sound of creaking and straining and then a section of the wall opened. A small room lay behind. It was large enough to contain a pallet and a narrow table with a pitcher and other domestic articles; and, because it was located between Macio's apartment and the great hearth in the dining room, it had the advantage of being warm at all times.

The apparatus which moved the paneling was cumbersome

and rusty and as easy to detect as the drawstrings in a magician's cloak. The little priest placed the candle, which Macio had given him, on the table and looked about him with a reminiscent smile.

"This is the fourth time I have been a guest in the hideaway," he said. "I think it likely that I have been the only one to seek the security it offers."

"You, and the children when they were small enough to play games of make-believe."

Ildico entered at this point with a platter of food. The little priest smiled. "Whenever I begin to imagine myself above the weaknesses of the flesh," he said, "my stomach takes me in hand and shows me my folly. I confess, my daughter, that I am very hungry. I have eaten nothing today save a piece of cheese and a swallow of goat's milk." He looked up at her with affectionate approval. "Ah, time is such a disrupter of families! It turns little girls into beautiful women and then tears them away from those who love them. You will not have this daughter of the sun with you much longer, my old friend."

"Very little longer, I fear," answered Macio. "I had a reminder of it this morning and have not yet fully recovered from the blow." He turned to his daughter. "The good father has come a long way and is very weary. We must leave him to his supper, and then the comfort of his couch."

The next evening, as soon as the sun had vanished from the western sky, Bustato went over the house with two helpers and proceeded to close all the shutters and lock the doors, ending in the dining hall where he fastened the bolts with a particular vigor. Then he set torches alight in iron sconces along the walls and placed lighted candles on the table.

Bustato then drew a bench away from the table and seated himself comfortably in the center. The two helpers placed themselves with equal nonchalance on each side of him.

Almost immediately thereafter the servants began to stream in. A stranger to plateau ways would have been amazed by the number of them. There were cooks and their assistants, chamber women, cellarers and wine drawers, ax and, as well, chimney men, horse trainers, grooms, field hands and workers from the manure pits who very humbly took seats at a distance from everyone else. They all wore the Roymarck livery, a band of blue around the neck of the tunic and the Roymarck horse embroidered on the right sleeve. There were enough of them to make it certain that no one had to work very hard: there were, clearly, three pairs of hands for every job. The ruddy-faced men and the buxom women looked well fed and content.

When Macio came in, followed by the three members of his family, the servants were seated in a solemn semicircle. They did not get up nor did they indulge in any form of greeting. A bench had been kept clear in the center and here the head of the household seated himself with Roric on one side and Laudio on the other. Ildico had changed from the rose-colored riding clothes which she had worn all day into a white pallium which almost reached the floor and allowed no more than an occasional glimpse of her white sandals. She chose to seat herself beside Brynno, the overseer. They carried on a discussion in whispers, her blonde head with a pink ribbon around it nodding earnestly, until the head of the family turned a stern and reproachful face in their direction.

Macio looked about him then and broke the silence officially. "Is everyone here?"

Craning necks uncovered the fact that only old Blurki had not put in an appearance. He was a misshapen, ill-tempered curmudgeon with a sharp tongue in his head who served as jester for the household and further enhanced his value by doing sundry chores about the place. He was responsible for bait for the fishermen, he kept the hearths blazing when once lighted and, if he failed to earn one loud and general laugh during the course of an evening, he would have to stay up to wash and dry all the flagons and drinking mugs and hang them up on nails in a beam across one end of the long room. Whenever this happened he would mutter bitterly over the task about the knuckleheads, the ninny-noodles, the suetguts who did not know a good joke when they heard it.

"I placed him outside as lookout," said Bustato. To justify his choice, he added, "He always sings off the pitch."

"Then give the signal," said Macio.

The man who sat nearest the hearth tapped with his knuckles on the wall. There was the same sound of creaking and straining as the dilapidated machinery proceeded reluctantly to do its work. In a moment Father Simon in his full robes stepped out into the light of the long dining hall and walked slowly to a position in front of the rows of benches. The whole company rose and began to sing a hymn, one of the very early ones which had been falling into disuse as ritual had developed in the services of the Church.

The little priest, singing louder than any of them in a bass voice surprisingly robust in one of his stature, looked about him and felt his heart fill with a deep sense of happiness.

"How firm they are in the faith!" he thought. "I was right to come here and to stay, even in the face of the early discouragements. My poor efforts have been bounteously rewarded. No longer do they worship their Wotan, the All-Father, or Thor the Thunderer. They have lost all belief in Asgard, the city of the Alamanni gods, and all fear of the coming of Ragnarok, the day of dreadful strife. They are Christians and happy in the teachings of the Lord Jesus Christ. Stecklius may harry me from the plateau but he cannot dim the belief and the peace I read in every pair of eyes before me."

CHAPTER II

1

THE MAN Who Wanted the World was moody and irritable. In the murky closeness of the partially subterranean room where he worked, sprawling on a bench without a back, he glared at Onegesius, his chief minister and aide.

"You say the last of them, this German prince, has arrived. Why are you sure he is the last?"

It was his custom to demand explanations many times and, if any divergence could be detected from previous versions, he would explode into rage. "Even you—the only one I have trusted —you are now trying to deceive me!" Knowing this, Onegesius proceeded warily with what he had to tell. "*Mursa*, there are ten of them in my hands now. The German arrived this morning in chains. Our men are watching in all parts of the empire for any further signs of disobedience. But there have been none. The other rulers are showing readiness to meet the full demands you have laid on them for soldiers, horses and money. But be sure of this, O King of Kings: our men have not lost any of their vigilance. They are watching. They see everything, they hear everything. If there is any sign of change, we will know at once."

They were referring to the heads of states which had been submerged in the conquering advance of the Huns; first under Rugilas and now under the great, the omnipotent, Attila. The ten prisoners were chiefs of Teutonic countries or kings of racial pockets in Scythia or even *skiptouchoi*, the barons of the Sarmatian people. They had refused to supply Attila with the sinews of war.

For the better part of a year the Scourge of God (a title which Attila accepted with considerable inner satisfaction when it was first applied to him) had been working without cessation on his plans to assemble the largest army the world had ever seen. The strain had not impaired the strength of his thickset body but it had taken toll of his nerves. His eyes had always been sunk deep beneath his bushy brows; and now they gleamed like a wild beast's in the darkness of its lair or, more nearly perhaps, like fireflies in the eye sockets of a skull.

"They must die!" he cried, in a sudden fury. "There must be no delay in teaching the world a lesson."

"They have not been tried, Great Tanjou."

"Their guilt is clear to me. Nothing else matters."

Onegesius was a man of good address but he was a subordinate by nature and a timeserver by acquired instinct. He had never pitted his ideas or his convictions against those of his master. But on this occasion he was shocked into a hasty word of protest.

"But surely, O Lord of the Earth and the Skies, it would be wise not—to be too hasty. Some of them, as you know, are the heads of powerful states. If their guilt could be established before you took their lives——"

"No!" Attila's heavy fist fell on the flimsy table at which he sat. "There is no time. In six weeks, in two months at the most, I must have my army ready. I must be prepared to march. To hold a trial and then see that the evidence was used to influence the minds of people would take all of that time. It is a swift lesson they need. A sharp and terrible one. These heads of states who disregarded my orders must pay the price of their treason at once. Then there will be haste to obey me."

He got to his feet and began to pace up and down. His legs were short in proportion to the rest of his body and the extreme heaviness of his torso made the disparity seem greater. He was in a physical sense a Hun of Huns: his head was as round as a melon, his eyes were small and with an almost porcine suggestion about them, his nose was short and with a slightly comic upturn. He was not in any sense a comic figure, however. There was power, cruel and inexorable, in every line of him. Men felt terror on seeing him rather than an inclination to laugh.

"What I shall do"—he spoke as though he had a full audience of his subordinate rulers about him instead of one subservient official—"is to make of their deaths a great spectacle. Listen to me, Onegesius, and make certain that you carry out my orders without slip or omission. Summon everyone tonight to the square. There must be a special place, raised above the rest, for the heads of states who have obeyed me, and for the generals and the officers of my household. There must be another space kept clear where all eyes can rest on it. Here there will be a row of ten seats and the block will be set up in front of them. I shall not be there. For the moment I have ceased to be one of you. I am the power above who has decreed the punishment." He suddenly threw out both of his arms and cried in an angry voice, "I am too weighed down with burdens caused by the disloyal conduct of these men to waste time in seeing them die!"

He fell into a silence while he continued to pace the room, with a rolling gait like a sailor's.

"The first night—tonight—only two of them will die. Lots will be drawn beside the block while the ten traitors watch. The two whose names come out will have their heads chopped off at once. Tomorrow night there will be the same ceremony and two more will die by lot. This will continue until they have all paid the penalty of their disobedience. Onegesius, you are to find ways of making this a spectacle which no one in the world will forget. Perhaps it should be decreed that the ten traitors sit in that grim and uneasy row in sackcloth. I leave all that to you."

Onegesius did not venture any further opposition. "It is your will, Great Tanjou," he said. "It shall be done."

2

At noon each day Attila repaired to the Court of the Royal Wives. Hun women were not subjected to the strict rules of the East which confined women to the harem and turned them into closely swathed wraiths with faces hidden from alien eyes. The wives of Attila's bowlegged warriors were free to come and go, to gossip, to stand in their doorways and toss insults at passers-by. But these rules had to be amended where the royal household was concerned. The leader of the Hun people had too many wives for that. Infidelity would soon raise its head if this large accumulation of neglected womankind were allowed to mix freely with the world. Accordingly they were kept in a town within a town, a collection of small houses behind a twelve-foot log wall. Behind this wall they were allowed every liberty accorded the wives of general or councilor or bowman.

Usually Attila donned his best attire for this pleasant daily function, a tunic of blue silk which fell to his knees and was elaborately embroidered with gold, and a three-cornered hat centered with a large ruby and an eagle's feather. But it had been most unseasonably hot and all through his hours of toil that morning the great conqueror had worn nothing to cover his thick torso. He rose slowly to his feet and scowled at the sun.

"I am pressed for time and in any event it is too hot to dress," he grumbled. "My little lotus blossoms will have to take me as I am." He looked about him and called in a sharp tone: "Giso!"

His personal attendant, who had not been visible for hours, appeared instantaneously. He was fat and greasy and, even in a race noted for the flatness of its snouts, he had undisputably the ugliest of all human noses. He walked with a stiffness of gait which would have puzzled anyone who did not know that Giso had been born a slave. It was the amiable custom of the Huns to cut the sinews in the heels of their slaves to prevent them from running away.

The attendant stopped short and regarded his master with a questioning eye.

"Has the blue tunic worn out at last?"

"The blue tunic is as good as ever." Attila was parsimonious to an extreme degree, grudging every coin which had to be spent for anything save the maintenance of his great army. The garment in question was the only one he possessed which had any pretensions to elegance. It had served on all state occasions for many years.

Giso was the only man in the Hun empire who dared to trifle with the white-hot temper of Attila. He grinned broadly. "What a pleasure this is going to be!" he said in a low tone, but one loud enough to carry to the imperial ears. "What a treat for all the little hearts fluttering so furiously behind the high wall."

Attila eyed him with every evidence of distaste. "I sicken of your stale jokes," he said. "Someday soon—it may be this very day —a spirit will make its way up into the clouds. The head it carries tucked under its arm will be yours."

Giso always knew when he had gone too far. He was prompt to make his peace. "I will not care," he said, "if it is from one of the seven hills of Rome that my spirit takes its departure. But I must see you standing there with all the world at your feet before I die."

They turned their steps, debating bitterly as they went, to the center of the huge clutter of plain log buildings which made up the capital of Attila. Guards with drawn swords stood outside the gate of the Court of the Royal Wives and they shouted, "The Lord of the Earth, the Mighty Tanjou!" as soon as the half-naked figure of Attila appeared there. The cry could be heard repeated from all parts of the temple of femininity until the loud beating of a brass gong drowned out other sounds.

It had once been the custom for all of the wives to rush out from their small houses on his arrival, dressed in their best, and most shrill and excited in their welcome. Attila had enjoyed this kind of reception at first. He liked to pat and pinch the ones nearest him and to bandy coarse jokes with them. Gradually, however, he had lost his taste for it, finding it easier to select his wife for a day and a night without all of them clamoring for his attention. It happened that he had taken forcible possession of a Grecian city in the course of his quarrels with Constantinople some two years before and one of the prisoners was a Roman official named Genisarius. It was known to Attila, who gleaned every little bit of information which might be useful from the reports of his spies, that Genisarius had been in charge of a royal household and had kept it in ease and quiet. The apprehensive prisoner was placed accordingly in charge of the busy village of the conqueror's wives, and with the use of systems of his own had brought peace out of chaos.

Attila was conscious that scores of bright eyes were watching him from the corners of windows and by other surreptitious methods. This pleased him and he strutted a little and puffed out his deep chest. He was not well pleased, however, when he saw that a member of his huge establishment had seen fit to disobey the order openly. In a small back yard there was a patch of red which resolved itself on closer scrutiny into the figure of one of his wives. She was leaning on the bark fence and watching him intently.

The fact that this particular wife was the possessor of a dark and lively eye and was moreover of a pleasant plumpness did nothing to diminish Attila's displeasure. He racked his mind to recall her name and finally succeeded.

"That is Attamina, is it not?"

Giso nodded. "Attamina it is, and if you have any desire for my opinion, she is one of the best of the lot."

"I seldom desire your opinion, and certainly not in this."

Not daunted in the least, Giso volunteered some information about the solitary and somewhat pathetic figure in the bare yard. "You got her in one of those towns in Moesia that we sacked so thoroughly. The place had been burned and we thought everyone was dead. The officer you sent to investigate came across this one hunting through the refuse for food. Her face was black and she was nearly naked and she spat like a wolf cub when he dragged her in so you could look her over." Giso gave his head an admiring nod. "Ah, Mighty Tanjou, what an eye you have for them! You said at once, 'She will be worth while when she has been cleaned up. Bring her back after she has been washed and fed.'"

"She *was* worth looking at," declared Attila, with a reminiscent twinkle.

"You have not sent for her," said Giso, after making a mental calculation, "for more than three years."

The good humor which had been slowly winning its way to the surface in the royal mind deserted him completely at this. "Oaf and slave!" he cried. "Is it concern of yours what I do about my wives? I will not have you spying and keeping count on me in this way!" He looked in the direction of the disobedient wife and was startled to see her raise her hand in a wave of greeting. "She has never learned to obey," he said, in a grumble of annoyance. "Still, I must call her in again. I've been forgetting how diverting she used to be. She *was* like a wolf cub." He frowned at Giso as an indication that his lack of tact had not been forgiven. "Go and warn her that the laws of the household are not to be broken in this way."

Most of the houses were small, containing not more than one room, but there was one which towered above the others and had rounded pillars at each corner. This was the house of Cerca, who had been the favorite wife for some years because she was the mother of his oldest son, Ellac. There were many rooms in Cerca's house and the furnishings were quite luxurious. She was not subject to the rules which bound the other wives. This was made evident when she came down the steps to greet him as he passed.

Cerca was no longer young. There were wide streaks of white in her hair (apparently she scorned the use of dye to which most women resorted) but she had kept herself slender. Her richly embroidered dress of scarlet and gold was in good taste. She smiled invitingly.

"I have seen little of you of late, O Great Tanjou," she said. Her voice was pleasantly modulated.

Attila stopped. "Has it not come to your ears that I am raising the largest army the world has ever seen? That I am on the point of embarking on the greatest war in all history?"

The favorite wife smiled. "I listen eagerly to everything I can hear about your plans. But, O Mighty King, you so seldom see me when you visit us now. Sometimes you notice me and smile. Sometimes you brush past me as though I do not exist."

"My mind is filled with many things," muttered Attila. It was clear that he was uneasy. It was no secret to those about him that this fierce and unforgiving man was indecisive in matters which pertained to his wives. He often tried to evade the issues which the size of his household created.

The fine dark eyes of Cerca compelled him to look at her. "I must talk with you," she said, in a tone half pleading, half insistent. "Have you forgotten the long talks we used to have? There was a time when you thought my opinion worth while and you liked to tell me about yourself. You even told me how much you hated that Roman boy Aetius, and how you became uncomfortable and silent when he was around and displaying his graces. I think perhaps, O Mighty Lord and Master, I was the only one you ever confided in to that extent."

Attila frowned at her impatiently. "Why are you stopping me to tell me this?" he demanded.

Cerca answered in an eager tone. "I have a reason, O Great Tanjou. It is about Ellac. Our son. Your first son, O Attila. He is afraid of you. When he is with me, or with his young companions, he is gay and full of life. He has the same masterful ways as his father. But when he sits by your couch, he is silent. You will come to think of him, I am afraid, as dull and lacking in spirit.

But that would be wrong. Oh, so very wrong! Ellac is a true son and copy of his father."

"I do not understand the boy," admitted the Hun leader.

"It may be that you have come to prefer other sons." The face of this wife, who was still counted the favorite although Attila seldom summoned her now to his own palace, had flushed with resentment. "I hear it is being said."

Attila had been on the point of brushing by her but at this he stopped. "What is being said?" he demanded to know. "Who is saying it? Have you been listening to those two brothers of yours?" He shook his head angrily. "They have always been dissatisfied. They both thought I should find governorships for them in the provinces. They even thought I should give them high commands in the army. They are nothing but troublemakers!"

"Attila, my lord!" cried the wife. "This has nothing to do with my family. My brothers have said nothing to me. It is a matter between you and me. I want you to pay more attention to Ellac, to find out for yourself how fine he is." She reached out and grasped one of his arms. "This I ask of you, O Attila. Take your eldest son, take Ellac with you when you ride to this war. He is old enough. And it is his right to be with you."

Attila paused and proceeded to give this suggestion the fullest consideration. "I am getting old," he said, finally. "It is time my soldiers saw a son riding with me." He nodded his head. "Yes, it is his right. He is my first son. He is the only one old enough to go." He gave Cerca a somewhat grudging look. "There. Does that satisfy you?"

The face of the favorite wife lighted up. "It is all that I ask, O King," she said. Then she touched his arm again, lightly, pleadingly. "Unless—O My Master, unless you can find it in your heart to take me back into your good favor again! I know it is much to ask because you have so many wives. But I love only you."

Attila said, "Humph!" and brushed by her. The matter was settled and he wanted no more talk about it.

He made his way to a central building of considerable size and even some pretension to beauty; it had been designed by a Chinese architect. Professing to scorn all culture, the emperor had been known to say that when he reached Constantinople and Rome he would not see this structure's equal. It had a red tiled roof and the interior was cool and aseptic with marble walls and floors.

Genisarius sat at a table, nervously fingering a pile of parchment sheets. He was a small man with a skin as dead white as a reptile's eggs in contrast with the wiry blackness of his hair and beard. Beside him sat a plump and attractive woman whose eyes were now a faded gray and whose hair showed traces of white through the inexpertly applied dye. This was Aja, who had once been the favorite wife, many years before, and who now acted in the capacity of a household duenna. There was a third occupant of the room, a slender girl who sat in a corner with her head lowered and did not look up when he entered.

Genisarius and Aja prostrated themselves on the floor immediately, intoning, "O Great Tanjou, we are your unworthy servants." For perhaps the only time since he had seized the reins of absolute rule this caused him annoyance.

"Get up!" he ordered, irritably. "Do you think I enjoy seeing nothing of my people but the backs of their heads and their big rumps sticking up in the air? It is not edifying."

The woman rose promptly. "There was a time, Mighty and Unconquerable One," she said, tartly, "when you couldn't see enough of mine."

Attila grinned at her audacity. This was the kind of talk he liked to have with his wives. "It was not any broader then than the spread of my two hands. And now see what you have done to yourself by so much guzzling of these rich sweets from the East and the honey tarts of the Romans." This proof of his own wit dissolved the vapors of ill humor in the great man's mind. "I am glad to see you, Aja, my partridge. I am glad to see you standing on your feet and looking at me with those queer eyes of yours. Not," hastily, "that I want the custom abolished. No word of what I have just said is to go out of this room. It is because I like to relax when I am with you. You know, don't you, my Aja, that I have always liked you?"

"Yes, O Master. Though you don't show it often."

"You held me longer than any of them. It was your uncanny light eyes and the sharpness of your tongue. You could always make me laugh. And you are one of my own people, the daughter of a brave soldier. Ah, if you had only given me a son!"

"I can't give you a son now, O Master. But I can still make you laugh."

This was a mistake on her part. Attila fell back into a defensive attitude at once. "You have had your turn," he said. He took notice for the first time of the girl in the corner. With a frown he motioned in her direction and asked in a whisper, "Which one is that?"

"That is the girl they sent you from Tiflis. Two years ago. Her father was a wealthy Armenian merchant and a Christian. The girl is a Christian too."

Attila nodded his head. "I recall her now. She is pretty enough but the wind would carry her away if my horsemen tried to toss her from lance to lance. And she could not speak the language. I saw her once only." He paused and a trace of his earlier irritability returned. "What can you do with a wife who says nothing and stares at you reproachfully with large eyes like raisins in a steamed pudding?"

Aja explained the situation in a whisper, although this was an unnecessary precaution. It was clear that the girl would not understand what they were saying. "She has not picked up one word of the language since. She lives by herself, never saying a word to anyone. She has been very unhappy because the others are beginning to play tricks on her. Last night"—Aja hesitated, fearing that he would not like the information she must now convey to him—"last night she tried to kill herself. She took a knife off her plate and drove it into her side. The knife did not get very far because it struck a rib."

Attila studied the bent figure of the girl with a puzzled frown. It was clear that he was uncertain what to do about this situation. "What tricks do the others play?" he asked.

"Well, sometimes they pretend to be Christians and they begin to sing hymns when she is with them."

The master of the household did not seem at all pleased. "One droopy hen like this might infect the whole flock," he said, in a grumbling tone. "And I have to confess to you, Aja, that I—I feel sorry for her. Those great dark eyes of hers keep coming back to me, now that I think of her again." He nodded his head in sudden decision. "For the first time I am going to get rid of a wife. But, make no mistake about this, I am going to make my generosity pay me well. We shall make a deal with that rich moneylending father of hers. His daughter will be restored to him if he pays us handsomely enough. I would not be surprised if I got the cost of equipping a whole company of horsemen out of this. Begin the negotiations at once, Genisarius."

This was the first intimation on his part that he was aware of the presence of Genisarius. The latter had been teetering nervously on his feet and dreading the moment when this would happen. Attila's eyes seemed to pounce on several piles of papers which, he knew, were there for his attention.

"You pinfeather from a black gander!" he roared. "You have your usual lists, I see. Names, names, names! Complaints about my wives and sly hints. You will drive me mad someday."

Genisarius said nothing but Aja went to his defense. "You have sixty wives!" she charged. "And nothing will suit you but to know everything that goes on. So, O Lord of All the World, you must have lists with names and accusations and sly hints." She stepped closer and confronted him, hands on hips. "I have said it before to you and now I say it again. You have too many wives. Get rid of most of them. Keep no more than, say, twenty. No man needs more than twenty wives."

"Because I am sending one of them away, you think I am ready to get along with as few as a fat thief of a goldsmith or a spindle-shanked bureau clerk?" Attila was now thoroughly angry. He glared at this wife who through all the years had remained his real favorite. "Take care or I will get rid of you. The kind things I said to you have gone to your empty head. It never pays to be kind, particularly to a wife." His frown became blacker. "Don't you know by this time, Aja, that I never give up anything that is mine? Not a foot of land, not an inch of shore, not a single little round gold dinar of the tribute they send me." He turned and barked at the palpitating Genisarius. "I'll not be bothered with you today. Take all your lists and your reports away, you ugly little mole. All I want of you now is a wife to sit beside me today and share my wine cup. What suggestion have you to offer me?"

Aja took it upon herself to answer. "There is a surprise." She walked to an inner door and gently tapped on a gong which had been taken from the palace of a Chinese prince. The servant who came in response received whispered instructions and the onetime favorite turned back then to face Attila.

"This one, O Lord of the Earth and the Skies, came this morning. With the prisoners from the north."

Attila asked suspiciously: "Is she young? Will she amuse me? Is her hair as yellow as the gold that this black spider," with a contemptuous gesture in the direction of Genisarius, "steals out of the accounts?"

"You must judge for yourself."

The girl in the corner had not moved. Her head had not been raised once. Attila motioned awkwardly in her direction. "Get that one out before the other comes," he whispered. "And let her know, if you can find a way, that she is being sent home."

The girl who was escorted in a few minutes later complied with all his demands. She was quite young and her eyes were blue; and it was clear they had once been accustomed to laughter even though the shadows of sadness gathered about them now. Her hair was not the dead yellow of gold but as vibrant and alive as a daffodil warmed to life under a spring sun. She wore a dress of green with slashings and gores and braidings of yellow to match her hair. It was made of the best silk from the East, for it frothed about her with every step and rustled in a way that was pleasant and exciting.

"She brought the green robe with her," explained Aja, noting a frown on Attila's face. But the latter had not been thinking of costs. He had frowned in bemusement over the beauty of the newcomer.

"Does she speak the language?" he asked in a whisper.

"A little. You must talk clearly and not be impatient if she is slow in finding her words."

Nothing was farther from the great man's intention than to display impatience. He took the little prisoner by the hand and led her to a corner of the room where he began to whisper.

"What is your name?"

"Swanhilde, O King."

"It is a pretty name. It is worthy of you. Do you find it hard to understand me?"

"No, O King."

"It is a good thing you speak the language, my child. We will get along well. It is hard to like a wife who does not know what you are saying and who just sits and stares at you."

She spoke with some hesitation. "But it is only a few words I know. Not yet many."

Her way of speaking the Hun language with its staccato and guttural qualities both pleased and amused him. There was a quaintness in her pronunciation of words which made him want to pat her pink cheeks. "I am going to like you very much," he said. He gave her the benefit of his very best attempt at a smile. His eyes gleamed and his lips formed a perfect sickle under his small nose. "Are you afraid of me?"

"Yes," answered the girl. "I am much frightened."

"That is good too. A wife, if she is to be a good wife, must fear her husband." How cool she looked! How slender and lovely! He took her face in his hands and gave it a playful shake. Then he looked up at the other occupants of the room. "I shall marry her at once. There must be no delay. You will make the arrangements, Genisarius." The conqueror stepped back and feasted his eyes on the surprise which this day had yielded. "I am well pleased. I am so well pleased that I must think of a suitable present for my new little wife."

But it was not to be as simple a matter as that. The bride-to-be hesitated and then she said in a low tone, so low that only the ears of the emperor could catch what she was saying, "Have you not been told that I am the daughter of Athalaric, the king of the southern Thuringians?"

Athalaric of Thuringia! He was one of the ten who had been condemned to a quick death a bare hour before!

"O Master of the World!" pleaded the girl. "If you want me as your wife, I will gladly take the vows. I will follow your custom and hand the whip to you at the same time. I will be a good wife to you. But I understood what you said about a present for me. Please, O Attila, make my present the liberty of my father! He has been a good king, a brave king, and oh, he has been the finest and kindest of fathers. To keep him a prisoner will be a sad thing for the people he rules and a sadder thing for me. It would break my heart."

Attila took her roughly by the arm and led her into a small

adjoining room. "Remain here," he said. Then he returned to the main apartment and confronted Aja and Genisarius.

"Why did you not tell me she is the daughter of one of the prisoners?"

"I was sure you knew," answered Aja.

"I was not told that any members of Athalaric's family had been brought with him."

"She was brought because the officers who made her a prisoner were sure you would be interested in her."

Attila's face now showed the sense of frustration which had taken possession of him. He asked, "Does the girl know her father is to die?"

Aja shook her head. "I think she fears the worst but she has not been told of what is to take place tonight."

The emperor spoke in a brooding tone. "The girl is beautiful. She is everything I want in a wife. I am sure I would love her more than any wife I ever had. But I cannot change this decision I have made because of—of a domestic consideration. I cannot spare Athalaric and behead the rest of them."

"I could talk to her," suggested Aja.

"No! That would do no good. I must talk to her myself." He looked at the woman who had been the first of his favorite wives and to whom he had given the compensation of a little authority when he relegated her to the shelf. His expression was one of angry puzzlement. "Why does the most desirable of all women have to be the daughter of a traitor!"

"There are other beautiful women in the world," Aja reminded him.

His manner showed increasing vehemence. "I could never want any other as much as I want this one."

He returned to the small side room. Swanhilde had been seated but she sprang nervously to her feet when he entered. Her face was pale and her cheeks gave the impression of having grown suddenly thin through the emotional strain she was experiencing.

"My little golden flower!" said Attila. "I want you to know that already I love you very much. But this also I must tell you. Your father and nine other rulers disregarded my orders to provide me with their full share of men and supplies. What am I to do? I cannot allow this disobedience to start in other parts of my dominions. My child, all ten of them must die."

"No, no!" The girl's eyes became distended with terror. "You cannot mean it. Oh, Great Attila, you are saying this to frighten me. You said you liked your wives to live in fear of you."

"I wish I could save you pain by being lenient with your father, traitor though he is. But, my poor little lotus blossom, I cannot change my mind about this. Because of personal feelings I cannot alter decisions of state." He took her by both hands roughly and possessively. "Listen to me. You are only a child. You will outlive what seems to you a tragedy now. You may even forget in time. All men must die sooner or later, even kings and rulers, even Attila, who is the greatest of them all. Are you listening to me?" He gave her a shake. "Come, listen with the greatest care. I needed no more than one glance at you to know that you will be my real wife, the one to stand beside me and sit near my throne and share in my approaching triumphs and glories. No woman ever has had the chance I am offering you. I shall make you, my lovely Swanhilde, the queen of all the world!"

She sank to her knees before him. "I will be your slave if you will spare my father. My good, my generous, my kind and loving father! If you kill him, I shall perish of grief. If someone must die, let me die in his place. Would it not be as much of a lesson to other rulers who perhaps have daughters too?"

He shook his head. "I cannot change what has been decided."

"Then let me die with him!" The girl was weeping hysterically now and clinging fiercely to his hands. "If my father cannot live, I will not want to live. O Great Attila, believe me when I say he was loyal to you but that he thought also of the welfare of his own people. Promise me this much: that you will give more thought to it."

Attila was not accustomed to debating his intentions at such length as this. "Give thought to it yourself," he declared, in a brusque voice. "I have known you a few minutes only but I have offered you a share in the kingdoms of the earth. I am accustomed to giving orders and not to explaining them, and I have no more to say than this: if you refuse my offer for a sentimental reason, you are not the woman I want beside me."

3

Attila did not allow these distressing complications in his personal life to interfere with his work. After leaving the Court of the Royal Wives, he sat in the open and held his daily Justice in the Gate, listening to complaints and settling disputes. He displayed good judgment and a sense of fairness in the decisions he rendered. His semi-nakedness did not disturb him at all, nor did it seem to give concern to those who came before him. After the last litigant had left, he retired to his great dining hall where in solitary state he consumed a knuckle of cold fat mutton and a handful of dried dates. He then went below for a consultation with a group of his officers.

They were seated about a long table, these thickset subordinates, and although they had emulated him in wearing no clothes above the waist, all of them had retained their high leather boots; which, having been well oiled and tallowed, stank most abominably. It was difficult for them, quite clearly, to sit on benches beside a high table when the racial habits of many generations had accustomed them to sitting only in a saddle or squatting on the ground. The feet of some of them did not touch the floor but swung back and forth like those of small boys on a school bench.

After listening for some minutes to a discussion of the routing of the armies from the East through the mountainous country called Dacia which lay to the north of the Eastern Roman Empire, Attila concluded there were things about them which he disliked more than the odor of their boots. He rose impatiently to his feet.

"What folly is this I have been hearing?" he demanded. "These orders you talk of sending will throw my dominions into disorder. We will have all my armies from the East marching through Dacia at once and crowding each other off the roads. They will eat the country bare like a cloud of locusts. They will halt to fight each other. I am not summoning these armies to war among themselves at fords and crossroads. They are to march against a common enemy." His eyes roved along the line of ugly, dwarfish faces at the table; he was contemptuous now and red with anger at their folly. "Wars are won by getting the best armies to the

most favorable of battlefields. You, my sagacious ones, will foun-
der my troops in Pannonian bogs and lose whole armies in the
passes of the Carpates Mountains. I have heard enough of this
for one day. I had hoped to get these details settled without calling on the Coated One, who is engaged in other work. But I see
he will have to be set to untangling these knots you have tied
between you."

The expressions on his generals' faces made it clear that whatever liking they may have had for this favorite tactician and assistant known as the Coated One had now been thoroughly
dissipated. They said nothing but exchanged glances more eloquent of their feelings than any words.

Attila felt no concern over the resentments of his lieutenants.
With a gesture he dissolved the meeting and watched them
shuffle out. Then, without realizing that he was allowing himself
to indulge in the vice of idleness, he dropped into a deep study.
For the length of time that he sat beside the deserted council
table his face fell into repose. It became less grotesque. Viewed
at this moment, it seemed almost to have a trace of nobility about
it as well as strength and cruelty. There was something about
him to induce a reluctant admiration.

Attila became conscious finally of the passage of time and also
of the presence of someone else in the room. He turned and saw
Giso standing inside the door. He frowned at the intruder.

"When did you come?"

"Half an hour ago. I did not dare interrupt the great thoughts
which filled your head."

The man who aspired to crush the earth beneath his heel gave
a scornful snort. "Why do you think it worth your while to tell me
lies? You could not have been in this room more than two or three
minutes. The meeting has just ended."

Giso gestured with both hands. "You are the Master of Life and
Death and cannot be wrong. This makes it clear that the truth is
not in me and that I have uttered a great and deliberate lie."

"What brought you?"

Giso did not hesitate to answer this question with his customary
glibness in spite of the doubtful mood of his master. "I knew you
would need me. The able soldiers who left the presence half an
hour ago—forgive me, O Great Tanjou—who left you two minutes

ago, had faces red with mortification. It was clear they had heard some painful truths. From this I concluded that their labors had brought forth no results and that you would have to call in a certain young Illyrian whose name is Nicolan of the Ildeburghs but who is usually called Togalatus, which means the Coated One. I came to report that the Coated One is expected to return this evening. As he is always on time, it may be taken for granted that he will be here in a few hours."

"He will have to work all night to straighten out this tangle and get a proper set of orders prepared."

For a moment it seemed that Attila was going to relapse into the mood of abstraction from which he had roused himself. Then he shook it off and, getting to his feet, began to stalk briskly about the room on his stumpy bowed legs. After completing several turns, he stopped in front of his attendant.

"I have reached a decision," he said. His eyes had lighted up and it was clear that this decision, whatever it might be, filled him with pleasure and excitement.

"I knew it was coming." Giso nodded his head with a corresponding eagerness. "It is about the ten prisoners."

At most times Attila was brusque in his manner and curt in his speech. He had, nevertheless, a curious gift for words which he could call upon when necessity arose. On the few occasions when he used it, his face would light up, his gestures would become eloquent, his speech would flow easily and convincingly. So it had been on the never-to-be-forgotten day when he presented himself to the chiefs of the Huns with the newly discovered Sword of Mars in his hands and had claimed their undivided fealty.

He began to speak now with an uplifted hand. "I have decided thus. Two only of the prisoners are to die. Who the two are will depend on the drawing of the lots tonight. I shall make no effort to control the decision. The executions will be carried out as I had planned except for one change. When the heads of the unlucky pair are in the basket, a message will be read to the people from the"—he paused for a moment and then began to describe himself with the candid insight he sometimes liked to display—"from this strange and harsh divinity who rules so large a part of the world. This contradictory man of destiny, who has been known to put the populations of great cities to the sword and to devastate whole countries but who does so because of state necessity and not through sheer cruelty, will show a side of himself which few men have suspected. His magnanimity. The message will pardon the other eight. This unexpected generosity will astonish everyone. It will leave the eight survivors with a sense of gratitude. The multitude of spectators will be thrilled and excited. They will even forget they are not to have the pleasure of seeing the rest die."

Giso found himself carried away with unqualified enthusiasm. "Mighty Tanjou!" he cried. "It is perfect! By such acts as this a great ruler commands the loyalty of those under him. All through the empire there will be nothing but praise for what you have done."

Attila nodded. "But they will find in my generosity no encouragement for further disobedience."

"It will be as sharp a lesson as lopping off all ten of the heads." Giso paused for several moments and then added in a tone which might best be described as sly, "Of course, there will be only nine names in the box from which the two are drawn."

Attila had gone back to his pacing but at that he swung around so suddenly that his inadequate legs threatened to fail in their task of supporting his heavy body.

"What do you mean?"

The sharpness of his tone caused the loquacious Giso to pause and consider. "Well, O King, it would be natural for you not to risk having the father of the beautiful German princess selected as one of the two chop-chop victims."

"You think I would resort to trickery?"

"It would not be trickery, Mighty King. You would be sparing this lovely young woman from the grief of losing the father she loves so much."

A curious change had been coming over the ruler of the Hun empire. He seemed almost to have accomplished the miracle of adding a cubit to his stature. A light which could be defined only as mystical had come into his eyes. Motives which could not be defined by any words had taken possession of him, racial beliefs which had governed his people when they lived their nomadic lives on the cold plains of northern Asia.

"Giso, you were with me when I carried into the kuraltai of my chiefs the sword which the gods had delivered into my hands, the Sword of Mars. Where else could it have been found save in the long grazing grass where the flocks of the Huns fed? That it was now mine meant that the hand of the god of war had touched my shoulder. It meant I must rule the Hun dominions alone and no longer share them with my brother Bleda. You knew then, even as I did, that my fate was hanging in the balance. Suppose they had not believed in the sword and in the strange way it had been entrusted to me? Then I would have died instead of Bleda and this great empire would never have been drawn together and welded into a mighty force. It was a chance that I took. But I did not hesitate to risk the decision of the dice of fate."

Giso knew the whole story, the real story, of the finding of the Sword of Mars. Nevertheless, he was carried away by his master's emotional statement. "Yes, Mighty Lord!" he said, in a rapt tone. "You have always listened to the voices which whisper in your ear and in none others."

"Do you think then that I would resort to trickery in the drawing of the lots tonight?" demanded Attila. "There is too much at stake. This lovely child, for whom I have conceived a passion which astonishes me, will be my wife if her father is spared. If he is chosen as one of the two to die"—the eyes of the great leader seemed to become lost in a strange fanaticism—"then I will know it was not intended I should have her as a wife, or that she should ride with me when I lead my armies to the conquest of the world." He seemed to lose all consciousness of his audience of one. "When it is a matter of state, I will lie and cheat and connive. I will resort to any measure. There are no limits to what I will do to achieve my ends. But this is different. Here the strange powers which have always guided me must be considered. If I took this decision into my own hands, would I not be risking their anger? This is for them to decide."

Giso had quickly relapsed into his normal frame of mind. "But it would be very easy, Master, to make the drawing come out as you want it. You desire this beautiful princess. Make sure you get her."

Attila shook off the mood in which he had been held. But he also shook his head and gave no indication of a change of purpose.

"My mind is made up, Giso. Let me hear no more from you." Then he added as though he found himself in need of reassurance, "The odds, after all, are very much in my favor. Five to one." He turned and gestured toward the papers and reports strewn over the surface of the table. "It may be I shall be occupied when the Coated One returns. A wedding night is not to be interrupted lightly. I shall depend on you to meet him and bring him here. Tell him my generals have failed to work out plans for the arrival of the armies from the East. He will know what is expected of him. And now send Onegesius to me."

When Attila had explained his new plan to Onegesius, the latter made the same suggestion about holding one name out of the box. This sent the emperor into another long and excited explanation of why he was leaving the decision to the forces which dictated so many of the most important things in his life. But Onegesius thought he knew his master better than that. As he left the presence, he said to himself: "But there will be only nine names in the box. I am not going to risk the blame if things should go wrong."

CHAPTER III

1

THE CANTONMENT of Attila, which he called his capital, lay on a flat and exposed plain between the Danube and the Theiss, scorning to take advantage of the defensive value of river and hill. There had been two reasons for placing it here. The Huns fought best on horseback and so the openness of the space gave them a chance to take full advantage of their cavalry strength in the event of attack. This was a point of such importance that no heed had been paid to other dangers, to the fact that the crude and hastily built town lay wide open to the assault of the sun under which it baked uncomfortably in the summer, without a single tree to shade it. In winter the cold winds blew down between the two rivers and raged about the wooden walls of the town, relentless and bitter.

The second reason for the selection of this site was of equal importance. This was the land known as the Great March, where the Marcomanni had lived, the bold bordermen who had never been conquered by the Romans. The leader who was now throwing down the gage of battle to the city on the Tiber could not have selected a better place for his headquarters than this plain which had never known the tramp of the legions.

Although the armies which Attila was gathering were for the most part in tented camps farther west and along the river, the imminence of war had turned the cantonment into a teeming city. The wives of the emperor, watching over the walls of their enclosure, saw soldiers stalking the streets by the thousands: great golden-haired fellows in gaudy tunics who came from the north and whose size and coloring caused the dark eyes of the women, having so small a share each in one husband, to widen and smolder; mounted warriors from the Hun horde who kept together in camps to the south; dark little men from the east with white robes flapping against naked, hairy legs and their hands ever on the hilts of sickle-shaped swords. Thousands of horses were staked out on the plains in all directions and it often seemed to the people of the town itself that the feeding of the steeds on which Attila and his men would ride to the conquest of the world was more important than the keeping of adequate food supplies for them. They did not complain of this. It was in all their minds that very soon now they would share in the rape of the world. "Woman," husbands would say to their wives, "you will sleep with me someday on a fine wide bed in which a drunken Roman emperor has lain." They talked of the great jewels and fabrics they would have, of the golden goblets from which they would drink rich, cool wine, of the slaves they would have at their beck and call. "Someday soon," Onegesius had once boasted, "the man who waits on me will be a Roman senator. I shall not spare the whip on his fat, white back."

During the afternoon of the day when Attila ordered the execution of the disobedient rulers and then fell in love with the daughter of one of them, a blare of trumpets was heard at the outer gate of the wooden town. Three melodious and unmistakable notes had been sounded. Men and women dropped their work and ran in the direction of the gate, shouting exuberantly to one another. Well they might, for this familiar fanfare meant that Micca the Mede had arrived with his caravan.

Micca was a mystery, even to Attila and Onegesius, who had been seeking for a long time to find the truth about his antecedents. He was an old man, tall and rather gaunt, with a silky beard, a benevolent eye, and a flow of talk in which learning joined with blandishment. He smiled a great deal and he was generous with his presents. It followed that all over the known world men spoke well of Micca and welcomed his visits. After trading was finished for the day, people would gather about him or sit in circles at his feet, and he would tell them long stories. No weaver of tales in a market place was more a master of drama and suspense than Micca. He never failed to hold his audiences in fascinated silence.

He was the most successful trader of the day and men assumed that he was enormously wealthy. The caravan with which he traveled consisted of a string of pack horses and half a dozen carts with four wheels which were painted a bright vermilion. What goods did he deal in? Everything. He sold jewelry, cloth, and silks from the East, weapons of all kinds, medicines and charms, articles of toilet, even confectionery and dried fruit. There was nothing, seemingly, that anyone might want which could not be produced from inside one of the vermilion carts. He went everywhere, it seemed. Reports would have him in Constantinople, in Rome, in cities of the East such as Antioch and Aleppo and Jerusalem, and sometimes even from towns in Gaul and Spain. But there was regularity in all his wanderings. He came three times a year to Attila's headquarters as faithfully and surely as a planet on its orbit. He was never early, he was never late. It was rumored that he owned caravans as well which plied back and forth in the Far East and that he had trading establishments in all cities.

The caravan did not enter through the gate, about which were grouped the buildings of the elaborate establishment of Onegesius. The vermilion carts were drawn up in a semicircle no more than a spit and a stride outside. Planks were produced and placed on trestles to form long tables. The goods were piled up high on the tables for the inspection of the people who came pouring out through the gate as soon as the three notes were sounded on the trumpets a second time.

The Huns no longer roved the plains and drove their flocks back and forth with the seasons. They had come into power and great affluence. But at heart they were still herdsmen. They had no skill in their fingers and no knowledge of handicrafts. In a very crude way they could fashion garments out of the skins of animals but if they wanted articles of cloth, linen, or silk they had to depend on barter. The coming of Micca was, therefore, both a pleasant interlude and an event of economic importance in their lives. They swarmed around his tables with hungry eyes, making their offers to his assistants with impatience and arrogance.

On this occasion Micca himself opened the proceedings with an exhibition for the benefit of the children. Calling them about him, he raised his hands to show that they were empty. Next he elevated them above his head until the sleeves dropped back to his armpits, proving that he had nothing concealed. Then, suddenly, there appeared in one of his hands a piece of elastic skin. This he blew up until it became a large head of Bilbil, the Wicked God, whose nose was as long as the snout of a wild boar and who had a forked tail. Tying up the end, he sent the little balloon floating out over the heads of the children. This he did half a dozen times until the young ones were running in all directions, waiting for the balloons to collapse and fall into their hands, crying excitedly, "Bilbil, come down!" and "Let me get hold of your tail, old wicked one."

The people of the town watched Micca while he performed a few tricks for their amusement. Heads could be seen all along the wall of the Court of the Royal Wives. Attila's little partridges were watching with a rather wistful interest; but not until Micca and his helpers had exhausted the possibilities of the town would they visit the Court. Trading there would not be very remunerative. Attila was close with his wives and they would have to pay for the few trinkets they bought out of their own meager savings.

2

Attila's palace, although it stood behind high wooden walls, was not large. To the eyes of his followers it seemed imposing, for it had gates with captured standards floating high up in the air, as well as the Hun royal standard with its crude symbol of the Gray Turul. The materials which had gone into the building of it had been planed and molded and even carved. Inside it consisted of a long room where the Great Tanjou dined with his staff. At one end was a raised platform with curtains screening it off from the rest of the room, and here Attila slept on a huge square bed which had come into the possession of his uncle Rugilas in the looting of a Byzantine city and had been brought all the way here on a wheeled platform with six horses dragging it. Beneath the dais were a number of small rooms, one of which served the great ruler when he immersed himself in the details of governing his loose-jointed empire.

It was in this corner, which was no more than ten feet square, that Attila now sat in a low chair behind a marble table which had once been a source of pride in some Grecian palace. He was

so busily engaged that he grunted impatiently when Giso parted
the curtains and entered.

"He has come," announced the attendant, in a cautious tone.
"He is out there, looking at the bed. I think he is wondering if
all your wives sleep in it at once."

"Who do you mean?"

"Who do I mean? Who else could I mean but that gentle-
speaking old ewe-neck who has just arrived." Giso's tone changed
to a grating whisper. "I mean that ferret in the guise of a harmless
mole, that grasping offspring of a father with no legal heirs. I
mean Micca the Mede."

Attila said without looking up, "Have him come in."

Giso seemed to resent the whole proceeding. "There is someone
else with him. The new one is to come in first."

"If it is so desired."

Giso was unwilling to leave the matter there. "If you saw a
woman wearing a spiked helmet, you would not believe her a
Roman soldier. This other one is wearing Micca's livery but you
can tell at a glance that he does not belong. Then who is he? And
what does he want?"

"Bring him to me and I will soon find out," said Attila, sharply.

The man who was ushered in immediately thereafter was small
and shrunken in frame like a pod which has withered on the vine.
He wore the coarse linen tunic with broad red stripes around the
neck and hem which constituted the livery of Micca but it was
obvious that he did not belong with the men of bulky thews and
horny hands who labored in the pay of the itinerant merchant.
He was more like an official in some governmental department
or a public scrivener, albeit he carried himself with considerable
dignity.

"My name, O Great and All-Powerful Attila, is Hyacinthus,"
said the little man, in a voice which seemed to confirm this identification. "I am a servant—I may say a trusted one, or I would not
be here on this mission—of the Princess Honoria."

Attila raised his head at this and gave his visitor a long and
steady look. "The Princess Honoria? Do you mean the sister of
my royal brother, the emperor of Rome?"

"Yes, O Mighty King. I am the bearer of a letter for you."
Hyacinthus produced the letter from a receptacle hidden under

his belt. He placed it on the table before the Hun ruler and then laid beside it a gold ring. "The ring is from my mistress, the princess. A mark of her respect and a proof that the letter is in her own hand."

Attila lifted the ring and gave it a quick examination. It was a plain circlet of gold, inscribed with the royal insignia. He recognized the markings and so nodded his head in acceptance of the authenticity of the letter. His mind was filled with speculations. Why should the Princess Honoria write to him? Was this just another effort to dissuade him from the invasion he was planning while the whole world watched and trembled? He tried to recall a story he had heard years before about the Princess Honoria but it eluded him.

"If the Great One does not read Latin——" began the envoy.

"I do not!" declared Attila, with a brusqueness of tone which placed the language of Rome far beneath his notice.

"Then may I read it to you, O King of Kings? The message it contains is most confidential and important. As you must be aware, the princess, my mistress, has been held in confinement for a number of years because of an episode which caused offense to her mother and to her brother, the august emperor."

The episode in question came back into Attila's mind. The princess had been indiscreet. She had taken as a lover a steward in her household. The fellow's name had been Eugenius and he had been a poor kind of lover for a princess of the Theodosian line. The man, quite properly, had been executed and nothing more had been heard of the princess except that she was being held in some kind of honorable but strict confinement. Attila's interest in the nature of the message from this lady of indiscretions began to mount rapidly.

Hyacinthus proceeded to read the missive in precise, clipped tones. It was in effect an offer of the hand of Honoria in marriage if he, Attila, Mighty Lord of the East, would rescue her from the irksome life to which she had been condemned and restore to her the estates and honors of which she had been deprived. Having completed the reading of the note, which was commendably brief, the envoy proceeded to explain that his mistress was watched so closely that it had been very difficult to get the letter out of the household. He, Hyacinthus, had found it necessary to don the disguise of a trader in the train of Micca in order to bring it to the mighty ruler for whose eyes alone it was intended. It would be wise, he added, with a shake of his close-cropped head, if the Lord Attila would keep the letter from all other eyes.

"I expect to die for the part I have played in bringing this to you, O King of Kings," declared Hyacinthus, with a dignity of resignation which raised him at once in the respect of his royal listener. "I will be well reconciled to my fate if I can be sure that the secret of my mistress' design does not become known because of any slip or mistake on my part."

Attila had by now recalled the whole story. His impression at the time had been that Honoria was no better than a royal wanton, allowing full rein to the degenerate strain which flowed in her blood. She had been young and beautiful when she behaved with such rashness; at least she had been credited with a dark and vivid charm. . . . When his armies reached Rome, he said to himself, he would not need her consent, which she now tendered with a hint of condescension. He would make her one of his wives if he so desired. It was more likely that he would apportion her to one of his generals, for she was beyond the age where he found women interesting. While these thoughts crossed his mind, however, he was aware that in the back of his mind there was a feeling of pride that a Roman princess was willing to marry him of her own wish and accord.

Fearing that this sense of gratification, of which he was ashamed but which he could not suppress, would show in his manner or in the tone of his voice, Attila answered in a voice which he kept sharp and official. He would give due consideration, he informed the messenger, to the contents of the letter from the Princess Honoria and would find a way to convey his answer to her in due course.

As he spoke, his eyes were considering the articles of great rarity and value which covered a large part of the surface of the table. These were from the loot of generations. Even in the smallest and humblest houses in the town such trophies would be found. Selecting a ring with a fine opal, his parsimonious instincts rebelling at the necessity, he handed it to Hyacinthus as a reward for the risk he had assumed. With a gesture of dismissal, he then brought the talk to an end.

3

Attila summoned Giso with a rap of impatient knuckles on a small Chinese gong as the door closed on the diminutive but proudly carried back of Hyacinthus. The attendant came to the door and paused there.

"You have the ears of a fox," said Attila. "What have they heard about the Princess Honoria?"

Giso closed the door behind him. "The impatient one? She is the worst of the lot." He paused and smirked. "It is necessary to keep that one under lock and key. She has become a mystery because no more than a handful of people know where she is being held."

Attila was frowning. He had hoped for a different report. "I know where she is being held."

"So! That was what brought Little Hips to see you." Giso made a sweeping gesture. "It is all nonsense to speak well of her. The princess is an open door where anyone can knock and enter."

The temper of the Hun leader flared up suddenly. "You are a fool!" he cried. "Send Micca in to see me. And keep out of my sight yourself or I will be tempted to shorten you by the length of your head."

"I am a fool," said Giso, cheerfully.

Micca entered the room and stood before the Hun ruler with his head bent and his eyes on the floor. There was a rigidity about his long back which suggested uneasiness and more than a hint of wariness in his warm dark eyes.

"O Mighty Attila, born of the heavens and the earth, established by the sun and the moon, I am your humble servant," he said.

"Begin," said Attila.

Micca proceeded then to demonstrate that the caravan in which he made his rounds and the wide empire of trade he had established were no more than a blind to cover up his real function in life. Micca was a spy, a very handsomely paid spy no doubt, in the employ of the man who proposed soon to plant his broad and heavy foot on the neck of civilization. "The world trembles, O Great Tanjou," said the merchant. "There is no

longer any doubt in Constantinople or Rome or Ravenna. They
know you will strike soon. But where will the blow fall? That is
the speculation which keeps the world occupied. Nothing else is
spoken of. It is generally believed that you will hurl your strength
at Rome. The city cringes in fear. A Roman bishop, to whom I
sell many strange articles—strange for a churchman to need—
bought nothing from me on my last visit there no more than two
weeks ago. His face was ashen, his hands trembled. He said to
me, 'I need nothing because soon I shall perish in the flames of
Rome.'"

Attila heard this statement with a mental smacking of lips.
He savored for several moments the feeling of pride it aroused in
him and then directed the attention of his visitor to a matter of
immediate concern. "What can you tell me about the Princess
Honoria?"

Micca's eyes narrowed. He realized that he must now walk on
thin ice. What was it this Hun wanted to hear?

"Hyacinthus has been cunning enough, O Master of the Earth,
to keep all his secrets from me," he began, cautiously. "I knew
only that he desired to talk to you of the princess. Perhaps I
could supplement what he has told you if I had some knowledge
of his mission." There was a pause which Attila did not show any
inclination to break. "This much I can say: that she is kept somewhere in the high hills between Rome and Ravenna. She has a
considerable household and she abides in comfort and dignity;
but she may not set a foot outside the marble walls of her palace."

"What is your opinion of her?"

Micca answered without delay or reserve. "She has a wise head
and a strong mind. If she should ever emerge and gain the upper
hand of the emperor—it is not impossible—all Rome would shake
with the exercise of her will."

"What of her person?"

Micca gave this matter some thought. "If I pause it is because
four years have passed since I saw the princess with my own eyes.
One can never be sure of what four years will do to a woman.
When I saw her, she was—what word shall I use?—she was intoxicating. She was slender and she carried herself with a regal
air. Perhaps it is misleading to put the effect of her in such words.
She was queenly, it is true, but at the same time she was—ah,

she was completely feminine and alluring! Men's eyes did not leave her."

"All that you say means nothing," declared Attila. "Queens and princesses are always praised to the skies. You are told that one is beautiful and when you see her you find her eyes dull and her skin muddy. You are told that one has a regal figure and you find that she has the grace of a hippo in the Nile. I have been misled often by this light which blinds men's eyes and now I want the truth."

Micca answered with an emphatic nod of his head. "When I last saw her she was beautiful, O Heaven-Born. What is she now? I cannot tell."

"Is she dark or fair?"

"She is dark, O Great King. Her eyes were like a pool glistening under the moon. Her hair was black but lustrous. Ah, yes, Proud and Mighty One, she was a picture to set one dreaming."

"Has there been any further scandal about her?"

Micca could have told of the stories whispered by men lolling on their couches in the bathing houses of Rome, in fact wherever they met in their hours of leisure. He had reached the conclusion, however, that Attila wanted to hear the opposite of this. On that account he decided to dissemble.

"If there has been talk, it has not come to my ears."

"What you mean is that other stories are being told about her."

"They have not been told to me. But consider this, O Great Tanjou: a woman who has once been indiscreet is always thereafter a mark for vicious tongues. Men state as fact what they want to believe."

"That is true," said Attila. "One must not be misled by the loose tongues of fools." The Hun ruler digested what he had been told for a few moments. He did not trust this tall old man standing with bent back before him. Micca always had a purpose in what he said. It happened, however, that he had stated what Attila wanted to hear.

"And now for matters of more importance. What word have you of Aetius?"

Aetius was the dictator of Rome. As a boy he had been sent as a hostage to the court of Rugilas. He and Attila had been much of an age. They rode together and they fought and wrestled. They ran races and competed in all manner of games, the fleet and slender Roman boy and the strong, thickset Attila. Aetius always won, except when it came to a sheer test of strength. He was a superior type, handsome, lithe, charming, educated, always ready to recite from the poets or to sing and to play on the lute.

There was a curious flatness in the tone of Attila in propounding this question. He did not intend to convey any hint by his voice of the feelings he held for the man who now controlled the destinies of Rome. All over the world it was believed that he and Aetius were still the closest of friends. Micca, uncanny in the accuracy of his judgments and perceptions, knew better than this. He knew that Attila hated Aetius, that he had always hated him.

Micca answered in a voice which conveyed no intimation of the knowledge he carried in his shrewd head. "The Emperor Valentinian grows more irked every day because he must bow to the will of this general. The mother of the emperor hates Aetius because he killed her favorite in his climb to power. Yet Aetius is more firmly established than ever before and this is because of you, O Heaven-Born."

Attila nodded. "Naturally. He is the best general they have and they must place their reliance in him to face me if I decide to strike at Rome. But let me tell you this, Micca of the Medes. They must not be too sure of the genius of Aetius. He is not a Scipio Africanus or a Caesar. He is not even a Pompey."

"You will have an opportunity soon to judge him as he is today. He intends to pay you a visit."

Attila was taken completely by surprise. He leaned forward and stared hard at the itinerant merchant.

"He is coming here?"

"Yes, O King of Kings."

Attila did not speak for several moments. "That is strange. Does he not realize he will be placing himself in my power?"

"Aetius," declared the merchant, "is a man of rare parts. No one is more gifted. But he has one weakness in his fine armor. He has a great conceit of himself. Tell him that he is not another Caesar and he would hate you all the rest of his life. Will the Unconquerable Lord of the Earth and the Skies permit a poor vendor of trifles to speak in full candor?"

Attila nodded his head. "Proceed."

"Aetius will come here to meet you without fear. It is firmly in his mind that he can bend you to his will if he can meet you again face to face. He is certain he can dissuade you from your purpose of invading Italy. He is convinced, of course, that such is your plan."

There was a pause. Attila had listened with the impassivity of a statue. His eyes, fixed on the merchant, were without expression. "How much he would like to know if it *is* my plan," he thought. Aloud he said only, "Go on."

"He will bring proposals."

"Yes."

"He has other courses to suggest. The one on which he counts most is a plan for you to invade northern Africa. He will be prepared to offer you a free hand against the Vandals there under Gaiseric. He will even be prepared to lend you assistance should you want it. He will unquestionably agree that Carthage should remain in your hands."

"It is a great prize."

"Yes, Mighty King. Carthage has become again one of the greatest cities of the world."

After a long silence, Attila began to ask questions. He grilled the merchant for two hours about the preparations the Romans were making to resist attack. How large would their armies be? Was help expected from Constantinople? Where would the legions be concentrated? How soon would their concentrations be completed? Micca was well informed on all points. He responded with a wealth of detailed information. Attila, watching him and weighing his answers, became convinced that he was hearing the truth. He made no notes but his mind was busy storing up every morsel of fact and rumor. He was mentally setting down the number of the legions, the names of the commanders, the places where they were stationed.

To an onlooker it would have seemed curious that the relationship between the two men had changed. No longer were they master and man, the ruler of so much of the earth and the spy who served him. They were so absorbed in their talk that such considerations had been laid aside. Attila asked his questions and commented on the replies he received in a low and rapid voice, the tenseness of his expression demonstrating the depth of his interest. Sometimes he appeared angry, sometimes he was jubilant; occasionally even he was amused and his broad face would light up and the sickle smile would appear. Micca talked with equal absorption, and he not only answered the questions thrown at him so abruptly but asked some of his own. It was a case of two men who knew their respective trades meeting on what was, for the moment, common ground.

Micca had continued to stand, however, and he gave a sigh of relief when Attila announced that he had no further questions. The merchant said: "I am weary, O Mighty King, born of the earth and the stars. We were in the saddle by daybreak and I have had nothing to eat since."

Attila got to his feet. He had become again the ruler, holding the power of life and death in his hands. His mind was busily reviewing what he had heard. "This man grows more useful all the time," he was saying to himself. "I must continue to use him, even though I am sure now that he spies for Aetius as well as for me. Perhaps he betrays both of us to that soft lot in Constantinople; those stupid drones who ride in their gold chariots behind their fat white mules. How daringly he asked me questions, seeking for information he could sell. He is playing us all against each other and raking in his rewards with both hands. What a pleasure it would be to have him covered with honey and staked out for the ants to finish."

He studied the merchant closely and the wrinkles tightened about his eyes and all hint of humanity left his face. He was saying to himself, "This smooth and daring rat will pay me one visit too many. He will come to me when I have no further need of him. Then I will burn out his eyes with red-hot spear points and I will cut off his ears. I will send him back to my good friend Aetius—that very good friend of my youth—and with him will go a note that I give him to the Romans exclusively so that he can see and hear for them."

Then he smiled again, a wild and exultant grin. He was thinking that when this time came Aetius would himself be dead, his body rotting with the soldiers who had fallen beside him.

"You shall have an honored place at my board," he said to the merchant.

CHAPTER IV

1

DURING the final stages of his talk with Micca the Mede, Attila had been fully conscious of the rapid advance of the hours. The first stars of evening were in the sky when the bent back of the tall merchant vanished through the door. He glanced up then at the small window above him.

"It is over," he said to himself. "The names have been drawn and two of them have lost their heads."

There was no suggestion of suspense about him. He was sure that his supreme luck had continued, that the gods to whom he deferred in his mind had looked upon his inner wishes; and so he had no doubts as to the outcome of the drawing. In any case, had not the odds been five to one? When had he needed better than that?

"Because I have spared her father, my little Swanhilde will be very grateful," he said to himself. "How her lovely eyes will shine! Tonight I shall have her sit beside me at the board so that my bold fighters will be able to feast their eyes on her."

It was with a satisfied spirit that he addressed himself to the Adoration of the Moon, which was his practice each evening. Turning to the window, he looked up at the orb which was showing its broad face above the line of the log wall.

"O Moon," he said, in a solemn voice, "this is Attila, the son of Mundzuk, who was the son of Turda, the son of——" He proceeded to enumerate the whole of his lineage, carrying the line back for a score of generations. "O Moon, who guided my people when they lived on the cold plains and who has been watching us march to the conquest of the world, continue to give us of your support now that the great test is at hand. O Moon, cold and clear and so very old and wise, give me of your counsel, direct my feet into the right path. See to it that I do not fail in the great task ahead of me. See that I do not become weak. Today I was guilty of a weakness. Let it not happen again. I must be hard as well as strong.

"Do this for me, O Moon, and I pledge that I shall burn none of the cities of mine enemies until the hours of the day are spent. So that thou, O Moon, will ride up into the sky in time to see the high flames greet you like sacrificial fires and as proof that thy servant has been working in thy behalf."

His voice went on, sometimes rising to an almost ecstatic pitch, sometimes falling into a mumble as a mood of incoherence settled upon him. Finally he lowered his arms and turned to take up again the mundane affairs of life. He realized that he was hungry.

Onegesius was waiting for him outside the door. The night was closing in so rapidly that a servant stood behind the latter with a flaming torch to light the way up the narrow steps leading to the dais. Attila could hear the stamping of impatient feet on the floor above his head. His officers, back from the pleasure and excitement of the executions, were hungry also.

"It is over," he said, with a nod to Onegesius.

"Yes, O King of Kings," was the answer. "I followed your orders. The crowd was large and there was much excitement. The people seemed pleased that the rest are to be spared."

"Who were the unlucky ones?"

If the light cast by the torch had not been so unsteady Attila would have been aware that his assistant was pale and very nervous. Onegesius swallowed uneasily before answering.

"The first one was Galata of Eastern Sarmatia." There was a pause. "He whimpered when his name was called. The guards had to take him by the arms and lead him to the block."

"He was always a troublesome fellow. I'm glad he was one of them. Who was the other?"

"The second one—was Athalaric of Thuringia."

The eyes of Attila blazed with the wild surge of emotions which filled him on receiving this intelligence but before he could speak Onegesius hurried into an explanation. "There was some trickery about it, O Great Master," he said. "I had disobeyed your orders because I—I knew you did not want Athalaric to die. I did not put his name in the box. I held it out. See." He fumbled at his belt and produced a slip of parchment on which appeared the name of the ruler of Thuringia. "But when the two slips were drawn, one of them carried the name of Athalaric. What could I do then? I could not protest that there had been a mistake, that it was not your desire that he should die. I could not say that someone had maliciously juggled the slips. All I could do was to stand there and watch Athalaric die."

Attila asked in a voice of suppressed fury: "How could it have happened? Who could have done it?" He examined the slip. "It is clear that someone was determined that Athalaric should die. Could it have been *them*? Is this the proof that it was not intended for me to have this girl as my new wife? Have the gods turned their faces from me? It is possible that *your* trickery angered them."

"No, no!" cried Onegesius. "I know it was someone who had a part in the drawing. There were several who had the chance to substitute the slip. I had arranged things so that it would not be known that one name was not in the box. As soon as two had been drawn, the rest were emptied out and burned at once. Then the two names were read. There were four who took part in the ceremony of the drawing. O Great Tanjou, there can be no doubt that it was the work of human hands. It will not be hard to get at the truth."

There was a moment of tense silence. Attila kept his eyes on the ground and so his assistant could only guess at the nature of the conflict going on in his mind. Would he believe what he had been told? Or would he decide that he, Onegesius, must be punished because he had angered the gods?

"Who would play me such a trick?" asked Attila, finally.

Onegesius breathed more freely. He was not to be made the scapegoat after all. "Are there not many," he said, "who would prefer you not to have another wife, one so beautiful she would have all your favor and who would give you sons you would prefer to those you have now?"

Attila looked up at this. "It is possible." He tensed his fingers as though they clasped the soft neck of the guilty one. But he dropped no hint of what he proposed to do. After a long silence, he asked in an almost normal tone, "Did he die well?"

"He died bravely, Great Tanjou. It was a contrast to the sorry ending of Galata."

"Do not tell me yet the names of those who helped in the drawing. I must think." Then he asked abruptly: "What of the girl? Where is she?"

"She has given way to her grief. Aja says that she cried out repeatedly that life holds nothing for her now, that she wants to die."

Attila grunted. "I want no wife beside me who snivels and cries," he said. "Perhaps tomorrow she will come to her senses. We shall wait and see."

Attila stumbled once as he climbed the dark stairs. He struck at the wall with an impatient hand. "Can it be that the gods are turning their faces from me?" he asked himself. "Is it a warning? Perhaps I have not striven hard enough; for the wise man knows that he must keep on pleasing the gods with accomplishments. He cannot sit down and expect them to favor him."

The clamor from the hall stopped suddenly. There was complete silence when Attila reached the last step leading up from the lower depths where decisions of world-shaking importance were made. He paused, wondering what had happened to close all the mouths of his raucous warriors. Then he heard a single voice raised and recognized it as that of Micca.

"Many hundred years ago," the itinerant merchant was saying in the full and rounded tones of the professional storyteller, "when Sargon was king of Babylon and the world was at his feet, there was a poor tailor who plied his trade in a small booth inside the gates of the city. This unfortunate man had a family of three sons who were thin and ill nourished because their father was too poor to buy them the food they needed. When it came his time to die, this poor man, who had worked so hard with such meager rewards, realized that he owned only three articles which he could leave to his three sons, a needle, a length of thread and a piece of wax. He summoned his oldest son to his bedside and gave him his choice——"

"A stop must be put to this," said Attila to himself. "It is womanish pap for my warriors to hear."

2

When the curtain was drawn back and Attila appeared at the top of the steps leading down to the main room of the palace, Micca's voice trailed off into silence. The leader of the Huns raised a hand in salute and immediately the fighting men who made up the company sprang to their feet and cheered wildly. "O Mighty Leader, may the gods direct your feet on the way to Rome! O Attila, live forever!"

He descended three steps and then stopped. Again he raised an arm, this time as a demand for silence.

"You saw two men die tonight who had refused to obey my orders," he called. "I have pardoned the others. And now, I trust, there will be no more disunion in the ranks. There will be nothing but eagerness and obedience when the earth begins to tremble under the marching feet of my armies!"

The room went wild with excitement. The blond German warriors of the north joined with the squat fighting men from the east in cheering the king who had united all the barbarian races. They waved their swords in the air as he descended the rest of the steps and walked to the elevated table at the head of the room.

"Lead us to Rome!" his followers were chanting with almost maniacal excitement. "To Rome! To Rome! To Rome! Our swords thirst for the blood of the sons of Caesar! Our arrows cry out to be launched against the tyrants! Against those who laugh at us and call us barbarian!"

Attila seated himself. Raising both arms, he commanded silence and invited his fighting men to seat themselves at the smaller tables which filled the room. They obeyed with alacrity, being both hungry and thirsty. Their master then looked about him with satisfaction. The bloody lesson of the evening had produced the desired effect. In the eyes of the men about him he could see nothing but eagerness for the battles which lay ahead, no hint of holding back, of disobedience. This was what he wanted to see. "*My* men," he thought, "are the best fighters in the world. They will crush the Roman squares and smother in blood the legions of these effete fools."

His eyes found other reasons for satisfaction. The tables were covered with looted treasures: tall jeweled standing cups, gold and silver vessels filled with salt and with spices from the East for those who had learned to like them, and long golden platters from which other kings had once partaken of meat. The wooden walls of the hall were covered with trophies and the round pillars holding up the ceiling were draped with rich silks. The objects on which his covetous eye rested had been wrested by bloody hands from marble halls where refinement ruled: tapestries, mirrors of polished silver, the crowns and scepters of conquered kings now dead, the great curved swords of leaders vanquished long before. There was always pride in his eyes when he viewed these fruits of conquest.

His own table and chair were small and simple in design but they were placed high above all others in the room. He noticed as he took his place that, for the first time, a second chair had been placed beside his. The exalted feelings, which had welled up inside him as he responded to the welcome of his warriors, subsided and he felt suddenly downcast; for he had ordered that Swanhilde was to sit beside him. The chair was empty.

He said to himself with a grim determination: "I must make my peace with her. It will not be easy, for the child is filled with courage and spirit. I must see her in the morning."

Before the heaping platters of meat could be brought in, there was a ceremony to be observed. Attila nodded to Onegesius, who shared a table directly beneath the dais with Micca, as a special guest. Onegesius rose to his feet and called in a loud voice:

"Linicenthus!"

One of the eight subsidiary rulers, who had been pardoned a bare hour before, got up from somewhere in the rear and walked to the steps beneath the dais of Attila. The ruler lifted a plain cup of ivywood, the only one on his table, for he insisted on being served in the simplest manner. The cupbearer filled it with rich wine from the sun-baked region called Tokaz. The emperor touched his lips to the brim and the cupbearer then bore it to the kneeling Linicenthus. The latter quaffed the wine and then said in a loud voice:

"O Mighty Emperor, who will one day rule all of the earth and the seas and the skies above us! O Favorite of the Gods, to thee I give thanks for the great boon of life I have received at thy hands. To thee I pledge my undying fealty and my promise to lead my men under your banners when we march against the common enemy."

All eight of the pardoned rulers were summoned in turn and expressed their allegiance in similar words. They were proud men, kings in their own right and long accustomed to rule; but they displayed no hesitation in their obeisances to this barbarian from the East who had forced them into submission. The lesson taught them had been a sharp one but it had been completely effective.

The ceremony over, the room burst suddenly into the kind of activity for which all the rude warriors had been waiting. The servants came into the room in a long procession, carrying platters of roasted meat high above their heads. There were dozens of haunches of beef and mutton as well as spitted chickens and ducks, and dishes of steaming stews. Every pair of eyes in the room lighted up at this welcome sight; all save those of the man who sat alone above them, for Attila could not stifle a feeling of dismay at the amount of food he must offer each night to his men. He was a light eater himself. On this occasion he took no more than a morsel of baked lamb. The ivywood cup was not refilled. It was apparent to everyone in the room that he was in a strange mood but this did not serve to dampen the feelings of his followers. The hall was filled with their loud voices as they slashed and cut at the warm roasts and tore the chickens apart with greasy fingers. Their feasting did not prevent them, however, from keeping wary eyes in the direction of the solitary figure seated high above them; and so, when he raised a hand abruptly in the air, an almost immediate silence fell on the room.

Attila pushed the wooden cup to one side, perhaps as a hint that the feasting and drinking should come to an end. Beneath him the seat which Micca had occupied was empty and a feeling of resentment took possession of him. "He has contempt for us," he thought. "He left the table as soon as he dared."

Every eye in the place was fixed on his face. Attila forced himself to put the action of Micca out of his mind. He looked about him slowly.

"What better way is there for justice to be done than in the presence of my splendid warriors?" he asked. He was pitching his voice high so that everyone in the hall could hear. "All of you know that Uldin of the Bulgars, who deserted to the enemy some months ago, has been captured and is now a prisoner here. I am of a mind to settle the case at once." He glanced down at Onegesius. "Have him brought in."

There had been continuous desertions since the Hun yoke had been forced on the land of mighty rivers and great forests which stretched from the Black Sea to the Rhine. Men who found they could not exist under barbarian rule had sought freedom outside the borders. Attila's pride had been ruffled by the volume of the desertions and he had included demands for the forcible return of the runaways in all of the peremptory exactions he laid on his southern neighbors. The few who had been sent back in response had been promptly crucified in the open squares of Hun cantonments or at much-traveled crossroads. Of those who had fled, the one for whom the Hun leader felt the deepest hatred was Uldin of the Bulgars, and his capture had been accepted as a personal triumph.

While he waited Attila licked his lips with eagerness. "So!" he thought. "At last he comes before me. Uldin the proud, Uldin the superior, Uldin the troublemaker! Now we will see how he bears himself in the face of death, this prince of unrest, this leader of discord!"

The man who was brought in by two tall guards, with his arms tied behind his back, was garbed in Dacian costume with a long-sleeved tunic and wide trousers. He was young and tall and apparently of unusual strength. His eyes surveyed the eagerly grinning company with nothing but scorn and then came to rest on the single figure seated on the dais. There was no hint of fear in them.

"Uldin of the Bulgars," said Attila, licking his lips a second time and staring down at the prisoner, his voice alarmingly low, "you think poorly of us. You call us barbarians."

The prisoner answered in a clear and high voice. "Yes, O Attila. I think poorly of you. I have called you barbarians so loudly and openly that all the world has heard."

"You have had the boldness to write me in similar terms. When you wrote this letter you were enjoying what you believed to be the secure sanctuary of the court at Constantinople. You did not seem to know how far my arm can stretch and that you might face the consequences of such audacity. Perhaps you now regret that you wrote it."

"I do not regret it, O Attila."

The emperor continued to speak in a restrained voice. "Do you mean you would not have taken more care in choosing your words if you had known you would be caught and brought before me thus?"

"That is what I mean."

"It seems," said Attila, looking along the rows of fierce and ugly faces below him, "that this proud young man sets small value on life. It is well that he does." He leaned over the table and fixed his eyes on the unrepentant captive. "You will die in the morning, O Uldin of the Bulgars. The Romans, who seem to you so much more worthy of your praise than my people, invented a cruel way of getting rid of their enemies and their criminals. They nailed them to a cross and left them there to die slowly in torment. You, O Uldin, will die by this method your friends have used so much. At break of day you will be crucified in the open square where two other men lost their heads tonight. I shall give permission for the troops in the camps along the river to come in relays and see how traitors die."

The prisoner said nothing for a moment. Perhaps the knowledge of what lay ahead of him caused his courage to desert him briefly. When he spoke, however, it was without any evidence of fear either in voice or manner.

"Crucifixion is a death reserved for criminals," he said. "I am a king."

"In my eyes, you are a criminal. The worst kind of criminal. You have disobeyed my laws."

"If I am subject to the laws of the Huns," cried the condemned man, "then I may demand that you allow me to fight for my life. There is a law which says so. I believe it is called the Law of Sangaree."

A voice from somewhere in the hall spoke up eagerly. "That is right. Let him fight for his life under the Law." Another voice joined in. "But he must fight any champion sent in against him, armed with any weapon, while he himself has nothing but a knife the length of his forearm." The idea was being joyously accepted throughout the room as a measure of entertainment as well as a demonstration of a right which any of them might sometime demand. Greasy hands waved beef bones in the air and clamored for the fight to take place at once. The name of a champion to face the young king was introduced by one of the most vociferous and was at once taken up by the rest. "Ivar! He's the one we want. Ivar the Briton! Send him in to attend to this black Macedonian who demands his rights under the Law."

Attila was not pleased with the turn things had taken. He would have preferred to make the death of Uldin a long-drawn-out one so that all his men within marching distance could come in and see the traitor writhing on the cross. But he was too shrewd to disregard the wishes of his men, particularly when they were invoking a law of long standing, one of the few which had survived from earlier centuries.

"Ivar the Briton is not here," he stated. "He accompanied the Coated One and may not return until tomorrow. He will not be in time to fight this upstart who invokes a law older than any of his own." All of the company were standing now, some with their jaws still filled with food, others voluble in their demands for a furious clash of champions at once. "Who will volunteer, then, to fight this man under the Law of Sangaree?"

There was no immediate response. The still hungry company stared in unison at the stalwart king of the Bulgars and silently reckoned him a mighty champion even when armed with nothing more potent than a knife the length of a forearm.

"If no one comes forward to fight him," declared Attila, in a voice of bitter impatience, "he will die by the method I have ordered."

Uldin, fearing that he would lose his chance to die on his feet in combat under the rules prescribed by the Law, glanced at the angry faces about him. When he realized that no one was coming forward, he cried in a taunting voice: "Are you all afraid of me? Do you hesitate to meet me even though I shall be armed with nothing better than a fish scaler? Has your courage deserted all of you? Or is it that Huns prefer to fight in great numbers and have no stomach for the kind of conflict that brave men welcome?"

The dark faces of Attila's warriors showed bitter resentment at his words but each man waited, nevertheless, for some other champion to step forward. Uldin was a foot taller than any of them, and his arm, which would clutch the knife, was long and powerful.

"Is it because I am tall and straight and you are squat and crooked?" cried Uldin, who was now deliberately baiting them into action against him. "Are you all afraid to face me with the advantages the Law gives you? Listen, then, to what I propose. I am ready to fight any two of you under the same conditions. Two of you, armed to the teeth, and I with no more than my slender blade. Come, O brave warriors from the East. Is my proposal not a fair one? Do you think it lacking in boldness? Select your two champions at once and remove the ropes from my arms so we can settle the issue while the great Attila looks on."

A huge ebony figure had emerged from the door which had served the servants in their trips to and from the kitchen. He had a white cap on his round head and in his hands was a long rod of iron which he had been using as a spit in preparing the dinner. This was Black Scyles, the head cook. Making his way through the room until he stood directly behind the captive, Black Scyles waved the iron spit in the air with a savagery which told how much he would enjoy employing it on the head of the proud Bulgar.

It may have been that Attila now desired to bring the episode to a quick ending. It would stand as an indelible reflection on the courage of his Hun warriors if no contest under the Law took place. Better, then, to let Uldin die at once before it became too evident that no champion was going to volunteer.

Attila's smoldering eye caught the excited orb of the man with the spit. He raised the forefinger of his hand which rested on the table. Black Scyles accepted this as a command. He gave the iron bar a flourish in the air and brought it down on the head of the young king.

For a moment the tall figure did not move, although it was clear from the sound of the blow that the skull had been fractured. Then the inert body seemed to fold slowly and sway forward. It fell with a thud to the floor.

Immediately the eager fighting men in the room went into action. With drawn daggers they converged on the spot where Uldin of the Bulgars lay, his head in a rapidly spreading pool of blood. There was a savage scramble to get near enough to plant a blow in the unresisting flesh. Like a pack of pariah dogs, they fought and snarled over the body of the man who had taunted them openly. When the rage to be in at the kill had been satisfied, the object on the floor bore little resemblance to anything human.

Attila waved a hand to the servants who had come out in a mad hurry from the dark kitchens where they blew on the coals and tended the spits, to stand in the doorway and stare with eyes white-rimmed in their smoke-blackened faces.

"Carry it out," he ordered. "The executioner has been saved the necessity of killing this disobedient dog."

3

It has already been told that Micca the Mede left the dining hall early. He made his way with sure steps to one of the large tents pitched on the plain outside the gate. It belonged, obviously, to someone of importance, for it stood fifteen feet high and was at least thirty feet across, and it was most snugly covered with the thick felt which made it cool in summer and warm in winter. The itinerant merchant lifted the flap and asked, "May a humble purveyor of simple goods enter the home of the honorable and influential Berend, son of Cham?"

The thickset man seated behind the pile of ashes, which had accumulated during the winter, nodded his head in welcome but did not get to his feet, for a Hun used his legs as little as possible. "Come in, O Worthy Micca," he said, in a reedy voice.

There were guests in the tent already, half a dozen men wearing their round felt hats crowned with red tassels pulled down over their brows. They gave no sign of recognition, it being the role and the sole privilege of Berend to greet the newcomer. A group of women, seated with their backs against the matting of steppe grass which formed the inner lining of the tent, were not so decorous. Looking out at the visitor from under lines stretched along the lattice and weighed down with joints of beef and lamb, dried fish, and bags of meal and flour, they nodded their heads and smiled in anticipation of a pleasant evening in the company of the great storyteller. The women were more of a type than the men and distinctly more rewarding to the eye, their black eyes smiling in round faces bronzed by the winds, and all of them as lively and as plump as pea hens.

The man seated on Berend's right moved over to accord that place of honor to the latest arrival. When Micca had seated himself cross-legged beside his host, he seemed like some great snowy bird which had plummeted down by mistake into a convention of jackdaws.

It was the rule that conversation should proceed from the point of interruption and visitors remain discreetly silent for several moments; long enough to gain some inkling of the opinions of the earlier arrivals before venturing any of their own. Micca observed this point of etiquette and to his surprise discovered that they were not discussing the double execution of the evening. Instead they were deep in a problem which concerned all of them very much. What steps were to be taken to conserve the trade of Rome when that city went down in violence and the inhabitants were put to the sword? Only one of the guests shared with Berend the gnomelike proportions of the Hun, the round yellow face and the deep-sunken eyes. The rest were of various nationalities, men who had deserted their own lands for good reasons and taken service with Attila. None of them were fighting men. They were money-changers, traders, merchants of one kind or another, all intensely acquisitive and bitterly selfish.

They were trying to find some way of preventing any stoppage of the wealth which flowed into Rome from all parts of the empire. The spout through which the gold and the loot poured so abundantly must be kept in operation after Roman domination had been ended.

Micca listened with an uneasiness which he did not allow to show on his face. "This is the final proof," he said to himself. "There is not in any of them a trace of doubt that it is Rome Attila will attack this time. They are so sure, they do not think it necessary to pretend before me, a Roman citizen." Thinking of the huge encampments he had seen on the plains, he wondered if Aetius would be able to put armies in the field strong enough to stem the tide. He shared an opinion held by everyone in Rome, that Aetius was an adroit leader and a soldier of sound parts but that he lacked the genius of the great captains of the past. He was not even placed on a par with a more recent commander, Stilicho.

It was Berend who introduced a new note into the discussion. "We must remember this," he said, in guttural tones of deep earnestness, "that we are no longer nomads. Never again will we strike our tents and follow the turn of the seasons. The time has come for us to sink our roots into the rich soil of the south as deeply as we sink the sword into the ground when we go to war."

"Not the plow!" cried his fellow Hun, Barich. "The plow is the sign of servitude. Let the rest of the world stay in slavery to toil. We must rule the world from our saddles!"

"Victory, O Barich, has its penalties," declared Berend. "It will be from Rome that we rule the world and not from here. Attila will sit in the palace of Valentinian. The rest of us will fold up our felt tents for the last time and content ourselves with marble walls. The plow will become the symbol of the kind of life that victory will fasten on us."

"Do you mean," cried his compatriot, "that we must start to live as the Romans do? That we must squat every day in these great steaming baths? That we must live on peacocks' tongues and the eggs of fishes?"

"They say a bath is very pleasant," said Berend, with a broad grin. "But you have not grasped what I mean, Barich. I think it will be well to talk about something else. Perhaps our honored guest will tell us a story."

So Micca proceeded to tell stories. The men who sat behind the ashes forgot their deep concern in the trade of the world as his skilled tongue wove its spell. The lively round eyes of the women, like dead-ripe plums, were fixed on his face with a fascination which was evinced in squeals of astonishment and little trills of fear. He was selecting his stories with such foresight that at the end of each he could lead his hearers on to discuss the points raised and he could then ask them questions. The group in the tent (where it was pleasantly cool because the top had been opened) did not realize how cleverly he interjected his questions or the satisfaction he took in the information gleaned from their replies.

Finally the tall old man felt that he had gone as far as he dared with this subtle interrogation. He bowed to his host and begged permission to withdraw. Getting to his feet, he said: "If Rome falls as you expect, I will see you there. Saddened and impoverished, of course, but with goods still to offer you—for I am a trader, not a soldier—and perhaps new stories to tell. If Rome does not fall—and you cannot blame me if I, a citizen of the empire, entertain doubts on that score—I will continue to come here and, I hope, to be greeted as an old friend. Whichever way it is to be, I trust that you will all abide in the best of health."

The moon was high in the heavens when he emerged, and at its fullest. There had been a time, and not far in the past, when the nomads from the Eastern steppes had been impelled by moons such as this to take to the saddle and to race their horses madly while their plump wives joined hands in circles and danced and sang. The light had other effects and when a man spoke of his April son or his August daughter he was not referring to the months in which his children arrived. The tents which now stretched in all directions, seemingly without end, looked ghostly in this strange light. Micca himself, with his white robes swishing about his ankles and his long silver hair falling over his shoulders, was like a wraith. He made his way toward the gates of the city where there was much noise and confusion. Booths had been set up for the dispensing of strong drinks and a company of dancing girls were wriggling and galumphing in a singularly graceless manner. As he paced slowly from one group to another, he became aware that someone was following him. Stopping finally and, without turning, he asked in a low voice:

"Is it you?"

"Yes, my lord Micca."

"No names! You must cure this habit or sometime you will utter a name when it will cause serious harm. Have you news for my ear?"

"Yes, my lord."

"Come, then, to my tent behind the first of the red wagons."

Half an hour later, in darkness because no lamp had been lighted in the tent, Micca sat down with the man who had been following him and listened to the whispers in which the latter delivered his report. If the darkness had been less complete, it would have been seen that the merchant was wearing an impatient frown.

"It comes to this," he said, finally. "You have done nothing."

"My lord Micca!" protested the visitor. "I have done everything that is possible. By the beards of my ancestors, I swear that I have not been held back by any fear or lack of willingness for the task. You do not realize the dangers and the difficulties I face. I must wait for the proper opportunity to present itself."

"There must be no more waiting."

Micca's voice carried a distinct note of warning. After a moment of silence, he continued in the same tone. "You see the armies this man is gathering. You know that he aims to attack Rome. There is only one way to avert the blow. Attila must die."

He got to his feet and closed the flap of the tent, after gazing intently to make sure that no listeners lurked outside. Then he produced a lamp from somewhere in the darkness and lighted it. Holding it above his head, he scrutinized his visitor closely.

What he saw was a lean, hawk-billed face staring at him apprehensively from the framework of a white turban and a bushy black beard. The attitude of the visitor, seated cross-legged on the ground, made it clear that he suffered from an extreme uneasiness of mind.

"Ala Sartuk," said Micca, "you agreed to carry out the mission I proposed to you. You accepted gold in advance. Do you know the source from which the gold came? From a very high source, Ala Sartuk. The man whose gold you took could reach out and pluck you from any hiding place to which you might scuttle."

The man responded in a sulky voice. "I agreed to do your bidding. I took the gold you offered. But I did not know how carefully he is guarded. Even if I succeeded in getting within striking distance, I would be cut to pieces before I could do more than raise my knife."

"A way can be found," declared Micca. "But before I tell you of the plan in my mind, I must make it clear to you that you will not be allowed to step down—nor to delay any longer. We have a reason much more potent than gold to drive you into action. Are you aware that your father in Moesia and your two brothers have joined the deserters and are now in Roman territory? If I give the word they will be returned to Attila to be dealt with— in the usual way. If that happens, their deaths will be laid at your door." Micca raised his fine head and stared hard at his visitor. "That is not all. There is the attractive widow of a certain money-changer, the rich man who absconded and was brought back to die. She also will be returned if we are driven to extreme measures. Am I not right in assuming that you, Ala Sartuk, are more concerned over the welfare of the beauteous widow than in saving your own skin? You would not like her to suffer the fate that the Huns reserve for female captives?" There was a brief silence during which the rolling eyes of Ala Sartuk vainly searched the face of the merchant for signs of relenting. Then Micca continued. "It would avail you nothing to go to Attila's men and say that Micca the Mede is plotting his death. I would die, of course; but you would die also and in due course the two brothers who would be sent back—that has been arranged for, of course. The rich widow woman would become the property of some greasy Hun."

Silence fell on the tent and then the visitor asked in a whining voice: "Is your magic equal to finding me a way to get within striking distance of the great khan?"

"I grant you that the difficulties here are great," said the merchant, his manner and voice still completely unruffled. "But some information came to my ears today. The Tanjou plans an excursion. He will ride into a country where the population is thin and the woods are thick and dark. His plan is being kept a secret and he will travel with a small company. Under such circumstances he is likely to relax his vigilance at times. I have arranged that you are to leave for this country at once. There is a man of some wealth and position who will receive you. He will help to find you the opportunity. Your escape has been provided for, if you accomplish your mission."

A long silence fell between them. The fingers of Ala Sartuk plucked at his glossy beard and his uneasy eyes kept darting about in all directions.

"I will do it," he said, finally.

Micca nodded his head in satisfaction. "There will be more gold for you if you succeed," he promised. "And when the Hun empire has dissolved into nothingness—which is inevitable after Attila's iron hand has been removed—you will be regarded as a benefactor of the whole human race. Nothing will be too good for you, no praise too high." He paused and then asked in an anxious tone: "Have you kept your skill with the knife?"

Ala Sartuk flexed the muscles of his right arm with an irritable nod. "Carry the lamp to the other end of the tent," he instructed. "Place it on the chest over there. Then step clear."

Micca did as he was bid and was quick to step well back as soon as he had deposited the lamp on the end of the chest. Ala Sartuk had produced a knife from his belt. He felt the edge of it and then gave it a single flourish above his head. His arm whipped forward.

Darkness descended on the interior of the tent. The knife had cut the tallow in two.

"An easy target," said the knife thrower, with a trace of self-satisfaction in his voice. "The neck of Attila will be a more difficult one."

CHAPTER V

1

ATTILA wakened at dawn. He had a great dread of the dark and it was his custom to have a lighted torch beside his bed. At regular intervals during the night a servant would come in to make sure it was still burning. But this time there had been a slip. He awakened in complete darkness and lay in bed for several moments without stirring, wondering what had happened.

Black Scyles had heard the first signs of life in the royal bed and now made his way up the steps. He carried a goblet of hot milk. Attila quaffed the milk in quick gulps.

The ebony countenance of Black Scyles was stretched wide in a gratified smile. "I broke the head of that one with a single blow," he boasted. "He was dead, that bad man, before he reached the floor."

"You did well," said the Hun ruler. "There will be a reward for you."

The royal cook had been promised rewards before but none of them had ever been received. It would be the same this time; still, he was glad that the terrible master was pleased.

Giso heard the sound of voices in the bedchamber and put in a prompt appearance. Attila grunted at him. "Onegesius. I want him."

"The ever watchful Onegesius, as it happens, is a late sleeper. He is not like you, master, who wakes up with the sun—with a head full of schemes." Giso motioned in the direction of the great hall below. "Perhaps he's down there. Many of them drank too much and went to sleep on the floor."

He walked to the curtain and drew aside a corner of it in order to survey the scene. He began to count, a twitch of scorn on his lips. "Twenty-three," he announced. "Faugh! How they snore!" His eyes darted quickly over the bodies of Hun officers sleeping off their potions on the rushes like pigs in a sty. "Onegesius is there. And he seems to be in very bad company. His two closest companions belong to the lucky eight. His head is cradled on the broad morass of warm suet which Nonnus from Burgundy calls his stomach. His feet rest on the bony countenance of Menalippe the Goth. I will go down and rouse him."

He clumped loudly down the steps. They heard a sound of splashing water below and in a few moments Onegesius joined them. He was soaked from head to foot but his eyes were still heavy with sleep. Attila snapped one palm against the other and both Giso and Black Scyles disappeared.

"I have work for you," said Attila. He lowered his small feet to the floor and began to don his clothes with swift and careless movements. "An embassy must set out at once for Rome. Select three of our ablest men, all of whom must be well known to the Romans. They are to go direct to the emperor and demand at once the person of my promised wife, the Princess Honoria. They must demand also that I receive with her one half of all the dominions of Rome which are rightly hers by inheritance. The emperor will refuse both demands, of course, with great indignation; and I shall have a perfect pretext for going to war."

Onegesius had listened in a state of amazement and mental confusion. "I do not understand, Great Tanjou," he said. "You say Princess Honoria is your promised bride? I have heard nothing of such an arrangement."

"It is a matter of a few hours only," explained Attila. He held up the ring. "There it is: the pledge of her understanding and agreement. She sent an envoy to me, the man Hyacinthus who came in the train of Micca, disguised as a seller of linens and silks. She promises her hand in marriage if I can recover for her the liberty which has been taken from her and the honors of which she has been robbed."

Onegesius was still bewildered. "The last word heard of the princess," he said, "she was to be married to some convenient old cuckold in Rome. As for her inheritance, she has little or none. There are no lands she can claim under the Laws of the Twelve Tables."

Attila had finished his toilet. "It is your greatest weakness," he said, "that you are too concerned with facts. The princess has no inheritance of any size to claim. I am well aware of this but it does not prevent me from claiming half of the dominions of Rome. You have been with me long enough, surely, to understand that my policies are based on an understanding of human weaknesses. The greater the lie you tell, the more likely you are to convince people that you are telling the truth. The more absurd the claim you make, the more you will get in the end. These are my rules and it is time you understood them, Onegesius. First, never be guilty of telling the truth if a lie will serve your purpose better; and never be content with a small lie, make it such a resounding one that in the end people will be brought to believe by its very size and audacity. Second, no half measures where claims are concerned. Claim everything at first, even if your grounds are weak; and recede from your initial position very slowly. Do you understand now?"

Onegesius nodded, although it was clear that he was still uncertain about such audacity. "Is it your intention, then," he asked, "to take the princess as your wife?"

It was Attila's turn to express uncertainty. "I am not sure," he said. "It may be sufficient to demand her hand in marriage, a claim which the Emperor Valentinian will reject with scorn. If it should come about that marriage with her would strengthen my hand, I would most decidedly take her as a wife. It would be a distasteful matter for me." He looked questioningly at his assistant. "Do you not see advantages for me in marrying a princess of the imperial Roman family?"

"I see a disadvantage," declared Onegesius, shocked into honesty by the nature of Attila's stand. "You have always demanded virginity in your wives. Do you intend now to wed a woman who is notorious for her loss of inexperience? Do you not fear that the world will laugh at you for accepting such a wanton bride?"

Attila raised both arms in the air in sheer exasperation. "You have heard nothing, you have learned nothing. If I found it necessary to marry this woman of easy consent, I would have a story to tell which would make the world believe her a woman of spotless purity." He lowered one arm and pointed a finger triumphantly at his assistant. "I have the story ready now. I will announce to the world that Honoria has been the victim of her brother's greed. As an excuse to seize all her honors and lands, he invented the story of her dalliance with the household officer. To make the first lie hold, he now systematically spreads stories of her continued wantonness. Tell that to the world loud enough and often enough," cried Attila, triumphantly, "and in time the Emperor Valentinian himself will be wondering if it is not true after all."

Onegesius was beginning to understand and admire his master's philosophy. "Perhaps your story is the truth," he said.

"Perhaps it is. How do we know?"

"When, O Great Tanjou, do you want the embassy to start?"

"Tonight," said Attila. "At the same time, send word to Constantinople, and to all other courts of any importance, of the claims we are pressing on that vicious simpleton, the emperor of Rome."

2

Giso came back to announce an early visitor. "The best one," he said, "your favorite—and mine."

It was Aja who followed him into the room. She had come in such a hurry that there had been no time to apply any of the customary aids to appearance. Her face looked gray and old. Her robe hung limply on her plump frame and did nothing to conceal the fact that she waddled.

"O Mighty Lord of All the Earth," she began, "we regret you have suffered the misfortune of which I must speak. It is in no sense the fault of anyone——"

"Speak up!" commanded Attila, sharply, when she did not continue. Then, his mind leaping quickly to a conclusion, he said, "You are trying to tell me that the girl is dead."

Unable for the moment to command the use of her tongue, Aja did no more than nod.

Attila stared at her so long and with such a fixed and somber air that the woman found it hard not to scream with terror. When he spoke, however, it was to say no more than, "I have been expecting this." A few moments more of silence followed and then he asked, "Had my orders been followed?"

Aja compelled her tongue to resume its function. "Yes, Great Tanjou. She was so overcome with grief that she wept for hours.

I had her watched as you had instructed. Two women remained with her until she fell asleep from exhaustion."

"Then how did it happen?"

"It must have been that she wakened during the night and tried to escape. It was no more than a quarter of an hour ago that her body was found under the wall. She had been struck by an arrow and it had gone right through her body. The sentry knew nothing about it. He swears that he heard nothing and it is true, O Great Tanjou, that his quiver is still full. He did not shoot the arrow."

Onegesius drew his master to one side. Attila seemed stunned by what he had heard. His face was the color of tallow and his eyes were dull. "This is the work of those who juggled with the slips in the drawing. They have found a way to kill her as well as her father."

The Hun leader muttered, "It may be as you say."

"The time has come for speaking openly. This is the work of one of your wives who has borne you a son, and her dependents who count on his favors later. They have seen to it that this most dangerous of all new rivals has been removed from their path." He took a quick look at his master's face to see how far he dared go. "Four of them have borne you sons. Do you believe any one of the four capable of this?"

Attila nodded his head slowly. "Yes. Any one of the four. They are all full of pride and ambition and as fierce as a lioness with a single cub. Even Cerca—perhaps more likely my quiet Cerca than any of the others. We must find the guilty one at once. . . . Onegesius, get all the evidence and bring the guilty ones to me. We must be very sure before we act." He was speaking in a low and almost breathless tone. "I must be certain which is the guilty one. And when we are certain, we must act quietly. I do not want any open scandal about this. I do not want the world to know that one of my wives could plot so against me. The guilty one and her brothers—or whoever may be involved—will disappear and never be heard of again. It will be a mystery and it will never be explained. The sentry must die at once."

"Yes," said Onegesius. "I will see to that first."

"It will be supposed we are convinced he shot the arrow." Attila paused for a moment as though conjuring up in his mind the scene which had resulted in Swanhilde's death. "See that he is put to death quickly and easily. It is likely he has been a good soldier. His death will lull suspicions and make it easier for you to get at the truth."

Attila had been holding the blue tunic in one hand. Now he turned and tossed it on the bed. "I cannot dress in my finery when that little creature lies dead with an arrow through her pretty body." He walked over to face Aja directly. "Do they think I can be prevented from choosing new wives as I see fit?" he cried in a sudden fury. "Take this word back to those scheming, treacherous women who abide with you in the Court. The one who brought about the death of this innocent child must hear the news at once. I am going to take a new wife. Can you guess who she is? It is the sister of the emperor of Rome! Tell them that from this hour forward things will be different. There will be only one wife, my illustrious and patrician bride, the Princess Honoria. She will sit beside me and have a palace of her own, with ladies to attend her and a huge staff of servants. She will have her own company of guards. The rest of you will be no better than concubines. Tell all that to them, my Aja, and watch how their covetous faces will turn white and how dread will come into their spiteful eyes. Go, and spread the tidings among them at once."

When Aja had taken her departure, in such a hurry that she did not pause for the customary obeisances, Attila's mood changed. He looked sad and tired. "I meant what I said, Onegesius," he declared, with a nod. "I am going to have one wife, to rule beside me in proper state. She will be the empress of the world, my true *yen-chi*. If what Micca says about the princess is in any sense true, she will be the one. But I think instead this new wife will be someone you will find for me." He laid a hand on his assistant's shoulder and gave it a peremptory shake. "Yes, you are going to find her for me."

"I? Where am I to find her?" cried Onegesius.

"I am laying an injunction on you. You must find for me a wife who will so chain my fancy that I shall be able to forget the little one who was killed last night. Search the whole world over if necessary. Look everywhere. Send the word out that we will give a great reward to anyone who can tell us where she is, this beautiful woman we seek. It is a difficult task I have entrusted to you, Onegesius, for the memory of Swanhilde will be hard to drive from my mind.

"She will need to be even more beautiful," he went on, after a pause. "Her hair must be fair. It must be as bright and golden as the light of the sun. I will have none of your girls from the East with their lively black eyes. The Court is full of that kind now. She must have blue eyes, as blue as the sky. She must be slender. I am weary of your full-breasted pigeons. Do you know where you can find me such a wife, Onegesius?"

The officer shook his head. "I know of none such, O King of Kings," he said. "But I shall find her for you."

For the first time Attila's voice took on a grim and menacing note. "Find her quickly then. I will tolerate no delay. It must be made possible for me to forget."

CHAPTER VI

1

IT WAS a relief for Attila to turn his mind back to military matters. He stumped on his short legs down the stairs to the offices under his bedchamber. He found the Coated One in the room where the consultation had been held with his generals the previous morning. Nicolan of the Ildeburghs had been working all night but had finally completed his labors. Four deep piles of parchment notes lay on the long table, one for each of the armies still to march in from the East.

He was a young man. Tall, slender (he looked light of frame, at least, in the company of thickset Huns), dark of eye and hair. He had something of the Greek about him, an intelligent eye, a good brow, a pair of hands which looked almost delicate. This impression, that he might be more at home at a sculptor's bench or in front of an artist's canvas, was quickly contradicted by his air and manner. He was a man of action, intensely alive and full of energy, quick of movement and keen of perception. He was, in fact, much like a well-tempered blade, with the sharpest of edges and a handsome burnished pommel.

"I am finished, Great Khan," he reported. He gestured toward the piles of notes. "The orders are there."

Attila did not have to question him. He knew that the four documents contained full and explicit orders. The armies still in the East would know when to start, which roads to take, how far to march each day, where to find food depots and supplies of water, when and where to ford rivers. Every detail would be set down clearly. The four bodies of troops would cross Dacia in turn and follow each other down the line of the Danube. There would be no interfering with other armies and no confusion. The orders would be concise and clear and easy to understand; more important still, they would be easy to follow, at least they would never demand the impossible or leave a commander with any excuse for failure.

"They must be dispatched at once," said Attila, in a gratified voice. Then he glanced at his proficient assistant. "You are weary?"

"A little, O King."

The sun was already blazing in at the windows and the atmosphere of the room was warm and humid. Nicolan wore, nevertheless, a tunic of cloth which was fastened closely about his neck. He tried to clear his eyes of the symptoms of weariness by rubbing a hand across them.

Attila seated himself at the end of the table. "I will reward you," he said, "with another difficult mission. You must be back in the saddle at an early hour of the afternoon."

Nicolan nodded easily. "A few hours' sleep. Then I'll be ready to start." He proceeded then to demonstrate that he did not share the fear in which the ruler was so universally held. "There was a reward promised me long ago and it is now overdue. The return of my lands, O King of Kings. The Finninalders should be forced to give them up. They made an illegal deal with Vannius to take them over after the killing of my father. It was an infamous transaction, O Mighty King. Vannius had no legal grounds for seizing the lands in the first place. Of the money paid by the Finninalders, not a single sesterce went into the funds of the state. Vannius kept it all. You, the head of the state, were robbed also. Has not the time come to right all this?"

Attila frowned heavily. It was some time before he replied. "I am not sufficiently acquainted with the facts. I can do no more than make you another promise, that this will be looked into in due course."

Nicolan was not willing to drop the matter as easily as that. "You have made that promise to me several times already," he said. His face had taken on an angry flush. "Have I not served you well? I am not asking for a reward, O Great Tanjou, I am asking only for justice."

"You must not press me!" exclaimed Attila, with a rising inflection of voice. "We are preparing for war. When we have won our victory, there will be lands and wealth to be distributed and I promise that you will have a large share. Would you not prefer estates on the warm hills of Italy to these lands about which you give me no peace?"

Nicolan shook his head. "There is nothing in the world that I want save the lands of my father."

"That is where I am sending you. Come. Let the matter go for the time being. Perform the mission on which I send you and then we shall talk further about your lands." A brusque motion of his hand indicated that the matter was closed. "It is curious that I have never set foot in this country from which you come, although it lies at my very back door. All I know about it for certain is that your people raise fine horses. There is a rumor as well that your women are more than passing fair."

Nicolan nodded his head proudly. "We raise the finest horses in the world, O Mighty Tanjou."

"The finest? A sweeping claim. Have you not been with us long enough to know that the horses we breed are the best in the world?"

"Come to the plateau country, O King, and see for yourself," said Nicolan, eagerly. "Our horses have as much speed as the Arabs' and more endurance. They are large and handsome. Truly their equal is not to be found elsewhere."

"You will say next," declared Attila, impatiently, "that your people ride as well as mine."

Nicolan nodded again. "I think I may say so in all truth. They ride best without saddles and they never use reins."

Attila laughed. "I will concede that they raise good talkers up on these plains of yours. Well, I shall see for myself soon and be able to judge of the merits of both men and horses. I shall visit this great country within the next fortnight. It is not only because you have such fine horses. I desire also to find myself a new wife, one with golden hair and a face that is pink and white, and a figure that is as slender as a reed. I am told you are a dark race but that sometimes your women are born with hair like the sun. I am curious to see both with my own eyes—the great horses which are so fast and the beautiful women with the sunshine in their hair."

Nicolan's face had grown grave. He saw good reason now for wishing that Attila was not going to pay a visit to the land on the high plain. When the latter ceased speaking, he asked, "Do you want me to go with you, Great Tanjou?"

Attila shook his head. "I want you to go first. When I set out, the fact cannot be concealed. Men have a cleverness for concealing what they do not want me to see. All the best horses would be out of sight before my own mount set a hoof across the border line. The beautiful daughters would cease to exist. I know their little tricks, these subjects of mine! And so I want you to go first and have a report for me when I arrive on what you have seen."

"You want me to spy out the land," said Nicolan, in a suspiciously quiet voice.

Attila caught the intonation of his voice and the royal eyes began to simmer. "Is it that you do not want to serve me in this? That you put the interests of your own people above mine?"

The young man from the plains looked his much-feared and hated master squarely in the eye. He was fully aware that the temper of the ruler of half the world might erupt at any moment like a volcano. "It is true, O King, that I have no stomach for such a task," he said. "But I will ride ahead of you and give you an honest report of what I see nevertheless. Will you permit me to tell you why?"

Attila motioned him to proceed. Nicolan got to his feet and stripped off his tunic. He then turned so that the emperor of the Huns could see his back. It was a mass of ugly scars, crossed and recrossed, and deep and still angry in appearance, although it was clear that the wounds which made them had been inflicted years before.

"People shudder when they see my back and so I never expose it to view. That is why I have earned for myself the name of Togalatus, the Coated One. The Romans did that to me, O King of Kings." Nicolan was speaking in a low voice. He stopped long enough to replace the tunic. "They killed my father and they carried off my mother and me to Rome where we were sold as slaves. My lovely and gentle mother died, which was fortunate for her. She could not stand the life. I was a slave first in the household of Aetius——"

Attila's eyes took on a sudden gleam when he heard this. "In the household of Aetius? My old, my great friend, Aetius? Tell me, Togalatus, what kind of master did you find him?"

Nicolan answered quietly. "You have seen my back. Is it necessary for me to say anything more? Except this: because Aetius will be in command of the armies of Rome, I am ready to help in getting all the horses necessary for the campaigns against him."

Attila began to speak in a reminiscent tone, which was at the same time sly and full of resentment. "He was such a handsome and gifted boy, that old friend of mine. He could outrun me on his long legs. He could read and speak several languages and he could play the lute and sing in a fine, clear voice. How he used to laugh when he beat me at something!" He turned to Nicolan. "Did this feeling you have for him enter into your work last night and make these orders sound in every particular and free from any error?"

Nicolan nodded curtly and with a sudden flush in his cheeks. "I was doubly careful, O King. That is why I took so long on the work. I was making certain that your armies from the East would arrive in time and in good condition for the work ahead of them."

Attila had forgotten the tragedy of the early morning. He indulged in a triumphant cackle. "I see it was a fortunate thing that you, my young Togalatus, were given to Aetius when the Romans carried you off."

2

When the ruler of the Huns had taken his departure there was a sudden movement in a pile of rugs under the table at which he had been seated. They were tossed aside and a copper-haired man with a broad and engaging face crawled out. When he got to his feet, it was apparent that he towered over most men by many full inches. He stretched his long thewed arms and yawned.

"I am hungry," he announced.

"You are always hungry, Ivar," said Nicolan.

The Briton, who would have been matched against Uldin of the Bulgars if he had been obtainable in the early evening hours, laughed in an amiable tone. "I have a large body to feed, my busy, scribbling friend. Do you suppose we can get some food quickly?"

Nicolan went to the door and called: "Scyles, you lazy scoundrel! Bring us food at once. The best you have and plenty of it. If you have any doubts, go right up to the man whose feet I hear on the floor above me. He will tell you we must have whatever we want. *That*," he said, when he had come back to stand beside his friend who bettered his height by nearly half a head, "will be the one reward I get for the work I did last night. Did you hear what we were saying, the mighty one and I?"

Ivar nodded. "I wakened just as the great bringer of death and destruction came in. I decided it would be best to stay where I was and not bring myself to his attention. And so I heard everything he said." He then asked a question in a serious tone of voice. "Nick, good friend, will you do as he has ordered? I mean about spying out the land for him?"

The young man from the plains who now served as Attila's chief tactician answered in a tone of equal gravity. "You heard what I told him. Have you any thoughts in the matter?"

The pleasant face of the tall Briton showed that he was entertaining serious doubts. "I am not certain," he said, frowning. "It is a hard thing to go against your own people."

Nicolan agreed to this. "Yes, it is a hard thing. But my people are in a very difficult position. There we are, high up on the plain and no more than a handful as compared with the races around us. It has been impossible to stay independent. First, it was the Romans who engulfed us and despoiled us, and then introduced their customs and abominations among us. Then came the Huns. For generations we have had masters to obey. Most of my people prefer the Romans to the Huns. I do not. They don't know as I do how lazy, cruel, degenerate, haughty and corrupt the Romans have become. The Huns have strength at least. If I must serve, I would rather serve a strong man than a dancing master and pimp."

"But, good friend," said the Briton, "this is a question not of which one you must serve, but of how far you must serve. I have never told you much about myself. My father was the slave of a rich holder of land in the fen country. He wore an iron collar around his neck and when I was big enough to walk they came and forged one around *my* neck. They made it large enough to last all my life, they thought, but they did not know I would grow so large. Before I was fifteen, they had to come again and file it off and put a larger collar around my neck. When they saw how strong I had become, they sold me to a Roman trader who thought he could offer me as a gladiator. But Rome had become Christian and the fighting of gladiators in the forum was prohibited before I could be trained for it." His eyes had assumed a faraway look. "You might think I do not owe that country of mine any loyalty. It gave me nothing but blows and withheld the right from me to stand up and call myself a man. And yet, good friend, it calls to me. I think all the time of the soft air, the greenness of the grass, the sweet fields which yielded so much good food that even I, a slave, had plenty to eat." He gave his head an emphatic shake. "I could not do anything to hurt that country of mine. I shall go back someday soon."

"I love my country as much as you do," declared Nicolan. "The air is just as sweet, the fields as rich. There is nothing in life I would rather do than watch the Trumping of the Baws. There is a girl back there I want to see again, although she may be married now; a girl with yellow hair and a fine spark in her eyes." He dropped a hand on his friend's great shoulder. "Let this be consolation for you, my huge Ivar. I had already decided that the first thing I will do when I reach my own land is to visit a Christian priest. He has been there ever since I was a boy but he had to stay in concealment much of the time because Attila has no liking for missionaries. He comes from the island where you were born."

Ivar frowned in a puzzled way. "Why should a British priest come to your country to make Christians out of you? Why did he not stay and do the same for our own people?"

"I shall ask him that when I see him," said Nicolan, smiling. "He is very wise and he sees into the heart of things. I will tell him what is demanded of me and ask him what I am to do. He will know, that smiling old priest. And whatever he says, I shall do. Does that satisfy you?"

Black Scyles arrived at this moment with a dish containing a most savory mixture of meats. In his other hand was a bowl of *camus*, a heady Hun brew. These he placed on the table and in a trice the hungry Briton was seated in front of them.

"It is no wonder you are so big, master, when you have such a big appetite," said the cook. "That Bulgar, now, you would have found him an easy mouthful to swallow if you been there, eh, master?"

On their return the evening before, the pair had been told of what had happened in the great hall. The Briton nodded without any pause in his eating. "I think it would not have been too hard, Scyles. But I am glad you finished him instead of me."

Nicolan found that he had no appetite. When the cook had left, he walked over to the narrow window high up under the ceiling through which the warm sun was shining. Stripping off his tunic a second time, he seated himself where the welcome rays could reach his scarred back, believing that the heat might be beneficial to it.

The loss of a full night's sleep and the warmth of the sun on his back put him into a reflective mood. His mind strayed back to the past and he began to recall everything which had happened to him since that day of horror when the Roman slave trader with the villainous scar on his face had come to the house of the Ildeburghs. He could still feel some of the panic he had experienced then, he could hear the cries of the frightened servants, the wild neighing of the horses, and old Maffa screeching her maledictions.

CHAPTER VII

1

OLD MAFFA screamed her wild curses in words which no one, not even those whose memories went far back, could understand! One of the soldiers had soon ended that. A gesture from the fat and freckled hand of the renegade Roman who had been placed in charge of the plateau country had sent the soldier over to the angry old woman. A swift stroke of his blunt sword, which drove the point forward no more than a few inches, had torn a great hole in her throat and had silenced forever the ancient nurse of the Ildeburghs.

Nicolan had wakened early that morning. In fact, he had slept very little, being too much concerned over an emotional discussion he had heard between his father and mother the evening before. His mother, his wise and lovely mother, had been urging Saladar of the Ildeburghs to adopt a more conciliatory attitude toward Vannius, as the turntunic Roman was now called, although all men knew his real name was L. Pontius Oriens and that he had absconded from Rome when his peculations in the royal funds had been discovered. Attila had handed him the country to govern with the understanding that large funds were to be raised. Vannius had not only done this, finding ingenious excuses for accusing the leading families of legal infringements and seizing their lands and horses, but he had managed as well to fatten his own purse beyond all reason. No man had ever been more hated than this evil-tempered tyrant who had set up a household, with many coarse yellow-skinned wives from the East, in the heart of the plateau.

"Saladar, Saladar!" Nicolan's mother had cried in the course of the discussion. Her dark eyes were filled with an urgent fear. "You must learn to bend a little. You are at this man's mercy. If you continue to answer him so sharply, he will take away everything we have. I do not mind that. It is the fear that he may take your life which makes it impossible for me to sleep of nights."

"Amanina," answered Saladar in an affectionate tone. "I do not like to see you so disturbed, my dearest wife. But I must tell you once and for all that I cannot pander to this servant of the evil gods. It is not in my nature to bend my back to him, this double-tongued traitor and thief! The demands he makes on me drive me into a fury. Not even to make things easier for you, my sweet Amanina, can I give in to him."

"But, my lord and husband, I fear only for your safety. Do you think I care about the lands and the horses and the little bits of gold we have saved? No, no, Saladar, I would face a penniless future rather than see you bend your knee to this evil monster. But your life, O my Saladar, is more precious than our pride. It is needful that you give in to him. Perhaps just a little, my loved one. Flatter his pride. O Saladar, Saladar! I beg you to do this."

It was not yet daybreak when Nicolan decided he would no longer toss uneasily on his hard couch. He rose and dressed in the dark, uttering an angry ejaculation when he stubbed his foot against the ivory base of his bed. The Ildeburghs had been wealthy for generations and their low U-shaped house was filled with luxurious appointments. It was still so dark that he had to walk cautiously as he bent his steps in the direction of the western meadows where the baws were being pastured. His thoughts were now concerned only with the fine yearlings they would have for the Trumping this year. It was seldom, in fact, that his mind held any other thought. Being a true son of his race, and only fifteen years of age, he regarded horses as the only interest worth a man's attention.

A word of explanation is required at this point. The language employed by the people of the plateau had been added to constantly over the years, words being borrowed from the other races they had encountered in their slow westward migration. One of the words thus acquired was "baw." It had meant in one tongue a pack horse, in another a friend. As a horse and a friend were practically synonymous terms with the people of the plateau, the word had gradually been applied to the yearlings, particularly at the time when, with much sounding of trumpets, the landowners brought the best of their stock for a match and testing every spring. In another week the Trumping would take place and Nicolan spent all of his time currying the best of their yearlings, and discussing their chances with Sido, the overseer. Sido's long whip, which curled constantly about the legs and backs of his helpers, had never been known to cause a quiver on an equine hide.

It was dark and still when Nicolan reached the entrance to the west meadows. Putting two fingers in his mouth, he emitted a loud whistle. Instantly there came neighings from all points and the staccato beating of hoofs as the yearlings came running in his direction. Nicolan grinned proudly to himself. "The fine little fellows!" he said. "They know me."

Soon they were all about him. The sun had lifted an inquiring yellow eyebrow over the eastern rim and he could now see their up-pointed ears and their long graceful legs. "My pets!" he said, reaching out to rumple the manes of the two nearest him. "Are you going to make me proud at the Trumping? Are you going to win all the prizes, my fast little fellows?"

"What's this?" demanded a sharp voice from the darkness behind him. It was clear from the tone of Sido's voice that he was angry.

"It's Nicolan. I came down to see how our young men were getting along."

He could hear the long whip of the overseer swishing in the air about him. "And what good could you do in this darkness? All you have done is to get me out of bed in a great sweat and fear that someone was trying to steal them," declared Sido. "I could not see who you were and in another second this whip of mine would have cut a strip of flesh off your back. And well you would have deserved it!" He added in a grumbling tone, "I would not have been slow to let you feel the weight of it, Master Nick, if I had caught you up to any tricks."

Nicolan knew this only too well. On many occasions he had felt the sting of the overseer's whip on his legs.

"But they know my whistle," he said, exultantly, nodding his head at Sido in the dark. "Did you hear them come across? They were over the meadows in a shorter time than any other lot have ever been able to do. I think, Sido, we will sweep the Trumping this year."

Sido responded in a grumbling tone. "They are not bad, it is true. Their eyes are the right color—there isn't a hint of blue in any of them. Their throats are neat and clean. Their pasterns have the right slope and their backs are strong. When they have their growth, they will stand higher than the Arabians. All this is good but it is still too early to be sure about them. The judges will have to guess, as they always do."

"It will not be hard for them to guess right when they look at this lot," declared Nicolan, confidently.

The sun had come up enough so that he could see the amulet around each slender neck, a protection against poison and evil charms.

It was at this moment that a wild and frightening wave of sound reached their ears: men's voices raised in anger and fear, the shrill cries of women, the clash of sword on shield, the frenzied neighing of horses. It came from the direction of the house. Recalling the discussion of the precious evening, Nicolan jumped at once to a conclusion. The hated Vannius had arrived to take possession of the Ildeburgh properties and his father was resisting by force of arms. Without pausing for a moment's thought, the boy turned and ran in the direction from which the sound had come.

Sido knew also what the clamor meant. The blow which had been anticipated so long had fallen at last. He could not be of any help in the fighting, he said to himself; it would be over before he could get there. But he could perform one service at least, he could get some of the best horses into the hiding place which had been provided in the Black Clough for such an emergency. Sighting one of his assistants on the far side of the meadow, he cupped his hands over his lips and shouted instructions to him. In a very few minutes the horses had been collected into a compact body and were being driven off down a narrow gulley.

The fighting had come to a tragic end by the time Nicolan emerged on the green plateau where the house of the Ildeburghs stood. Resistance had been brief, because the lookout man posted in the cover of trees which commanded the road had fallen into a doze and had been knocked into insensibility by a blow on the head with the flat of a Roman blade before he could sound the alarm. Saladar, who slept lightly, had rushed out sword in hand when the first iron-shod hoof sounded on the stone of the road; and this had been accepted as full justification for a murderous attack on him, under which he had gone down. Three of his men had shared his fate later.

When Nicolan arrived on the scene he saw first of all his mother standing defiantly before Vannius, her arms bound behind her back, her face cold with grief and despair. The body of his father lay where he had fallen. The world came down in sudden and complete ruin about the boy and he did not resist when two of the governor's men seized him roughly and dragged him up to stand beside his pale mother.

Vannius was sprawled in a wide chair which had been brought out from the house for his convenience. It was a beautiful thing of chaste Grecian design and in it his bloated body looked macabre and out of place. His face had once been finely cut but was now coarsened by years of indulgence and grotesquely mapped by purple veins.

"Is this the son?" he asked, in a thick voice.

When assured that Nicolan was the heir to the Ildeburgh lands and honors, he gave a negligent gesture of his hand toward the limp body of Saladar. "Everything this traitor owned is to be confiscated," he said. His yellowish eyeballs rolled slowly and sickly in the direction of Nicolan. "The boy will be disposed of with the mother. That is, of course, if Trigetius, who seems to believe in one-sided bargains with all the profit for him, can be induced to make a reasonable offer."

In a voice which the boy did not recognize, so drained was it of all human quality, Amanina whispered in her son's ear, "We are to be sold as slaves."

Nicolan became aware at the same moment of a man beside the chair where Vannius slouched obesely, a Roman with an acquisitive squint and a scar on one cheek which lent his face a villainous expression. This, he knew, must be Trigetius. Everyone in the plateau lands had heard of him. He was a slave trader and the most unscrupulous of them all.

The slave trader made his face still more hideous by frowning as he pondered the problem. Finally he named a figure.

"It is not enough, my hardfisted Trigetius," declared the governor. "The widow is worth that much alone without considering the value of the boy."

Trigetius did not need to look again at the still and tragic figure of Amanina, having already assessed her as a highly valuable commodity who would sell at a very fine profit to some elderly Roman on the watch for desirable feminine slaves. He turned instead to study the boy. "He's thin," he commented, in a disparaging tone. "You can count all his ribs. There would be little bidding for him."

"I appeal to Attila!" cried Nicolan, roused to a sudden fury of courage. "My father had broken no laws. You have killed him so that his voice cannot speak in his own defense."

The eyes of Vannius looked again in his direction. "I sit here in Attila's stead and I am vested fully with his powers," he declared. "When you appeal to Attila, you appeal to me. Get that into your head, impudent stripling."

"He does not know the things you do in his name!" cried the boy. "They say it is his desire to be fair to those who live under his rule."

"The comb of this young cock needs cutting," said Vannius, dropping all pretense of dignity and speaking in an angry voice. "I know no fate worse than to confide him to the care of the considerate Trigetius, who will know how to curb his tongue and humble his pride. Because of what he has dared say to me, I shall argue no longer over terms for this pair. I make you a fair and easy proposition, O kind Trigetius. Throw in that opal you wear around your neck and I will accept your price."

The trader with the ugly scar detached the jewel from the heavy gold chain around his neck. "I will give the stone only," he said. "The chain is worth more than the skinny hide of this —this very rash young upstart." He dropped the opal into the fat cushion formed by the governor's cupped hand. "The deal, then, is made. I will pay you in Roman gold, which I am sure, O Vannius, you would demand of me in any case. May I say that on the whole I am content to part with the stone. I suspect it has brought me bad luck. . . ."

"Nicolan, say nothing more," whispered Amanina in her son's ear. "You will only bring more misfortune on your head if you rouse their anger in this way."

The eyes of Trigetius seemed to draw closer together as they went from mother to son. He motioned to a servant. "Truss the boy's arms. We are leaving at once and I do not want any attempt to run away. If he makes as much as one false step, let him taste for his breakfast the fine flavor of the bullwhip."

2

By the end of the day the party of the Roman trader had been swelled by the acquisition of more prisoners who were being sold into slavery, a dozen or more men and women too frightened to whisper among themselves; some of them were being disposed of by owners of their own race and blood. They had not yet left the plateau and Trigetius decided for safety's sake to camp well off the road. He set two of his men to act as sentries while the rest prepared a meal over a carefully screened fire. Neither Nicolan nor his mother had any appetite, which brought the trader over to give them a curt piece of advice. "If you faint on the road tomorrow for lack of food or if you lag, you must expect the consequences. The medicine I serve to slaves is sharp."

"I have looked this day on the dead face of my husband," said Amanina.

The trader nodded his head. "You will think better of it tomorrow when hunger drives grief out of your head." He looked at her with a shrewd eye in his scarred face. "You are a woman of family. Sit down and I will tell you something for your own good." He squatted down first, lifting his long linen robe over a pair of lean and hirsute knees. Much gesturing with both hands provided an accompaniment to what he proceeded to tell her. "Trading in slaves is my business and I make it pay me well. I am not a hard man but I never let sentiment interfere with what I do. My field is in the border provinces and in sections where the Romans have lost their hold. The more unsettled a part is, the easier it becomes to pick up slaves at low prices. Mostly I buy children. The parents sell them. When their families get too large, they turn over some of them to me. Children are no trouble. One tickling with the whip and all the foolishness goes out of them. But I make the best profit with women like you—wellborn, good to look at, and with a pleasant cushioning of the bones. You may find this hard to believe but it is true that our interests are identical. You want a good master and an easy way of living and I make my best profit when I find these for you." He nodded his head slowly. "With the great families in Rome there are always nice occupations for female slaves. I might find someone who is looking for an *auro praepositia* and that would suit you well because all they have to do is to keep the gold plate and see that it is well burnished. There are always *lectors* who read to the family. Then there is the *corinthiaria* who looks after the brazen vases. A little lower—but still quite respectable, oh, indeed yes— are the *structia* who see to the making of the ornamental confectionery and the *panicoctaria* who make fine cakes." A sly look came into his eyes. "There are still easier posts about which I need not tell you anything, for I see you are a woman of delicate scruples. There are many buyers in Rome for this kind of slave and sometimes they pay high, very high indeed; the older the buyer, the higher the price."

Amanina did not answer. She was holding her head down in the deepest shame, her hands clutched in her lap.

"But if you don't watch yourself, woman, I will have to sell you to a lower kind of family; as an *auditia* who cleans the house or a *cubicularia* who works in the bedchambers. That is what happens when you get to weeping and pining and letting your hips get thin and hollow and your neck stringy. It is hard to give women away when they are like that."

Nicolan, standing close at hand, said at this point, "My mother is unhappy and ill. I demand that you leave her alone."

Trigetius got slowly to his feet, an angry frown in his close-set eyes. "I was trying to be helpful when I should have turned you both over to my men for a sound whipping. It is always with young cocks like you that I have trouble. Let this be a lesson to you." He raised the whip in his hand and brought it down across the boy's shoulders. A hot, excruciating pain surged through Nicolan's body and instinctively he shrank away. "Do you want twenty more like that? I will see that you get them if you open your mouth again."

All through the next day Nicolan's shoulder and neck pained him so much that he tramped beside his mother in a dazed and unhappy silence. He thought mostly of his father, his mood swinging from a furious and desperate rage to the numbness of despair. His bonds had been removed after the first few hours on the road but he kept his hands with conscious firmness against his sides. When they reached their camping place for the night, and the rest of the prisoners were consuming the coarse fare which had been provided for them, a far from palatable concoction of pulse and corn, heavily salted, he moved his position close enough to his mother to be able to whisper in her ear.

"We cannot stand this," he said. "We must contrive to escape. I have no idea how it can be done but there must be a way. We will find it in time. And that means we must be able to make our way back. I have been thinking about it and I am going to draw a map."

His mother shook her head in despair. "Nicolan, you must not build your hopes this way!" she whispered. "It will not be too hard for you, my fine son. You will grow taller and stronger and in time you will be able to buy your freedom. They say that Rome is filled with freedmen and that many of them are powerful and wealthy. If you tried to run away, my son, and they caught you, they would nail you to a cross. It is what they always do." She shuddered. "Some men of our race have died that way. You must promise me to be sensible. What"—a tear, the first he had seen her shed, was on her cheek—"what good would come of returning to our home? They would take us again and sell us to other masters."

"Mother, what will become of you?"

"My son, it does not matter. I lost all desire to live when I saw your father go down under their swords."

Nicolan sat in thought for a long time before speaking again. "I do not want to add to your grief. It may be as you say, that it is impossible to escape. But I am going to make the map. It will keep my mind occupied, at least."

The next night, after everyone had fallen into a sleep of complete exhaustion, he made his way with great stealth to the fire. Here he found a charred twig in the ashes and returned with it to his place. His mother, on his urging, had ripped a strip from the bottom of the one spare robe she had been permitted to bring. Taking a small piece of it, he proceeded to make a map of the ground they had covered since leaving the familiar homeland.

He was discovering something about himself which made it easy to complete the task. His eyes were adept at gauging distances and judging the levels of roads as well as the height of the land. Now he found that his hand had an unsuspected skill in transferring everything he had seen in the fullest detail to the white material. When the drawing was finished, he was certain that it would be an easy matter to follow the instructions he had set down.

Each day thereafter he kept his eye on the course of the road, noting each detail of the trail which seemed important and carefully estimating the distances. Each night he took another square of the material and set down what he had observed. The pieces were numbered and stowed away under his belt.

3

One of the other slaves was a tall man of middle years who answered to the name of Sarus. Usually Nicolan walked beside his mother but one day he found himself at the foot of the line where Sarus, who had bad feet, was always to be found. They fell into talk and the limping elder man told his story to the boy: how he had been born and raised in Illyricum, that he was a free man but had married a pretty slave girl. Amaga had borne him two sons and her hard master had claimed them as his property. When they were old enough, they had been sold to a slave dealer.

"My Amaga is dead," said the unhappy father. "When I learned that my two sons had been bought by a senator in Rome, I decided I must follow them by any means at all. I must see them. I must be in a position to help them. Perhaps someday I might even be able to buy them free. But I couldn't do any of these things from Illyricum." He gave his head a saddened and weary shake. "There was only one thing to do. I sold myself to Trigetius. With the money he paid me—he drove a hard bargain—I may be able to purchase the freedom of my poor little sons. If I can find them."

"What will happen to you then?" asked Nicolan.

Sarus turned on him a face which was transfigured with emotion. "Nothing else will matter," he cried, "if I can get them free!"

The day came finally when they saw on the horizon the walls

of the great city which the change-seeking Romans had built close to the waters of the Adriatic as a rival to Rome. It was apparent at first glance that Ravenna was already a great accomplishment, for the roofs of white marble palaces and the towering spires of churches showed above the walls. Sarus as usual was hobbling along in the rear and he raised the stick, which gave some aid to his legs, as a signal to Nicolan to drop back.

"Have you heard?" asked Sarus, in a whisper when they were pacing along together.

"I have heard nothing."

"We are to be offered for sale here in Ravenna."

Nicolan looked at his companion and saw that his face was drawn into lines of suffering and despair.

"But Trigetius won't offer you," he said. "He made you a promise. That you would be taken to Rome."

"A promise made to a slave is nothing," said Sarus, bitterly. "It can be broken in the next breath." He groaned in desperation of spirit. "He has chosen Ravenna because so many of the wealthiest Romans are coming here now that the old woman"—he was referring to Galla Placidia, the mother of the emperor—"has made it her home. It is said that even the emperor is talking of moving here. Prices of everything are going up. Slaves bring a better price here than in Rome." Disregarding the proximity of one of the guards with a heavy whip in his hand, the unfortunate father cried out in a loud voice: "Alas, my poor little sons! I shall never see them again!"

To give him some comfort, Nicolan pointed out that in all probability the wealthy Romans, who would bid for slaves on the market at Ravenna, kept up establishments in Rome as well. He might still hope to be taken to the capital of the empire.

"I have thought of that," said Sarus. "I get some small comfort out of it."

The next day the male slaves, who had slept in the courtyard of an inn outside the city walls, where the smell of stagnant water in the canals which had been dug to drain the fens around the new city filled their nostrils unpleasantly, were ordered to discard their clothes. They were then instructed to take turns in stepping with both feet into a bucket containing white paint.

After doing this, they sat in rows on the damp cobbles with their feet raised on pieces of wood to give the paint a chance to dry.

Nicolan asked the meaning of this strange proceeding of the man seated next to him. "This," was the answer, pointing to their whitened feet and ankles, "means we are barbarians and have been brought across the bounds of what they call their empire. The buyers—the slavering, stinking beasts who will come and look us over and poke their fingers into our stomachs—know about us, without being told, from things like this. Someday Marha will look down and see what we suffer and we will dip *his* fingers into molten lead and poke them into *their* stomachs!"

"Will we be offered for sale naked?"

The other slave nodded. "They want to see what they are buying."

"The women too?"

"As naked as the day they came into the world. That's what brings the buyers out. Lots of them come to the slave market every day. They get more pleasure out of it than anything. Many of them, without a copper coin among the lot of them, stand around and buy the naked girls with their eyes."

Nicolan was so filled with angry emotion that he wanted to cry out against such abominations. He was asking himself if his mother would be compelled to undergo this ordeal. He was sure that, if they made her stand nude in the market place, she would die of the shame. Never would she be able to survive such humiliation as this. He raised his wrists and stared at the chains which bound them together. Was there nothing he could do? He called to the guard who stood over them and demanded a word with Trigetius.

The guard laughed and gave his whip a swish in the air. "A word with the master? Foolish little slave, I will curl the ends of my whip around your skinny ribs if I hear another word out of you."

The slave market was circular in shape, with benches two feet high around the outside. Trigetius had rented half of the space and had planted spears in the ground at each end with a rope looped from handle to handle. Nicolan was halfway of the section where the men stood on display. He had not dared turn his eyes in the direction of the women. A card with a price on it had been pasted to the skin of his waist but he refused to imitate the others and bend his head to find what valuation the astute Trigetius had placed on him. He kept his head up and his eyes fixed on the sky above the white marble portal of the Slave Exchange.

Buyers and mere lookers were walking up and down in front of the benches. They congregated for the most part where Trigetius showed his wares and most of their talk was of the healthy men and buxom women he had brought. Occasionally a buyer would step up to flex a muscle.

"You will never sell," said the man next to Nicolan, in a whisper. "You're not worth the price he has put on you. What were you, the son of a German king or a Sarmatian baron?"

Nicolan passed over the ill will behind the remark. "What is the price fixed on Sarus?" he asked. That unhappy man was standing at one end of the line and it was easy to see from the pallor of his cheeks and the lines about his eyes that he was a prey to the deepest fears.

"Low," was the answer. "He will be the first to go."

This proved to be an accurate guess. An old Roman with a predatory nose raised a hand in front of Sarus and snapped his fingers as a sign that he would pay the price. The pale Sarus, unable at first to believe that this great misfortune had come his way, had to be shoved off the bench, landing in a heap at his new master's feet.

A few minutes later one of the guards came to a stop in front of Nicolan.

"Get down," he said.

"Have I been bought?" asked Nicolan.

"Didn't you hear what I said?" demanded the guard, angrily. "I told you to get down. Yes, you have been bought. I don't know why. You don't look as though you had a good day's work in you."

Nicolan got his courage up to the point of looking at the other end of the line where the women stood. There were many gaps already. His mother was not there.

His first reaction was one of hope. Had Trigetius, in deference to his mother's station in life, exempted her from appearing on the slave market? If that were the case, he would take her on to Rome and dispose of her there. The possibility of this was dismissed almost immediately from his mind. It was much more likely that Trigetius had found a purchaser for her at an early stage and that she had already been claimed by her master.

His mother was looking forward to death with such a fierce desire that gradually he had come to feel some reconciliation to this as a solution. He could do nothing for her, no matter how passionately and continuously he turned over every possibility in his mind. There was no one to whom he might appeal. They had been dragged into a world where the kings of conquered countries labored as slaves for the dominant race and heroes died under the lash of cruel overseers. If there was nothing they could do, what hope was there for him? One only: he might be able to seize the sword of the tall black attendant who stood in the center of the market and slash about him until he was cut down and killed. This suicidal gesture would not abate his mother's sufferings a single jot.

"Follow me," said the guard.

He was taken back to the underground room in the Slave Exchange where those who had been sold were held until claimed. A few moments later Trigetius came and squatted down beside him.

"I have done well with you," he stated, with a satisfied nod of his head. "You have been sold to Aetius."

At this most unexpected announcement, Nicolan turned and stared at the dealer. Aetius was the master of Rome. By the death of Boniface eight years before the only rival had been removed from the path of the ambitious Roman who had spent his youth at the Hun court and had later become the best of the imperial generals. Despite the hostility of Placidia, the mother of the weak young emperor, Aetius had acquired a control over Roman affairs which amounted to dictatorship.

The trader nodded his head again. "This will be a great chance for you. As you can read and write, you may be advanced in his service. Aetius is the greatest man in the world today—barring, of course, that monster up there. I have sold him many slaves and so I know him well. He depends on my judgment and it required no more than my recommendation to close the deal with his agent, who came out yesterday."

"What will he do with me?"

Trigetius raised both hands with the palms up. "Who am I to

say what the great Aetius will do? He has need of men with
education since he has his hands on all the departments now. The
young emperor is a slack-bellied glutton and fool and Aetius never
consults him any more. The old woman"—Nicolan knew he was
referring to Placidia—"hates him like poison but there is nothing
she can do. They say she bites her nails with rage in her palace at
Ravenna and swears that someday she will have his head brought
to her on a charger. But Aetius goes right on governing the
empire."

"What have you done with my mother?"

Trigetius was twisting a quill in his teeth with an air of oily
affability. "I sold her," he said. "It was settled last night by private
treaty. Her owner is a wealthy man of advanced years who has
a house in Ravenna as well as in Rome. He will be an indulgent
master, if she will be sensible about it."

"I am afraid my mother is indifferent to what may happen to
her."

"I had been noticing that her health was not good. That is why
I decided to make a quick sale." Trigetius nodded with pride in
his own sagacity. "There are doses you can give slaves before ex-
posing them for sale. It puts color in the cheeks and brightens
up the eyes. A young girl can be made to look very lively and all
the buyers will bid for her. I seldom do it because I have a reputation to maintain. Your mother is a comely woman and she could
still be sold without going to such lengths. The old bag of bones
who bought her was quite pleased with her."

Nicolan, holding himself under a tight rein, asked in a low
tone, "Will I be able to see her before we are separated?"

"There is still time. I grant you this favor because I have done
well enough with both of you. You will tell the steward of Aetius
that I was lenient and considerate." Trigetius got to his feet.
"Come with me."

His mother was sitting by herself in a corner of the room where
the women were held. The chains had been removed from her
ankles and wrists. Nicolan seated himself beside her.

"Do you know that we have both been sold?" he asked.

"Yes, my son. You are being taken to Rome. Surely, in the
household of such a great man, you will have fair treatment."

"I have no idea what it will be like."

"Be careful and sensible, my poor son. You are young and you must think of the future."

"I think only of you. Mother, Mother, what will happen to you? Have you seen this man they call your master?"

"No, not yet." She leaned over and stroked his hand gently. "My son, it does not matter about me. I think only of the release which will come to me very soon now. I think of rejoining your father in the land to which his spirit has gone." She roused herself sufficiently to turn and look at him with deep love in her eyes. "My son, I am afraid that I am a better wife than mother. My thoughts have all been of the husband who died before my eyes and not of the son who must go on living in this cruel world."

"That is as it should be, Mother," said Nicolan. "A man must stand on his own two feet in this world, even if they are painted white. Have no fears for me. Somehow I will escape. And I promise that I will take a full measure of revenge. And this I promise too, that I shall love and reverence you to my last hour of life."

CHAPTER VIII

1

ALTHOUGH Rome sat quiescently under his eye and the provinces trembled at his nod, Aetius was an upstart. He had been born in Silistria, which was a dark and barbarian land along the Lower Danube. His father was one Gaudentius, who had risen to be called the Count of Africa although it was certain that not one drop of pure Roman blood pulsed in his veins. It was a custom among the members of the great old families to ask each other in cautious whispers: "Aetius? Where was Aetius yesterday?" and the answer was, "Where he will be tomorrow."

When this able and ambitious man found it necessary to locate himself suitably in the capital of the great empire over which he now ruled, he discovered that a palisade of pride ringed the Palatine Hill. Here stood the palaces of dead and gone emperors with the homes of the great families clustering about them. Not as much as an inch of land was for sale or subject to confiscation. And yet where else but on the Palatine could a man of his stature live? Even with the power he had gathered into his hands, the best Aetius could do was to take a scrubby piece of land on the slope. It was close to the spot where Cicero had once lived in considerable pomp but there was no consolation in that when it was found that a house built on this site would of necessity cling precariously to the sloping earth. When Aetius finished with the raising of his far from pretentious walls, it was found that the entrance road would be too steep for any form of conveyance. The carriages and curtained litters in which visitors arrived had to remain, therefore, on the crest while the passengers approached the plain stone entrance on foot, with the aid of an iron railing. Some arrived in a belligerent mood but mostly they were reduced to a proper degree of humility by the experience.

The palace of Aetius was, therefore, the least imposing as well as the least comfortable on this mighty citadel of privilege where the riches from the rape of a world were squandered. The *vestibulum,* which was always crowded to the point of extreme discomfort, was almost bare of furnishings. The best accommodation it offered was a ledge around the walls and this was crowded at all hours. There was never a moment seemingly when this inhospitable stone did not accommodate the soft posterior of a senator and the lean, tough shanks of at least one general.

As though conscious of his obscure beginnings, Aetius had shown the good taste not to follow any of the fads and fashions of the moment. He had not filled the saloons of his aseptically new house with *imagines majorum,* the waxen masks of ancestors, real or imaginary, with which social climbers bolstered their claims. He had not placed on his walls a single relic of the departed great, a form of antique for which all right-thinking patricians competed bitterly. If Aetius accompanied a prominent visitor to the door before dismissing him, he never tarried beside a prayer rug on the wall to say, "Do you find it hard to believe that the lovely knees of Helen, yes, *the* Helen, pressed this many hundreds of times?" or with even greater arrogance, "This sword, which cost me a fortune, I assure you, knew the touch of the hand of great Caesar."

The only distinctive feature of the house, perhaps, was a strong stone lodge at one side which was surrounded by a moat and could be approached only by a single drawbridge. Here Aetius slept and, when he had retired for the night, the bridge was raised and bolted securely to the wall. He shared with all dictators a desire to sleep in well-guarded isolation.

In spite of its drawbacks the house was well adapted to the needs of its owner. Most of the visitors came on matters of business or political concern. They would be taken for a brief minute or two into the small spare room where the dictator sat. They would be questioned sharply and to the point and dismissed as soon as the question at issue had been resolved. Aetius tried to see everyone who called and so had won for himself the good will of the common people, which he was sensible enough to value above the condescension of the patricians.

A visitor who looked about him in this Spartan house and took note of the cedarwood cabinets, fitted with pigeonholes and cubicles and stuffed with notes, and observed the busy secretaries and scriveners who came and went in silent absorption, could not fail to realize that the owner had dedicated himself to work. If they enjoyed the opportunity of watching him closely they would come in time to know that his was not the kind of genius which excelled in brilliant improvisation and arrived at results by daring expedients; that, instead, the great Aetius, who without doubt *was* a genius, was systematic and thorough to a degree. He took no decision until he had carefully considered everything bearing on it. He possessed so much common sense, in fact, that secretly he had no belief in the accepted superstitions of the day. Before going into battle he consulted the auguries in deference to the universal belief in the need but he took his course from the information his scouts and spies had brought instead of following the conclusions adduced by a study of the quivering entrails of newly killed poultry.

A day came which was memorable only to a slave newly arrived in Rome who had stared about him at the great marble palaces and the high public buildings as well as the malodorous caverns where the poor lived and had found himself in a welter of emotions, excitement, incredulity, shock, and resentment. In the early afternoon of this day, Aetius escorted a visitor through the *atrium* and out to the entrance, above which stretched that difficult road so hard to ascend. The visitor was a tall and stooped man in his late middle years with a friendly eye which saw everything going on about him.

"Micca," said the dictator of Rome, in a careful whisper, "you have brought me much information which will be useful and for which I thank you. Come back again after you have paid your visits to Constantinople and to that—that man of envy and scorn, that boaster and bully who will someday cause us great trouble. I depend much on the news you glean for me. On your way, stop at Ravenna and find what the old woman is thinking and doing. She seems consistent in one thing only, her hatred of me."

"The—the personage to whom you refer is not hard to understand, O Great Aetius," said the trader. "If you persevere in the opinion you have just expressed, you will never be at fault where she is concerned." He continued then in a tone for all to hear.

"I thank you for the commissions you have been generous enough to confide to me. I shall strive to please you with what I obtain."

The *vocator*, whose duty it was to keep account of all visitors and inform his master in advance of their names and occupations so that Aetius could greet them with familiarity, said to the great man as he returned from dismissing Micca the Mede: "There is a new slave. The one purchased from Trigetius. He is the son of a wealthy landowner on the Alföld. The father is recently deceased."

"That one," said Aetius, pausing. He was so thorough in his methods that no detail was too insignificant for his attention. He even made it a point to see each new slave. "Who are still waiting to speak with me?"

The *vocator* went over the list. A score or more were waiting for a chance to see the master of Rome. None, however, was of first importance and Aetius decided they could all wait. He would have a look at the slave first.

Nicolan was surprised at his initial glimpse of the ruler of Rome. Aetius was the handsomest man he had ever seen. The boy who had roused the enmity of his stunted playmate Attila had grown into an imposing figure, with a high and finely proportioned forehead, a straight nose, an animated eye. On second glance it became apparent that his good looks were limited by an expression of extreme severity. He never smiled and when he spoke it was in cold and contained tones. Behind the animation of his eye was a hint of calculation.

The ruler of the empire studied a note which the *vocator* had placed in his hand. "I see here," he said, without raising his eyes, "that you read and write."

"Yes, my lord Aetius," answered Nicolan.

"Do you know anything of this new way of writing?"

"I understand the shorthand."

"Who taught you?"

Nicolan hesitated. "A priest. A very learned man who came from one of the islands of the west and who studied it in a book."

"A missionary, I judge. The first one I have heard of who seems to have some practical sense. It is good you can write the short way. I have a few here who use it but not as many as I would like.

You come from the plains below the Danube. Have you ever seen the emperor of the Huns?"

"No, my lord Aetius."

"Have you seen this renegade who has been put in control of your country? He goes by the name of Vannius."

"Once, my lord. On the morning he killed my father and sold my mother and me to the trader."

"And what is your opinion of him?"

"He is a cruel and ignorant tyrant. If he escapes retribution long enough, I will strangle him someday."

Aetius handed the note back to the *vocator* and addressed Nicolan without turning in his direction. "I asked the question to see if you would be foolhardy enough to answer. The first lesson you must learn, it seems, is that a slave has no opinions." He turned to the *vocator* and said in a matter-of-fact tone: "I will make it light this time. Tell the bailiff five lashes only. Take him away."

The prompter asked, "What work is he to be given?"

"When he recovers from the effect of the lashes, the bailiff will put him to copying."

"What class is he to be in?"

"The lowest," instructed Aetius. "This one needs to be taught humility."

2

Sitting where the warmth of the rising sun bore down so gratefully on his scarred back, Nicolan found that his recollections of living in the lowest classification of slavery in the household of Aetius, apart from several episodes of sheer horror, had to do mostly with food. He was always hungry. The meals served twice a day were scanty and at times unpalatable. The first consisted invariably of a porridge-like substance made of wheat which was supposed to be nutritious but certainly was not pleasing to the taste. The second, served in midafternoon, was rather more substantial: thick slices of a heavy brown bread with a few shreds of gristly meat or cheese made of goat's milk, and a cup of thin sour wine to wash it down.

To make it harder for those who subsisted on this monotonous fare, they were drafted for service in the kitchens when Aetius entertained and the sights and smells would drive them almost mad with craving. Nicolan served on many occasions in the preparation of the gargantuan feasts which the dictator served to groups of prominent Romans. Once he was delegated to stuff the stomach of a boar, which had been spitted whole on a huge turning-iron, with deliciously roasted sausages. Another time he was put to work with the dessert squad, far away from the great hot fires where the roasts were preparing, and he spent several hours of temptation in filling field-fares with dried grapes and almonds and luscious tarts with fresh fruit heavily sugared and then embedded in cushions of brown custard. There was an almost irresistible impulse in him to seize a morsel of this wonderful food and cram it into his mouth. Fortunately he never yielded to the desire. Sharp eyes scrutinized the laboring ranks of the slaves and any surreptitious munching of food would bring a cry of "Thief!" or "Birds in the cherry tree!" The bailiff had one method only in dealing with such cases. He would say, "Five lashes," or, if it were a second offense, "Ten lashes."

The sentences of the bailiff were always carried out immediately. First the Punishment Bell would ring, sounding three sharp notes somewhat like the swish of the lash, and all members of the household who were free at the moment would repair to the kitchen court which had been built out somewhat precariously from the base of the building. The delinquent would be stripped to the waist and compelled to kneel. A tall eunuch from Numidia applied the whip. He was so skillful that, if he so desired, he could make the lash curl about the flesh of the victim without causing excessive pain. But more frequently, when he disliked the offender or felt complete indifference, he would let the rawhide crash down on the shrinking backs with an effect like the impact of white-hot metal bars.

Nicolan's first taste of the whip had not been too great an ordeal. At any rate he had managed to sustain it without emitting a sound. His second was a much different matter. The grapevine of the slaves, which distributed news of the outside world as well as the gossip of the household, had brought him word that his mother was dead. Her life had ended in Rome within a fortnight of her sale to the wealthy landowner. She had not followed the warning of Trigetius, quite clearly, and had been subjected to the disciplinary lash. The son's grief had been violently expressed and the bailiff, informed of the threats he had uttered, departed from his usual formula by saying, "Ten lashes." This time the eunuch allowed the heavy whip to cut the skin and Nicolan fainted as the last of the ten stripes descended on the shrinking flesh of his back and shoulders. He was in the hospital of the household for several weeks before his strength came back.

In course of time he was promoted to a higher level in the slave scale, owing to the proficiency he showed in his work. This meant that he no longer slept in a room below the level of the ground on a mound of dank straw. He had a narrow bed to himself in a long ward which accommodated nearly seventy of the higher-ranking slaves. There was a long tiled bath in the adjoining chamber, capable of use by half a dozen adults at the same time. This had to be shared with the female slaves and an arrangement had been made whereby the women had the sole right to the bath until two in the afternoon, after which it was exclusively for the use of the men. He took his meals with the same privileged group in a stone chamber from which could be heard the clatter and confusion of the kitchen. The food was better, although inclined to be coarse at times and monotonous always.

To his surprise, he found the conversation at meals interesting. For the most part the high-placed slaves discussed the affairs of the household and of business generally. There was continuous reference to the uses they were making of their *peculium,* the reward they were allowed to make and keep. Sometimes they conversed on such matters as world politics, the arts, the leaders of Rome, religion, and philosophy. Nicolan was surprised at the intelligence they displayed. Comparing their talk with the languid and insipid tattle in the great dining room above, he got the impression that slaves were more alert of mind and enterprising of spirit than the masters of the world who lolled in the absurd existence of luxury and privilege they had created for themselves.

Nicolan was put into the copying room first, and here he worked with such speed and proficiency that in a short time he was promoted to secretarial work. As a final upward step he began to take dictation from Aetius himself. The tall, stern Roman recognized him without a doubt (he never forgot a face) but he gave no evidence of interest or recollection when Nicolan entered his room for the first time. It was soon apparent, however, that he had been well satisfied. Within a week Nicolan was doing all his work.

Aetius dictated with great speed, saying "Letter" or "Note," and plunging at once into a flow of well-conceived and trenchant sentences. Sometimes he would pause and rub the end of his fine long nose with a forefinger but for the most part he was never at a loss for a phrase. To keep up with him, the fingers of the young slave had to move as fast as the legs of a charging soldier of the legion.

It was by reason of his frequent attendance in the small workroom of the master, from the window of which a view could be had of most of the great city, that Nicolan became the sharer of a secret. Conscious of the contempt of the patrician families, Aetius was planning to raise himself high above them all. His idea was one of great audacity: to divorce his wife and take in wedlock in her place the sister of the emperor, the young and vivacious Princess Honoria.

The dictator discussed this scheme with several of his closest adherents, senators and men high in the army and the governmental services. The consultations were carried on in whispers but otherwise no effort was made to keep the secretary, sitting at his small table in a corner, from knowing. He was a slave and was under the strictest obligation to divulge nothing that concerned his master. There was less danger in him than in the four walls which enclosed them as they whispered about the plan.

Nicolan was not interested at all. What did it matter that his master, who made no effort to win affection or foster allegiance in his own household, was hatching a scheme to raise himself to a place in the imperial family? Everything that happened in this proud and wealthy city, this center of corruption and hypocrisy and wickedness, everything he heard and saw and felt, added to his hatred for Rome and the Romans. Once he said to himself that Rome was like a dying leper clothed in shimmering silk and wearing a jeweled crown; and the phrase stayed in his mind and he often repeated it to himself, with a sense of pride that he had coined it.

The men consulted by Aetius seemed to favor his idea. It

would consolidate his position, they told him, more securely than anything else he could do. Only one of them raised a doubt. "What of the old woman?" he asked. "You will never get her to consent."

Aetius smiled at this. "Nothing will give me more pleasure than to go over her head. I will have the matter settled with the emperor before she has any inkling of it."

Within a very short time it was announced that the Princess Honoria, who had been sharing the semi-retirement of her mother in Ravenna since the rise of Aetius had taken all power out of the hands of Placidia, would pay a visit to Rome. The manner of Aetius became gay, in fact it might have been termed frisky, as he set himself to planning a suitable gift for the lovely guest. He summoned the best jewelers of Rome to make suggestions but listened to their ideas with impatience. None of them could think of anything but necklaces and tiaras and bracelets, all of which would involve him in enormous expense without achieving any suggestion of thoughtful planning. It happened that Micca the Mede was in Rome at this juncture and the desire of Aetius came to his ears. It happened also that Nicolan was with his master when the itinerant merchant was admitted. Micca, wearing a confident smile, had a bundle under one arm, carefully swathed in silk wrappings.

"O Great Aetius!" said Micca, bowing as he stood in the doorway. "I am told you have need of a gift and it came to my mind that there was in my possession an article which might seem to you well suited."

The habitual cold expression on the face of Aetius showed some sign of amelioration. "It is true that I need a gift of great rarity," he said. "I have been in despair of finding it."

"If my lord Aetius will permit me to show him what I have ——" Micca moved close to the marble table at which Aetius labored so many hours of the day. He placed the bundle on one corner and proceeded to remove the silk wrappings. When the final cover had been taken off, there was revealed a tall urnlike vessel of surpassing beauty which possessed not one but four lips. It was whiter than the most translucent chalcedony and was decorated with rubies set in a scroll of delicate silver work. It was so lovely that even the practical-minded Aetius fell under its spell completely and did not trust a finger to touch it. Obviously it was very old and everything about it spoke of great associations in the past.

"What is the purpose of it?" asked Aetius, after several moments of silent contemplation.

"See, my lord Aetius." Micca touched a finger to the inside of one of the lips and a delicate spray of perfume was the result. "That is balsam. Inside there are four sections and each contains a different perfume. It is"—even the old merchant seemed to stand somewhat in awe of this ancient and lovely thing—"my lord Aetius, it is certain that it is very old. It came from the East and the story I have been told is that it once belonged to an emperor in China. I confess that I have no proof of this. The body, as you see, is of white jade and the rubies are flawless." He hesitated and then added, "I can conceive of no finer gift."

Aetius was both pleased and excited. He got up and moved around the table in order to see the urn from every angle. He even smiled, a fleeting effort which was entirely muscular and carried no hint of inner warmth.

"What is the price?" he asked.

Micca answered in a tone of velvety unction. "The price, my lord, is very high. Let me put it this way. The price is your continued confidence in me. It can be expressed only in terms of my appreciation of the honor you do me. If it pleases you, it is yours. I give it freely and gladly. There can be no question of any other kind of payment between us."

After Micca had left the room, leaving the urn on the table where the eyes of Aetius could rest on it with mounting and intense satisfaction, the real ruler of the empire began to plan the note which was to accompany it. He took the greatest care in the phrasing and paused often in search of the right word. It was clear that the astute mind behind the severe dark eyes was now deeply committed to the idea, and that this man, who had seized the reins of real power from the worthless emperor and his ambitious mother, was now determined to win the highest of honors for himself. Had not Placidia herself been given as her second husband an Illyrian general named Constantius, whose achievements had in no way equaled those of Aetius and who had been, moreover, a loutish and sullen figure? And had not Constantius been made joint emperor with Placidia's brother at the same time that she was given the title of Augusta? Was it presumptuous to think that history might repeat itself?

3

The sight of Ivar breakfasting at the other end of the room made Nicolan's thoughts turn to the first time that he had seen the tall Briton. Although he had been involved immediately thereafter in a nightmare of suffering, he could still recall the meeting with a depth of affectionate feeling. He smiled across the room at his friend and Ivar paused long enough in his prodigious eating to smile back.

Aetius had decided to send a large number of secondary gifts with the jade urn, a few small pieces of jewelry, some bolts of oriental cloth, as well as fruit and flowers in great profusion. Each article was to be carried by a slave on an embroidered cushion of green velvet and Nicolan found that he had been selected as one of the bearers. Those honored in this way were attired in special livery for the occasion, consisting of a white robe with a stripe of green across the breast and on the lower hem, and new sandals with green thongs. They were instructed minutely in what they were to do.

They were ushered into a high-pillared room in the royal palace and in a few minutes the princess entered, followed by a bevy of her maids and several important-looking officers of the imperial household. She spoke in a very sweet voice to the young general who had been selected to make the presentation. Nicolan was taller than most of the other slaves and so was stationed in the rear rank, holding one of the cushions on which reposed a vial of true nard, a most aromatic perfume. To his own surprise he found that he was quite curious about the sister of the emperor.

The Princess Honoria was a slender girl with enormous black eyes and a manner which could not be described as effusive but which certainly strayed beyond the narrow confines set for royal dignity. She smiled often and she made it clear that she was delighted with the urn. Her approbation seemed to extend to the young general as well, who had black hair curling closely over his head and a handsome bronzed face. As he knelt before her she allowed her fan to touch his shoulder; the merest touch, of course, which could have been accidental but obviously was not. When it became Nicolan's turn to climb the three marble steps and sink on one knee in front of her, with his head carefully lowered, he found himself carried away on a wave of sheer intoxication. Seen close at hand, she was undeniably lovely. Was his imagination playing him tricks or had the long black eyelashes fluttered as he sank to his knees and held out the cushion on both hands? It had not happened, of course, and a fine piece of presumption it was on his part to have conceived it. But what followed was not imagination at all.

Before one of her ladies could lift the vial for her inspection and then deposit it with the rest, the princess said in a voice quite as sweet as the tone she had used for the young soldier, "How lovely!" and lowered her head to test its fragrance. She had beautiful hair, as dusky as her eyes and with a soft natural wave. He was conscious of a faint but intoxicating perfume which made the contents of the vial seem coarse and ordinary. While her head was thus bent close to his he heard a voice speak to him in a tone so low that he again suspected it was something he had conjured up in his mind.

This was what he heard, or what he believed he heard: "What a pity you are a slave—and not *my* slave!"

His head swam and he wondered how he was going to get sufficient control of himself to rise and walk backward down the marble steps. Before he had recovered any degree of his self-possession, she raised her head and said in a casual voice, "It is nard and *not* one of my favorites." This had the effect of bringing Nicolan back to earth. He raised himself from his kneeling position and reached his place in the line without any mistake.

A few minutes later the ceremony was over. With a final smile, which she tried to distribute impartially over all the occupants of the room, the slender princess disappeared. Nicolan began to breathe naturally again. "I wonder," he asked himself, "if she spoke to the others like that?" The thought was dismissed instantly. He was sure she had not.

The slaves were led to a dark room in the rear of the palace where a single jug of *mulsum* had been provided for their refreshment. The freemen of the party were partaking of food and wine from a well-laden table in another room. When it came to Nicolan's turn to take a sup, he shook his head. He knew from the color of the wine that it was inferior *mulsum* and suspected that it was not real Falernian wine which had been mixed with the honey water in making it.

At this moment a tall young man, wearing the livery of the princess, entered the room and glanced about him. Nicolan had noticed him during the ceremony and had been impressed not only with the strength of his bare arms and the fine lines of his powerful legs but much more by the steadiness of his dark gray eyes. Once their glances had crossed and both had smiled instantly and instinctively. It was as though they had met and had said to each other, "We are going to be friends."

The tall slave, for he wore the badge of servitude on his shoulder, walked over to where Nicolan was standing. "You refuse the *mulsum*," he said, speaking in halting Latin words and with a marked accent. "You are wise. It is thin and very sweet."

"I had a disinclination for it apart from its quality," answered Nicolan.

"It is clear you have not been a slave long. Did they paint your feet when they brought you to Rome?"

Nicolan nodded. "They did that in Ravenna. I come from the north, the country of the Upper Danube."

"I come from much farther north. From Britain. Perhaps you do not know of it—an island north of Gaul. A large and very fine island." The tall slave motioned in the direction of the wine jug, which was now empty. "I have been a slave all my life and so I am not so much concerned at being treated in this way."

"I saw you upstairs. I thought what a gladiator you might have been before they closed the arenas."

"I saw you too. I said to myself, 'I like him and I must see him before he leaves.'"

This friendly speech brought tears to Nicolan's eyes. It was the only kind thing which had been said to him since that morning of wrath when Vannius had appeared so suddenly and had put an end to everything worth while in his life. Since then he had been surrounded by the stern and critical faces of those who had authority over him and the ill will of the other slaves who resented his elevation to the post he now filled in the household.

He had almost reached the stage of believing that all kindliness had fled the world and decency had become a thing of the past.

"If we could only be together!" he said, impulsively. "I have been alone now for three years. I have no friends, none even to wish me well. I have been very unhappy."

"My name is Ivar," said the Briton. "And yours, my new friend?"

"Nicolan. My father was a landowner and a breeder of fine horses."

Ivar did not volunteer any information about his own background. Perhaps he thought it sufficient that he had already said he had been born a slave. He remarked with a thoughtful nod of the head: "It would be very fine if we could be together, as you say. But I am afraid that cannot be. I have a fear of Rome; and it seems unlikely that I will ever be sold here. Would you prefer to be in Ravenna?" He shook his head emphatically. "It would not be good. It is better for you, and safer, where you are."

A sharp word of command from the bailiff who was in charge of the party brought this brief conversation to an end. Nicolan fell into line with the others. Looking back over his shoulder, he received a quick smile, a nod of the head, and a wave of a hand from the young Briton.

The interest which he had felt when the lovely eyes of the princess had smiled for him was gone. It was not of her charms he was thinking as he marched from the palace. He was thinking instead of Ivar, of the friendliness in his wide-spaced eyes, of the genuine quality of his slow smile.

The slaves of Aetius walked back to his palace on the slope of the hill in double files. Nicolan found himself paired with a man of sandy complexion and inquisitive eyes whom he recognized as the anointer of the household, the *unctor*. As was customary with one of his occupation, the *unctor* was in a talkative mood.

"What do you think of her?" he asked. Without waiting for a reply, he proceeded to give his own opinion of the Princess Honoria. "I like them more substantial myself. She's all eyes and no hips." He looked up suddenly to ask, "What did she say to you?"

"To me?" Nicolan was caught off guard by the question. "Do you mean the princess? She said nothing to me."

"That is odd," said the *unctor*. "I was sure I saw her lips move. Others thought so too." He gave a sly nod. "She wants to captivate every man she sees, although they say she is really in love with that big slave. The one who talked to you."

Nicolan turned an incredulous face on his companion at this. "You must be wrong. I am sure he has never looked at her. Not in that way. He must know what the penalty would be."

"I am glad I am not in the shoes of that one." The anointer shook his sandy head with emphasis. "He belongs to her and he must obey orders. But would he be spared on that account? Not if the old woman got a hint of what was going on. But the princess is a sly one. She has little ways of her own. It will be a good thing for you, Master Clerk, if she never sees you again. You caught her eye; there could be no mistake about that." He grinned up at his taller companion. "I would like to know what it was she said to you."

No secrets could be kept in a household containing over one hundred slaves. Nothing escaped so many curious eyes; and they loved, in addition, to prattle and gossip, so that in time a grain of truth would become a toothsome pudding of fiction. It was soon known in the palace on the slope of the Palatine that the master proposed to set his wife aside and take instead the beautiful royal princess. This created a great deal of discussion, much of it unfavorable, for they knew that royal slaves could never be given their freedom.

Aetius had intended to keep his plan a secret until certain necessary arrangements could be completed but the news swept over Rome and two things happened immediately. The visit of the princess was cut short and she was sent back to Ravenna in a great hurry, and Aetius was summoned to the palace of the emperor. He came away from this interview with a red face and an air of suppressed fury. How the word got out can only be conjectured but soon all Rome knew that for once the puppet ruler had asserted himself. He had made it clear to Aetius that he must abandon the idea of allying himself with the royal family.

Nicolan was busy copying letters at his small table in the corner when Aetius came in. He did not look up, it being a rule of the household that slaves never spoke unless addressed directly. His ears told him, however, that something had gone wrong. There was anger in the footsteps of the master.

"It seems," said the dictator of Rome, who had just learned that his dictatorial powers stopped short of controlling the personal affairs of the royal family, "that word of things I plan is reaching the outside. What I say here in confidence today is shouted to the housetops tomorrow. Now, who can be responsible for this?"

Nicolan went on with his copying but his hand had become unsteady. He sensed grave danger for himself. A slave had no defense against any charge his master might care to bring.

Aetius stared down at his desk in a bitter silence. Everything had seemed to be going well. He had seen the princess twice and had talked to her at some length. Honoria had found him interesting. She had become quite gay and had fluttered her eyelashes at him. Later she had confided to one of her maids that she thought him handsome. And now this had happened! Aetius thought of the absurd pretense of dignity the emperor had assumed during their interview, how he had puffed out his pasty cheeks and refused to discuss the plan at all.

"Are you the one?" he demanded of Nicolan.

"No, my lord Aetius! No, no!" exclaimed the latter. "I never repeat what I hear. I swear that this is the truth."

Aetius pointed an accusing finger at him. "You write the letters. You hear what I say to visitors. All the documents go through your hands. Who else is there to suspect but you?"

Nicolan realized now the full danger which confronted him. He was completely in the dark as to what had gone wrong and so had no way of defending himself save by protesting his innocence again.

"I am faithful to your interests, my lord!" he declared. "I do not gossip with the rest of the household. I have never given anyone a hint of what happens here."

"I am told the princess whispered in your ear when she was receiving my gifts." This seemed to have galled him particularly, that the princess who might have been his wife and shared with him in time the throne of imperial Rome had shown interest in a slave. "It all fits in! Yes, I think you are the one, my sly and silent one. It is a good thing I have found you out so soon."

He began to pace up and down the room. He had fancied the

princess and this added to his need to pay off the score. What if she was as flirtatious as people said? He would have been able to tame her. Each time he turned in his angry pacing, he scowled at his silent and apprehensive clerk. With each turn it seemed that his belief in the guilt of the latter had become more firmly established in his mind. Finally he halted and summoned an attendant by a sharp clap of his hands. To the *ostiarius* who answered the summons he gave a brief word of instruction. "Take him to the bailiff!" pointing to Nicolan. "He is to be punished."

"How many lashes, my lord?"

Aetius had gone to his seat behind the marble table but at this he got again to his feet. It was as though he could not keep still. Ever since he had emerged from his painful interview with the emperor ("That weak fool!" he kept repeating to himself), he had been like a bull with a lance head in its hide. He needed an outlet for his inner rage; and, guilty or not, he had found his victim.

"How many?" he cried, with a flourish of his arms. "It would be impossible to name a number high enough for the wrong he has done me. How many lashes for treachery? Tell the bailiff he is to have fifty."

The eyes of the *ostiarius* opened wide with incredulity and he stammered a comment. "My lord Aetius, no man could live after fifty strokes!"

"Are you questioning my orders?" demanded the master of the household. "As for this one, who has sold me to my foes, I am not at all concerned over his chances for survival."

4

Nicolan lived through a period of semiconsciousness during which he suffered without respite and from which he rallied for a very few minutes at a time to a realization that he had survived the punishment after all. The pain in his lacerated back was so terrible that he would welcome a return to the comatose condition from which he had been roused. His mind was incapable of coherent thought but it was possessed of one strong desire, that he be allowed to leave his mutilated body and be through with life.

Later he was able to recall something of what had filled his fevered mind during the long spell when he hovered between life and death. It had to do entirely with the people of Rome: their arrogance, their cruelty, their corrupt ways, their lack of the great qualities which in earlier centuries had carried them to the mastery of the world. His thoughts had gone around and around like a squirrel in a cage: from the feasts that Aetius arranged for his guests (as all wealthy and powerful Romans did) and the great succession of rich and costly dishes which the slaves brought in to the little circle of lolling sybarites, to the picture of the slums of the great city where the poor lived like beasts and fought viciously for food; from the magnificence of the great white palaces on the Palatine to the malodorous stews of Subura; from the armies of Rome recruited almost entirely from among barbarian mercenaries who were willing to sell their great bodies and sword arms for Roman gold, to the futilities of the Romans themselves, the effeminacy of the marble baths, the strumming of lutes in palm groves, the inconsequential chatter about cloudy philosophies. He came back continuously through days and weeks of delirium and suffering to one thought. Why did not the world see that allegiance need no longer be paid to a master race which had become so effete and helpless?

There was one stage, a lengthy one, when his mind was concerned entirely with a conversation he had heard, as he sat in the cabinet of Aetius and wrote industriously at his small table, a talk between Aetius and a priest. He never found out who the priest was. The room had been silent and then suddenly he had looked up and a tall old man with a high brow and sunken temples and a pair of burning eyes was standing in the open door, holding a forefinger above his head.

"I have come to rebuke you, O Great Aetius," said the old priest.

At this point the picture always became blurred in the sick mind of the young slave. He would hear the voice of the old man crying out that the people of Rome no longer gave heed to the teachings of Christ and Aetius replying in a cool and cynical tone that the teachings of Christ were needed in their place but they had no place in the governing of an empire. Aetius kept repeating, "Nothing counts but the power and the glory of Rome." Over and over again he said this, shaking his head angrily when the old man preached at him passionately of the need for fairness and honesty and the practice of Christian virtues. When he had first listened to this talk, Nicolan had thought of Father Simon, who preached the same things to the people of the plains; and sometimes now in his disordered mind it became Father Simon and not the strange priest who was talking to Aetius. But whether it was Father Simon or the strange priest, no impression was made on the cold-eyed head of the state. Nicolan wanted to cry out to Aetius that he was wrong, that ideals were more necessary, and more effective in the course of time, than legions of armed mercenaries. But because he had said nothing when he heard the talk in the first place, his tongue now stuck to the roof of his mouth.

His mind would come back to a moment of sanity from this confused clatter of tongues and he would say aloud: "That is why Alaric got to Rome and why Attila will beat the Romans now. They think of nothing but the power of gold. They are proud of their selfishness, they boast of it; but it will be their downfall."

The periods of consciousness became longer and finally he made a final and complete emergence into sanity. For days he lay without any movement and with no will or desire to take up the matter of living; for, although the agony in his back had dwindled to a condition of numbness, any movement would start it again. At first he did not care where he was, knowing that people were about him but not concerned as to who they were, that voices sounded in his ears without rousing in him any desire to know what they said. A conviction was growing in him, in spite of this apathy, that he was going to live. At first he was vaguely reluctant to go back to the bitter existence from which he had so nearly escaped. It was not until the physical forces in his body took control that he began to welcome the idea of living again.

When his mind reached this state of acceptance, he began gradually to take an interest in what was going on about him. He was being kept, he realized, in the sickroom of the palace. In any establishment where there were servants by the score, it was necessary to have facilities for the care of the sick. Aetius had done as little about this as possible. The room he had set aside was small and low of ceiling, with one window opening on the kitchen court and a second over the steep slope of the hill. It contained two beds of considerable size, both of which were usually filled with two or even three patients. Nicolan found that he was sharing one of them with a kitchen slave from the East who was suffering from some strange and violent malady. It came to Nicolan finally that the man was insane and that he himself would have to watch with great care to escape injury. The man tossed and groaned and indulged in wild and incoherent tirades. Sometimes he would sit up with a glitter in his eyes and begin to sway back and forth as he sang a song over and over again in a gabble of unfamiliar words. This was, had the involuntary listener known, the riding song of a great people of the East and it went something like this:

> The sun dies each day in the west.
> It is submerged in the waters,
> Or it sinks into the cover of the hills.
> Even thus must die the foes of the Hiong-Nu.

In his more violent moments he would spring up and charge about the room with a heavy wooden club (he clutched it so firmly in his sleep that it had been found impossible to take it away from him) in both hands. He would shout and scream and beat at the wall with the club; while the guards would watch anxiously from the doorway and not venture into the room until this mood had subsided.

In the other bed were two very sick men who seemed to be dying. At any rate they lay quietly with closed eyes and never spoke. One of them had spells of coughing and the sponge which lay in a basin beside the bed was becoming constantly redder from the blood which was swabbed off his face.

A day came finally when Nicolan had the sickroom to himself. He was not sure but he thought that the two patients in the other bed had died. The day before the madman from the East, still clutching the club in his hand, had leaped out of the window and had gone rolling down the hill. No one cared enough about what had happened to him to inform the sole remaining occupant of the hospital.

The household physician came in late in the afternoon and seemed surprised to find Nicolan in sole possession of the room. He stared at the empty bed but made no comment. He had served in many of the campaigns of Aetius and was called Old Crack-Bones behind his back because he was a little abrupt and rough in his methods. The term, however, was applied with respect for the veteran, who was said to have a certain degree of kindliness buried deep inside him.

The physician took possession of the only chair and seemed disposed to talk.

"Did you know you were given up for dead after the full number of lashes had been applied?" he asked. "I had been away and when I returned it was all over. Your body was lying in the middle of the kitchen court. Aetius was having guests and everyone was too busy to spare any time for you. Besides it had started to rain heavily and the idea seemed to be that you could stay there until the storm was over. I had spent too many nights going over battlefields with a torch and finding a few survivors in the piles of corpses to take anything for granted. I went out and found that you were still breathing. You were nearly gone; another half hour and the tiny spark of life would have flickered out." He shook his head in wonder. "I still cannot understand how you survived. If you had been a stouter and stronger man you would have gone under early." He was silent for a moment and then asked, "Have you had a sight of your back?"

Nicolan shook his head. "I have been afraid to look. Is it badly marked?"

"It is a mass of deep scars from just below your shoulders to the waist. I must warn you that it is not sightly."

"Will they be permanent?"

Old Crack-Bones nodded. "You will have them to your dying day. The angry color will be lost in time but the deep welts and ridges will remain. Well, you must count yourself lucky. You are still alive."

Nicolan said in a somber tone: "I see no great luck in that. But for this boon—and in time I hope to see it in that light—I have you to thank. I want you to know that I am grateful."

"You are a young man," said the physician, gruffly. "I hear you are quick and clever with the pen. You will earn your freedom someday." He gave his head a satisfied nod. "Yes, I saved your life. But I am not foolish enough to take any pride in that. I have saved the lives of thousands; and most of them, I am compelled to say, were quite worthless. Your case was not hard because I am highly skilled in matters of the bodily exterior—in setting bones and healing wounds and in cutting off arms and legs. I have even dug splinters of metal out of skulls and seen the owners stalking around afterward in perfect health and with no more intelligence under the skull than they had before. But here, my young friend, is the tragedy of it: I can save others but I can do nothing for myself. You see, we who are physicians know nothing of what goes on inside the human body. What causes all these fevers and diseases? All we can do is guess. We say, perhaps, that an evil spirit has taken possession of the sick body. Or that the man is being punished for his sins. At this very moment I have in my right side a pain as though my bowels are being explored with a red-hot iron. It is an inflammation of some kind. What can be done for it? Nothing. If I were one of my own patients, I would be trying all manner of silly helps but knowing in my own mind they would be of no use. I do not bother to find relief for myself. In a few days perhaps I shall be as dead as one of the eels they are skinning for great Aetius' supper tonight."

He got slowly and painfully to his feet. "All that you need," he said, "is to get some flesh back on your bones. What food have they brought you today?"

"Nothing," answered Nicolan. "No one has been in all day. I have had the place to myself."

"Are you very hungry?"

Nicolan discovered that he was. It was the first time that he had been conscious of a healthy desire for food.

Old Crack-Bones motioned across the kitchen court. The deep caverns, where strange and costly dishes were being prepared, were filled with light and vibrant with noise. "Aetius has many guests tonight," said the veteran. "Many great people. He has been entertaining much lately. They say he feels the need to live down that great blow to his prestige—the refusal of the emperor to have him as a brother-in-law." He glanced back at Nicolan. "He has found out at last that you are still alive. Never a question has passed his lips, although usually he demands to know everything that goes on in this vast household of his. The impression is that he was a little ashamed of the fit of temper which led to your punishment. I don't know about that. If it's so, it is the first time in his life that he has regretted anything he has done."

Nicolan made no comment. He forgot his hunger, he allowed everything in his mind to be carried away in the wave of hate which had swept over him.

"Two days ago I took him the list of slaves, to discuss with him the health of the household. We do this once a month. He began to skim it quickly and when he came to your name—I knew because I was watching him—he stopped and looked up at me with a surprise he could not conceal. But he said nothing. He dropped his eyes at once and went on down the list. He asked no questions about you. I'm told he has discovered the truth and knows now that you were innocent. If that is any satisfaction to you."

Nicolan did not reply at once. "It is not a sense of satisfaction I feel," he said, finally.

Old Crack-Bones put a hand to his side. "This pain!" he groaned. "I am told he will take you back when you get out of here. Which will be in a day or so. Is there satisfaction in that?"

Nicolan felt his lips tighten. "No. None whatever. But I am a slave and so I will have to obey."

The veteran walked to the door. "I will speak to the *promus*," he said. "He has a heart somewhere in his huge body and will send you food. But I am afraid you will have to wait until the master and his guests have been served. That will be a long time, for the first course has just gone up."

It took a long time indeed to serve Aetius and his guests. The shadows of night had settled about the palace walls and the incessant drone of night insects rose from the hillside before a kitchen slave, a coal-black man with a broad smile, brought in a platter and placed it on the table with a cheerful clatter. "Sick man nearly starved?" he inquired. One glance at the platter convinced Nicolan that the results had more than justified the delay. A wonderful odor reached him from a beef rib, sprinkled, he was sure, with the very best *garum*. There was also a capon leg, brown and crisp, and beside that a little nest of fresh red berries in a basket of flaky pastry.

"I am sure this will complete my cure," he said, to the friendly waiter. "My heartfelt thanks to the *promus* and to you. I have nothing else to offer."

He continued to stare at the platter with incredulous eyes after the waiter had gone. Not since the morning when he had been seized and sold as a slave had he been allowed to partake of such rare food. But when he sat down to it, with a lighted wick floating in oil at his elbow, he found that the habit of hearty eating had left him. He was content with the capon leg and a single mouthful of the beef.

While he was eating he became conscious of sounds on the hillside below the window. He laid the beef rib back on the platter and listened. The sounds continued, and he decided that someone was stealthily climbing up the rocky slope. Was it the madman coming back? He considered this highly unlikely, for there had been no caution or stealth in that unfortunate man.

Nicolan got to his feet, surprised to find that so much of the stiffness had left him and that even his scarred back responded to the dictates of his will. Taking the lamp in one hand, he walked to the window and looked down the hillside.

The climber had been keeping an eye on the window. Nicolan saw him flatten himself against the earth where he remained for several moments without making a move.

"Who is it?" he asked, in a careful whisper.

There was no immediate response. Then a cautious voice asked, "Nicolan?"

"Yes. This is Nicolan."

"Are you alone?"

"Yes. There is no telling how long it will last but I think it unlikely that anyone will come now until morning."

"Then I will come up."

It was Ivar. Nicolan thought he had identified the voice and as soon as the head of the climber came within the circle of light he recognized the reddish hair and broad brow of the Briton. To prevent any other eyes in the palace from seeing what was happening, he carried the lamp away from the window and placed it back on the table.

Ivar threw a muscular leg over the sill and dropped his feet to the floor with an exclamation of satisfaction.

"My good friend, this is very lucky," he said. "I have been getting reports of you, in a roundabout way, and have wanted to come for a long time. How fortunate that when I do come I find you all alone."

"You are taking a great risk," said Nicolan, anxiously.

Ivar did not seem concerned. "For three weeks," he said, "I have been existing in the greatest danger. I have become accustomed to it." His eyes went to the table and remained fixed on the platter of food with such fascination that for several moments he said nothing more. "My friend," he whispered, then, his nostrils twitching as the fine odor of the beef reached them. "During those three weeks I have had small chances to eat. I am sure that another week of it would see the end of me. Would it be too much to ask that I be allowed a mouthful of—of what I see on the table?"

"It is all yours," answered Nicolan. "I have eaten all I want."

The tall Briton approached the table with wary steps, almost like an animal stalking its prey. Then he dropped into the chair and began to eat like a hungry dog, gulping the food without pausing to savor its richness. After a few moments he compelled himself to stop and looked up at Nicolan with a hint of moisture in his eyes.

"Have I died and gone to Valhalla?" he asked. "Never in my life have I known such rapture." He scooped up the last remnants of the beef and then fell to on the berries and pastry. When the last crumb had vanished he sat back in the chair and looked at Nicolan with a sudden change of mood.

"I have run away," he said.

Nicolan gave vent to a startled exclamation. It was almost impossible for a runaway slave to get out of Italy and the penalty for those who tried and failed was death by the most painful method which could be devised. Few made the attempt, although it was the most widely discussed of all subjects when groups of slaves got together.

"Do you know the risk you are running?" he asked.

The Briton nodded his head. "There was nothing else left for me. Things had reached a stage where I could no longer stay." He did not volunteer any further information but Nicolan, remembering what he had heard about the preference of the Princess Honoria for the brawny Briton, did not need to be told. "I ran away before the party started back for Ravenna. For three weeks I have been hiding in the hills east of the city." He motioned over his shoulder with a thumb. "An ex-slave, a Briton who is married to a Roman woman, owns a herd up there. He told me of a cave where I would be safe and he has given me food once in a while. He did the best he could for me but his wife is a saving woman without any kindliness or sympathy and she watches the food like a hawk. I have been slowly starving." He glanced questioningly at Nicolan before continuing with his halting speech. "I waited because I thought you might go with me. After what you have been through, you might feel disposed to risk it. What do you think? Do you want to make the try—and are you strong enough now? I think I have strength enough for the two of us. If you were to tire, I could carry you on my back."

Nicolan was thinking hard. "Is the risk any greater than what I face in staying?" he was asking himself. "This man who bought me has the power of life and death in his hands and he does not hesitate to use it. Could I hope to survive if he had another of his evil tantrums?" A second consideration took possession of his mind. "This is the best chance I will ever have. Never again will there be a comrade as brave and strong as this one to share the risks. It is a case of now or never. If I refuse to go, I will have to live in Rome as a slave for the rest of my life."

"I do not want to urge you," said Ivar, after a long pause, during which Nicolan had continued to weigh all sides of the problem. "It is better for two to go than one. You see, all the walking must be done by night. During the day you sleep; one watching while the other gets his turn of rest. You have to beg your food or steal it." He gave his head a brisk nod. "I have a plan. My friend, the Briton up there in the hills, says it would be mad to attempt to get away by land. No one could hope to go all the way up through the hill country and then cross the Lombardy Plain. You will lose your way a hundred times and always you have to be asking directions. No matter how careful you are, you are sure to be caught sooner or later. The best way is to get to the coast by the most direct route and work passage on one of the ships. The captains are always short of men and they do not ask questions. My friend up there has given me the names of two captains who would be willing to risk taking us. Unfortunately they both ply the eastern routes and never sail for the Pillars of Hercules."

Nicolan had heard much discussion of this point. "But they say that life on the ships is no better than slavery. In some ways it is worse. You sleep in the hold and your food is full of worms, and the captain gives the lash if you don't jump to obey him. And when you get to an Eastern port, you do not understand the languages you hear spoken. You have a few coins only in your purse—for the captain always cheats you of most of the pay you have earned—and so all you can do is to hang around the water front and wait for another ship ready to take you on. You hope that someday a ship will be sailing for your own country, so that you can get home, but you never find one. After a while you give up hope and spend your life in the ships. The conditions are worse than anything you have to endure here." Nicolan shook his head emphatically. "I see no sense in changing from one set of chains to another. If we are going to risk our lives in running away, we must see the prospect of freedom at the end of it." His mood changed to one of eagerness. "I would rather die than stay. It is over three years since my mother and I were carried off and sold as slaves here in Rome; and the thought of escaping has never been out of my mind. And *I* have a plan, a better one, I think, than getting away to sea."

He went to a place beside his bed where his clothes and belt were hanging on a peg. From the purse under the buckle of the belt, he produced two small coins and a long strip of papyrus which had been carefully folded up inside. He shook this out and Ivar saw that it was a map.

"This will make it possible for us to get away by land," said Nicolan, confidently. He proceeded to tell how he had made the original map, laboring over the campfires after all the others had gone to sleep. When he started to work at copying, and had access to paper and ink, he had redrawn the original with the utmost care, using small squares as in the first instance and then sewing them together, to make the long and legibly marked strip which he now held in his hands. "With the help of this," he declared, "we will never have to risk asking questions. We will travel by night and sleep in concealment during the day and, if we use proper care, we will never be seen. All the information we will need is here."

Ivar took the map into his hands and studied it carefully. Then he looked up. His eyes, which had seemed to Nicolan quiet and reserved, had lighted up. "Then you will go with me?"

Nicolan did not hesitate. "Yes, my friend, I am ready to try. The only reason I had for not saying so at once was that I wondered if I had the strength. I do not want to be a drag on you."

Ivar got to his feet, his face shining with relief and excitement. "Then why do we linger? Let us be on our way."

5

It was five weeks later. The two ragged, barefooted, and weary men had followed the directions on the map which Nicolan had drawn and had not found it at fault. Traveling always by night, they had been able to make their way in the darkness without ever taking the risk of asking directions. On no more than half a dozen occasions had they spoken to strangers and each time it had been when hunger drove them to beg at the isolated huts of sheepherders. They had found that the lonely men who tended their flocks in the hills were kind and willing to help. On one occasion, they met with a demonstration of kindness that played a great part in the success of their flight but this story will be told later. The food obtained in this way had been eked out by fruit picked at night in orchards and berries found in the woods. They had been lucky enough a few times to catch fish in the streams they passed.

And now it was apparent that they had reached a land where the law of Rome no longer ran. Nicolan pointed to a bend in the road ahead of them. A man on horseback had come into view.

"A Hun," he said.

Ivar made a shade of his hands and stared with intense interest at the approaching horseman. He perceived that the Hun was wearing a hat of red felt, that his legs were cased in long riding boots, and that a circular sword was stuck through the front of his belt.

"So, this is one of them, the men who want to conquer the world," he said. "He seems to ride with skill."

"Skill enough. But wait until we come to *my* country. That is where men know how to ride—and have the best horses in the world for their riding."

The tall Briton turned to his companion with a quizzical grin. "A suspicion has been in my mind for some time. Now it has become a certainty. You have been purposely edging us toward the more easterly roads. I supposed at first we were going to your country, up there on the plateau to the west, but somehow there was always a reason for taking a different road; one which turned out to be in this direction and took us across the Danube. You wanted to come where we seem to be now—in the center of the Hun country. Is it not so?"

"It is so." Nicolan frowned in deep thought, keeping his eye in the meantime on the horseman who was now pounding down the road at a fast pace. "When I sat in the room of Aetius, and saw what was done and heard everything that was said, I learned many things. I learned things which I kept sealed up in my mind and never divulged, although I was offered up to death on the mere suspicion that I had done so. One thing I learned was that Aetius is certain he must fight the Huns someday. It will not be for some years but he is already making preparations for it. He is certain he will beat them when Attila finally attacks Rome but he does not think it will be easy. He despises Attila but is beginning to fear him also." There was a pause, as they stumped along together on stiff and weary legs. "Ivar, if there is war between the Huns and that degenerate race who will be led by Aetius, I want to fight on the side of Attila."

He had never come out so openly before. The Briton looked at him with a protesting frown. "Nick, good friend," he said, "you must not let your personal grievances sway you in this matter."

"I have grievances, many and bitter ones," declared Nicolan. "But it is not only because I have been so badly used myself that I feel like this. I spent all my spare time in Rome looking at the way people lived, the high and the low alike. Never before has there been such a display of wealth and such terrible poverty. The poor are no better than slaves. All the loot of the world is being spent by a few hundred families. But that was not all. What galled me most was the spirit of Rome. These proud and cruel people are concerned only with gain. They no longer have ideals and they make a boast of it. Each man wants to beat all the others in a race for power and wealth. That is what they consider worth while. Ivar, this we both know in our hearts: the world cannot go on without sincerity and decency, it will fall into ruins when it ceases to be guided by ideals."

"And so you want to see Rome pulled down," said Ivar, thoughtfully. "What is to replace her?"

"I am no prophet. I don't try to look that far ahead. I am concerned with one thought only—to help in the defeat of that corrupt world we have left behind us. Anything that replaces it will be an improvement."

When the Hun horseman drew rein in front of them there were other riders following him down the road and raising a cloud of dust. He exploded into a clatter of words which seemed definitely hostile.

Nicolan said, "We speak Latin," without making any impression on the Hun, then pointed to himself with one hand and motioned with it in the direction of the west, saying "Bakony" several times. The horseman understood this and gave his round head an affirmative bob. Nicolan pointed then at Ivar and waved his hand high to indicate the far north, saying: "Britain. Island. Britain." The Hun shook his head impatiently. This was beyond him.

When more of the riders had come up, they formed themselves into an escort for the two strangers and wheeled about to return by the road they had used in their approach. They jabbered among themselves and scowled at the pair on foot, motioning for more speed and even producing their swords in threatening gestures.

"It seems that we are prisoners," said Ivar.

"Attila's main city is not far from here. That is where they are taking us."

"I wish they would show a little more concern for our weary legs," complained the Briton.

"The Huns are born to the saddle and have nothing but contempt for the human leg," explained Nicolan. "A few of the Hun words I knew as a boy are coming back to me. As far as I can make out, they think we are spies. They are pleased with themselves for capturing us."

"They expect for us an early death," said Ivar. "And they are pleased at the prospect."

The Hun cantonment was in an early stage of its development. It sprawled over a wide stretch of flat land but it lacked the im-

petus of impending war to turn into the great beehive of activity
it was to become later. However, a standard flaunting the turul
floated over the main gate to let the world know, or as much of
the world as came that way, that its prospective master was here.
It was clearly a very busy place behind its wooden walls, for they
could hear even at a distance the hum of human voices aided by
the neighing of horses and the barking of dogs. There was an impression in more civilized parts that Hun dogs lacked the power
to bark but the canine population of Attila's city seemed determined to give the lie to this story.

A troop of horsemen, carrying spears and leather targets,
emerged from the front gate. They came out at top speed, as
though an inclined drawbridge had been there to lend them im-
petus, an impression strengthened by the thunder of the hoofs.
They swept down the road toward the newcomers and then began to gallop about them, curvetting their horses and shouting
like madmen. Their antics raised such a dust that it was impossible to see anything of the road and even the royal standard
above the wooden gates was blotted from view.

"Are they mad?" asked Ivar, anxiously. It was clear that he had
never participated before in such a frenzied welcome.

"Yes. But also they are calculating and cunning. You can never
tell what they will do next but you must never underestimate
them."

One of the mad horsemen rode at Ivar with leveled spear and
did not divert the point until the last possible moment. It ripped
a piece of cloth from his sleeve. The horses, small and stocky and
with savage heads, seemed to be entering into the sport. They
kicked up their heels and neighed viciously.

"We came here of our own free will, good friend," said Ivar.
"And I begin to think it was a very great mistake to do so."

The eyes of the two travelers, which had gazed on the white
palaces of Rome and the glories of the Colosseum, saw the capital
of Attila as a mean and tawdry place. His palace, which seemed
so great to his followers, was little more than a frame hut enlarged
many times over; with wooden pillars, it was true, and a pointed
roof and some carved beams. The mounted escort, which had
brought them in through the gate of the city, still screaming and

gesticulating with their spears, dropped back now and disappeared from sight. The two captives were led through the dining hall, which impressed them somewhat with its size, and down the steps into the warren of small offices where Attila spent his days.

It was difficult to enter his own special cabinet because a map had just been carried in and was occupying the whole of one wall. The Scourge of God was wearing a blue tunic (*the* blue tunic which was new then and shiny with its rich embroideries) and sitting behind his small table. His harsh and unblinking eyes studied the prisoners with an unfriendliness which added to their mental discomfort. An interpreter began to question them in Latin, addressing himself first to Ivar, whose great bulk had already created much comment. The latter explained their status and told of their long flight. Nicolan, standing at one side, fixed his eyes on the map.

Attila sat in silence during this stage of the interrogation. At first he had given his attention to the magnificent physique of the Briton. Then he shifted his position slightly and looked at Nicolan, who was still studying the map. It showed the network of roads between Rome and the natural barrier of the Alps. He was tracing with his eye the course they had followed in their escape from Italy.

It had been assumed by the two travelers that the Hun emperor was depending entirely on the interpreter but to their great surprise he suddenly spoke up, using the Roman language with an easy if not a scholarly intonation.

"My map makers are the best in the world," he said. He motioned to the chart on the wall and addressed a question to Nicolan. "You, who are so much interested in this one, what do you think of it?"

Nicolan, much to his own surprise, had no feeling of fear for this great conqueror who was gradually gathering the dominions of the world into his control. He addressed his answer directly to Attila. "I have never seen a better one. It is beautifully drawn and with the most complete detail. It is true to scale. But it must also be said, O Mighty Emperor, that it is very inaccurate."

The high note of Attila's laughter filled the room at this remark but no one made the mistake of thinking him amused.

"This young cock is not afraid to flap his wings and crow," he said. The corners of his mouth drew down as he savored his displeasure. "So, my map is inaccurate! What does an escaped slave know of the making of military maps and of the roads to Rome?"

Nicolan was now aware of a tensity in the room. He had had the effrontery to criticize something which Attila prized highly. It became clear to him, as he glanced at the flush around the deeply embedded eyes of the emperor and at the uneasiness of the Hun officials in the room, that he must justify what he had said or face unpleasant consequences.

"Perhaps I have spoken without sufficient care, O Great Emperor," he said. "But it is true that we made our way during the hours of darkness from Rome to the border. We never made a mistake. We knew the distances and the turn of the roads. It was never necessary for us to retrace our steps and we never had to make inquiries."

"You have made this journey many times?" asked Attila.

"No, Your Imperial Greatness. Once before only. We had a map I made on my first trip over the roads."

Attila was beginning to show some trace of amusement. "How old were you when you made this map?" he demanded to know.

"I was fifteen years of age."

"And this chart you drew is more accurate than what my skilled map makers have been able to do for me?" He gave a quick look around the room and grinned at his officers. "You have more impudence in you than a Roman scholar who pretends to know everything." His eye came back to Nicolan. "Where is this map which is so wonderfully accurate?"

Nicolan produced the much-thumbed and worn map from under his belt. In response to an impatient demand, he crossed the room and laid it on the table before the emperor. The latter studied it for a few moments.

"Onegesius," he said, "bring my map makers in. We must get to the bottom of this. No, I have a better idea. Bring in the observers I have used on the roads to Rome. We will find what they say about it first."

The room had to be partially cleared to make room for the military observers who were ushered in a few minutes later by the black-a-vised Onegesius. Even the proud officer, who had brought in the prisoners and who had not yet received so much as a glance from his master, was among those banished. The experts studied the handsome map on the wall and Nicolan's creased and flimsy strip of papyrus. They contrasted the two on specific points, they ran their fingers along the course of roads, they traced the outlines of mountains and rivers. Then they whispered and conferred and, with every evidence of reluctance, came to a decision.

"It is true, O Mighty Tanjou," said one of them, "that in some points of detail the official map is not—it is not exactly as we recall the roads to be. This opinion we give because it is always your desire to have information that is fully correct. It is not our desire to find fault with the skilled hands which made the map."

"Are these faults serious? Are they wrong by yards or by miles?"

"By—by many miles in some cases."

"Do you find similar mistakes in this?" Attila pointed, with no attempt to conceal his annoyance, at Nicolan's map.

The spokesman hesitated. "It is done in miniature, O Mighty Tanjou, and so it is hard to judge. But on the hasty examination we have made, we find no faults to call to your attention."

Nicolan heaved an inner sigh of relief. The storm had been weathered, the wrath of Attila averted. He looked at the figure behind the table and saw that the head of the Hun empire had not bolted the information fed him by his military observers but was disposed to digest it slowly. He asked many questions, all of them very much to the point.

"It is clear I must have some serious words with my map makers," said Attila, finally. He squared around and stared hard at Nicolan. "Your self-confidence may be no more than the audacity of youth. I hope so. It is my present feeling that you, with your little maps which have confounded my experts, could be useful to me."

"My friend and I came to your capital, O Great Emperor," said Nicolan, "in the hope that we could take service with you."

Attila turned his head in Ivar's direction. "I can use this great ox," he said. "Although he resembles nothing so much as a chestnut stallion, I am inclined to think he comes from the island of the Black Singers." The accuracy of this guess brought a bow of assent from Ivar. Attila had so much confidence in his own uncanny powers of observation that he always expected to be right. He turned his attention back to Nicolan.

"You come of a stubborn race," he said. "They raise horses but by nature they resemble the mule more. I have found it necessary to be very severe with them. Will you be as stubborn as the rest or will you be ready to serve me in any capacity I may suggest?"

Nicolan decided that no better time for frankness would ever present itself. "I am placing a price on my services, O Great Emperor," he said. Even the anxious expression that he detected on Ivar's face did not deter him from continuing. "Vannius, acting as your agent, killed my father and confiscated our lands. He sold my mother and me into slavery. I am asking that the injustices he did be rectified and that the lands of my father be restored to me."

Attila assumed a defensive attitude at once, it being foreign to his nature to relinquish anything of which he had taken possession. "I am not aware of the circumstances," he said, in a grumbling tone. "Vannius is dead. He was a liar and a thief. When I found he was taking more out of your country for himself than for me, I had his head cut off. It has been a great regret with me ever since that I allowed that greasy traitor such an easy death." He studied Nicolan with a calculating eye. "Your impudence passes all bounds but I cannot help feeling some regard for the way you set forth your demands, preposterous though they are. We will leave the matter this way; when you have proven your worth to me, we will discuss what kind of reward you have earned. It may be that your lands will be awarded to you; but, my bold young bantling, you must not think I am making you any promises. When I make a promise I keep it; and so I am chary about committing myself." He said abruptly to Onegesius: "Now you may bring in the envoy from Constantinople. Have this map removed from my sight first. I do not want to lay eyes on it again until the mistakes in it have been rectified."

The memories ended at this point. The warmth of the sun pouring down on Nicolan's back through the high window had conquered him. He fell sound asleep and his rhythmic breathing caused Ivar to get up from the table. Brushing a hand across his lips, the tall Briton proceeded to make his friend comfortable, placing a bearskin from the floor back of his head and one in the small of his back. The chair was not the kind of couch one would choose after a full night's work but it was much better than anything they had enjoyed during the long weeks of their flight from slavery.

CHAPTER IX

1

BEFORE the sun had completed its climb above the horizon on a warm morning some weeks later, Nicolan and his invariable companion reached a part of the country which lay in a bend of a legendary river, one of the great waterways, which centuries later would be called the Blue Danube, although it would have been nearer the truth to speak of it as jade green or brown or even black. This corner of the Bakony lands, with its thick forests and small lakes and umber hills, proved so exhilarating to Nicolan that he put his horse to a gallop, watching the while with busily questing eyes. Suddenly he hauled in his mount and pointed a finger. In the center of a clearing ahead of them stood a long and rambling wooden structure with smoke pouring from one of its chimneys. The house was surrounded by a palisade of pointed logs, and the presence of an ornate framework over the entrance lent to it a hint of the Orient. His mood changed immediately.

"Mine!" he said. There was a choking sensation in his throat and he found it hard to speak. "My father died inside the gate when Vannius made his surprise attack. I was off there in the pasture lands when they struck." He sat in silence for several moments. "This is worth everything—the insults they have heaped on me, the threats, the angry looks, the refusals to give me their lists. To come at the end to the place where I was born!"

The weeks they had spent in surveying the Bakony lands with an eye to the man power and, more important still, the horse supplies had been difficult ones. Nicolan had been received with open hostility. He had been reviled as a traitor to his own people. It had been necessary to resort to threats to get the information he needed from his stony-faced compatriots. As it was his intention to fight for the most lenient terms for them, he had felt the injustice of this deeply; but he had said little in his own defense.

"Is this our last stop?" asked Ivar.

The Briton was not accustomed to riding and had found it necessary to use a high-backed saddle, thus presenting a somewhat ludicrous contrast to Nicolan, who had discarded his gear on reaching his native land, it being the custom there to ride bareback. Ivar seemed glad of the chance to rest after the jolting he had sustained in the course of their climb from the plains below.

Nicolan shook his head in response to his companion's question. "We do not stop here," he said. "Yesterday Ranno of the Finninalders gave me the information I needed." He paused for a long moment of bitter reflection. "I won't set foot on Ildeburgh land until I come to claim it as my own! May the gods speed that day!"

He looked about him and sighed deeply. The plateau was flat and rich but relieved of any hint of monotony by clumps of alder, willow, and acacia trees. The grass was thick and green. His eyes picked out other colors which had delighted him as a boy, the blue of wild hickory like a reflection of the sky, a hint of violet, and the red and yellow of the first pasqueflowers. Far off in the distance, against the proscenium of the sky, were the jagged peaks of purple hills.

"Only Macio of the Roymarcks remains to be seen," he said, finally. "I've tried to arrange our movements to reach him today so we can watch the races. I want to see this fabulous Harthager in action."

He withdrew his lance from its rest and scooped up some of the turf. "Look at it!" he said. "There's nothing richer in the world! Someday all this will be mine. But there's only one way I can claim it. By serving Attila. If he is beaten by Rome, the legions will march north again and this country will be portioned out to their leaders. Some great captain will take it or a soft-bellied army contractor will buy it in. On the other hand, if by some miracle my country became independent again, the Finninalders will be left securely in possession. They've become a powerful family, the second, I expect, in wealth and influence. I have no kinsmen left to back me in my claims. I couldn't hope to oust them. So, Attila is my only hope." He turned to Ivar, his expression set and hard. "You keep at me, my friend, demanding why I ride with the Huns. I've given you many reasons, all of them good. Now I give you another, a purely personal reason, a selfish one, if you like. I am taking the only course open to me to regain my inheritance."

The Briton nodded his head. "That's an answer all men can understand. Even I, who wore the iron collar of slavery in my cradle, can sympathize with you."

Half an hour later they reached the crest of a hill. Below them lay a stretch of flat country with the red roof of a rambling house barely visible above a nest of trees.

"The land of the Roymarcks," said Nicolan. "We were neighbors for many generations and I think my people always felt jealous of them. They were so rich and powerful. But all that changed for me when Macio's youngest daughter was born."

At this moment his attention was attracted by a horse and rider emerging from the shadows about the house with the red roof. He saw that the rider was a woman. The sun was climbing high and, by straining his eyes, he perceived that she was slender and young and that her hair streamed out behind in a golden cascade.

"It is Ildico," he said to himself. Although it was many years since he had seen her, he was delighted with this chance of meeting her again. "Ride on, Ivar. Wait for me in that clump of trees where the road turns in."

He set his mount to a swift gallop to catch the rider on the horse which was as black as midnight and he smiled as he recalled the many times he had sat in tongue-tied silence and worshiped this high-spirited young daughter of Macio. Could anyone have been as much in love as he was then, or as incapable of expressing his feelings?

The girl gave no indication that she was aware of his presence, even when he came pounding up behind her, except for one quick glance from eyes of such beauty that he caught his breath. She swung away from the main trail and followed a narrow road which wound up into the western hills, thus forcing him to drop back where his eyes became filled with dust. They rode thus for the better part of a mile. Then the road widened on attaining the crest of the ridge and he was able to pull up abreast. All his attention had been focused on the girl, noting every detail of her blue riding jacket and taking in with a sense of delight the grace of her carriage and the slender line of her back, but he had been conscious at the same time that she was riding a remarkable horse. "What a magnificent fellow!" he thought.

They galloped together for some distance, the dark eyes of the man never leaving the face of the girl. For her part she looked straight ahead but there was a hint in her attitude of acceptance of his presence. Finally she turned for a quick glance and then, with an imperceptible pressure of her knee, brought her mount to a slower pace. For the first time their eyes met squarely.

"We could have left you behind," she said. "It would have been very easy. I held Harthager in because he is going to race this afternoon and it wouldn't do to give him more than a short run." She continued to look at him intently. "I know who you are."

"*You* are Ildico of the Roymarcks," said Nicolan. "It is easy for me to recognize you. But if you know who I am, you have a very good memory."

"I think you are Nicolan of the Ildeburghs. The boy who was carried away to Rome." Her expression became one of defiance. "The one who has sold himself to the Huns."

Nicolan did not meet this challenge at once. He was studying her face. She lacked the long narrowness of feature which was almost universally encountered on the plateau; instead her brow was broad, her nose rather short and delicately modeled, her cleft chin of sufficient width to suggest character and determination. Her beauty thrilled and at the same time frightened him. "There can be no doubt about it, she is the one Attila is looking for," he thought. "One glance will be all he needs." This possibility disturbed him so much that he began to think of ways and means of keeping her out of the emperor's vision. "She should be sent away," he thought.

He became conscious that she was holding her chin very high and that every line of her was taut with disapproval. "I am well aware," he said, by way of answer to her unspoken charge, "that I am not held in high esteem here."

"My brother Roric is the only one who has a good word for you."

Nicolan flushed with pleasure. "He was my best friend when

we were boys. It makes me happy to know he is still my friend."

"Don't count too much on it. My father is very bitter about you."

Nicolan was watching her with the closest attention, noting her mannerisms, the way her eyes closed when she smiled, her habit of gesturing as she talked. One of the oldest proverbs of the plateau country came into his mind. "A man may reach the highest peak," he quoted, "but still be blinded when he looks into the sun."

She retorted quickly, "Then it is wiser not to look."

"Sometimes," he said, "one look is worth a life of blindness. I am here for such a short time that I must take advantage of the few chances I'll have."

"Perhaps Father will relent and let me talk to you at the races. You *are* coming?"

He was realizing that her opinion was more important to him than the combined voice of the plateau people. It seemed of the utmost importance to make his position clear to her. "Those who hate me stay at home and curry horses instead of riding them to the wars. But I—I ride on the greatest adventure the world has ever seen. Do you understand, Ildico? Attila will conquer the world. Is it a time to be staying home and tossing manure?"

"Is it a time," she countered quickly, "to be fighting for the oppressor of your own people?"

"The Romans oppressed us before the Huns came," declared Nicolan. "We have one choice only, a choice of masters. I know that most of our people prefer the yoke of Rome. I do not. I've served under it and I know what it's like. I will ride with Attila when he leads his armies to the plains of Lombardy. I hope to be there when the last flapping is heard of the wings of the twelfth vulture." He had not taken his eyes from her face for a moment. "And in the upturning I shall recover the lands stolen from my father."

Ildico was now watching him with an intentness which equaled his own. "You are wrong and blind," she said. "But even if you are so very blind, I think you are honest." Suddenly she began to smile. "How much you have changed! You were such a quiet boy."

He turned then and studied her mount. "This must be the

great Harthager I've heard so much about. Isn't it unusual to take him out for such a brisk run on the day of the races?"

Ildico shook her head. "He needs the exercise. Father and Roric will be angry with me because they don't think he does. Old Brynno will be furious. I know better than all of them." Her voice had risen to a vehement pitch. "Do you believe that horses always know when they are going to race?"

"Of course. They have ways of knowing things. Do you suppose they talk among themselves?"

"Yes," said the girl, eagerly. "I've heard them."

"They know when there's going to be a battle. I've visited the horse lines before a brush and it's always the same—ears twitching, eyes looking afar off, a curious low whinnying from all parts of the line. What's more, a horse knows if he is going to be killed. He is very quiet and he doesn't eat and his tail hangs limply."

"Oh, the poor fellows!" cried Ildico. "I feel sorrier for them than I do for the men who are killed in battle. It's the men who make the wars, not the horses."

"Then you are sure Harthager knows he's to race today?"

"I am sure he does."

Harthager was strong enough to toss off the slender figure perched on his back with one rearing motion of his strong legs. The black was holding his head up and pawing menacingly in his anxiety to be off.

"This morning I knew he wanted me to take him out. You see, we understand each other. We have talks. He has ways of telling me things. He whinnies as soon as I go in and you would be surprised if you knew how much difference he can put into it. When he needs exercise, he taps on the door of his stall with one of his hoofs. This morning he never stopped—tap, tap, tap, tap! He could hardly wait to get out. He was telling me that he was boiling with energy and had to work some of it off. He was saying to me, 'Take me for a run in the hills. Then I will rest and this afternoon I will run as I have never done before.' He meant it. You'll see that he will win with the greatest ease."

"I hope to be there to see it."

The girl gave him a rather disturbed look. "If you come, I shall treat you the same as any other guest," she said. "Father will be very angry with me. His eyes will be as black as thunderclouds. I am afraid there will be scenes afterward. But I don't believe I shall let that influence me, Nicolan. I am *so* pleased you are here."

2

Nicolan rode to the spot which he had appointed as the meeting place with Ivar but found it deserted. Several minutes elapsed before his tall companion returned. The Briton pointed back over his shoulder.

"She's come. The woman with the red hair."

Nicolan frowned in disbelief. "You don't mean the widow of Tergeste?"

Ivar nodded. "Do you see the tents behind that clump of trees? That's where she's camping. I saw them arrive; a dozen horsemen at the least and half that many pack horses. She travels in state. I went down and watched from behind the trees. She was riding a white horse with gold trappings and she was giving them orders like a slave overseer."

"She must be mad to ride this far north of the border. I think, Ivar, we must visit the beautiful widow again and give her some advice. Do you suppose she'll remember us?"

Half a dozen tents made of silk in the broadest shades of red and blue and yellow had already been pitched on the flat ground beyond the trees. The servants were now engaged in watering the horses at a small stream some distance away and the blaspheming incidental to this labor came clearly to the ears of the two visitors.

A mahogany-colored slave at the entrance to the largest of the tents did not address them but waved his arms in admonition. "He's probably had his tongue cut out," said Ivar, in a tone of compassion.

"We desire to see the Lady Eugenia," said Nicolan to the silent slave.

The mute bowed and vanished inside. In a matter of seconds another man of bronze skin came to look them over.

"Who are you?" he asked.

"We are officers of the Great Tanjou, Attila, master of the world and emperor of the skies."

The man vanished in turn. Coming back after some delay, he

opened the flap wide and said, "Mistress will see servants of the great khan."

The interior of the pavilion had already been completely settled in a manner as luxurious as any Roman villa. There were rich rugs on the ground and there was a couch of noble proportions behind which stood a tall mirror of polished metal. The mistress, in a gown of green and gold, was seated on a corner of the couch while a third male slave plied comb and tongs on her hair.

The widow of Tergeste was a woman of indeterminate age, handsome enough to be in her early twenties but with sufficient proof of experience in her large brown eyes to be much farther along on the highway of the years. The red of her hair was instantly suspect but even the most critical observer would have to acknowledge that the application of the dye had been most skillful.

She gave Nicolan an appraising look and then motioned to both servants to retire.

"I know you," she said, in a voice of deep undertones. "You are the poor starved rat who came in the dead of the night, tapping on the door of my little place in the hills above Aquileia. There were two of you, a pair of runaway slaves. You begged piteously for food."

"Yes, my lady. We were seeking liberty. You were most kind to us. You saved our lives."

The widow rose to her feet and walked toward them, her voluminous skirts trailing behind her. She looked hard in the direction of Ivar, who had remained just inside the door.

"Is that the great silent ox you had with you the first time?"

"Yes, that is Ivar."

"He's turned into a Hercules, hasn't he?" She motioned imperiously to the Briton to come closer. "You're a handsome fellow after all. A very handsome fellow. I didn't suspect it, you were such a bag of bones before. Phoebus Apollo, how I like big men!" She turned briskly in Nicolan's direction. "And now what brings you here? You're not in any need from the looks of you. I understand that you are in the pay of the Scourge of God. Has it been a case of escaping from one master to fall into the clutches of another?"

"No, my lady. We are free men. But you are right. We are

with Attila's forces. We are here because I have matters to discuss with Macio of the Roymarcks. When we saw your tents, we decided to pay our respects first; and also to give you some information."

She showed signs of an eager interest at the mention of Macio. "I also have come to see him. Rumors reached my ears that he has raised a fabulous black horse. Have you been lucky enough to see this Harthager?"

"We had a look at him in action not more than half an hour ago."

"Tell me, young man, is he as fast as they say?"

"My lady, he has quicksilver in his heels. He carries a set of bellows as powerful as the steed Apollo drives across the sky each day."

A determined light showed in the alert eyes of the widow. "I must have him! I am going to offer the old man a price he won't be able to refuse. Where is this Macio to be found?"

"You have pitched your camp on his land, my lady. His house can be seen from the top of the slope east of here."

"Then I must go to him at once. But, first, what is the information you have for me?"

"You will be well advised to leave immediately. Attila is coming. He's riding through this country and can be expected here in a few hours."

She gestured carelessly. "That for your Attila. I am not afraid. Everyone, even this terrible Hun, knows about the widow of Tergeste. I come and go as I please."

"He is no respecter of persons," urged Nicolan, earnestly. "You may not know that we are in a state of war. He wouldn't hesitate to despoil even as great a lady as you. It's possible he would think you a spy or, at the least, he might hold you for ransom. My advice is to pack and leave at once."

"Not until I've seen Macio and bought this fabulous Harthager. I tell you, young man, I have a mission to perform, a duty—to convince the stupid Romans, with their thick heads of solid stone, that they won't keep the people satisfied much longer with the kind of entertainment they offer in the circuses. They've all turned Christian so they can't offer a tasty massacre any more. And they don't seem to know that horse racing is the greatest sport in the world—when it's well done. They stick to chariot races or sometimes they turn the horses loose with clowns and tumblers on their backs, skipping from horse to horse and dancing and lying down. Why can't they see that a proper race, with a rider on each horse, is the most exciting thing in the world? They have them everywhere in the world, except in Rome. Even in Greece, and *that* shows how slow we Romans are. Sutphus of Epirus holds races every year and contestants come from all over. I was there last year with a roan I thought very well of. I lost a fortune. One hundred thousand sesterces! And that's a lot, even for the widow of Tergeste. Now I must buy Macio's black and return to Epirus for my revenge. I can't wait to see the weasel face of Sutphus when the black runs away from the field! That's why I'm here and nothing will persuade me to leave until I've bought him."

"Attila will take Harthager for himself." Nicolan was struck with a sudden thought. He paused to give it careful consideration and then added in eager tones: "I believe, my lady, that I have a plan. I'm certain no power on heaven or earth would induce the old man to sell his great colt but he might be willing to lend him. He might see the wisdom of having the black out of the way *before alien eyes can rest on him.* You would have to swear to bring him back as soon as the war was over. It would be necessary to work quickly. Every minute counts."

The widow's eyes had opened wide with excited speculation. "Do you think he would agree?"

"I don't know. I'm inclined to think so. He doesn't want this great colt carried off to be slaughtered in the war. Of course, he would insist on sending a trainer along with you whose word would be law where the black's concerned." Suddenly he clapped one hand on the palm of the other. "I have it! He could put his daughter in your care, or both daughters for that matter. On the understanding that you would take them away with you in an hour's time and get them over there into Roman territory as fast as your horses can travel."

The widow nodded her head in understanding. "This will be no place for young girls."

"All fathers with unmarried daughters are in a panic. Particularly when the daughters are beautiful."

"I take it that Macio's daughters are particularly good to look upon," said the Lady Eugenia, with a shrewd smile.

"I've seen one of them only, the younger, Ildico. She's as beautiful as a sun goddess." He paused for a moment. "I think she could take charge of the colt. I saw her ride him this morning."

"I will agree to any conditions!" cried the widow. "Anything which makes it possible for me to race Harthager in Epirus. Come, young man, take me to your Macio of the Roymarcks and expound the plan to him."

"The expounding of the plan I leave to you. In fact, I think it would be wise not to mention me. I am, after all, Attila's man. He would think it ill of me to lose him such chances. He is most partial to girls with golden hair. One glance at Ildico would be enough to stoke his desire to the blazing point. Go, then, to the old man and lay *your* plan before him." He glanced about him. "And set your servants to packing at once. There won't be any time to lose if Macio agrees. Attila has a habit of arriving early."

"You have a shrewd head on your shoulders, young man." The widow paused, frowning at the silent Ivar. "Doesn't this great hulk of flesh ever say anything? He has done nothing but stare at me since he came in."

"It is his way of showing how much he admires you."

"Well," said the widow, patting the tall superstructure of her gleaming hair. "I could teach him some better ways of showing it. A thought occurs to me. If I am to take the girl and the horse with me, why don't I take him as well? I could make good use of him. And I would pay him better than Attila."

"You do me too much honor, my lady," said Ivar, hastily. "There is active duty ahead of us. I am better suited to that."

"Don't think that serving me isn't active duty. It's been compared to fighting a campaign. But I pay well. Your pockets would always be as full as your stomach. Think it over. I might be a very partial mistress to you."

3

From the cover of the trees, the two friends watched the departure of the widow's augmented party an hour or so later. It had not taken long to convince Macio of the wisdom of a plan by which he could remove his golden-haired daughter from danger and by the same stroke keep Harthager out of the ruthless hands of the Hun. The widow had talked to him first; and, although no mention was made of her visit when Nicolan had been admitted later, there had been an obvious relief in his attitude. It had been a brief talk he allowed the advance representative of Attila. No more, in fact, than, "Here is my stock sheet and, here, a list of the men on my land. Is there anything else you need?" His tone had been hostile and Nicolan was certain that the old man had no inkling that the plan was his and not the widow's. On leaving, Nicolan asked if there would be any objection to his presence at the races. Macio's answer had been a gruff and unfriendly "None."

From where they stood, they could see that Ildico, with her yellow hair well concealed under a velvet bonnet, was riding beside Harthager. She kept her head inclined in his direction. It may have been that she was endeavoring to console him for the undignified way he had been muffled up in an old blanket quite unfitting one of his high station, and that lime had been used to trace a disguising white star on his nose.

"It is strange," said Nicolan, "that he sends Ildico only and keeps his other daughter home. Do you suppose he doesn't care enough about her? Laudio might well find favor in Attila's eye. I remember her as a comely girl. She had dark hair and eyes but her skin was fair and delicate. I wonder, now, what Laudio thinks of this? She always had a temper of her own."

The party, proceeding at a brisk trot, was soon lost sight of in the trees which clustered along the winding road. Nicolan watched with fixed attention until the tail of the last horse had vanished from sight. Then he turned a sober face to his companion.

"I may never see her again," he said.

Ivar could afford to be philosophic about such matters, having as yet no interest in them. "I concede that she is pleasant to the eye," he said. "But the world is full of lovely women. You will have many chances to console yourself."

"Perhaps it's just as well," acknowledged Nicolan, in gloomy undertones. "It's certain the Roymarcks will never forgive me. What bitterness the old man showed me this morning! His eyes seemed to look right through me." He sighed deeply and it was several moments before he continued. "One thing is certain. If she does return, she'll find me dead or master of the lands of the Ildeburghs!"

CHAPTER X

1

ATTILA did not arrive early. Nicolan kept one eye on the races that afternoon and one on the eastern road, from which direction the Hun leader was due to appear. Lacking the zest which would have been loaned by the participation of the much-discussed Harthager, the races were rather dull. Ranno of the Finninalders won more than the Roymarck entries, an unexpected turn which did not seem to displease Laudio, who rode beside the winner. She was looking almost as lovely as her younger sister in a pink-colored riding jacket and black high boots.

The afternoon passed and no cloud of dust rose from the eastern road to proclaim the approach of Attila.

When the last race had been run, Nicolan said to his companion: "Something has happened to change his plans. There's nothing left for us but to ride back to headquarters."

As they turned their horses, however, a stir among the spectators caused him to rein in. "What's this?" he asked. Then in a tone which had an undercurrent of excitement, he added: "I believe, my friend, we are going to see a Duel of the Whips. We must wait for this! Prepare for the most stirring and terrifying spectacle you have ever watched."

The spectators had drawn closer in, leaving an oblong space of perhaps one hundred and fifty yards in length. A mounted contestant appeared at each end of the space, riding bareback, of course. Each had a heavy whip of most unusual length wound around his wrist and a poniard in his belt. Macio presented himself at one side and made an announcement, pointing first to one of the opponents and then to the other. A deep murmur arose from the watchers.

"In a Duel of the Whips," explained Nicolan to his companion, "they maneuver for position and try to curl the whip around the neck of the other man, in order to drag him from his horse. Those whips are twenty feet long and you will be surprised at the skill they show with them. Boys are trained to the use of them from the time they are five years old, because anyone may find himself involved in a duel. When one is dragged to the ground, he is no longer allowed to defend himself. His opponent can do either of two things. He can extend the boon of life to the prostrate man or dispatch him with the knife at his belt. Generally they use the knife; because feelings run deep." He stopped suddenly and drew in his breath. "I know one of them. The tall one at the other end. Rathel of the Dotterspeares. He was a gentle and quiet boy and we were close friends. But he was never very strong and I'm afraid this—this will go badly for him."

They dismounted and made their way to the front rank of spectators. Nicolan decided to get what information he could from the man nearest him, a small fellow with a cap on his head as pointed as his inquisitive nose.

"What is the quarrel?" he asked.

"Sparkan claims the girl that Rathel is to marry was promised to him by her father when she was in the cradle. Both fathers are dead now, and so there is nothing for Rathel to do but fight him. It won't be an even duel. Sparkan has fought with the Whips several times and has always killed his man." He looked up at this point and discovered the identity of the one he addressed. His expression changed, becoming dark and angry. "Is this any concern of yours, Nicolan of the Ildeburghs?"

Nicolan answered in a quiet voice, "Rathel was my friend."

"A friend no longer! He's going to die out there but I'm sure he wouldn't change places with you."

The duel had started. The man Sparkan was tall and heavy of frame. He controlled his mount with practiced ease and sureness and his dark eyes never left the figure of his opponent. There was deadly stealth in the way he held his whip. Half a dozen times it whipped out like the head of a cobra striking from its coils and each time it missed by no more than an inch. Rathel was showing horsemanship of a high order also, although he gave the impression of being continuously on the defensive. Only once did he succeed in getting behind his opponent, the position from which the whip could be used to best advantage, and the cast he made from there was far from accurate.

"My poor Rathel!" breathed Nicolan. "There can be only one end to this!"

The end came almost immediately. The black-maned Sparkan gained the coveted position and his rawhide whistled across the intervening space, winding itself about the neck of the unfortunate Rathel. A single tug brought the latter to the ground. He lay where he had fallen, according to the rule, and made no effort to regain his feet. His poniard he had already cast aside.

There was an animal eagerness in the speed with which the victor sprang to the ground and an urge to kill in the way he released his knife. Nicolan turned his eyes away. In a moment he heard a deep sigh rise from those about him and the frightened cries of women.

"One stroke only!" said Ivar. "It was murder, as surely as the dispatch of a gladiator when the thumbs were turned down."

"My poor friend!" said Nicolan. Although he was not of the Christian faith, he whispered, "May God be kind to him."

The spectators seemed too stunned to move and the small figure of a priest in a gray robe had to fight a way in to the cleared space. He ran to the center of the course and dropped on his knees beside the dying man.

"That is Father Simon," said Nicolan. "The priest we tried to find at Belise Scaur as we came through; the one I hoped would relay word of Attila's demands in advance of us. He's risking his life by showing himself publicly in this way."

The priest repeated a prayer over the recumbent body and made the sign of the cross.

"I call on all of you to witness that he lived long enough for absolution," said the priest. "He had not brought himself to the true faith, my poor Rathel of the Dotterspeares, but he was a good and honest man, and a sweetness of spirit kept him always in the straight path. In the end he knew himself a sinner and his eyes begged forgiveness before he betook himself to the life beyond. May the merciful Son of Heaven receive him into eternal peace."

The kinsmen of Rathel took charge of the body. The patriarch of the clan anointed the brow and cheeks and then placed on the

head a white cap. The victim was encased in a stiff white vest-
ment and his arms were crossed on his chest, with his knife in
the right hand. The whip he had used was wound around his
wrist so that he would depart to spirit land with the proof on him
that he had died in a duel, thus ensuring the cordiality of his
reception. Finally they grouped themselves about him and intoned a long and high dirge. The girl who was to have married
him watched from a distance, her head bowed in grief. When
Sparkan approached her, smiling triumphantly, his bloodstained
knife back in its place, she turned in a sudden hysterical anger
and waved him away.

2

The emotional effect of what he had seen took hold, at this
stage, of the man in the peaked cap. He pointed an accusing
finger at Nicolan.

"There's the one!" he cried. "He should have been killed in
there and not Rathel. He deserves death, this traitor who is selling
his own people to the Huns."

Men who had been on the point of reaching their horses and
starting away came to a halt. The shrill words had struck home.
They fell into vociferous groups, they muttered, they raised their
fists and rattled the daggers in their belts.

"Death to the traitor!" cried a high clear voice from the heart
of the crowd.

The spectators began to move forward slowly but with frowning and ominous purpose. Nicolan felt no fear at first. Here, he
realized, was his chance. The accusation had been hurled at him
openly; so now he could defend himself with equal openness.
Everyone would hear what he had to say, and perhaps they would
understand.

"Do you want your Roman masters back?" he demanded.
"Vannius was a Roman. Do you want his like, sitting over you
again like a greedy vulture? Do any of you want to be sold as
slaves in Rome as I was? Do you want to feel the whips of Roman
overseers on your backs?"

"The whip!" The word was taken up by the shrill little man
who had started the trouble. "Would this spy of the Huns have

the courage to stand up to one of our own people in a Duel of the Whips?"

"Yes!" cried Nicolan, letting himself be carried away. "But you all know that the skill we are taught with the whip as boys can be kept only by constant practice. I have not had a whip in my hands since I was carried away to Rome."

"We know you for a coward, Nicolan of the Ildeburghs!" cried a voice. "Your heart is weak and you have only a wily tongue for reasons and excuses."

"When I have had a chance to get the feel of it again, I will ride against anyone you pick!" declared Nicolan.

"Against Ranno of the Finninalders?"

"Yes, against Ranno of the Finninalders." Then a sudden surge of anger caused Nicolan to throw all caution to the winds. "He above all others. I ask nothing better than a chance to fight Ranno. Ranno whose father connived with Vannius for the murder of *my* father. You all know that he was in the plot with Vannius. That he stood aside when my mother and I were taken away and sold as slaves! Many of you here must remember my brave father and my gentle mother. Can any of you believe that the Ildeburgh lands should remain in the hands of Ranno? Think back over the years and remember what this treacherous family has done! Yes, I'll fight with Ranno. I will fight him with the best will in the world!"

By this time the crowds had gathered thickly about them. Nicolan's words, seemingly, had not had much effect. He saw nothing but angry eyes and savagely nodding heads. Some had drawn their knives and were waving them in the air.

"Cut him to pieces!"

"Hang him on the highest tree in the grove!"

"Don't listen to his prating about the past. It's what he's doing today that counts!"

"This is the end of me!" said Nicolan to himself. "I should have kept a still tongue." And yet a sense of exultation weighed above the fear he felt. If he had to die, this was one way he might have chosen: defending himself against his accusers, crying out the truth about the evil Finninalders.

He drew his dagger to defend himself, although he realized it would be of little use in the struggle. The hostile ring was already within a few feet of him. And then he heard the voice of Ivar raised above the clamor.

"Stand back!" the Briton was shouting.

Nicolan did not realize that his friend had gone into action until he saw Ivar plunge against the advancing line of angry men. The hands of the huge islander closed on the necks of the two nearest him. With apparent ease he raised both of them in the air, cracked their heads together, and threw them into the ranks of their fellows. The impact was great enough to crumple up the line and to sweep many off their feet. The advance came to a momentary halt.

"I do not speak your words!" cried the Briton. He threw off his tunic and raised his naked arms in the air, flexing his great muscles as he did so. "But I think you will understand me. Listen. I am a mighty fellow. Those two who lie there so quietly, they are not hurt. I was easy with them. But I will not be easy with the rest of you. Oh yes, you would kill me. There are many of you and you have weapons. But before I died, I would kill plenty of you. It would be unpleasant deaths you would suffer."

The advance had not been resumed and Ivar looked along the line of lowering faces. No one met his glance, not wishing to be picked for a further demonstration of his strength. "Let me give you advice. Stay where you are. Why should many of you trade your lives for mine and that of my friend?"

Another voice was heard at this point, that of Macio. He had ridden up in great haste, shouting to the mob to break up. He drove his horse into the midst of them, opening a lane to the danger center. Here he reined in and glanced about him with an eye which blazed angrily.

"Men of Bakony!" he cried. "Since when have you become cowards? A hundred of you prepared to attack two men! This is not the way of our people. Listen to me, my friends. These men are guests. No harm shall come to them while they stand on land of mine. Enough of this! Stand back, all of you, or my sword will be drawn in their defense."

The men who had lost their footing rose slowly, grumbling angrily; but the rest fell back and seemed uncertain what to do. Some of them, clearly enough, were now ashamed of the part they had been prepared to play.

"Are we to be told what to do?" asked the querulous voice of the man in the peaked cap.

Macio turned fiercely in his direction. "So, you are here, Marklius of the Pens? I am sure you started all this. Wherever you show your sniveling nose, there is trouble. Be off, you thief with the double tongue, or I'll see that you suffer for the evil-doing you have been forgiven in the past!"

Another voice joined in. Ranno rode up to the edge of the crowd.

"What is this I have heard?" he asked. "That I am being challenged to a duel?"

He dismounted, throwing the reins to a bystander. There were six plumes in his bonnet, one for each race he had won that afternoon. Macio had won four but he was not wearing them. The step of the newcomer was both jaunty and confident.

He confronted Nicolan with a supercilious smile. "I greet an old comrade," he said. "You were once Nicolan of the Ildeburghs but now you are Nicolan the Hun, the traitor who comes to spy out the land. Can it be that you are in earnest, that you desire to match your skill and your courage against mine?"

"It must be as clear to you, Ranno, as it is to me that sooner or later we must put our differences to an armed test," said Nicolan. "You stand in my shoes. You hold the land that belongs to me and refuse to let it go. For this I must kill you."

Ranno moved closer and studied him with a show of mock alarm. He slapped one hand against his thigh, encased in sky-blue hose.

"There is still plenty of light. What better time could there be for it than now? Come, let's make a memorable day of it. A second Duel of the Whips!"

"What eagerness you show, brave Ranno! You are ready to fight a man who has not had a whip in his hand for ten years. You would make short work of me, my honorable son of an honorable father. I have no intention of throwing my life away. I still have too much to do. I must prove, first, that your father was with Vannius in plotting the death of my father. I must confront you with proof of the infamous transaction which gave you our lands. I must show that I am now the rightful owner. When all that has been done, then I shall be prepared to meet you in a Duel of the Whips."

"He is right, Ranno," declared Macio, in a voice which left no doubt of his disapproval of the stand taken by the man who aspired to marry his daughter. "Have you forgotten that Rathel was granted three months for training when Sparkan challenged him? It has always been the rule."

"If his impatience cannot be slaked," said Nicolan, "let me point out that we each carry sword and dagger. Why not fight now with these weapons? I am ready if he is."

But Ranno, it developed, did not want to fight on such terms. He would wait, he declared, until they could use the whips.

3

When the two friends had mounted their horses, they found that Macio was waiting for further talk with them. He was now accompanied by his daughter Laudio.

"A word with you," he said to Nicolan. "For your ears only."

"Is it your purpose, dear Father," asked Laudio, in a bitter tone, "to explain why you sent Ildico away and left me to face whatever may befall us in the wars?"

"Peace, child!" said Macio. "You know the reason."

"All our people are wondering!" cried the girl, her slate-colored eyes flashing in her resentment. "Are you going to proclaim it to them? They are smiling behind the back of the oldest daughter who was not thought worth the effort to save!"

"Laudio, Laudio!"

"It doesn't surprise me," persisted Laudio. "You have always preferred her. Ever since she was born. You've shown it in a thousand ways, my father. You wouldn't have cared if I had been taken from you, to live in horrible slavery among the Huns. But Ildico, your favorite, your beloved child with the golden hair! Ildico must be sent to safety, even though it may bring down the wrath of Attila on all of us!"

Macio laid a hand on the reins of Nicolan's horse and led the way at a walk to a distance where they could speak without being heard. He disregarded his daughter's outbreak and proceeded to speak of other matters.

"I cannot ask you to sit at my table tonight," he said. "If I did, none of my other guests would break bread with us. There would be the three of us only, you and I and Father Simon. They are strong to hold a grudge, these people of ours. You have seen that today." He continued in a hesitant tone. "Since Attila has not come to state his demands, what are we to expect? Will all our horses be taken? And all our young men?"

"I am hoping he will accept the requisition lists I have prepared," answered Nicolan. "If he does, no breeder of horses will be left without adequate stock to maintain his strain. The drain on the man power will be heavy. What can you expect? It is war; one half of the world fighting the other half. Young men capable of bearing arms must respond to the call. I must turn in the lists I have prepared."

"What share of our horses would be left to us?"

"If Attila accepts my list, nearly a third will be left you."

For several moments Macio made no comment. He was thinking no doubt of the fine sires and mares and the promising youngsters he would lose, for horses do not come back from wars. Finally he gave a brief nod of his head. "I must be honest and tell you that your plan is more lenient than I dared hope for. None of our people expected to escape as lightly as that. If he agrees, you will have done us a service." He hesitated again. "But you must not expect any gratitude from them. As I said, we are a stiff-necked people. They can see one thing only; that you are an officer with the Hun. You may lap them all about in privilege and luxury and they will still cry shame on you." He made a gesture as though to brush the topic aside. "Tell me, Nicolan of the Ildeburghs, how did it come about that you knew the widow of Tergeste?"

"Ivar and I were running away from slavery in Rome. We hadn't eaten for days and we were so weak that we could barely walk. When we reached the walls of the city of Aquileia, we knew that we couldn't go on. An old woman, whose aid we asked, said the widow had a kind heart and would be ready to help us. She took us after dark to a large place in the hills beyond the walls. The old woman left us outside while she pleaded our case with the widow. At first the Lady Eugenia, so we were told later, was not of a mind to interfere. We were runaway slaves and she was one of the largest owners in the empire. If hers ran away, she would think ill of anyone who aided them. But she agreed to hear us and, when we had told our story and she had seen the scars on my back, she relented. Ah, how generous she was! She kept us with her three days, hidden in a room where none of her people would know. She brought food to us herself. Then she sent us off, with money in our belts and a supply of food for several days. It was because of her goodness of heart that we managed in the end to escape across the line to freedom."

"I learned something just now which made me think you saw her this morning."

"Yes, my lord Macio."

After a moment's silence, the old man went on. "That Attila did not come after all is beyond the mark. I am happy that my daughter and my great horse are well on the way to a sanctuary where the hand of the Hun cannot reach them."

"It was wise to send them. Word would have reached the ears of Attila about them before very long. While we speak of this, I would advise that you pick out your two best horses at once and send them to him as a personal gift. Inform him that Harthager is racing in the south and that you plan to send him one of the great black's get for each of the royal sons when Harthager becomes a sire."

"An excellent idea. The plan that the widow proposed to me this morning was so sound that I fell in line with it at once. I did not ask if she had discussed it with you. If the scheme was hatched in that long head of yours, I knew you would not want it known. So all I can say to you is this: that I think it was your forethought which has benefited me so mightily and I want you to know that I am grateful."

CHAPTER XI

1

NICOLAN was not left long in doubt as to the reason for Attila's change of plan. He heard it as soon as he rode through the gate of the teeming city in the bend of the river. The officer in charge of the guard leaned out through the open window of his small wooden cubicle and accosted him.

"Have you heard what's afoot?" he asked.

"I have heard nothing."

"Aetius is on his way north. With a small guard only. He arrives tomorrow."

Nicolan was taken aback at this news. "The Roman leader?"

"None other. He has twelve horsemen with him. No more."

Nicolan turned to study the officer, his lips puckered as though he were indulging in a silent whistle.

"How is it that you know this, Eppigus?" he asked.

"Everyone knows. The word has spread like fire in a grain field. The great khan is preparing a reception." The officer nodded eagerly. "I would like to know what kind of a reception it is going to be. What manner of death do you think he plans for the bold Roman?"

Nicolan brushed this aside. "Your nose is a short one, Eppigus, and yet you cannot see beyond it. What would you say if a great banquet was held for the Roman and he was then permitted to return to Rome?"

The officer laughed loudly. "You are a fool, Togalatus!" he said. He withdrew inside but almost immediately his head reappeared. "Your folly made me forget. I have an order for you. You are to report at once to the great khan."

When Nicolan was admitted, Attila was sitting by the side of his bed, wearing no more than a pair of loose woolen drawers. He stifled a yawn.

"What reports have you?"

Nicolan produced his lists. Attila looked first at the horse requisitions and slitted one eye thoughtfully as he considered the total. "I agree," he said, finally. "It is a large enough supply. We must not be greedy. There will be other wars."

"Macio's great black had been sent to race at Epirus. It will be no loss. A race horse is flighty and full of moods, so it's of no use for the cavalry. The old man promises you the first four of Harthager's get when he's used in the stud. One for each of your sons, Great Tanjou. I brought with me his two finest chargers, which he desires you to have for your personal use."

Attila grunted. "He is being suspiciously generous, this Macio. What is he concealing? I must give some thought to this later."

The emperor of the Huns looked up sharply at Nicolan. "I've had a report of a woman riding south on a black horse. A young woman with hair as yellow as sunshine on the desert. It was no more than a glimpse my lookouts had of her. The party she was with turned off the trail immediately as though not wanting to be seen. They all said she was beautiful. Was she real, think you? Is she the wife I've been seeking? Or was she a vision supplied by Them?" He was back on his old belief that great powers in the spirit world watched over him and were always ready to reward or punish him according to his deserts. Then he gave his head a negative shake. "No, no. If They intended it as a promise, the vision would have appeared to me. Then who was she?"

"Women often look beautiful at a distance but lose in charm at closer view."

"Not this one. My men swear her like has never been seen before. If she is flesh and bones, I shall find her. I believe she may be the divinely gifted one who alone is fit to share the throne I shall set up in Rome."

After a pause for reflection, he considered and approved the statement of available man power. He yawned again and then indulged in a disgusted frown. "Can it be that I am human after all? That I share the weaknesses of ordinary men? True, I rode all last night; but that has never tired me before. Why, then, do I find myself for the first time in my life yowking for sleep like a thin-flanked bridegroom?" He held up a hand. "I am giving Aetius a reception. It will be the finest ever held. A festival, in truth. It will not be anything like the wine-tasting festivals for the twice-born Dionysos. . . . You see? The Greeks call me an ignorant barbarian but I know all about their insipid and woman-ish annals. . . . This one will leave a far different taste on the tongue of my boyhood friend." He looked at Nicolan intently. "I shall want you here. You are to play a part in it."

When the two friends were inside the gate and settled in their quarters, Ivar began to ask questions.

"Is the man mad to trust himself into the hands of Attila?"

"He is mad—or very wise. I don't know which it is. Aetius is very sure of the strength of his position and he doesn't believe Attila will dare lay violent hands on him. He has a great deal to gain—or so he thinks—by getting into close contact. Perhaps he thinks he can persuade Attila not to attack Rome, to lead his armies somewhere else—against Constantinople, or North Africa, or even against the Visigoths in Gaul. Or failing that, he hopes to get some inkling as to how Attila will proceed against Rome. You see, the people of Gaul are bitterly antagonistic to the Huns and they might decide to attack if Attila moves his army into Italy. That leaves our great man with a hard decision. Should he leave his flank exposed or should he strike at Gaul first; and then, having brushed them aside, get to grips with the empire? Which he will do is a problem which keeps Aetius awake at nights, I am sure. He won't decide where to mobilize his forces until he knows Attila's purpose. Perhaps he expects to get to the bottom of it while he's here."

The same questions were being asked all over the noisy city. The men who tramped bowlegged through the narrow passages and the plump, black-eyed women who peered out from doorways all wanted to know what Attila would do to this bold Roman who was placing his head voluntarily in the lion's jaw. They all had the same idea, that their leader should take full advantage of his opponent's foolhardiness. Nothing less would suit them than the sight of the handsome head of Aetius decorating the end of a pike over the city gate.

2

It was indeed a handsome and imposing head that the dictator of Rome carried on his shoulders when he arrived with his handful of mounted men. It was a familiar scene which greeted his eyes and he gave no indication of fear or indecision. He addressed the captain of the guard in the Hun tongue, smiling in a friendly way and avoiding any show of discontent when Onegesius came to greet him and not Attila. The hours he had to spend in a small house near the inner city of imperial wives before any message reached him did not seem to ruffle his good nature. This much, at least, he had expected when he decided on his gamble.

He felt better about it, without a doubt, when he was ushered that night into the great hall in Attila's palace by attendants who bowed to him and said, "Attila is *my* lord and *thy* lord." The leader of the Huns had outdone himself for the occasion. Everything in the way of a trophy had been brought out and put on display. The walls were covered with flags and tapestries and prayer rugs. The tables glistened with silver and gold. Among the guests already seated were the heads of eight states, most of them endowed with royal titles. There were generals and ministers and wealthy merchants and religious figures. There were even women present; not wives, for that would have opened the doors too wide, with men's matrimonial inclinations running into high numbers; but voluptuous creatures all of them, in glowing yellows and rich reds, who had been brought from points as far distant as Constantinople, the home of well-mannered courtesans. Attila himself would have been disappointed, nevertheless, had he searched among them for the beautiful golden wife he sought.

Remembering the days when he had been a youthful hostage at the barbarously frugal court of Attila's uncle, Aetius was both surprised and amused at the efforts made to impress him. He recognized one of the women and said to himself, "Now where next will my little Pulchra appear?"

None of the kings had been invited to occupy the empty chair on the dais beside that of Attila. Aetius was escorted there and was received with a few words of welcome in far from gracious tones. Aetius looked about him and recognized some of the faces, in addition to the blonde Pulchra. He began to feel much easier in his mind over the outcome of his rash venture.

"Talk!" said Attila. "That's what you came for."

"Yes. I came to talk. I recall that I talked a great deal in the old days. You said very little. You sat and looked at me and kept your thoughts to yourself."

"You had nothing but contempt for me."

There was a long pause. "That is true," said Aetius. "I resented being sent as a hostage. I never forgave my father for allowing me to be selected."

"I hated you," Attila said. "You were tall and well dressed. Your nose was high and straight and women admired you. You were a scholar and I hadn't learned to read. My hatred has grown with the years."

Aetius nodded. "If I had not been sure you hated me, I would never have dared pay you this visit."

Attila stared with a complete lack of comprehension at his uninvited guest. "What reasoning is that?" he demanded. "Is this the talk you Romans call subtle? I don't understand it."

Although the room below them was filled with talk and sounds of laughter, all eyes were fixed on the two men who had met under these extraordinary circumstances and who might settle between them the fate of the world.

"It is simple," the Roman said. "Let me explain. In five years, perhaps, both Attila and Aetius will be dead. You may fall in battle or you may succumb to the heavy inroads you make on your strength. As for me, I will fall, as Caesar did, to the knives of conspirators. I live in constant danger of assassination. What happens to us in these few remaining years is not everything. In the hundreds of years to follow, men will study the history of these dramatic days, and ask what manner of man the great conqueror Attila was and, in lesser degree, the upstart Aetius. I know how deep your pride runs, O Attila. You do not want the men of the future to scoff at you as a barbarian. You will not let them say you feared me so much that you had me killed. No, no! Your pride demands that you show your supremacy over the hated Aetius on the field of battle. I had to be very sure of the depth of your hatred before I could thrust myself into your power in this way."

The spectators sensed that the air was charged with tension. The food was left untouched and they watched with almost breathless interest. Conversation died down to a drone and then ceased, until nothing was heard in the long hall but the shuffle of the servingmen's feet.

Attila had listened to his antagonist with a sense of shock. What Aetius said was true. The leader of the Huns had not realized before how true it was. There would be a savage pleasure in ordering the death of Aetius but the satisfaction it brought him would be momentary. It would be small compared to the great triumph he longed to achieve over his rival on the field of battle. The ugly, slower-witted boy must win the ultimate victory over the handsome and glib youth from Rome. He must prove his mastery in the greatest test of all. To kill Aetius now would be to rob himself of the chance for that supreme achievement.

Attila gave his round and ill-shaped head a fierce nod. "You are right. I hate you too much to kill you now."

"Then," said Aetius, "I shall talk, as you demanded. There is much to say. I must make it clear, first, that I come in the hope that we can save the world more struggle and bloodshed at the moment. We must clash ultimately, you and I, but must it be so soon? Should we not consider first the easy spoils the world offers to the great power we both command?"

Attila looked scornfully at the imposing figure beside him in the spotless white toga. "I, the youngest nephew in my uncle's house, I rule now over more of the world than Alexander had under his sway. Everything I have achieved has been by struggle and bloodshed. You, my Aetius, are the master of Rome. How did you achieve that? By struggle and bloodshed."

"No, no, I am not the master of Rome. I serve the Emperor Valentinian."

Attila, the more honest of the two, gave his shaggy head an impatient shake. "Why then are you here if you are no more than servant to that slothful and stupid son of degenerate parents? I have no time to waste on go-betweens. Is it in your power to reach decisions? If it is not, you waste my time; and that I cannot forgive."

Aetius hesitated. He was practiced in the suave exchanges of diplomacy and the bluntness of the Hun leader disturbed him.

"I have the power to make decisions," he said, finally.

Attila grunted and settled into his high-backed chair, stretching his bandy legs under the table. "Then talk," he said. What

Aetius proceeded to say was a masterpiece of carefully phrased suggestion. He did not go to the extent of offering Constantinople as a better target than Rome but he hinted at the ripeness of the Byzantine plum. He was more direct when he turned attention to North Africa. Here was a rich field for the scythe of the conqueror, one moreover where Roman and Hun might labor together as allies. He advanced a cleverly conceived plan of campaign, placing it before his listener with the hesitancy of one who pretended to know himself in the presence of the great master of strategy.

Attila listened and grunted and said nothing. It was not until the sweep of the Roman's argument subsided into a trickle of words that he roused himself.

"First," he said, "we have matters to settle. Matters over which Rome has boggled and squirmed and refused to act." He glanced about the room until he saw the face of Nicolan at a seat near the far end of the hall. He gestured to the latter to come forward.

Nicolan obeyed with much inward reluctance, certain that his former master would recognize him and foreseeing dangerous complications.

"Do you know this man?" Attila asked the Roman visitor when Nicolan stood before them.

The handsome features of Aetius hardened when he looked down at Nicolan.

"I know him," he said. "He is a slave of mine. He ran away from my household in Rome some years ago. I did not believe a slave could escape from the city alive and so I was sure he had been killed!"

"Do you claim him?"

"Of course. He is my property."

"Then I will give him to you. To do with as you wish. Crucify him as a lesson to other slaves. Or take him back and make use of him. I have found him helpful."

Nicolan knew that he faced death in its most terrible guise. There was no hint of mercy in the set features of the Roman dictator. Then he studied the face of Attila and was conscious that something was being held back. He heard the Hun leader say: "But there must be a fair exchange. I have a long list of those who have run away from my dominions and are now in sanctuary with you. These must be handed over to me. I have put Nicolan at the top of the list of those I am prepared to return to you because he is of the greatest value to me. Here is the other list. Look it over carefully."

Aetius took both lists and his face flushed as he glanced at the names of those Attila demanded in exchange.

"You do not mean it!" he cried. "You have here, at the very top, the name of the Princess Honoria."

"She desires to become my wife but is held a prisoner by orders of the emperor," declared Attila. "I demand that she be sent to me as the first condition of any discussion about our future relations."

The face of Aetius showed how unexpected this demand was. "You ask the impossible. The Lady Honoria is a princess of the imperial line. The Emperor Valentinian would never consent."

The watchful eyes below, whether they belonged to Teuton king, Sarmatian overlord, or plain foot soldier, were fixed with sudden alarm on the two figures seated above them. They saw Attila take the two sheets, which he and his guest had been studying, and tear them to pieces. They saw him turn to Aetius and say something with an air which did not suggest amity.

What Attila had said was, "Now I shall talk." He brushed aside a serving arm which would have filled his drinking cup. He had taken no more than a few mouthfuls all evening. "You are not ignorant of the fact that I am preparing for war. For the last twenty-four hours of your ride you were in country covered by the tents of my warriors. I have assembled here the greatest army ever seen on the face of the earth; and still they come. Where do I plan to strike? That is what brought you here. You hope to find some proof of my plans, or to trap me into an admission. I find no fault with this. I have my own spies everywhere. Perhaps I should be proud that Aetius, the master of Rome, has thought it necessary to act as his own spy." He paused and then threw a question at the visitor. "What conclusions have you reached?"

"You are preparing to attack Rome. I am so certain of it that I am here in an effort to convince you that nothing but ill can come of it—for you as well as for Rome. Have you taken into consideration the advantages which always rest with the defenders? The desperation, the patriotic fervor which makes men excel themselves, the intimate knowledge of every foot of terrain, the relative ease of feeding the defending armies? All these advantages were on the side of Rome when Hannibal attacked her. And Hannibal failed."

"I know all this. I am still certain I shall beat you, Aetius, and raze the walls of your great city."

"The haruspices have been at work. They agree that your purpose is to attack us. They agree also that you will fail. And die in the attempt."

"What methods do they use, these haruspices of yours?"

"The study of the entrails of the newly killed. Not animals. Not slaves. They use the bodies of young maidens."

The watchers, who had sensed a growing tension between the two men on the dais, were disturbed to see Attila throw back his head at this point and indulge in a roar of laughter. He seldom laughed. There were many in the room, in fact, who had never seen him give way to mirth. His laughter now, it must be said, had little suggestion of mirth about it. Beginning with a curious low-throated chuckle, the sound mounted slowly until it reached torrential volume. It was not infectious in any sense; it was, instead, fearsome, horrendous, unhuman.

"I am the barbarian," said Attila, when his laughter ended. "You are the cultured scholar, the man of wide knowledge. Yet you believe in divination, in the prying of priestly fingers into the vitals of dead things to learn what the future holds. I laugh at such folly. I, the barbarian, depend only on my own judgment, based on experience—and on the reports of my spies and my advance troops. Oh, I let the priests perform their functions. The people around me believe in them. And now, Aetius, as between us, which is the real barbarian?"

Aetius disregarded this question. He asked, "What method of divination do your priests use?"

"The Flight of the Arrow. Human sacrifice, naturally. At the instant of death, the victim shows what she has seen beyond this life. It is done, not by the writhing of her bowels, but by the direction of an arrow. It has been used by my people for centuries. It is interesting to watch. Shall we try it, O my friend from the so-called world of learning and culture?"

Aetius found it hard to conceal his eagerness. A fanatical light appeared back of the sternness of his eyes. "Yes, O Attila. Summon your priests and let us learn what they can tell us."

The hall was cleared, save for Attila's generals and chief advisers, as well as two of the party accompanying the Roman leader, and the heads of allied states—perhaps twenty spectators in all. The curtain closing off the raised area of the hall was rolled back. Attila's bed was shoved to one side. Then a metal bar, with a pair of sandals permanently attached in the center, was brought in. It was then noticed that the wall at the far end of the hall, a distance of perhaps eighty feet, was covered with a map of the world.

Attila raised a hand in the air. "Bring in the maiden," he commanded.

A pretty young girl, with flowers in her dark hair and draped across her white tunic, was led in. She struggled to free her arms from the viselike grip of priestly fingers.

"Is she of the right age?" asked Attila.

"Yes, Great Tanjou."

"I cannot judge from this distance if she is lovely enough to please the gods."

"Yes, Lord of the Earth and Skies. The maiden is surpassing fair."

"She is not a slave?"

"No. Her father was a sheepherder. He resisted our demand for her and was killed in the struggle. This will make it a double sacrifice and so please the gods. Even Marha, the One of Terror, will be pleased."

"Does she know what is expected of her?"

"Fear has taken her in its grip. She trembles like a young fawn. It is the right mood, Great Tanjou."

The feet of the girl were placed in the sandals and an iron ring was attached to one of them. Another ring was placed around the neck of the victim, and the two were then attached by a bowstring of unusual strength. An arrow, more than four feet long, was fitted into a notch around her waist.

"May her departing spirit direct the arrow truly!" cried one of the priests. "May we thus wrest from the gods the knowledge of where the victory of Attila will be won! Pull!"

Two powerful Hun bowmen began to draw back on the string.

The girl screamed in terror and pain. They continued to pull until it seemed certain that her head and heels would meet. Then there was heard a sharp and sickening crack. The girl's body collapsed, her head striking the floor but the rest of her body contorted unnaturally by the anchoring of her feet to the bar. Her back had been broken.

The arrow sped with great velocity in the direction of the map. It struck into the wall with such force that the feathered end quivered visibly.

"Where has it struck?" demanded Attila.

One of the priests pointed with a long black finger. The head of the arrow was firmly imbedded in a circle of red which marked where the City of the Seven Hills lay on the river Tiber.

"Rome!" he cried.

Attila spoke in a mocking tone to Aetius, whose face had turned pale. "Was it trickery? Or have the gods spoken?"

"The truth has been revealed."

"You came here convinced you knew my purpose. So you have learned nothing from this that you didn't believe before. Now I have a word of advice for you, O Aetius. Get to horse at once. A guard will accompany you beyond the point where my armies are encamped. You must ride all night. My people do not like to see you here. Nor do I."

His voice rose to a shrill pitch and he began to give vent to his real feelings. "Some of my people remember you as I do—the boy from Rome who laughed at us. They still call you by the names we made for you then, 'The Poet,' 'The Long Nose,' 'Little Half-ass,' and 'The Skin Bather.' My people are demanding your blood. Get away at once while your head is still on your shoulders." He turned savagely on the Roman leader. "I won't be able to control my impulse to have you killed if you are here when the sun rises!"

3

After the departure of Aetius, the work of mobilization proceeded at an increased rate of speed. More armies came in from the north, made up of tall men with dull yellow hair and carrying rude weapons. Horses were delivered from the Alföld. Nicolan found himself so immersed in detail that he had time for nothing but work. He slept in snatches and read reports at his meals. He was surprised, therefore, to receive a summons from Attila and to discover that what the emperor desired to discuss was the unknown young woman who had been seen by his advance horsemen.

"I have had later reports," said the Hun leader. "The party reached Aquileia. There, instead of turning down the south road to Ravenna, they skirted the head of the sea and went to Tergeste."

"Did they all find her beautiful?"

"She was wearing her hair under a round felt cap like a boy. But one of my men saw her remove the cap and shake her hair loose for a moment. It was golden and her beauty was great enough to strike him dumb with wonder." Attila looked steadily at his assistant. "From the direction taken by the party, I am inclined to think they came from your country."

"The women of my country are dark," declared Nicolan. "Is it not more likely that the party came through my country on their way from the forest lands beyond the great river? There the women have hair the color of sunshine and they let it hang down their backs in long free tresses."

Attila fell into a thoughtful mood. "It is true that the lovely Swanhilde, who died so needlessly, came from the forest country. It may be that the wife I must find before I am crowned in Rome will come from the north. But I have a strange feeling about this beautiful girl who has appeared and disappeared so quickly. I think she will be seen again and that she will be the wife I have waited for so long."

"But, Great Tanjou, she seems to have vanished from sight."

"She is in Tergeste," declared Attila. "No one can leave there without my people knowing. They are watching. Someday soon, I shall have further word of her."

He then put the topic aside and plunged into arrangements for an immediate march. The die had been cast. They would strike first at the hostile people beyond the Rhine. Not until the armies of the Gauls had been broken would the drive on Rome begin.

CHAPTER XII

1

HALF a million men in leather jackets and red topknotted caps with bows over their shoulders were facing half a million other men in gray and brown under the eagles of Rome and the gaudy banners of the Visigoths. From where he stood behind the earthworks on a high point of the Catalaunian Plains, Nicolan could see, burning bright in the blackness of night, the bivouac fires of the enemy. The next morning these million men would converge and clash and perhaps a quarter of them would be murdered before the sun sank again. Nicolan watched the twinkling lights with a sense of personal guilt. He had known this to be inevitable and he had seen it approach without any qualms, even with equanimity, because the war might lead to the restoration of his rights and lands. Now, because of this, he felt as though the responsibility rested entirely on his shoulders and a feeling of fear took possession of him. For the first time he was uncertain of the stand he had taken.

Attila was sitting silently on his horse a short distance away. He thought better that way and it was clear that he had much to think about. The generals and rulers of conquered lands who were commanding their units under his direction had not been able to get a word out of him for an hour. The Hun leader was not the mere barbarian that the world pictured, with an urge to fight and kill and conquer. He was, on the contrary, thoroughly realistic and he knew that Aetius sat behind those myriads of campfires on the horizon and plotted cleverly the methods of attack he would follow the next day. He, Attila, had been caught somewhat off guard at the siege of Orléans, just as that city was ready to drop into his hands like a peach from a wall. At any rate he had been in a poor position to turn and give battle. A retreat had been necessary and now he had come to bay between the Seine and the Aube, waiting for Aetius to accept the gage of

battle. He was not happy. Those three brother princes, who were
extolled so highly for their gallantry, were no better than ox-
heads, he said to himself. They had allowed Torismond of the
Visigoths to seize a height of land on the left flank of the Huns.
The first necessity of the morning would be to dislodge Torismond
from his commanding position. Attila tore off the skins of field
mice which had been tailored together to make him a wrap, feeling a wave of anger mount inside him. These hotheaded sons
of weak fathers, what a price he paid for their adherence! This,
already: the archers of the enemy commanding his flank from that
captured hilltop, and the three gay fools carousing in their tents!

Nicolan knew the emotions which were smoldering in the
breast of the Hun leader and he was wondering if he dared to
approach him with a suggestion. He wanted to report that the
grade up the hill was less steep on the far left and an attack there
at dawn might scatter the Visigoths with one wild charge.

He heard someone behind him in the dark and a familiar voice
said: "Nicolan! I have come to offer my hand in friendship."

It was Roric of the Roymarcks, who had already distinguished
himself in several sharp encounters. Nicolan turned eagerly to
greet him.

"My old friend!" said Roric. "Tomorrow we may both die! I
do not want to pass over into the shades with this cloud between
us."

Nicolan's emotions were so stirred that his voice shook. "Roric,
I could not go to you," he said. "I knew how you felt about me.
How all of you felt. I couldn't face more rebuffs."

Roric was in a mood for open confession. "You were right
about all this. Here we are, all of our race, fighting for Attila. We refused to see the truth of the situation. All of us but
you. Nick, my good friend, I have felt tonight the stirring of the
wings about me. Tomorrow I shall die. I must say this to you
first. If you survive, promise me you will think of my people and
wrap the cloak of your foresight about them—my father and my
sisters and our great horses, as you did on one occasion we both
know of. Yes, my father told me it was you who saw the way
to get Ildico out of danger."

They shook hands gravely in the dark.

"I swear, Roric, to put their welfare above everything. But, come, you are in a despondent mood. Tomorrow, when the legions of Rome have fled in defeat, it will be another story."

"For you, I trust. But not for me. I have heard the voices whispering near me and the hands reaching in the dark. I am marked to die." Then the son of the Roymarcks shook off the heavy mood in which he had come. A hint even of elation came back into his voice. "Before we crossed over into this accursed Gaul, I had word from Gaddo the Kite. He had been sent to attend my sister. She sent him back. He knew they were being watched at Tergeste and suspected it was by agents of Attila. He brought the word that they had succeeded in getting away and had reached Epirus. Also he brought to my father a story of the race there."

"Was the little Ildico well and content?" asked Nicolan, eagerly.

"In the best of health and well content." Roric smiled broadly. "At first she was very angry because the other horse owners refused to let her ride Harthager. It would be an affront to every one of them, they swore, to have a woman ride against them. The widow of Tergeste shamed them out of that. 'So,' she said, 'it is now the men who fear the women. The world is turning topsy-turvy.' She offered to double her wagers and, of course, they grasped at that. Ildico could ride, they said, but she must not offend the proprieties. She must wear the cap and shoes of a paid rider." Roric paused to laugh. "What a picture she must have made, my little sister, swallowed up in one of those round felt hats and in boots twice too large!"

"But she won! I am sure she did."

"Trust her for that. It's a strange thing that Harthager always did his best when she was up, even better than when I rode him. She was very wise about the race, according to Gaddo. She took Harthager right out to the side, giving away twenty yards by doing it but making sure there would be no interference. It was not until they saw the finish post ahead that she began talking to him. They are close friends and he knows always what she says. I can just hear her saying in his ear, 'Now, great fellow, now is the time to show these earthborn horses that you are not mortal and that you were trained by the gods with the clouds for a course!' Harthager flattened himself out like a black thunderbolt and raced across the line many lengths ahead of the field. The widow

of Tergeste won back all she lost the year before and a pot of
profits." Roric's voice lifted to a less prudent pitch. "That little
Ildico! She lost her cap in the riding, and both shoes, and she
came back to the judges with her hair floating behind her like
a ruddy comet and her little pink toes turning up in her
excitement."

"You are a poet, friend Roric!" cried Nicolan. "What a picture
you have given me! I would have given an arm and ten years
of my life to be there."

"The widow has taken them, Ildico and the horse, into Greece
for more races. They will then go to Constantinople."

Nicolan nodded his head in deep satisfaction. "The war will
be over before they get back," he said.

Roric laid a compelling hand on Nicolan's arm. "Make your
peace with our people and go home when this is finished. I must
speak out and tell you what is in my mind. I want you to marry
Ildico. I am frightened of what I have seen in the eyes of Ranno
of the Finninalders. Go back where you belong, old friend.
Gather into your hands the reins that I—I shall drop tomorrow."

The hunched shoulders of Attila stirred and he began to speak.
Roric and Nicolan clasped hands, each with a lump in his throat,
and the former disappeared in the darkness. Nicolan walked forward to join the group around Attila, thinking there might be
orders for him. But the leader of the Huns was unaware of anyone about him. He was communing with Them and demanding
guidance for the desperate hours which stretched ahead.

2

No one pair of eyes can see much of a great battle. If engaged
in the thick of the fighting, a soldier discerns nothing but those
nearest him, the fierce eyes of the enemy, the swinging axes, the
thrusting spears; if a spectator, there is no more to be seen than
a segment of the battle line, a dust cloud, perhaps, rising from a
charge of horses, a frenzied rush of reinforcements being urged
down into the blood and turmoil.

Because of a duty imposed on him by Attila, Nicolan saw only
the terrain immediately in front of him; but here, as chance had
it, the fortunes of the battle were waged and finally decided.

It was in early morning and a mist still clung to the plains, obscuring all view of the enemy. The sound of the Roman trumpets, blaring thinly on the heavy air, seemed to come from far off but the voices of the Hun scouts issuing from the murk made it clear that the enemy lines had not been changed. Attila, tallowy of face and with smoldering fire in deep-sunken eyes, held up an importunate finger to Nicolan.

"For you I have orders," he said. "I shall lead the center in person and I must be kept advised of how the battle goes. From here, where you stand, you will direct the dispatch riders. There are a hundred of them and they will patrol the whole field behind the lines. They will bring you word of what they see and hear, and reports from my generals, and you will relay everything to me as fast as it comes in. When anything important is to be sent, give it to a dozen riders, to be sure that one at least of them will reach me."

Attila's servant Giso, as greasy and truculent as ever, appeared on a small and shaggy horse. He spoke to Nicolan out of the corner of his mouth. "Send some of them to me. I'll always be there. I won't be in the fighting. But *he*," motioning at Attila, "will be in the thick of it. The messages will be sure to reach me."

Attila heard and glared over his shoulder at Giso. "Has it come to this," he demanded, "that I need the help of half-witted servants?" Then he paused and ran a finger over the tiptilted bridge of his squat nose. He turned to Nicolan. "It is an idea, Togalatus. When the news is important and pressing, send one message to this imbecile. He will be looking after the safety of his skin and so he'll be alive to receive it. He may find ways of getting the messages to me which the dispatch riders wouldn't know."

Attila rode down to the front of the lines and his voice could be heard raised in exhortation to his followers. Nicolan kept his head turned in that direction but could hear no more than an occasional word. After a time there was silence, an almost complete lack of sound, and then suddenly a great roar rose from the ranks. The voices of troop commanders were heard, the trumpets blared forth with shrill excitement.

The battle was beginning.

3

The first message to reach Nicolan came from the left flank where the three princely brothers were in command, having roused themselves from the stupor induced by the night's heavy debauch. The face of the rider who brought it was covered with blood. He reined in his horse.

"Roric of the Roymarcks has been ordered to lead his horsemen up the northern slope to dislodge the Goths from the hilltop."

Nicolan found it hard to believe what he had heard. "Who gave such an insane order?" he demanded.

"Prince Tallimundi."

"Ivar!" cried Nicolan. "You were with me when I made a survey last night of the approaches. Am I mistaken in saying that the northern slope is the steepest of all?"

"It's impossible to get to the top there. The slope on the east is where the attack should be made. It's more gradual and it's well screened with trees."

"That is the information we gave to Attila and he agreed that the attack should be made on the east. He said also that it was work for foot soldiers. How can horsemen be expected to ride up such a steep slope? Go back," he said to the rider, "to the Prince Tallimundi and beseech him to countermand the order at once." Then he paused. A disturbing thought had become lodged in his mind. After the battle there would be inquiries made as to why certain things had been done or not done. He asked the rider, "What is your name?"

"Somutu."

"Somutu, keep in your mind everything which happens today. Remember what you say to the princes and what they say to you. It may be of great importance. And now lose no time in getting back. The fine horsemen under Roric are being sent to their deaths. Tell the princes I am advising the emperor of what has been done."

Nicolan turned then to a second rider. "Your name?"

"Passilis."

"Ride down to where the emperor has taken his station. Tell him of this order and of the steps I have taken. Tell him that this goes completely against the report I made to him last night and that the princes are making a fatal error. Say that I beg him to direct an attack by foot soldiers. Off! There isn't a moment to be lost."

Nicolan leaned over and spoke to Ivar in low tones. "We must keep an accurate memory of all the orders which pass through our hands and of the reports which reach us. The names of the riders, the exact orders they bring, the times when they are delivered."

Ivar nodded. "I'll attend to it. I have a good memory."

In a matter of perhaps ten minutes the man Somutu was back. His wounded cheek was still bleeding. He seemed very much disturbed.

"The charge had begun," he said breathlessly. "Roric was leading his men up the slope. They were finding it hard. The accursed Goths were sending arrows down on them like hailstones. The losses will be heavy, whether they carry the hill or not."

Nicolan felt sick of heart. "All of my friends are fighting up that hill. Somutu, what chance have they?"

"None who watch believe they have any chance at all." The rider continued with a puzzled frown. "And yet it's said that one of your own leaders came to the tent of the Tallimundis and suggested the charge."

Nicolan looked up. "When was this?"

"A few minutes before dawn, O Togalatus."

"Which of the leaders was it?"

"The name I heard was——" The rider hesitated. Then memory came to his assistance. "It was Ranno."

"Somutu!" cried Nicolan. "By the memory of your father and all of *his* fathers, by your fear of the vengeance of the gods, never let that name go out of your mind! You may be called upon later to tell what you know. You must be honest and tell then what you have told me. Ranno! Ranno of the Finninalders! Keep that firmly in your memory."

"That I will."

In a very few minutes a fresh dispatch rider brought the news that the attack on the hill had failed. Most of the horsemen had been killed in their futile effort to reach the top.

"How many died?" asked Nicolan, grimly.

"My lord Togalatus, I find it hard to tell you. Very few came back. None of the leaders. Roric went down among the first with an arrow in his eye."

There was a long silence, Nicolan finding nothing he could say. Then he asked, "What of Ranno?"

"There is no word of him."

A rider came up the slope from the extended position where Attila had drawn up the center. He put his horse in one leap over the earthworks and approached Nicolan.

"Orders from the emperor," he said. "To be sent Prince Tallimundi. These are his words: 'Withdraw horsemen from the attack and repair this disastrous mistake by sending foot soldiers to attack on the east. Lose not an instant in carrying out these instructions.'"

Nicolan gave his head a despairing shake. "Too late. The attack has been made and has failed. Few of the horsemen have returned." He looked at the rider, who had lost his cap in the heat of his gallop up the slope. "What is your name?"

"Allagrin."

"Make certain, Allagrin, that you remember the time when you delivered this message. Return now to the emperor and tell him his orders have been conveyed. Tell him also that the disastrous mistake of the three princes has cost him most of the attacking force." He motioned to a fresh rider. "Carry the emperor's message to Prince Tallimundi. Ride like the wind!"

"Foot soldiers are now attacking on the north slope," was the next report brought back. "The princes say there is not time now to mount an attack on the east."

"They'll find the time when they get that order from the emperor," said Nicolan, grimly. "How many of the horsemen came back?"

"Who can tell yet? A score perhaps. Not more. They were doomed before they moved out from the lines."

Nicolan felt the sympathetic hand of Ivar on his shoulder. "We'll find things are not as bad as they say. It's always the way, old friend. They exaggerate the losses."

4

The air was filled now with the excitement of an advance all along the line as Attila led his men into action. Ahead of the Hun leader was the weakest part of the army of Aetius, the Alani, commanded by a pusillanimous king named Sangiban. Aetius, with his Roman horsemen, was opposite the Hun right and he was showing an unexpected lack of activity. Nicolan tried to see what was happening there but the distance was too great. The first dispatch rider to arrive from that quarter had nothing to report. What was the Roman fox planning? Nicolan propounded this question to Onegesius, who was passing on his way to his own station on the right.

The latter shook his head scornfully. "Does it matter? Our Great Tanjou will win by breaking Sangiban like a dry twig. We will cut their army in two."

The strategy of Attila was now developing and the opinion of Onegesius seemed likely to be borne out. The emperor was counting on a quick breakthrough in the center and an enveloping movement to the left to drive Sangiban back on the soldiers of Theodoric, the gallant old Visigoth king, back of the hilltop, and so roll up that whole side of the field. The plan was succeeding so well that already a gap had opened between the panicky Sangiban and the Roman cohorts.

"Do you see?" chuckled Onegesius, who still lingered to watch. "The enemy center is broken. The battle is won."

But Nicolan was not convinced. "Aetius hasn't made a move yet. Do you think he will let himself be beaten as easily as this?"

Another chuckle from the confident Onegesius. "What can the stag do when the tiger breaks his back with one leap and sinks his teeth into the soft flesh of the neck?"

A dispatch rider galloped up from the left flank. "Good news!" he cried. "Old Theodoric is dead. He was wounded and fell out of his saddle. The hoofs of his own horse cut him to tattered shreds of bone."

"Do his own men know?"

"Yes. They seem to have lost heart. They're making no move to help Sangiban."

Nicolan's hand fell on the rump of the nearest horse. "In there!" he cried to the rider. "Get this word to the emperor!"

"The stone walls on the seven hills of Rome are shaking!" shouted Onegesius.

Nicolan did not share to the fullest the optimism which was showing in the Hun ranks. He expected to hear something from the Romans at any moment. There was danger, he felt, in the rapidity of Attila's success. If the Hun leader pursued the broken center of the enemy too far, the Romans would be left with nothing to oppose their advance. They could then in turn cut Attila's army in two. Nicolan was so conscious of the dire consequences of this possible turn of events that he took it on himself to send a rider to the emperor with word that the gap was becoming dangerously wide. Then he sent a second, a third, a fourth. The gap continued to widen and he dispatched horseman after horseman to warn Attila of the danger.

Aetius struck before anything was done to correct the situation. The Roman eagles came suddenly to life and moved forward. A battle song sounded exultantly from thousands of Roman throats as the armored horsemen charged up the slope to the earthworks. Then the move that Nicolan had feared was made. Part of the Roman forces were diverted to strike into Attila's unprotected flank.

None of the riders had returned and there was no way of telling if any of them had delivered his message. He continued to send them down into the murderous maelstrom where Attila was now desperately in danger of encirclement. Even Onegesius realized the seriousness of the situation which had developed. His piglike eyes glittering with fear, he clutched at Nicolan's shoulder.

"The tiger sprang too far!" he croaked. "The tusks are now goring his own ribs!"

But it was soon apparent that the Hun leader had not been carried so completely away by his easy success against Sangiban as to be unaware of the danger which now threatened. He checked his exultant, screeching horsemen from their eager pursuit of the Alani and swung them about to meet the new danger. The light Hun horsemen, clad in hardened leather and armed

THE DARKNESS AND THE DAWN 189

with their crescent-shaped swords, found themselves countering the armored Romans with their heavy metal swords and spears. It looked an uneven contest but the men from the East were agile and swift. They maneuvered their horses with the pressure of their knees and let the murderous blows of the Roman swords glance off their round shields while awaiting the chance to strike themselves. The legion lost as many men as the Huns in this struggle.

Nicolan could see that Attila had one purpose only now, to battle his way back to the position he had held when the struggle began and so consolidate his lines. If he could do this, the Roman advance would be stopped and the two armies would reach a stalemate. But this was not the kind of battle that the wild horsemen from the steppes liked to fight. No room here for mass maneuvering, for the hit-and-run tactics they could play so well. Instead they must fight their way through an ever lessening strip of ground, with the Romans pressing in on one side and the Goths on the other.

The battle had reached its climactic stage. The two armies had come into close conflict along the whole of the three-mile front. The air was filled with outpourings of hate and rage and anguish, the clash of arms, the screams of wounded horses. Men fell and were trampled underfoot, for the living and the whole were too busily engaged with bloodstained weapons to give ear to the agonized pleas of the wounded. Half a million men on one side of the Catalaunian Plains sought to kill the half million on the other side, and not a minute passed but the last breath ebbed from hundreds of broken bodies. Never before had the sun looked down on such a scene of mass murder as on this tragic day.

"Can Attila still be alive?" asked Nicolan, as he and Ivar stared with horror at this loosing of the forces of evil.

"I can still see his flag," was the answer. "The top shows over there. Can you make it out? That small patch of black and gold."

"I'm sure no messages can reach him." Nicolan shaded his eyes with one hand and studied the field. He then turned to his companion. "There's no use wasting the lives of any more of our riders. But I'm going down."

Despite Ivar's remonstrances, he vaulted his horse over the

earthworks and began to make his way through the Hun ranks.
It was hard work and highly dangerous. The first thought of the
surly soldiery he was trying to pass was to strike. He lost his cap,
the hoof of a bucking horse caught him on one leg, a swinging
scimitar cut through his sleeve and left a long wound on his arm.
His demands to be taken to Attila met with no response; none of
the fighting men had any idea of what was happening beyond
the range of a few yards. The ground was encumbered with
bodies, the grass was slippery with blood. The farther he rode into
the press, the slower his progress became. Finally, convinced that
the stage had been reached where nothing but brute force
counted, he turned back.

Perhaps his struggles had carried him close to the Roman lines.
Or it may have been that the armored legions, in their efforts to
cut the Hun army in two, had been gaining ground. Whatever
the reason, Nicolan suddenly found himself confronted by a tall
Roman who showed little more than a pair of angry fighting eyes
over the top of his great shield. A powerful arm was raised in the
air and a sword fell with the force and weight of a landslide on
the small shield which Nicolan carried on his left arm. His arm
seemed to wilt and the brunt of the blow was borne by his shoulder. Twice more the deadening weight of that mighty sword fell
upon him and Nicolan had no recourse but to yield ground, expecting each moment to be his last. A fourth blow slipped off
the surface of the shield, which had been turned sideways by the
weight of the previous one. This gave him an inkling of the defense to be used against this kind of attack; he must hold his
shield at an angle and thus deflect the blows.

The Roman was pressing hard to finish him and paying small
heed to defense himself. This provided Nicolan with a chance.
A quick jab with the point of his crescent sword found its target
in the bronzed neck of his antagonist. Blood spurted from the
wound like a fountain in play. The tall figure seemed to pause,
and then it swayed and fell backward out of the saddle.

A clump of dispatch riders were sitting their horses in anticipation of orders when Nicolan got back within the lines. Ivar was
among them.

"You're wounded!" he cried.

The hand with which Nicolan dabbed at his cheeks came away

red with blood. He had felt no pain. The tall Briton examined his face with anxious hands.

"A cut over the left eye," he said. "Not deep, fortunately. It's been bleeding freely. How did you get it?"

"I don't know."

While Nicolan talked to the riders, finding that they had no reports to be relayed, Ivar vanished in the rear. He came back in a few minutes with a rib bone of beef which he pressed into Nicolan's hands. "Black Scyles is behind there," he said. "He has enough food prepared for a score or so. The country behind us is stripped bare and there will be no more food as long as we stay here. The army will have to rest on empty stomachs."

Nicolan tore the meat from the bone with his teeth, realizing suddenly that he was ravenously hungry. After consuming half of it, he handed the bone back to Ivar, who began to gnaw at it eagerly.

"You picked the wrong horse, brave Togalatus," said a voice from behind them.

Nicolan turned and saw that Ranno had ridden up in the rear. There was a mocking light on the sallow face of the head of the Finninalders.

"The effete Romans seem to be winning themselves a battle."

"A battle," declared Nicolan, taking in his unstained riding jacket and his ease of manner, "in which you appear to have taken no part."

"On the contrary. I have just returned from scouting around their right flank. There was a fear that the Goths might be extending their lines to outflank us."

Nicolan said quickly, "Who gave you the order?"

"My commander, Roric."

"Then you started before the battle began. How fortunate for you. You have escaped all this bloody mess. Have you heard that nearly all our brothers and friends were killed in the first few minutes of the fighting?"

"I have been told the losses were heavy."

Nicolan wheeled his horse about and rode over to confront the seemingly unconcerned Ranno. "It is being said that it was on your advice that this insane attack on the northern slope was ordered."

"That is a lie!"

"I have reason to believe it is true. About this other order, the one which sent you out on an excursion into the quiet country-side, it's unfortunate Roric is dead and his testimony can't be had. I don't believe he gave it."

Ranno's hand was gripping the handle of his dagger. "A time will come when you will pay for these charges you are making!" he exclaimed.

"I have no doubt, gallant Ranno, that you will find ways of stealing the lands of those who have fallen today. Perhaps you had that in mind when you contrived to have our people sent to their deaths!"

The angry exchange of words ended at this point, for more riders arrived and Nicolan found it necessary to listen to their reports. By the time he was through with them, Ranno had disappeared.

Nicolan leaned over to speak to Ivar. "You heard what he said? He's prepared to deny that he spoke with Tallimundi. Can proofs of it be obtained?"

Ivar looked up with a worried frown. "If there is an investigation after the battle is over, there will be bitter recriminations. Will that fellow try to lay the blame on you?"

"I think it certain that he will."

"We have the word of the riders. I'll see if more proof of it can be found. . . ."

Ivar, who had been on foot all day, borrowed a horse and rode off on this quest.

In the meantime the tide of battle had turned. The pincers which had been closing on the Hun army of the center had been broken. The grim fighting men from the steppes were pouring back into the lines they had occupied before the fighting began. The Romans did not seem disposed to dispute the issue any further and the Goths, having no stomach for more fighting, had already fallen back.

"A drawn battle," thought Nicolan, standing in his stirrups to get a better view of the field.

Somutu had ridden up beside him. "It's being said, O Togalatus, that one man in every four has been killed. Never before has such a bloody battle been fought." He looked anxiously at Nicolan. "Will it be called a defeat for us?"

"This drive into the country of the Gauls was planned to stop any possibility of an attack from them when the march on Rome began. Their losses are so heavy that they won't be able to try anything of the kind; so that much has been accomplished. But will Attila now be able to recruit his forces sufficiently after this to attack Rome?"

"I am weary of war," sighed Somutu.

The tired Hun warriors were pouring over the embankment and crying loudly for food and drink. The legions of Rome were withdrawing into their former position. From all points of the bloodstained field rose the beseeching cries of the wounded. The wind had fallen and the standards on both sides of the line hung limply as though discouraged with this lack of result after a day of carnage.

5

Black Scyles saw the last morsel of food vanish and waved a black arm at the company of officers. "No more," he said, cheerfully. "You've done better than the poor devils out there. Not a bite for them." No single appetite had been satisfied but the grumbling men who wearily wiped their greasy hands on their leather jackets had one consolation. None of the generals or top advisers of the Hun leader had shared in the meal. They had been called into consultation and the debate still dragged on, Attila sitting his horse like a bronze statue with his aides grouped about him.

Nicolan had refused to eat. He sat on the ground with his hands pressed tightly against both ears to spare himself the anguished cries of the wounded. Ivar, sitting beside him, with his belt drawn tight to ease the pangs of hunger, tried to bring him to a more reasonable frame of mind.

"I hear there are as many as fifty thousand out there," he said. "All of them will be left to die. And there's nothing you can do about it. Even if we dragged a few of them in, it would do no good. Attila makes no provision for the care of the wounded. They would die of neglect anyway."

"I was eager for this war," said Nicolan. "I never acknowledged it—but I was. I thought it would give me the chance I've waited for. To render Attila such services he could no longer refuse to restore my lands. Yes, Ivar, that's how selfish I was." He shook his head bitterly. "Listen to them! Dying out there in torment and not a hand raised to help them! I feel that I'm as guilty as Attila himself."

A short silence fell between them. "Ivar!" said Nicolan, suddenly. "Do you suppose any of my people are lying wounded on that hillside? The men from my own country?"

"Like enough," answered the Briton. "It was the archers who stopped them; and arrows don't always kill." He looked compassionately at his companion. "You can't go. There will be orders for you any minute now. But I'll go and search the ground." He rose stiffly to his feet. "It may be too late. But I'll do my best."

The tall form of Ivar had hardly vanished in the darkness when the group about Attila broke up. The decision they had arrived at spread through the weary ranks with almost unbelievable speed. A retreat had been ordered. The bone-weary men sprang to their feet, accepting with gladness the prospect of interminable hours on the march in preference to another day of carnage on the terrible plains below.

Nicolan heard his name called and saw Attila's servant Giso weaving his way toward him through the darkness. "He wants you," said the servant.

Attila was alone when Nicolan approached him. The Hun leader was in the saddle still and he did not turn his head. There was a long moment of silence before he spoke.

"I've ordered a retreat."

"Yes, Great Tanjou."

"I want an opinion, an honest one. None of these others has the sense to speak up and tell me the truth. What will be said about this battle? Will it be said I was defeated?"

"How can it be? If you fight another day, both armies will be totally destroyed."

"That is true."

"And you cannot remain here because all our food supplies are exhausted."

"That also is true."

"Then how can it be regarded as anything but a drawn battle?"

Attila nodded his head. "A drawn battle it is. But those who fear me, and those who hate me—and who doesn't do one or the other?—will lift up their calflike faces to whatever gods they worship and sing praises because I have been defeated." He paused and then added in an angry voice, "They will say that the hated Aetius has won a victory!"

Under ordinary circumstances Nicolan would have said nothing more. He sensed, however, that Attila was hungry for reassurance. "The Goths," he said, "are still mourning their dead king. There are rumors that they are withdrawing."

"Yes, they are pulling back."

Nicolan ventured on an opinion. "Torismond, the oldest son, will want to get back and establish himself on the throne. It may be that the silence from his lines means he has already left the field. If that's true, can Aetius meet you on equal terms tomorrow?"

"My men can't fight on empty stomachs." Attila continued to stare into the dark but it was clear that his spirits had lifted. He began on an explanation of the battle. "As soon as I saw that Sangiban, that weak peacock, was in command of their center, I knew that Aetius had set a trap for me. He expected me to smash through Sangiban's lines and pursue him too far. At the right moment he would drive his legions behind me and cut my army in two. Well, I decided to gamble, to seem to play his game. I struck at Sangiban but I didn't intend to pursue him far. As soon as I had him on the run, I planned to wheel about and throw all the strength of my center and right against the Romans." He gave his head a somber shake. "But I was giving Aetius too much credit. In order to beat me thoroughly he should have waited longer to counterattack, but he did not wait. He moved first." Another shake of the head. "If one of us caught the perfect time to wheel on the other he would become the conqueror of the world." Suddenly he raised both of his arms in the air. "The fate of the earth hung as close in the balance as that!

"Three of the riders got through to me with your messages," he went on. "I said to myself, 'The little bat has sharp eyes. He sees it.' All the time I was watching the gap in the line widen and grow. I needed an extra quarter hour and then the next thing I would be tearing down the walls of Rome. I said to myself,

'Aetius will wait long enough to be sure.' But he didn't. He has the soul of a hyena which lives on the leavings of nobler beasts. He wasn't as bold as the gods are when they sit down to gamble. A draw was all he asked. He struck too soon; and it wasn't a great resounding blow, it was no more than a pounce. If he had been bold and decisive, I would have beaten him. But instead he was like a mouse nibbling at a cheese."

There was not a single star in the blackness of the sky. The cries of the doomed thousands who were dying on the plains filled their ears. All other sounds had ceased.

"We'll begin the retreat as soon as you can get out the marching orders," said Attila.

Nicolan's heart sank. He was so weary that he found it hard to sit up straight. Was he capable of many hours of concentrated effort? He flexed his hands, wondering if they would be equal to the strain.

Attila was peering intently into the darkness and listening, as well as he could. "The Romans are quiet," he said. "There are few fires lighted. What does that mean?" He turned again to Nicolan. "Send the three princes first. I don't want to see their drunken faces again. The Baltic tribes should go next, and then the Thuringians. You'll have to work out different routes for all of us. We destroyed the country we used in coming in. There won't be a head of cattle or a field of grain up that way."

"You burned everything to the ground," affirmed Nicolan. "There wasn't enough food left for a flock of crows."

"Don't lose any time about it," urged the Hun leader. "We must be well on our way before dawn. With good foraging in sight. I'll be the last to leave. I won't trust any but my own men to hold the rear."

Nicolan settled down to his task. A captured saddle, with high pommel and back, had to serve as his table and a small fire of sheep dung provided a light for the maps. He regretted the absence of Ivar, who always took in hand the task of deciphering the maps.

As he started work, he knew that he faced a crisis in his life. Could he serve any longer this master who, in order to conquer the world, was willing to destroy everything in it? Aetius lacked the power and vision to stop him. The road to Rome would soon lie straight ahead. But he, Nicolan, had the power in his hands to ruin Attila, if he dared use it.

"He has confidence in me and doesn't go over the orders," he said to himself. Attila had turned his horse and was directing the loading of the pack wagons. "I could send the armies up through that burned-over stretch. What chance would hundreds of thousands of starving men have, crossing a country which can't feed a single company? Attila is coming last and it wouldn't be discovered until it was too late. The first armies would have scattered to forage in all directions. Few of them would get back. The horses would starve and the pack wagons would have to be abandoned. Attila would have no army left. The world would be safe."

What would his punishment be if he were caught? The most dreadful death that Attila could devise.

The idea filled him with waves of conflicting emotion. He would be playing the role of a traitor and men would spit at his name. He would always thereafter carry a blood guilt as great as Attila's own, for he would condemn whole armies to death by starvation. On the other hand, he might save civilization. He would be remembered in history for what he had done.

He dropped his pen and stood up. He must be willing to try, he told himself, and to pay the price. Never had a man been offered such a chance before. He must not let it slip by.

He heard footsteps approaching in the dark and a voice, saying, "Where are you, Coated One?" He recognized the voice. It belonged to Baldar, one of Attila's younger aides.

"Here!" he said.

Baldar came into the light cast by the fire. "I am to help you," he said. "I can write. You give the directions and I will set them down. The Lord of All the Earth is afraid you won't be able to do it alone in time."

Was it that, or had the sly mind of Attila perceived the danger and provided against it? Whichever reason it was, the chance had been lost. The armies would have to be sent out along southerly roads. Nicolan said, "Sit here, then, Baldar. We must begin at once."

6

Shortly after midnight a great fire blazed up at the eastern end of the Hun lines. Nicolan's assistant lifted his head from his work. "What's that?" he asked. "Are they going to attack us?"

Two armies had already been started on their march to the Rhine and the orders for the two to follow had been prepared and delivered. Not a sound had come from the enemy on the other side of the bloodstained field, not a hint of interference or pursuit. Nicolan felt free to lay his labors aside for a few moments. He stood up and gazed at the sudden light.

"A funeral pyre, I think," he said. "It is a custom of my people. The bodies of brave men must not be left to rot in the field or to be eaten by beasts." A deep sense of sadness showed in his voice. "It's a large fire. That means there were many bodies to be burned."

Ivar brought confirmation of this when he joined them a few minutes later. It was the funeral pyre of the Bakony dead. The tall Briton seated himself on the ground and stared at Nicolan with a strained expression.

"A terrible thing to watch," he said. "I stayed as long as I could."

"It's been the custom of my people since the beginning of time," declared Nicolan.

"There were a dozen or more women. They were thrown into the fire with the bodies of the men."

Nicolan asked sharply: "Who ordered that? It was a custom centuries ago but it has not been done for as long as anyone can remember."

"The order came from Ranno. He's in command of what's left of them."

"Ranno!" This was what Nicolan had expected to hear but the announcement came, nevertheless, as a severe blow. "Then it means Roric is dead."

Ivar nodded unwillingly. "I fear so. I searched the slope from top to bottom but I found no trace of him. Of course it was dark and the bodies had all been stripped for the fine garments and the bits of finery they wore. I had seen Roric a few times only and so I could have been deceived. But many others had been looking for him and with no better luck."

Nicolan was finding it hard to hold back the tears which filled his eyes. "He knew he was going to die, my poor Roric," he whispered. "Last night he told me he had seen the signs. The Voices had spoken to him."

"There was a brief moment when we had hopes," said Ivar. "A girl who had accompanied him had a Christian cross he had worn under his breastplate. But one of the camp followers had found it and had given it to her. That was accepted as the final proof."

"The girl would be little Minah. She belonged to the Roymarcks and she was in love with him; so he brought her with him. What has happened to her?"

"She was burned with the rest. It was clear she wanted to die. She walked into the fire with her arms stretched out as though she expected to join him."

"Someday Ranno will pay for this!" declared Nicolan, bitterly.

There was a moment or two of silence. Then Nicolan shrugged hopelessly and returned to his work. The scratch of Baldar's pen went along unceasingly as he took down the instructions. The fire climbed still higher against the eastern sky.

"Was there an election for leader?" asked Nicolan, after a time.

Ivar shook his head. "Ranno was the only chief left. He took it on himself to issue the orders."

"Macio is an old man. He hasn't long to live. When he dies, Ranno will step into his shoes. Unless we can let the people know the truth about what happened here today."

"Somutu and Passilis are both alive. I've talked to them. They stand by what they told us."

"The witness we'll need most is Tallimundi. But he and his brothers are well on their way by this time." Nicolan paused. "I don't believe Roric gave instructions for Ranno to take that long and useless ride around the Goth wing. Ranno's a coward and he took that way of avoiding the fighting. But Roric is dead and the truth has been burned with him."

"There's still a chance. A slim one. Roric's servant, Bathgar, hasn't been seen. There was no trace of his body. If he turns up alive, he might remember what passed between the two men."

Nicolan nodded. "A staunch little fellow. What could have become of him? I'm certain, Ivar, he would be useful to us if we could find him. Keep your ears open."

Ivar had nothing more to say for several minutes. "The hilltop has been vacated," he said. "The Goths seem to have vanished."

"Has Ranno started back?"

"He left half an hour ago."

Nicolan said to himself: "There is one consolation in all this. Ildico is safe. We must make sure she doesn't return until Ranno's influence has been removed."

Book II

CHAPTER I

1

ATTILA, immersed in the work of assembling his armies for the march on Rome, heard a sound which caused him to stiffen to attention. He made no move. His eyes remained fixed on the document in front of him. But every sense was on the alert.

This room in his wooden palace, where he worked not less than sixteen hours a day, was supposed to be too well guarded for anyone to gain access secretly; and yet the emperor knew instinctively that the sound had not been made by any creature which crawled or flew on wings.

He heard the sound again and he knew that it was the cautious shuffle of a naked foot. Without pausing to look up, Attila threw himself full length on the floor. As he did so, he felt a metal edge pass the muscles of his neck like the black wings of warning which played so frequently about his couch of nights. The knife had missed by the smallest fraction of space and he heard the point imbed itself in the wooden partition behind him. As he fell, he kicked with one foot at the bell which always stood under his covered table, and the sharp clang it gave forth filled the room. Almost immediately (so carefully had his safety from attack been planned) there were guards about him, frightened, puzzled, murderously angry. The would-be assassin screeched as he sought the only escape left him by falling on the point of the long dagger he had carried in his belt.

Attila rose to his feet. The knife in the wall still quivered from the force with which it had been thrown. His assailant was no more than a lifeless bundle of gray cloak and turban, stained red with blood.

One of the guards gave the head a twist with his foot in order to see the bearded face under the turban. "It is Ala Sartuk," he said. "Never before has he missed his mark."

"How did this deadly cobra crawl in here?" demanded Attila, whose face was flushed and whose eyes darted fire.

No one could answer. The truth would never be known now, for Ala Sartuk himself was as dead as a skinned rat and would not be able to tell.

"I shall talk to Micca the Mede about this," declared the khan in dangerously calm tones. "Bring him to me."

The great trader was brought in soon thereafter. He was smiling, and as cool as the emeralds on his fingers and the clustered pearls in his belt.

"I am here at your command, O King of the World," he said, bowing obsequiously.

Attila motioned him to a cushion. The trader squatted with crossed shins, awaiting the purpose of the summons.

"You have heard of one Ala Sartuk?"

"He put a knife between my shoulder blades once and only a miracle kept me alive," answered Micca. "The man's trade is murder."

"He tried to kill me. An hour ago. I was saved by my own quickness and not by the vigilance of my slow-footed guards."

Micca the Mede could not entirely conceal the intensity of the interest with which he asked the question, "He has been caught, I trust?"

"He's dead. It's most unfortunate he was able to disembowel himself before the very eyes of my sluggish protectors." Attila swung his head around sharply in the direction of Micca. "He was in your pay!"

The trader answered with unruffled calm. "He was not in my pay, Mighty Khan. I haven't seen him since he tried to kill me."

Attila brushed the denial aside impatiently. "I have never been deceived about you, my glib teller of tales. You have brought me much useful information but I've always known you were in the pay of Aetius also. There's nothing new or strange about that. Rats who traffic in secrets can always be bought. But your treachery, Micca the Mede, has been particularly black. As long as you were useful to me, I winked at it but I said to myself that when your usefulness was over I would make you pay the price." His voice rose with a hint of triumph. "You are no longer of service to me. And there you sit!"

"Are you sure, Great Tanjou, that I can't be of use to you?"

"So sure, my smooth-tongued friend, that I shall now tell you how I plan to rid myself of you. You are to die the Death of the Inches."

The trader's eyebrows seemed to quiver slightly. "A method of execution," he said, "that your people brought from the Far East. I have heard it is very slow and painful."

"Judge for yourself. The first day the executioner cuts off the top joints of your fingers and toes. The second day he chops away the second joints. The third day he severs what is left. The fourth day the stumps of your hands and feet are removed. The fifth day you lose your arms at your elbows and your legs at the knees. Need I go on? Each day, as long as there is life left in you, something is cut away. Some of the victims are lucky and die of the agony in four or five days. Some last twice as long and do not expire until the neck itself is threatened. It is an ingenious method, don't you think? I may allow my people to pay for the privilege of watching you."

"No doubt the revenue from such a spectacle would be considerable," said Micca, with a not completely successful attempt at unconcern. "But you have not heard yet of the matters in which I can be of service to you."

"That you will waste your own time in telling me is of no concern save that you have little of it left," declared Attila. "But I can't afford to throw mine away. I think I shall arrange for the process of your dismemberment to begin tomorrow."

Micca shifted on his cushion, in evidence of the inner terror which possessed him. "You have been making continuous efforts to learn the whereabouts of the Princess Honoria. Without success. I can tell you where she is being held. I can even promise that such emissaries as you may appoint will have the chance to speak with her."

"So? I have given up all thought of approaching the Princess Honoria. The issue is now clearly drawn. I shall lead my armies against Rome in my own good time. The princess can be of no help to me."

"Not even as a pretext for declaring war on the empire?"

"Not even as a pretext. I need none. I shall plant the sword in the ground. The Sword of Mars which the great powers of earth and sky placed in my hands before I became the ruler of my people."

"I know that the princess, if made free, will proclaim to the world the justice of your cause."

"I thought she might be of use to me once but now I see no reason to spare you in order to reach her." Attila shook his head. "You will have to do better than that, my crafty seller of secrets. Much better. I am setting the price of your life very high. As high as the gallows I would raise for a lesser criminal than you."

"Then what think you of this?" asked the trader. "You have made no secret of your desire for a wife with hair of pure gold. I have been told that a score of candidates have been brought you and that you refused them all. It may be that you don't believe the gods will smile on your arms unless you have the right queen to share your throne in Rome. One with a head like the sun itself. This may or may not be true. But the rumor has reached my ears that you are making inquiries about a certain maiden who has traveled from city to city in the East, and who rides a great black horse. This I do know: that so far your agents have had no success."

Attila kept his head down to conceal the intense emotion which had been roused in him.

"Go on," said Attila.

"I can tell you the name of the girl and where she comes from," declared the trader, who now saw with inner relief that he had on his hook the most powerful fish in all the waters of the world. "I can tell you with whom she travels. I can even tell you where they now are."

"Is this girl married?"

"No, Great Tanjou."

The silence fell again over the room and remained unbroken for several more moments. "How can I know," demanded Attila, finally, "if you are in a position to supply this information? You may be playing for time."

"I have learned from long experience," said Micca, "that your word, once pledged, will not be broken. Keep me here, then, until such time as your agents have followed up the clues I shall give you. When you find I have told you the truth, I am to go free and

I am to receive a suitable reward as well. After all, I live by the sale of what I know."

Attila felt under the table with his foot and produced two sharp rings of the bell. When Giso answered the summons, he was ordered to produce a flagon of wine. "Dealing with you is dry work," the Hun leader said, scowling at Micca. "I am thirsty."

When the wine was placed in front of him, he drank deeply. He would then have wiped his lips with the back of his hand but, feeling the eyes of the immaculate trader on him, he made use of a cloth instead.

"It is agreed," he said.

2

When the room had emptied, Giso returned and stood in the doorway, fixing his master with a demanding eye.

"What is it now?" asked Attila.

"She is dead," was the answer.

The emperor's complete attention was captured at once. He tossed aside the documents, to which he had returned, and got to his feet.

"Cerca is dead?"

"An hour ago. She kept asking for you to the end. When they couldn't get your ear, her servants told her you had left for the East. I don't think she believed it."

"Was my son with her?"

The servant shook his head. "Not at the finish."

"Where has Ellac gone?"

"Hunting," answered Giso. He raised both hands in front of him, the palms turned upward. "What can you expect, O King? A death chamber is not a pleasant place for a youth of his years."

"She deserved no better than this," declared Attila. He fell deeply into thought and did not speak again for some moments. "If she had lived to a hundred, I would not have gone to her. Could she expect me to forgive her the part she played in the death of Swanhilde? Those grasping brothers of hers did it. One of them shot the arrow that killed the girl. I should have hanged them both. But I let them live for Cerca's sake. Was she told that?"

"Yes, Great Tanjou."

"Then," in a grumbling tone, "what more could she expect?"

"She too was ambitious," said Giso, after a pause. "She wanted to sit beside you on the throne. She asked you many times."

"Every time I went to her. She talked of nothing else! She demanded it of me."

"She was not asking for herself, O King. She wanted it that way so Ellac would be acknowledged as your successor and heir."

"I must see to it," said Attila, after giving the situation further thought, "that Ellac is taken away from those lying, belly-crawling uncles. They will be teaching him treason. They will be whispering in his ear, 'You will be emperor someday, so why wait?' I know them, those black traitors. If he has anything of them in him, he will listen. Giso, go at once and send Onegesius to me. I'll have both uncles sent to posts on the northern frontier." The thought was in his mind that Cerca's brothers would be exposed to all the fighting in the forest country until they got themselves killed. He could have no feeling of security about his son as long as they were alive. "I must have Ellac here with me now. He must be taught what it is to be a king's son, so he will make a strong king when his turn comes. Have the boy brought to me at once. And I rely on you to see that he doesn't go to his mother's burying. He must never speak to those uncles again."

"Yes, Tanjou. I leave at once to obey your orders." He did not go at once, however. "Ellac is a good boy."

"He is my son. But all I can be sure of yet is that he promises to grow tall," declared Attila. He gave his head a proud shake. "He has straight legs."

A moment later he added, "Bring the Coated One."

CHAPTER II

1

NICOLAN had ridden out that morning beyond the line of the tents. The most momentous decision of his life had to be made, and made at once. He rode with a loose rein, allowing his horse to go where it pleased, and for hours they had ridden far afield. When he finally turned back, he was as tired as though he had been through another battle. The decision had been reached and it would be adhered to, he told himself, without any regard for, or fear of, consequences.

There was a distinct change in the city since Attila had brought his army back. The men no longer swaggered like lords of the earth. The beady-eyed women did not stand in the doors and spit at alien passers-by. There even seemed to be a less jeering note in the cries of the children at play. There could be no doubt about it: the result of the battle of Châlons had sobered the Huns.

Nicolan was thinking of this as he passed in through the gates. He had been too intent to drop a coin for the lepers and their shrill imprecations assailed his ears as he rode in under the tall frame structure. "Something has happened," he said to himself, conscious of a change in the crowded streets. He had to dismount in order to make his way through. A bearded chief laid a hand on his shoulder and said in the mixture of tongues which had been evolved for general use, "An inch closer and there would be no emperor."

Nicolan looked around at him. "What are you saying?"

"You haven't heard then? About the attempt on Attila's life?"

"Again? It has been tried many times."

"But this was different. Perhaps there was help from inside. A black tribesman from beyond the paynim country got into the palace. The great khan was quick or he would be a dead man now."

"Did they catch the fellow?"

The chief shook his head. "He killed himself. It was a great pity. The execution would have been worth watching."

Nicolan was thinking: "I wondered when I saw the wagons of Micca the Mede outside. Can there be any connection?"

Giso came in great haste through the crowd, holding one hand above his head and demanding that everyone step back. His eyes were fixed on Nicolan.

"Togalatus!" he cried. "I have been looking for you. The Giver of All Light is demanding your presence. Where have you been?"

Nicolan waved an arm in the direction of the plains to the south of the tented city. "I have been riding."

"He will think that a poor excuse."

"What is his mood at the moment?"

"What would you expect?" Giso was aware that the gabble in the street had stopped to hear what he had to say and that all eyes were on him. He puffed out his chest and proceeded to make the most of it.

"He has gone back to work. Nothing can ever shake him. He is a man of iron."

"What of Micca the Mede?" asked an eager voice.

Giso looked sternly about him. "I cannot answer any questions."

"Here's another for you. Answer us this. What is being done with the brothers of Cerca?"

Giso raised his chin to an imperious angle and stared severely about him. "You know it is against all the rules to discuss the life of the palace."

The questioners were not to be put off. "It's said," cried one, "that Cerca is dead."

"Come with me, Togalatus," said Giso, in an effort to bring the questioning to an end.

They made their way to the palace entrance where a servant took charge of Nicolan's horse. "What a time we have had!" whispered Giso, conscious that there were ears close about him to hear every word said. They crossed a dark hall and began to descend the steps. Attila's servant placed his lips close to Nicolan's ear. "The guards are all under arrest and a new lot put in their places. He may hang them all. It doesn't seem possible that Ala Sartuk could get inside unless one of them had been bribed."

"Ala Sartuk!" exclaimed Nicolan. He was recalling something

he had heard on the occasion of Micca's previous visit. It had been rumored then that this skilled knife thrower had been seen in the company of the trader.

"There was much talk," confided Giso. "And Micca was summoned to the presence. He has been placed under guard but it is my opinion that he won't die. A wily one, that. He is never at a loss."

Attila was making no pretense at working when Nicolan was ushered in. He grunted once, sought among the papers in front of him, and selected one which he held out to his visitor.

"You had my promise," he said.

It was a legal transfer to Nicolan of the lands which had belonged to his father! The latter raised it with trembling hands and at first the words seemed blurred and indistinct. It was what he had worked for, the goal of all his plans and efforts, the reward for his willingness to bow before the dictates of a despotic master.

"Great Tanjou," he said, "I am so overwhelmed by your generosity that I can't find words to tell you how I feel."

"You earned it," said Attila.

It was strange, thought Nicolan, that this should happen immediately after his decision had been reached. He read the document a second time and then returned it to the donor.

"Great Khan," he said, "I repeat that it is most generous. But I—I cannot accept it."

Attila stared at him as though unable to believe the evidence of his ears.

"Are you mad?"

"No, Great Tanjou. It's because I realize the land is given me in the expectation that I will continue to be useful to you."

"You will always be useful to me," declared Attila. "You know what my plans are and the part I expect you to take."

"But," said Nicolan, "it is impossible for me to serve you longer."

The man who wanted the world stared at this member of his staff who had dared utter such words. "Don't you know," he demanded, "that no one leaves my service as long as he lives?"

"Great King, I would not be of use to you. I have discovered in myself what you will consider a great weakness. I've found that I hate war and can no longer have any part in it."

"Not even if I strip you of all rank and send you in to battle with my foot soldiers?"

"If it came to that," declared Nicolan, "I still would not fight. I would refuse to raise my spear and would let the first foeman I encountered slit my throat without raising an arm to defend myself."

Attila shoved away the documents in front of him with an impatient hand. "You have turned to religion," he charged. "To some sniveling form of belief in impotent gods."

"In one God, O King. There is only One."

"There are many gods and they are all alike."

"Will you allow me to explain what—what has happened?" asked Nicolan.

"Make it brief then. The subject sickens me."

Nicolan could see through the one narrow window a small square of blue, warm from the afternoon sun. This might be, he realized, his last chance to see men's greatest benefactor, the sky under which they lived and had their being.

"I can still hear the piteous cries of the wounded we left to die at Châlons," he said. "After all these months, it's hard for me to sleep. Whenever I speak of it, I get the same answer, 'Are they not well dead and rotting in the sun?' unless it is a Christian I ask. The answer then shows compassion."

"Christians!" cried Attila, his face showing a purplish tinge. "I might have known. Those womanish cowards, whining to a god who offers them nothing but a harp and a song! Don't you know, you fool, that it's only because the Romans have turned Christian that they can be beaten?"

"Christians are not cowards! Haven't you heard how bravely they suffered in the arena at Rome? They died under the tortures of Nero with sublime courage."

Attila, it was clear, was bitterly angry and yet a little mystified that one who had always seemed to him a cool thinker should now hold such views.

"Will their courage be equal to defending the walls of Rome against my armies?" he demanded.

Then he subsided into silence while he studied the face of his young aide with a somber concentration. Finally he said: "I don't want my armies straggling down the wrong roads and getting in each other's tracks. I have no one to take your place and so I have no intention of losing you. Where would you go? To Rome? Aetius, that cold and cruel demon, would have you nailed to a cross. I saw it in his eyes."

"There is only one place I want to go," declared Nicolan. "To the city where I can learn the true teachings of the man Jesus. To Jerusalem."

Attila was still suffering from an inability to believe what his aide was saying. "You would go all that distance to learn what a dead peasant said? You fool, you are suffering from a fit of madness! And yet there is no madness in your eyes. They are cool. Can it be you mean what you are saying?"

Attila got to his feet and stumped on his crooked legs about the room. Nicolan noticed that he seemed unsteady. His face was the color of tallow. Thick beads of perspiration covered his brow. It was certain, however, that his condition had nothing to do with the experiences he had been through earlier in the day. The same symptoms had been noticeable in him, in a lesser degree, for some time.

"I can't move against Rome for five months," he said. "Go, then, to this hot stone city, where the Christians fester in holes in the walls, and satisfy that prying mind of yours. Then come back. In two months!"

Nicolan shook his head. "No. I am through with war. With the treachery and the cruelty, and the butchery."

Attila allowed his anger to gain control of him. "Do you think you can leave me and escape punishment? There's no corner of the world small enough to hide you from my anger. Not even the lands which may lie beyond the Pillars."

"I am fully aware of the penalty I face. But could I live at peace with myself if I changed my mind?"

It became apparent at this point that a new thought had taken possession of Attila. He stood still and frowned at the muddy tips of his cowhide boots. Then he returned to his chair and sat down heavily. From there he studied Nicolan with a closer attention than he had yet bestowed on him.

"There is a mission which must be performed for me at once," he said. "It is highly dangerous and only a brave and resourceful man would undertake it. It wouldn't conflict with these tender scruples of yours. Will you go?"

"What would I be called on to do?"

"You would go into Roman territory. Do I need to remind you again that you would die a cruel death if you fell into the hands of Aetius?" Attila paused, not to give Nicolan an opportunity to reply but to consider more fully what he himself had in mind to propose. "If you took this bold venture in hand for me, you might get over these womanish ideas. You would probably come back cured, and that would be a good thing for both of us. I'll come straight to the point. I want you to see the Princess Honoria and discuss a plan with her. You might have to contrive her escape and bring her back with you. There will be a rich reward if you succeed. I might make you the governor of Jerusalem, where you could improve the lot of these Christians you love so much. I would fill your lap with the spoils of Rome." Suddenly the emperor threw back his head and laughed loudly. "I might even give you the princess. As your wife. I don't want her myself. I—I have other plans which I am already proceeding with. And from what I hear of that beautiful daughter of imperial Rome, she might prefer you to a barbarian like me.

"Don't give your answer yet," added Attila, when he saw that Nicolan was prepared to speak. "This will bear thinking over. We will talk of it again. Tomorrow morning. If you agree, you will be on your way south by noon."

2

Attila took one quick glance at him when he appeared the next morning and nodded his head with satisfaction.

"You are going," he said.

"Yes, Great Tanjou. I am going."

"That is good. I am glad you have come to your senses. Partly, at least. The rest will follow."

He picked up a knife with a short blade and began to trace a route on a map of the north of Italy which hung on the wall. "Here," he said, pointing to the pass in the mountains above the city of Aquileia which perched at the head of the Adriatic Sea. "This is the road to the plains of Lombardy. Here, on the east, we have a nest of islands which have collected where the great rivers of the north, the Po, the Brenta, and the Adige, empty into the sea. They are busy rivers and they bring much with them from the mountains to deposit at their mouths—rich earth and stones and wood. The islands have been formed from this silt. What do you know about these islands?"

"There is nothing to know," answered Nicolan.

"Ha!" exclaimed the emperor, triumphantly. "You do not know everything, then, my sharp young man. You think them uninhabited, no doubt?"

"I've always believed so."

"These islands," declared Attila, "are covered with tall pine trees. And in the shadow of the pines live many people. Fishermen who sell their catch to the mainland cities closest to hand. People who have salt pans and make a living from that. Fugitives. Malefactors, fleeing from justice, who take to the islands in these lagoons, where they drop out of sight like stones tossed into the sea. There are political runaways as well, men of rank and property who manage to live quite well in houses that are built for them. If Aetius spread a net around these islands, his catch would be a rich one!

"Now take this island," he went on, pointing to the center of the archipelago. "This is one of the oldest and it now has a solid foundation. Its trees are taller than any of the others. On this island, hidden away in the trees, is a palace of stone. It is built so low that no glimpse can be had of it from the water. No one knows it is there except the fishermen and the fugitives who skulk in the cover and dare not go ashore. And in that palace, with a large household, lives the Princess Honoria. A boat calls once a week with supplies. Visitors are never allowed to land. She sees no one with the exception of her personal servants. The beautiful old demon, her mother, decided to keep her there for the rest of her life. The mother is dead now, but the emperor is of the same mind."

Nicolan studied the map closely. "And that is where I am to go?"

"Yes. All the details have been arranged. You will take with you one of Micca's wagons, filled with goods. Three of his trained men, one a juggler and maker of magic, will accompany you as well as a few of my most reliable fighting men. I think it will be wise for you yourself to pose as a political refugee, looking for sanctuary. No suspicion must be aroused in the minds of the island guards or they will refuse to let you put foot ashore."

"Suppose they do refuse permission to land?"

"It's improbable. They have a dull existence and the chance to look over the goods and watch the juggler will be hard to resist. Micca has sent a wagon through the islands several times and found a welcome everywhere. If the guards remain stubborn, you will have to slip ashore at night and find some way of talking to the prisoner. That is a detail I leave to you."

Nicolan considered the matter carefully. "I think it will prove more difficult than you suppose," he said, finally.

Attila gestured casually. "No obstacle is ever great enough to stop a resourceful man."

"How will we get to the island?"

"Micca has a boat at Alimium which will be at your disposal."

"And what message do I carry to the princess?"

"I have made a list of the things I want you to say. You will read it now and commit all the points to memory. Then the list will be destroyed.

"And now," continued the emperor, "we come to the hardest part. When the princess has agreed to my terms, you must get her off the island at once. The fighting may start earlier than I first planned."

Nicolan looked at him with surprise when he heard this announcement. There was an air of suppressed excitement about Attila. His small eyes, sunk deep under brows which seemed shaggier than ever, were alive with it. He nodded his head several times.

"I have had confirmation from my scouts of rumors which reached me earlier," he said in a tone little above a whisper. "Aetius will have none of the allies who helped him at Châlons. He must fight alone this time. It's said he has little stomach for it and I've heard he can't sleep, this man who was once your master. Fear rides his shoulder like an evil spirit." His voice rose. "Now, now, we shall come to grips for the last time!"

Attila seated himself in his chair. He was silent for several moments and Nicolan was surprised to see that the outburst had drawn heavily on his reserves of strength. His hand trembled perceptibly as he brushed aside the documents on the table.

"When the Roman princess has agreed to my terms, you must bring her to me. That will mean men, boats, and money. You must go to Scalpius."

This was a completely new name and Nicolan looked his surprise at the reference. "In the city of Aquileia," went on Attila, "you will go to the market place. It will be full of beggars. Scalpius is one of them and he's the shrewdest knave of all. He's a coward and a hypocrite and a liar but he has more influence than anyone in the Lombardy country. I know. Because, you see, Scalpius is my man.

"Go to him," continued the emperor, "and he will supply you with whatever you need."

3

This is not the story of Nicolan's conversion. It may be taken for granted that, through all the time he thus found himself tangled in the web of circumstance, in the double-dealing, the treachery, and the cruelty, the germ planted in his mind by what he had lived through at Châlons was growing steadily, and that it finally reached the maturity of a steadfast faith. There was nothing unusual in his spiritual awakening. The message of Christ was spreading far and wide throughout the world. The missionaries were carrying the Word even to the savage lands which lay beyond the bounds of what was called civilization.

It may be permissible to cast forward and say that Attila never found himself with the power in his hands to make Nicolan, or anyone else for that matter, the governor of Jerusalem. It fell out also that Nicolan was not to find an opportunity to tramp the hot and dusty roads to the Holy City with the staff of a pilgrim in his hand. Thus he was deprived of the chance to sit at the feet of the fathers of the parent church. He had at all times, however, the privilege of meeting men of simple faith who expounded to him the teachings of Christ; and it may be that this was the truer path. Once a very poor man, who made his living as a scrivener in Aquileia, said to him: "There is much being said and done these days which people like me do not understand. There is a great man named Nestorius who preaches his own idea

of what we should believe. And then there is another learned man
in Egypt who says that Nestorius is wicked and wrong. I close my
ears to all this clamor. I know what Jesus preached to us on the
Mount. There is room for nothing else in my heart."

The Christian people, he had found, could be divided into two
classes. There were the militant ones who proclaimed their faith
to the skies and wanted to convert the whole world. And there
were the silent ones, content to believe in what the man Jesus
had taught and to live accordingly. Nicolan was one of the latter
class because he realized how much he had to learn. He needed
time to accustom himself to this change of heart. It was quite
clear to him that he could obtain the time only by agreeing to
the wishes of the great khan and it was this which led to his
acceptance of the role of emissary to the Princess Honoria, rather
than any fear of the consequences of refusal.

Nicolan and Ivar shared a small shed in the yard which enclosed Attila's palace. It had been used at first for the emperor's
special horses but the smells and the flies had become such a
nuisance that the four-legged tenants had been removed to stables
at a greater distance. Briefly thereafter the building had contained
chickens and then doves but it had been vacant for some time
when the two friends were given possession. Despite their determined efforts to clean the place, some of the odors of former oc-
cupancy still manifested themselves. The walls had been covered
with souvenirs and spoils of war—a battle flag, a cluster of pen-
nons in many colors, weapons of various kinds, a Roman shield,
a halter of silver, and a cloak from the very far East made of the
crests of birds.

After his talk with Attila, Nicolan ran across the yard and
opened the door with a hasty hand, having a short time only to
prepare for his journey down into the Adriatic. He found Ivar
seated in a corner.

"I'm going away!" he said, before he noticed that a stranger
was sitting on the floor.

"I am from the country which was once yours," said the
stranger, getting to his feet. "I belong to Macio of the Roymarcks
and my name is Hursta."

This identification of himself was accepted at once. He had

the thin bowed legs which come from a life in the saddle and his eyes, which he was using to stare at Nicolan from under his three-cornered brown cap, were dusky and heavily fringed with black lashes. He was quite young.

"What brings you here?"

"I come on orders from my master. He is not well. Since he heard of his son's death, he hasn't stirred from his couch. He lies there and broods."

"Does he still preside in the weekly courts of the Ferma?"

The man Hursta shook his head. "Not any more. He lacks the strength."

"Who has taken his place?"

"Ranno of the Finninalders."

Nicolan asked sharply, "Was he chosen by the Inner Council of the Ferma?"

The visitor shook his head a second time. "No meeting of the Council was called. Ranno assumed the duties, saying there could be no other choice." After a moment Hursta added, "There are so few of our chiefs left since the battle."

Nicolan remained silent for several moments. Then he asked, in an abrupt tone, "Is Ranno in good favor with the people?"

The visitor nodded affirmatively. "He is thought to be very wise for his years. Now that Roric is dead"—his eyes showed a hint of moisture which he brushed away—"Ranno is certain to succeed when my master dies."

"What is the news you have for me?"

The man lowered his voice. "A messenger reached my master. He was from the train of the lady of Tergeste and he had come a long distance. From the East."

"What word did he bring?" asked Nicolan, eagerly.

"It may be about the king—our great Harthager. Or it may be that some danger hangs over the Lady Ildico. My master gave me not so much as a hint and I could get nothing out of the messenger. All I know is that it's the desire of my master to tell you of it."

"Has he no one around him who can be trusted?"

"My lord, the servants of Macio would all gladly die for him. He knows that; but it must be that it is a matter not to be confided to slaves."

"In two hours I must leave on a mission for the emperor."
Nicolan gestured helplessly as he turned to Ivar. "It is a matter
of such importance and the need for secrecy is so great that it
was Attila's orders you were not to go with me. He thought your
size would be remarked and perhaps lead to trouble."

"Is there no chance of getting out of it?" asked Ivar.

"Two lives depend on my going. One is the life of Micca, who
is a greater rascal than anyone suspected. He will die a cruel and
lingering death if I don't succeed. I feel freer about the other life
because it happens to be my own."

"I think I see a way out of the difficulty," declared Ivar, at
once. "I could ride back with Hursta and talk with my lord Macio.
He might be willing to entrust me with a message. Then I could
join you as soon as you had completed your mission."

Nicolan turned the matter over in his mind. "It should not
take me long to carry out the emperor's orders. We could meet in
the mountain pass above Aquileia."

Ivar was giving the matter much careful thought. "Suppose you
found it impossible to join me? What would I do?"

"Wait. Wait for me as long as you dared."

"And if you did not come?"

"You would proceed then with whatever it was my lord Macio
desired us to do. By yourself."

"But would he have sufficient confidence in me for that? I am
not of your blood. I am a stranger from a far land."

"That is true. But he knows you are honest and strong. I think
he would be ready to leave it in your hands."

"Even if the message has to do with the safety of his daughter?"

"It is because I think it does concern Ildico that I can't sacrifice
my life by refusing to do Attila's bidding," declared Nicolan. "I
must contrive somehow to reach her. It occurs to me, Ivar, that
Macio might agree to allow Hursta to accompany you. If you had
to start before I arrived, you could leave him behind with the
necessary directions. There is an inn in a cover of trees about
fifteen miles above Aquileia. He could await me there. It is easy
to find because there is a cross above the door."

"Is there no possibility of postponing your mission?"

"Every moment of delay in starting on it lessens my chance
of meeting you in the pass."

CHAPTER III

1

A TIGHT-LIPPED Neapolitan, whose name was Priscius, was in charge of the trade wagon which set out that morning. A juggler was second in command but it was to the third member of the party that Nicolan paid the most attention. This was a tall young Arab who went attentively about his work and had nothing to say. He had features like chiseled marble and eyes which seemed to have fires banked behind them.

"This fellow Hussein," asked Nicolan, drawing the Neapolitan to one side. "What is he? The son of a long line of desert monarchs?"

"Exactly, Illustrious One. He was captured in a foray when he was a young boy. He has never said a word about himself since. But the other slaves from the desert countries tread lightly when he is about and speak in tones of respect. They know something but they refuse to tell."

Ten days later they followed the creaking wagon through the pass of Mount Ocra and saw ahead of them the tall Roman battlements which surrounded the city of Aquileia. Priscius, who rode beside Nicolan, sighed gustily with relief. "When I see those walls," he said, pointing with his whip, "I know I'm on Roman soil—and safe once more. They did a lot of loose talking back there about the ease with which they would capture this place. Ho, ho! I dare laugh at them now. This is a city which will never be captured. Not even by the mighty Attila." He added, as an additional reason for his increased ease of mind, "They have the best wines in the world here."

As they walked their horses under the northern gate, Nicolan was impressed by the size of the walls but even more so by the cleanness of the streets and the air of brisk prosperity. There had been no lepers at the gate and even the humblest water carrier wore his cape with self-respect and his blue Phrygian cap with the jaunty conviction that all was well with the world.

"They don't seem to know," he remarked to Priscius, "that war is going to break."

"They know," asserted Micca's assistant, "but they trust their walls."

The party found their way to the market place, which offered the first evidence of crowding and poverty. Nicolan dismounted and looked about him. The place teemed with noisy bargainers and along the walls were beggars, holding out their hands and intoning their monotonous cries. He looked the latter over carefully but at first found no one to meet the description supplied by Attila. Finally his eye encountered that of an occupant of a corner post. There was an air of humility about this particular bidder for baksheesh which made him look a second time.

He was surprised to hear the mysterious Hussein say at his shoulder, "When your master comes, the blood of these people will fill all the gutters."

"I'm afraid that's true," he answered, turning to study the fiercely proud profile. "I am told you came from the East."

"From a faraway land. I was young when they took me away but I seem to remember there was a city built in a great cleft in the desert. Its towers were higher than these"—motioning about him—"but some of them had been carved out of the rock walls."

"Petra," said Nicolan, who had heard of that strange city.

"I am not sure. But this I know: its temples are as finely carved as lace and in the walls are enamels as blue as the desert sky. I shall see it again someday, O Reader of Maps."

There was a moment's silence and then the young slave turned with sudden resolution. "It has been said you were sold into slavery as a boy."

"That is true. My father was killed and all our lands and stock were seized. My mother and I were sold into slavery. I served in the household of Aetius. In Rome."

"I have been told all that. It must be then that you can feel sympathy for me. I, O Togalatus, am the son of a king. I was captured and sold to Micca the Mede. I was young, perhaps as young as you were. Never since have I found the chance to let my father know where I am. He is an old man now and I fear he hasn't much longer to live. Soon it will be too late for anything to be done." He raised his eyes to meet the gaze of Nicolan. The latter could sense the deep emotion which filled this son of a proud race. "O Togalatus, give your aid to one who is in the same position you were! Help me break these bonds!"

There was a moment of silence between them and then Nicolan spoke in cautious tones. "It may be I can help you. Do you know that your master is in trouble?"

Hussein gave his head a discreet nod. "We heard something of that. I think it's because of it that I found the courage to speak to you."

"The outcome is still in doubt. I know that Attila believes Micca paid the assassin to attack him. In the end he may kill your master. In that case his belongings will be seized. I might arrange for you to be transferred to me. The chief obstacle is that I myself may not stand high in the emperor's favor. I may even share the fate of Micca."

The young slave now made it apparent that he had been giving close study to the prospect of escape. "Some of the ships from the ports of the East come to Ravenna," he said. "That is not far from here."

"Four days of stiff tramping," declared Nicolan, who thought in terms of armies on the march. "Longer, if you have to do all the traveling by night."

Hussein began to speak in impassioned whispers. "Help me, O Togalatus. You have broken your bonds: aid me to shake from my limbs these hateful chains which bind me in servitude. I, a king's son! If you help me, I make you a promise. Someday rewards will reach you. Precious stones, rich rugs, all the things we have in my land which will enrich you here. And above all else, you will have my gratitude for the rest of your life."

They had been crossing the square as they talked and they now stood directly in front of the corner where the humble beggar plied his trade. The latter looked up and Nicolan was amazed at the pathos of his face. His eyes beseeched help in the most piteous way. They were timid and honest and they seemed to say, "I am a forlorn creature, beaten down by the slings of misfortune; help me or I perish." He was sitting cross-legged on the ground and on one thin shank was a large and ugly sore, prominently displayed. The tunic he wore was ragged and threadbare, and far from clean.

Convinced that he had found his man, Nicolan dropped a coin in the beggar's dirty outstretched hand, saying in a whisper, *"The wings of the twelfth!"*

"May the gods bless you, noble stranger," whined the beggar. Then he added, in a whisper so low that it was hard to hear what he said: "In ten minutes I leave. Follow me. At a distance."

After stalking the stooped figure through the poorer quarter of the city, Nicolan saw Scalpius vanish into the shadows beside a small house. The house itself was mean and unobtrusive, and built against the stone of the outer wall. He approached with care and applied his knuckles lightly to the door. It opened immediately and he was summoned inside. The interior was so dark that he could see nothing at first. Scalpius addressed him in a cautious tone. "Stand where you are. I return at once." He was back almost immediately, carrying a lamp in which a small wick burned feebly. The light thus provided was enough to demonstrate two things: that the tiny room in which they stood was almost devoid of furnishings but spotlessly clean, and that the beggar himself had accomplished a quick transformation. He was now wearing a white tunic and his face and hands were clean. A still more startling change was soon apparent; the face which peered over the flickering flame had lost its professional air of entreaty and wore instead a sharp and sly expression.

"Sit down," said Scalpius.

There were no chairs or benches in the room so Nicolan squatted on the floor, an example which his host followed. In doing so, Scalpius bared both legs and the visitor was astonished to see no trace of the sore which had been so publicly displayed on the market place.

"A miraculous cure," said Nicolan, pointing to the healthy surface of the mendicant's shin.

The latter cackled. "Part of my stock in trade," he said. "I paint it on each morning. I am clever with the brush. It was my purpose to become an artist until I found I had a gift for winning sympathy. Since then I have not worked." There was a pause. "What brings you to me?"

Nicolan held out his hand with a small lozenge of tin cupped in the palm. Scalpius looked at it and then said in an urgent voice: "Put it away. Give me your message quickly and then begone. As long as you sit in my house, I can feel the rasp of the hangman's rope on my neck!"

Nicolan explained briefly the mission on which he was engaged. Scalpius listened attentively, nodding his bald head. The thick mane of hair which he had worn into the house had been a wig.

"You will have to act quickly," he said. "This is a city of fools. When they hear that Attila is going to strike soon, they laugh and point to the walls. But their hearts will change to water when they hear his armies are coming through the pass and they will scatter like frightened mice. Those who can afford it will cross the water and find shelter in Dalmatia. Those who can't will take refuge in the islands. The islands will be overrun with them and that is why I advise you to act quickly. Your princess will be in a sorry plight if she's left there until those starving rats come swarming ashore."

"Do you expect the hand of Attila to fall heavily on the city?"

"Aquileia will be destroyed," asserted Scalpius in a matter-of-fact tone.

"It's lucky then that you have no property to lose."

The mendicant's pride asserted itself in a scoffing ejaculation. "By the bolts of Jupiter, young man, you have no conception of the profits made in this trade. I know what is going to happen and for the past four months I have been selling everything I own. My houses, my shops, my farm with its fine fig trees, my ships, my camels. I shall leave very soon for the safety that only Dalmatia offers."

"You will take your household with you?"

"I have no household," asserted Scalpius. "I have neither wife nor child. Families are costly things. Since I clutched in my hand the first coin I ever earned, I have shared with no one. What is mine is mine. I never spend. I trade and, when needs must, I steal."

"But sooner or later you must die."

"I shall be buried beside my gold. That has been arranged: there it will be, at my side, in an iron box and so close my arm can touch it. The only regret I'll feel, when my time comes and they gird my bones in, will be that my arm will lack the power to touch the box, to open it, to fondle the coins."

Nicolan was astonished at the greed in the eyes which had seemed at first so honest and appealing. His interest lay, however, in the carrying out of his mission and he proceeded now to ask questions.

"You say the poor people of the city will take refuge on the islands. How will they subsist there?"

"They will starve," declared Scalpius, in a tone which seemed to carry a note of satisfaction. "It will do them little good to run away. What betters it to escape the sword of Attila and die of hunger on a stinking island? They will steal everything on the islands first; and that is why you must get this woman of Rome off before the trouble starts."

"We will need a larger boat than the one Micca has put at our disposal."

The beggar nodded. "I can provide for that. There is a trading ship which plies between the ports of Palestine and the Adriatic. It comes as far north as Ravenna. I can arrange to have it lie off the islands until the princess can be taken aboard." He paused to consider the plan in detail. "It will be too late to take her up through the pass into Hun country. Soon the roads will be black with the horsemen of Attila. It will be done this way instead. The princess will be left in a Dalmatian port and lodged in the household of a wine and oil merchant. He is rich—but he takes his orders from me. The woman can be delivered to Attila later. At Rome, or his own capital, or at any city where he makes his headquarters."

"I must see her first and gain her consent to what the emperor has planned."

"That," declared Scalpius, "will not be hard to get. She has nothing to lose, that wanton."

2

The party started that same afternoon down the Via Emilia, the great Roman road which would merge farther south with the Via Flaminia. The Lombardy Plain loomed ahead of them, that fabulously rich land which was sometimes called the breadbasket of Rome. The plain had been the first objective of all the planning done when Attila sat with his generals about him. To capture the cities which guarded it, to seize control of its great rivers and its broad and sunny acres, had been the purpose of all their scheming. When his armies held the plain, he might well feel assured that the fall of the city on the seven hills, which had once ruled the world, was the inevitable next step.

Nicolan was puzzled at the aspect of the countryside. The ground was hard, the fields brown instead of green. The cattle were finding it hard to get sustenance from the parched land. He remembered now that some of the reports he had seen from the observers kept by Attila in all parts of the Roman Empire had mentioned that the previous autumn had been a dry one and that the crops were likely to be sparse. There had been nothing, however, to prepare him for this. He kept his eyes busy as they rode down the broad highway, and was shocked at the ill favor Mother Nature was showing the usually fertile plain.

"It's going to be a lean year," he said to himself. "These brown pastures and sickly cattle will never feed the half million men that Attila will lead to the storming of Rome. Is he being misled?"

The farther south they rode, the more desolate the country became. The sun was growing stronger. The hillsides and the meadows turned a deeper yellow and the usually fast rivers, racing down from the mountains to the sea, were dwindling into mere trickles.

"This is all wrong," he thought. "Either the truth is being held back or Attila has made himself believe he can conquer famine as well as the armies of Aetius."

The herdsmen and the shepherds seemed to lack in vigor as much as the animals they tended. They appeared to watch endlessly, their eyes fixed on the north as though they expected to see at any moment the red hats of Attila's dreaded horsemen on the horizon. When questioned they all had the same thing to say. "Why doesn't he come?" they would ask. "That great man, that brave Aetius, who beat the Huns once! Is he going to leave us unprotected? Does he not know of our danger?"

For two days Nicolan rode in an almost complete silence, trying to make up his mind to the course he should take. If he turned back and convinced Attila of the danger of an invasion under such adverse conditions, he might succeed in bringing about a delay in the emperor's plans. Postponements, he knew, were dangerous things. It might prove impossible for Attila to keep his men under arms for another year; or, if he dispersed them, he might not succeed in assembling his strength again for the drive south. In that way civilization might be saved. On the other hand, if nothing was done to lay the true facts before him, the emperor would undoubtedly proceed with his campaign. It would almost certainly fail, and the Christian world would be saved. But at a terrible cost. The cities of the plain would be stormed and reduced to rubble, and the people of this rich and happy land would die in tens of thousands by the pagan sword.

Every mile they rode made it seem more certain that Attila's agents had failed to convey to him a proper picture of the conditions in Lombardy; but Nicolan could not persuade himself that his duty lay in turning back.

CHAPTER IV

1

THE BOAT which Micca maintained at Alimium was spacious enough to carry a large cargo. Nicolan went aboard in the disguise that Attila had suggested. Under a cape of gray cloth, which was as plain as the garb of the lowliest citizen, he allowed a glimpse to show of a once handsome toga, a little tarnished now and with rents in its golden embroidery. He could not be mistaken for anything but what he professed to be, a man of some position who sought a hiding place under the pines of the islands.

A damp breeze blew from the south across the green water and Nicolan watched the break of the waves about the prow with the fascination of a new beholder. He was sorry when Priscius joined him to point out that their destination lay straight ahead, a stone wharf on an island of some size. It was the largest in the group and, if either Nicolan or his companion had been gifted with the power to look ahead into the centuries to come, they would have been amazed to see a huge city built on this deposit of alluvial soil: a city with castellated buildings of stone and brick, of a strange beauty, and canals stretching in all directions with humpbacked bridges over them and pleasant craft plying along them in endless number. The conception of this city, which would be known to the world as Venice, would date back to something which was soon to happen and which Nicolan would witness with his own eyes, a frenzied rush of refugees from the mainland, fleeing the approach of the Hun armies, and an inclination later to remain where they were rather than return to the towns and villages which Attila had destroyed.

Nicolan's first glimpse of the island showed it to be flat and with no outward signs of life. It was amazing, however, how suddenly the landing pier swarmed with people when they turned in there. A vociferous individual, with a sword hanging at one side of his belt and the keys of authority at the other, motioned to them angrily to keep off.

"No strangers allowed here!" he bellowed. "It is an order of the strictest. Be on your way."

Paying no attention to these protests, Priscius steered in to a landing.

"Is it you, O Criplian?" he called, in a cheerful tone. "I have been here twice before and have not been refused. We have goods to offer you and our juggler is a veritable artist. You must see his magic." He whispered to Nicolan. "This man is in Micca's pay. He will help you. Swing over your shoulder this bag of goods I have made up for you. It will be necessary to go before the princess in the guise of a trader."

The island Cerberus gave no indication of friendliness. He scowled when the boat touched the landing place and regarded Nicolan with a sullen eye. "And who," he demanded, "is this fine gentleman? Who does not seem so fine at a second glance."

Nicolan took it on himself to answer. "I seek quiet and peace for a short time. And I have the means to pay for what I desire."

"They all have that," said the man carelessly. "Did you dip into the public funds or are you sought for trickery in private affairs? Do not give me an answer; it is better for me not to know. If these others are allowed ashore for a brief hour, you at least will remain where you are, my fine runaway patrician."

Nicolan stepped out on the wharf in spite of this injunction. He drew the man Criplian to one side. "'Though his feet may turn to the west, the head of a wise man inclines always to the east,'" he whispered.

The guard's manner lost some of its surliness. "So, you are the one," he muttered. "I will deal with you later."

When the cases of goods had been opened and the wares spread temptingly about for the inspection of the people of the island, female as well as male, and the juggler was testing his knives and other props, the man Criplian sought Nicolan, who had stationed himself at some distance.

"You are expected and all the arrangements are made," he said. "But, my fine swindler or thief, or whatever you may be, the money first."

Nicolan surreptitiously dropped a bag into his palm. It was heavy and it gave forth a musical jingle.

"You are sure it is all there?"

"It has not been opened since it was handed to me."

"I wouldn't trust you not to dip a hand in for yourself. I'll count it later. If it isn't right, I'll see to it that you don't leave the island alive." The bag vanished inside the man's loose and far from clean tunic. "Now you will listen. Stay in the cover of the trees while I pass on the word that you are here. There may be some delay; although I saw all of her maids feasting their eyes on the goods back there."

"I don't expect to complete my mission to your royal mistress——"

Criplian interrupted by hissing furiously through his teeth. "Be more careful, you fool. There is never talk of royalty here. She, the one we guard, is said to be an invalid. She is never seen by outside eyes. Put a guard on your tongue."

"Of course. I did not realize the care you have to take. What I meant to say was that I can't complete my mission with one conversation."

"I can keep you on the island for one night, if necessary. You will be hidden in a damp hole in the boat sheds. And you will obey my instructions to the letter."

In a very few minutes Criplian returned and beckoned to Nicolan. The latter followed him along a narrow path through the trees. They reached the palace, which was a low structure of white stone with barred windows high in the walls and copper-covered doors. A cool dark passage brought them to an inner court.

"Gracious lady," said Criplian, "this is the man. The messenger of whom I spoke."

A slender woman was reclining on a low couch, her eyes fixed on a barred gate which opened on a path to the water. She turned her dark eyes, languid under long black lashes, and Nicolan recognized her at once.

The princess had not changed much since the day when he had knelt before her with one of the gifts from the ambitious Aetius. She had, he thought, become more slender, which had the effect of making her eyes seem larger and of lending a fallacious note of nobility to her broad white brow. She was attired in a loose blue gown which obviously had seen much wear.

"Spread your goods out on the floor," instructed the guard, in an urgent whisper. "If anyone comes, play the part of the trader. And be prepared for rough handling in the manner of your going."

Nicolan obeyed instructions by emptying the bag and placing the contents in a semicircle about him. He was conscious of the interested scrutiny of the princess as he went about these precautions.

"This is a surprise," she said, when Criplian had left them alone. "You are different from what I expected—much, much different. I was prepared to receive a fierce Eastern warrior in a round red hat and with a curved scimitar." She looked at him more closely and her eyes opened wider. "I have seen you before. Where could it have been? And when?" She sat up straight on the couch and wrapped a bare arm around her knees. "I know! You were one of the slaves who brought me the gifts from my lord Aetius on my last visit to Rome. Such a long time ago!" She smiled and nodded her head. "I'm sure I can't be mistaken. I remarked you quite closely at the time."

"You are not mistaken, gracious lady. I presented you with a container of nard on a green velvet cushion."

"I never liked nard but I was much impressed with the bearer. Your station in life seems to have changed for the better. I have been hearing much about you. Rather remarkable things. But of course I did not connect the able lieutenant of Attila with the slave who waited on me that day."

"After I made my escape from Rome," said Nicolan, speaking in carefully low tones, "I found favor in the eyes of my lord Attila. He has thought well enough of me to entrust me with this most delicate mission."

The deep dark eyes of this princess, who had so offended her family by her indiscretion, were watching him intently. She toyed with a jeweled fan. "Are you not taking a great risk," she asked, "in venturing thus into Roman territory? What if you were caught? My lord Aetius is not of a forgiving nature."

"I realize the danger."

"We must see that your secret is well kept," said the princess, spreading the fan and watching him above it. "I am beginning to recall memories of that day in Rome. You seemed so very young as you knelt before me. I hoped you would look up. Some of the others had been bold enough to do that but you kept your eyes on the floor. Perhaps that was why I was guilty of a great indiscretion. I whispered to you."

"Yes, Your Highness. I shall always remember it."

The princess laughed lightly. "How indiscreet I was!" The archness of her manner was replaced by a more serious note. "I am always curious about my slaves. They come from all parts of the world and there is so often a deep mystery in their eyes as they serve me. I could not see your eyes that time but I could read that same mystery in the line of your brow and in your fine hands; and now I realize that I was right.

"You bring me, perhaps," she resumed, "another present? The one I desire most of everything in life—my liberty?"

"Yes, gracious lady. The Emperor Attila is prepared to gather his great armies and march on Rome in your behalf. But he must be sure he acts with your consent and understanding. There must be an alliance, a joining of interests."

He produced a small box from under his belt and raised the lid, revealing the gold ring which Hyacinthus had carried to Attila. "When you sent your trusted servant to the emperor with this token, you were of a mind to join him in the most sacred of all alliances."

The pale cheeks of the princess flushed. "May I speak freely to you? Will you regard what I tell you as given in confidence and not to be repeated?"

Nicolan bowed. "Yes, my lady."

The eyes of the princess had displayed a languishing softness under artfully employed lashes at the opening of their talk. Now her expression changed, suddenly and completely. She became direct and even realistic.

"My mother keeps me a prisoner. I can't move from this dull place. I'm sure she means to keep me here for the rest of my life. I am watched and spied upon. Oh, it is shameful! I was desperate when I wrote to Attila and ready to take any means of breaking my bonds. They keep me in the dark about everything. One of my maids heard that my mother is dead. Can you tell me if it's true?"

Nicolan did not feel free to tell her what he had heard. He shook his head.

"But," she went on, "his answer has been a long time in reaching me. May I ask you some questions?"

"If it is understood," said Nicolan, "that any answers I may give will also be treated in confidence."

"Naturally." The princess hesitated before proceeding. She closed the fan and then opened it again, seeming much interested in the pattern of the ivory. "What is the emperor like? Tell me of his appearance, of his habits and manners, of the court he keeps. I've heard so many stories about him that I don't know what to believe."

"In appearance he is a typical Hun. Need I say more on that point?"

She shook her head. "But is it possible one could like him?"

"I find it possible to admire him, my lady."

"Is he cruel?"

"He takes no pleasure in cruelty, as so many despots do. I am told he never sees an execution. But he has no hesitation in wiping out all the inhabitants of a city, even of a whole province, if he believes it will further his plans. He can decree the annihilation of thousands and still sleep well of nights."

"If I married him, what would my life be?"

"You would share the throne with him. If he took Rome, you would be crowned there. By this I mean you would occupy a chair beside him. He would never consult you about affairs of state. Sometimes he consults a lieutenant but it is always on matters of detail. Policy he decides himself."

"What would my position be as—as a wife?"

"Gracious lady, I must be completely frank. As a wife you would be one of forty. You would rank as his number-one wife but, on marrying you, he wouldn't put the others aside."

"Forty!" cried the princess, her face a picture of consternation.

"There have been nearly one hundred of them altogether. He is rather indulgent to them. Sometimes they have to be punished but I can't believe he would have one of them put to death. Still, they come and go. Some die. Some disappear."

"Do they have music? Plays? Do they read? To what extent are the gracious sides of life practiced?"

"There are no gracious sides to the life they live. There is music. Of a kind—strange, barbaric. I find it very hard on the ears. The race from which I spring happens to be quite a musical people."

"Well, what else? Do they use perfumes?"

"It's frowned upon as weak and degenerate. I believe it has to be brought in and sold secretly by traders like Micca the Mede. The Hun women are partial to one kind only. It has a thick, musky odor."

"What kind of baths do they have?"

"The only answer I can give to that," answered Nicolan, smiling, "is that I have heard there is a marble bath belonging to Attila and that it's the only one there."

"This is worse than I thought!" Honoria seemed thoroughly shocked. "What are his habits with this large harem?"

"His rule is to visit each day the inner city where they live together behind a high enclosing wall. He does this always in the morning and he selects his wife for the day. She is sent over to his palace and remains there. She sits beside him at the evening meal."

"And does she sleep with him?"

Nicolan nodded his head. "That is the rule. Occasionally he falls out with his wife for the day or she does something he doesn't like. In that case he sends her back and has her replaced."

"A different wife every night!" The princess was finding all this hard to believe. "You don't think he would change his way of living if he married me?"

"My lady, he never changes."

The manner of the princess altered perceptibly at this point. She sat up still straighter on the couch and a small spot of color showed in each cheek. An imperious note manifested itself in her voice.

"But if I, a princess of imperial Rome, became his wife, wouldn't everything be changed? Would it not be possible for me to set new fashions? To introduce all the gracious ways of living we have here? To have proper palaces and public baths built? To have civilized cooks and fine wines and the perfumes of the East? After all, I would be the mistress."

"Such things would be possible only," was the answer, "if Attila conquered Rome and established himself there. In that event, he and his people would try to adapt themselves to the new ways. You would be, in name at least, the empress of the world. Perhaps Attila would listen to you then in domestic matters. But only a soothsayer can tell whether this change would be permanent or how soon the conquering race would revert. It's my opinion that in less than a generation they would turn the palaces into pig byres and use the temples for their pagan rites, and stable their horses in the great arenas. If you went to him now as his queen, you would have to accept things as they are. You would live as the others do. It would not be—shall we say, a pleasant or brilliant life?"

The princess shuddered slightly and fell into a silence.

2

"Will you permit me now," asked Nicolan, "to tell you what the emperor proposes? He desires me to say first that he would be proud to have you as his wife but that from the standpoint of policy it might not be a wise solution. I am to tell you that he desires your open support. To make this possible, he will contrive to free you and settle you where the Roman power does not reach. He will provide for you extensive estates with an income adequate to maintain a court of your own. A match will be arranged with some king or ruler of a dependent state. A German, perhaps. Or a high-placed Dacian or Sarmatian. Even, a prince of the Eastern Empire. In making war on Rome he would openly espouse your right to a fair share of all the dominions of Rome and your interests would be watched closely in any treaty settlements which might become necessary. You would submit yourself to his protection and forgo any communications with your brother, the emperor of Rome, or any member of your family."

The princess had followed his explanation with a close and shrewd interest. She nodded her head at this point. "It seems to me this plan has much to commend it. But my brother, the emperor, will refuse to sanction any marriage which he has not made for me. We must expect that."

"He has made no effort to select a husband for you. That is the answer Attila will make if the question arises."

"Where will I live?"

"As far away from the Roman boundaries as possible. There must be no opportunity allowed them to get possession of your person again."

"My brother will be prepared to state that I am dead if you succeed in getting me out of their hands."

"That," declared Nicolan, "is one of the chief reasons why Attila feels you should be removed at once from the custody of your family. When he has set you up in state, it will be useless for them to claim you have died. It is highly desirable that you marry at once and have children to carry on your claims."

She remained in silent thought for several moments. "If Attila doesn't conquer Rome, what will my position be?" she asked, finally. "Will he discard me then as being of no further use? Will he brush my claims aside? Will he allow me to go on living on the scale you promise or will he confiscate my properties and send me into exile?"

"Who can say what a man with despotic powers will do under any given circumstances?" Nicolan was selecting his words carefully. "In matters of statecraft he is sly and devious. He makes use of any pretext and he seizes every advantage. But I believe that, once he has pledged his word, he will keep it. I have known him to fulfill promises where his inclination has been to evade them. In any event, what have you to lose in trusting yourself into his hands? At the worst, you will be exchanging one form of captivity for another."

"That is true. If my mother is still alive, I can expect nothing. And the emperor is equally unforgiving." The princess proceeded then to ask for more information on the point which, quite obviously, interested her most, her marriage. "Will I have any voice in the matter?" she asked. "Or will I be expected to accept any man the emperor may choose himself?"

"I raised that question and his answer was that he would consult your wishes and be agreeable to any decision you made, provided the man of your choice was the head of a state acknowledging his rule. Needless to state, he can't have you aligning yourself on the other side."

"Supposing," began the princess, looking up into his eyes for a full moment before allowing her own to fall, "that I prefer to follow the dictates of a romantic disposition? Would I be allowed to marry for love instead of reasons of state?"

"The emperor would have no objection if you married for love. Provided"—with a dry smile—"that you fell in love with the right king."

"Then I could not marry a man of lower station? Such as—a man of your rank?"

"I assure you, gracious lady, that is quite out of the question."

The Roman instinct for a proper bargain showed for a moment in the princess. "He is asking much of me. I must desert my family, my own race, to join him. Can I be certain he will be as generous as he promises? Will I live in proper dignity and luxury?"

Nicolan glanced around the little court. The walls were of plain stone with no trace of sculpture or adornment of any kind. There were no flowers growing and no plashing fountain, without which a Roman garden was a very shabby thing indeed. The couch on which the daughter of imperial Rome sat, or reposed or twisted according to her mood, and the chair which he occupied were of peasant design and workmanship. There was no hint of richness about the clothes she wore.

"A prisoner within four walls is hardly in a position to drive a close bargain," he reminded her.

The mercurial disposition of the prisoner showed itself then in a quick change of mood. The completely feminine and somewhat flirtatious attitude she had adopted at first was again reflected.

"If the life among the Huns is so crude, how can you bear it?" she asked.

"I am kept too hard at work to care much about how I live."

"They say the women are quite lively. Have you found them that way?"

"They are dark and squat. I keep far away from all of them."

"What a virtuous young man! All Romans sent to outpost work are supposed to console themselves. Even those who have wives and families. Are you wise to be so—so very strict?" Then she returned abruptly to more serious points of discussion. "Well. What is the next step?"

"Your decision," answered Nicolan. "What word am I to take back? It's possible I could manage to remain on the island if you desired the night to think it over and reach your conclusion. Criplian says he can hide me for that length of time."

The princess looked about her, at the plain stone walls, the clumsy furnishings, the path, so narrow and empty, leading down to the water. Not a sound reached them from any direction.

"This dreadful quiet!" she exclaimed. "It is always the same. No one comes near me except my servants. I never have a chance to talk. I sometimes hear voices in the distance but they are always rough and unfriendly. I shall go mad!" She dropped both feet to the ground and seemed on the point of rising. "I agree!" she cried. "It is a bitter thing to sell oneself to the enemy. But what can I do? Yes, I agree. I am prepared to sign."

Nicolan drew out the papers and handed them to her. "You are wise to decide at once. Every hour counts. At almost any time now you will be swamped by refugees. It will be a struggle for survival then."

The princess looked helplessly at the papers in her hands. "How am I to sign them? All the servants are out." Then she smiled briefly and rose to her feet. "I seem to remember seeing a reed pen somewhere about. I will look for it."

She left the room and returned in a few minutes with a triumphant smile. "They keep pens hidden from me since that one letter I wrote. But I was right! It was where I remembered seeing it. And here are the papers. Properly signed, I trust."

Nicolan accepted the documents with a low bow. "You have made a wise decision, great and gracious lady. I hope you will never have reason to regret it."

"When are we to leave?"

"It will be necessary to take the boat back and return with a larger one. And with more men. But it's a short sail. I think it possible to arrange it so we can get away before daybreak."

The beautiful eyes of the princess seemed to grow larger and darker with excitement. "So soon!" she exclaimed. "Ah, how happy I am to find you a leader of so much decision." She reached out and took one of his hands in both of hers. "Oh, tell me, is this just a wonderful dream? Or am I really going to be free? But, my kindest of captains, you will stay here. I don't believe I can bear to be left alone now."

Nicolan frowned with indecision. "It would be better if I went with them and saw to it that all the arrangements are properly carried out. Priscius is hard and shrewd. But——" He paused and studied her intently. "I can understand your desire not to face this alone. But can I make all necessary plans with your man Criplian before I leave?"

The princess gave her head an emphatic shake. "I will need you. This is a desperate step I am taking and I must have your support. If I am left alone, in the midst of these people who have always been so cruel and unfriendly, I may lose my courage."

After a moment of careful consideration, Nicolan nodded in agreement. "Very well, gracious lady. I can arrange everything with Priscius before he leaves. I would feel safer the other way. But, after all, your state of mind is important to us."

Her eyes were fixed on his as they reached this decision. The years seemed to have rolled from her shoulders, for she looked very much younger. Color was showing again in her cheeks.

"I think I feel some happiness for the first time since I was brought here."

A sound reached them from the gardens outside and her glance went to the gate through which the view of the grounds could be had. They remained fixed on something she had seen. One hand was raised to her mouth.

"Who is that?" she asked.

Nicolan stepped forward to get a view of the outside. A man was standing on the path and looking in at them. As soon as he realized that his presence had been detected, he turned quickly and vanished into the cover of the pine trees.

"Who was it?" she asked, again.

"A member of my party. A slave belonging to Micca the Mede. His name is Hussein."

"Can he be trusted not to tell?"

"Most certainly. I have no fear on that score."

"He was staring at me so intently. I turned in that direction because I could feel his eyes on me. Does he know who I am?"

"I don't believe so. Of course something may have been said. Hussein is a man of high honor. You spoke of feeling a mystery about so many slaves. There is a mystery about him. His father is a king. The ruler of a desert state. He was captured as a boy and he doesn't remember much about his early life."

"I knew it." The princess turned away and seemed to be striving to penetrate the green blanket on each side of the path. "He had a strange effect on me. How proud and stern he looked! I think he is the most beautiful man I have ever seen. More beautiful even than you."

CHAPTER V

1

NICOLAN was escorted by Criplian to a very small and dark room with one window, cut in the form of a crescent and immediately under the ceiling.

"Make no sound," he was cautioned. "Those chattering little fools will be coming back soon."

They sat for a few moments on the edge of a couch and discussed the arrangements for the escape.

"Our part may not be hard," said the major-domo. "Word has come to expect a rush of refugees from the mainland at any moment. Most of the guards will be kept all night at the wharves." He motioned over his shoulder with a thumb. "There's a cove on the other side. I've sent a man with Priscius to guide the boat in there. If they arrive before dawn, it will be a simple matter." He had a pronounced droop in one eyelid and Nicolan had noticed that it twitched whenever there was talk of money. At this point it seemed almost to flutter. "This is more than I bargained for. I'll have to be paid well."

"I know the arrangement made with you. The sum promised will be paid before we leave."

"It will not be enough."

"I was told you were hard to deal with. But the bargain has been made and you have said yourself that it will be a simple matter. I see no reason to give you more."

The villainous appearance loaned to the major-domo's face by his drooping lid seemed to become intensified. His fingers, long and crooked and covered with dark hair, clutched his belt with a tensile grip. "There is one reason. Priscius has left with your men. What is to prevent me from calling up the guards and ordering them to slit your throat?"

Nicolan did not show much concern. "What is to prevent you from doing that? Your greed, Master Criplian. You would be throwing away the reward promised you. I have an empty purse. Priscius will bring your money with him." He indulged in a short and unfriendly laugh. "Only one whose head was filled with mutton fat would put himself in *your* power."

"But you cannot afford to fail."

A long silence fell between them. Finally Nicolan rose to his feet. "This much I promise you," he said. "When the princess is safely aboard and there is no danger of armed interruption, I shall toss—from the side of the boat—a purse with something additional for you."

The drooping eyelid winked furiously. "How much?"

"That," said Nicolan, "is a point for me to decide. I shall give it some thought."

The major-domo made his way grumblingly to the door. "Don't expect much to eat. I'll have to slip by all those curious creatures with what I can get."

2

The establishment filled with much clatter of feet and confusion of talk, proof that the trading boat had left and the servants had returned. Criplian stepped inside and locked the door after him.

"She wants a talk with you," he said. "A long talk. It's not going to be easy. There's a staff of twenty-five here and all of them spies for Mother Rat-Tooth, the matron. Except two. The personal maids of the princess. Tina and Zasca. A faithful pair. She insists on taking them with her."

"Why is it necessary to keep so close a watch on an island like this?"

"To satisfy the court. The matron is under orders to visit the royal chamber at least twice every night. To see if she is there—and alone. Mother Rat-Tooth always goes at midnight and then sets her other visits at different times." The major-domo indulged in a grin which displayed a diminishing supply of his own teeth. "There are three baths in the house but none in the royal chamber. The princess has to walk down a long hall. The doors are locked at eleven and by half after the hour the household is sound asleep. She will come then and be back before midnight. If that doesn't suffice——"

Nicolan frowned uncertainly. "There will be chances to talk on the boat surely. Wouldn't that be better?"

"She says not. The boat will be crowded. There will be too many ears and eyes around you. What she has to say calls for strict secrecy."

"But remember this. The smallest slip, a careless footfall, a raised voice, an unexpected appearance of one of the staff, may cost us our lives. That of the princess also."

"I have said all that to her. She still insists." The major-domo removed his rod of office, the silver of which had turned to yellow from lack of polishing, from under his belt. He produced a sheet of parchment. "Wait. This is a plan of the building. Here is the room we're in. It is kept locked and is only used when there are visitors. I have the only key. And here, just a few doors down the hall, is the bath. She can pretend to visit the bath and slip in here instead.

"The matron," he went on, tucking the plan away from sight, "keeps a model of the place beside her bed with small clay figures to show where each servant sleeps and each guard is stationed. If she suspects anything, she can reach for a rope hanging over her bed and ring a bell loud enough to be heard all over the house, inside and out. That shows how careful we must be."

It was half after eleven when a key grated in the lock again. The princess came in with noiseless steps, followed by a plump little woman with a kind, round face. Honoria was still in the tunic she had worn in the afternoon but the addition of a few small pieces of jewelry lent a slight distinction to it. The languor of the afternoon had given place to an air of decision.

"My little Zasca knows only her own language," she said. "We may speak freely."

Nicolan remained standing while the princess seated herself on the edge of his couch. The maid sought the farthest corner and turned her back.

There was a brief pause. "I am going to place my fate in your hands," whispered Honoria. Another pause followed, a longer one. "If you have listened to all that has been said of me, you think me an idle and foolish woman. Perhaps that is what I am. But I still have friends in high places and I keep in contact with them, in spite of this sly and detestable matron, and all the unfriendly eyes around me. I am kept advised in affairs of state. When the threat from the Huns is removed——"

"That," he said, "will depend on military considerations."

"The cloud will lift. I am certain of it. And when that happens, there will be"—she paused—"there will be great changes in Rome."

Nicolan was still feeling surprise at the difference in her. The lackadaisical and flirtatious mood of the afternoon was gone. She appeared coolly intelligent and, certainly, well informed.

"My brother, the emperor, is an imbecile and a coward. The people of Rome will rid themselves of him without any delay."

To test her views further, Nicolan asked, "What of Aetius?"

"Ah, I am sorry for him. That unfortunate Aetius will lose, no matter what happens."

"If you are so certain Attila will be beaten, why are you going over to him?"

The princess replied promptly. "To save myself. If the emperor realizes the danger he faces, he will take steps to get rid of me. He will want one of his children to succeed. I must get myself out of his hands at once. And, of course, I have no intention of letting Attila select a husband for me. He will be in no position to keep his promises to me."

Nicolan could not refrain from smiling. "But, my lady," he said, "I am here as the emissary of Attila. What you are telling me is that you have no intention of living up to your share in this agreement."

She leaned forward and addressed him in the most serious of tones. "Don't you see that this agreement can be carried out only if Attila conquers Rome? Is he going to win? His chances get thinner every day. And if he retreats a second time, he will never lead another army against us. And don't you see also that what I am proposing to do will suit his own plans? I will be helping to destroy the confidence of the Roman people in their present leaders."

The same thought repeated itself in Nicolan's mind. "She has been listening to discreet counsel. I wonder who it is?"

"There is only one clause in the agreement which I intend to disregard. I am going to choose my own husband without consult-

ing him. You think it strange that I tell you all this? I have no
fear that you will go back to Attila and repeat everything to him.
In your heart you fear him and hate him."

"In my heart I fear and hate Rome."

"With good cause, no doubt. But listen with an open mind to
what I am going to say." She leaned still closer to him and took
possession of one of his hands. "My reputation is tarnished. They
will turn to me only if I have a man of great strength with me. At
one time I thought of Aetius. But not now. I have a better candidate in my mind. You!"

Nicolan's face was a study in emotions, with amazement up-
permost. "I am a nobody. A barbarian. An obscure member of
Attila's staff. What is more, I am young and untried."

"No," said the princess. "Not untried. Don't you know that the
march of the armies of Attila into Gaul was a masterpiece of
direction? The officers of Aetius knew that Attila had someone
with genius back of him. They discovered who it was. There has
been much talk of you among the Roman leaders. You stand high
in their esteem."

The mood of the princess changed completely. She looked up
at him as he towered over her with a return of warmth in her
beautiful eyes.

"And high in my esteem, my friend and captain. Ah, how
weak a word I have used! What we have been saying must be our
secret, shared with no other living soul. If we are careful and
wise in everything, and daring when the need arises, I can become empress and I can make you the dictator of Rome. You
can step into the place of Aetius."

Perceiving that he was still too startled to make any suitable
response, Honoria smiled with even greater warmth. "You are
modest. Rome has been ruled by many men of alien blood. None
of them, not even the great Stilicho, as able as you. Nor as
honorable."

The door opened and the other maid put her head inside with
apparent hesitation. "My mistress," she said, in a low mumble of
foreign words, "the clepsydra has stopped." This referred to the
water clock which was to be found in all large households. "I do
not know the time. I think it may be close to the hour."

Honoria rose slowly to her feet. She glanced up into his eyes at close range. "Do you remember what I said?" she asked. "That day when you knelt before me."

Nicolan reflected for a moment. "Yes. I remember what you said. It was this: 'What a pity you are a slave—and not *my* slave.'"

The face of the princess lighted up and she clapped her hands noiselessly. "You do remember it. Every word. I am pleased. I am delighted. Well, my Nicolan, you are no longer a slave. You are now a master. You may become with me the master of the world. And you are already the master of my heart."

Again Nicolan found himself speechless with surprise.

"Yes, you will marry me. That is my plan. Don't look at me as though you think I speak of impossibilities. It is true I am Augusta and so raised above all men, save those of equal birth. But didn't my mother marry Adolphus of the Goths? And isn't Pulcheria sharing the throne in the East with Marcian, who was a common soldier? It can be done again and I will have it no other way."

"I am overwhelmed, gracious lady," said Nicolan.

She glanced at the two maids to be sure their backs were turned. Then she clasped her arms about his neck and placed her cheek against his. "It was my hope we would part on sweeter terms. I fell in love almost from the moment you came to me this afternoon. It has never been like this before. Ah, how greatly I will love you! But—you see, don't you, that I can't risk the faintest whisper of scandal? Never again must there be cause for gossip about me. The stakes, my beautiful and brave captain, are too great."

Her arms tightened for a moment about him and then fell to her sides. "So now I must go. It is needful for me to be in my bed when that hateful old woman comes, prying and looking everywhere, and asking questions. In a few hours"—her eyes lighted up and became as bright as the few stars he could glimpse through the crescent window above—"I will be free. And with you. My life, I think, is just beginning."

3

Nicolan was wakened by the loud clangor of a bell. It rang so loudly that it seemed to fill the house. His first thought was that the matron had discovered what was afoot. If that were the case, he was caught in a trap. The door was too strong for the shoulder of a Goliath to force open and the window was not large enough to allow the passage of anything larger than a cat.

He sprang to his feet and slipped into his sandals. Then he clasped his sword belt about his waist. For a moment he listened and became conscious of voices at some distance in the house and the clatter of hurried feet. The room was in complete darkness and so it was clear that dawn had not yet come.

"Our only hope," he said to himself, "is that the boat will be early and that they can overcome the guards."

He had noticed when brought to the room that there was a pitcher of water in a corner. He sloshed his face in the water, which aroused his senses fully.

A hurried but furtive footstep came down the hall and halted outside the door. The key was turned and Criplian put his head inside. "The place is afire!" he said. "The princess is already out. Everyone is fighting the flames."

When Nicolan reached the hall he found it filled with smoke. It was impossible to see more than a few feet in any direction.

"What caused it?" he asked.

"Mother Rat-Tooth went early to the chamber of the princess and found one of the maids packing clothes. She hurried back to her own room and, in reaching up to pull the rope, she upset a candle which set fire to the model. The flames are spreading fast."

"Where is the princess?"

They had passed out through a rear door and Nicolan saw with relief that a faint touch of gray was lightening the sky in the east.

"She's with her two maids. Everyone else is helping to fight the flames."

"Bring them to the cove," Nicolan instructed. "Our only hope is that the boat will be coming in to take us. Are any there now?"

"Two small ones."

"I'll stand guard and try to hold up any pursuit. You smash one of the boats and take the princess and her maids off in the other. I'm a strong swimmer and may be able to overtake you. If I can hold the guards off long enough."

Standing back in a fringe of trees, Nicolan saw that the flames seemed confined to the interior. Clouds of smoke were pouring out of the doors and windows. Pandemonium had taken possession of the place. Hoarse voices shouted orders and hysterical ones screamed in fear and supplication. Belongings were being carried out and deposited on the grass. Nicolan's hopes rose. In this emergency the princess might be left unwatched.

Some time later, one of the maids, hurrying down a path with frantic speed, saw him standing in the cover of the trees and motioned him to follow. They reached a path and in a few moments they were in sight of the sandy shore of the cove. Here the major-domo was breaking the ribs of one of the boats while the princess and her second maid crouched in the other.

When Criplian gave the ax a final swing, Nicolan said to him: "Get in. I'll shove the boat off."

The sky seemed noticeably lighter and he stole a moment to gaze into the east. Yes, dawn was breaking. If the vessel came in on time, they could now get away. As he plunged through the waves with a hand on the stern of the boat, he risked a glance into the north. He detected something there more substantial than either sky or water.

"They're coming!" he said.

The two men began to row with every ounce of strength they possessed. The waves were running high and, with each plunge forward, an icy shower splashed over the boat, soaking the occupants thoroughly. The gray-black of the sky began to fade and a trace of pink showed in the east. The shadow to the north was taking positive form.

"I am free!" cried the princess. "I am free! I am free!"

4

The vessel provided for their escape was an ancient warship which had been converted to commercial uses. No oars protruded from the double row of banks, and reliance was placed entirely on sails for navigation. Three masts, no less, with square rigging, stood up against the damp clouds. The hull, from which all ornamentation had peeled long since, preserved a certain dignity by its castlelike proportions fore and aft.

The wind had freshened and the ship pitched and tossed. The two maids disappeared early, to suffer in some corner. The princess, wrapped in a soiled length of sailcloth over her wet garments, stood beside Nicolan on the upper deck.

"Have we far to go?" she asked, in an urgent tone.

"One hundred miles, I'm afraid. It's unusual for the *bora* to blow at this season but it gives us one advantage. There can be no pursuit."

To avoid falling on the slippery deck, she slipped an arm through his. "Will you go ashore with me?" she asked.

"Only long enough to see you delivered into the right hands. A wealthy Dalmatian merchant will be waiting for you. I must then return and report to Attila. I want to make certain, as far as I can, that the promises in the agreement are carried out."

"Yes," she said, in a weak tone which suggested that she was finding it necessary to keep her lips closed tightly together. "I suppose it is necessary. But I shall regret it. How can I trust anyone but you?"

"You will be in the best of hands."

"Oh, these dreadful waves! I am desperately ill. You will return as soon as possible?"

Nicolan hesitated. Then, keeping his eyes resolutely on the tossing gray of the sea, he answered, "No."

"No!" The surprise she felt at this answer seemed to revive her momentarily. "You must. I—I insist. I will not agree to anything else. What might keep you away?"

"There are other duties I must attend to."

"Has this been nothing but duty, then?"

"It has been a great honor," he protested.

"Have you given thought to what I said last night?"

"Yes, Princess. I lay awake for hours and thought of nothing else. But I realized in the end that I have one ambition only in life. To see my country free. Free of the shackles of Rome as well as the cruel chains of Attila. And, after that, to take back the lands which were stolen from me and raise fine horses as my forefathers did."

"No!" exclaimed Honoria, looking up at him with furious eyes. "You are not speaking the truth. No man could refuse the great chance I have offered you. Not to spend his life raising a few scrawny horses in some hidden corner in the hills!" She gave his arm an angry tug. "No, no! It is not that! There must be another woman. Answer me, is it not so?"

Nicolan hesitated for a second time. "I am not sure," he said, finally.

"Why can't you be sure?"

"There is one I knew as a small girl. I have seen her only once in the last fifteen years. How can I be sure about my feeling for her? And I have no reason to suppose she has any romantic attachment for me."

She had been watching him closely as he spoke. "I believe you are telling the truth. This, surely, is something you can toss aside. You will soon forget her if you stay with me now. I do not need the support of Attila any more. I am free. I have powerful friends where I am going. Come with me. I am running away. You must run away with me."

"Gracious lady, you will be well looked after. There will be many honest and brave men to see that no harm befalls you."

"I am not interested in honest and brave men. I might not like any of them. I *do* like you. And that counts more than all the honesty and bravery in the world."

"My lady, I am a soldier, a man of no rank. It is a sense of gratitude which makes you overlook my unworthiness." In an almost desperate effort to convince her, he added: "After you have enjoyed your freedom for a short time, you won't even remember me. You will be surrounded by men of suitable rank, admiring you, begging your favor. You will be a princess again, with your own household, your own court. You won't even see Hussein, who is one of those chosen to accompany you. At his own request."

Honoria was silent for a moment. "Do you mean that wonderful creature who stood on the path and stared in at me? The one you said was the son of a desert king?"

"Yes. I agreed to let him go with you in the hope that very soon you would give him his freedom."

There was a brief silence and then the princess indulged in a laugh of such faintness that it was clear she was succumbing again to the power of the angry sea. "I suspect you of craftiness. Is it possible you are offering me this young slave as—shall we say, a substitute?"

"Your Highness, I had no such thought. It was arranged before we came. Hussein is a prince in his own right. He has every good quality."

"And," she added, "he has eyes that burn like the sun and the face of a god! There is no use denying what you have in mind. It is all very transparent."

"I want him to have his freedom, so he may return to his own land before the old king dies. That was my sole reason. I beg you to be kind to him."

The princess suddenly recovered her energy sufficiently to pound at his chest with angrily doubled fists. "You are throwing away the world!" she cried. "I have come to you on my knees and you are casting me aside like a woman of the water front! You fool! You fool! You fool!"

The effort involved in this outburst was too great in her weak condition. She turned hurriedly and stumbled back into the shelter of the waling-pieces about the stern of the vessel.

5

If Nicolan had entertained any doubts as to what he should do, they were quickly resolved on his solitary ride up the broad highway to Aquileia. In spite of his sense of the need for haste, he made a few excursions inland to satisfy himself about the condition of the countryside. What he saw appalled him, for things were getting rapidly worse. The sun no longer rose with the benign smile of a benefactor but with a glaring intensity of heat which baked the fertile earth to clay. The crops were withering. The cherry trees were plagued with cobwebs and the apples and pears had wilted away. Even the olive trees looked sickly. The cattle suffered so much that their flanks had fallen in, and high in the sheep runs the piteous bleating never ceased.

He knew now that he must hurry to Attila's headquarters with warning of the true state of affairs. Perhaps there was still time to stop the slaughter and suffering of an indecisive war. The mission which Macio had wanted him to undertake would have to wait. The steady stream southward of pale-faced civilians, on horseback, astride mules and on laboring feet, had hurried his decision.

The walls of Aquileia still raised their confident turrets to the sky but the streets were empty and quiet. When Nicolan paid a visit to the house of Scalpius he found the shutters closed and the doors barred. The captain of the guard on the northern gate was the only one to volunteer him any information. "The first of the Huns have been seen in the pass," he whispered, with a shake of his head.

Nicolan could not believe that the armies of Attila were already on the move. He began to question the captain. "Who saw them?"

"All this morning people have been streaming down the road and begging to be let in. They think they'll be safe behind the walls."

"It was a patrol party they saw."

The captain shook his head. "The pass is filled with them. They were whooping and screeching with delight because there was no sign of a Roman army to dispute the pass with them. Most of them had human heads on their spear points and some of them were tossing them back and forth."

Nicolan touched a heel to his horse's flank. He nodded his thanks to the captain. "I'm too late!" he said to himself. "But I must do what I can."

The inn with the cross above the door was closed tight. Nicolan stood at the front entrance and shouted loudly without getting any immediate response. "They must be Christian," he said to himself, "and yet they too have flown the wrath to come." Then he heard a cautious hail from the cover of the trees and saw the head of the man Hursta peering around one of the trunks.

"Come out!" he called. "There's nothing to fear."

Hursta obeyed slowly. "The shadow of evil fills the pass," he said. "One more day and you would not have found me."

"My friend has gone, then, about my lord Macio's affairs?"

Hursta nodded. "It was a matter of much urgency. He left at once, striking for the east and not coming here to await your arrival."

"Tell me about it."

They betook themselves into the shelter of the woods and Hursta proceeded to tell what he knew. "First," he said, "one of Attila's men came into our country. He pried about and asked questions and made loud threats. He was there, he said, on the direct orders of the emperor who, it seemed, had heard stories about a girl with golden hair. And about a black horse. He soon got at the truth, of course, for among our people are many who can't keep their tongues from wagging. The man himself let a hint drop that was brought quickly to my lord Macio: that Attila knew they were in Constantinople and he had already dispatched a party to demand that the girl and the horse be handed over to him. My master saw one chance only to save the Lady Ildico. Someone must reach Constantinople first and get her away in time."

Nicolan listened to this explanation with a sinking of the heart. It was not only that Ildico was in grave danger, there was his deep regret also that he had lost this chance to serve her. When would such an opportunity rise again to display his devotion?

"I am not surprised that Ivar left without a moment's delay," he said. "If I had only been free to go!"

Hursta then went into an explanation of the plan which Macio had made for the rescue of his daughter, the execution of which had been entrusted to the tall Briton. The mountains which rose back of the fertile plains of Dalmatia could be crossed at various points, for the most part by roads which followed the rivers. The rivers were in such a hurry to reach the sea that many of them dropped out of sight in places and went underground, to emerge far below. Once, a long time before, a river lost itself in this way for many miles, using a deep and cavernous gorge through the roots of one of the tallest peaks. In course of time, however, there had been a diversion and the water had found a better way which wound around the base of the peak, and so the underground opening had not been used for many centuries.

"Have you heard of the Garizonda?" asked Hursta, in an awed tone of voice.

Nicolan shook his head. He had never heard of the Garizonda.

"It's the name of the underground route which the river once took. It is still there, they say, though few know where it begins or where it ends. It runs for mile after mile and it's said there are strange animals down there and sights to curdle the blood. There are high places, so high that the human eye can't see to the top. Great winds sweep through from one end to the other and it's impossible to keep torches lighted. It's said that strange sounds fill the place, as though the gods in the earth are enraged when mere mortals dare to set foot there.

"The Lady Elstrassa, long since dead, who was wife to Macio," went on Hursta, "was a native of Dalmatia and her family owned all the land around the southern exit of the Garizonda. She left my lord Macio a map which showed how to find both entrances. A copy of this map was given to the tall one."

Nicolan's face had become white with apprehension. "Do they intend to try it?" he asked. "It would be sure death for all of them. There wouldn't be air to breathe in the depths under a mountain."

"There are other openings," Hursta said. "Air gets in through cracks in the rock above."

"How can you be sure, since no one has attempted it for generations?" Nicolan was still unable to see any wisdom in the plan. "The old man must be mad! If they go in, they will never come out."

Hursta gave his head a shake. "It's the only way. They can't stay in Constantinople. The cowardly emperor would turn them over to Attila's men; he has pulp instead of a heart, that one. How else can they escape? The passes will be guarded. But this way, they vanish at the foot of the mountain and come out on the other side."

"But suppose they don't come out? What kind of a death would it be, trapped underground like that?"

"There are worse things than death, my lord Nicolan. Do you suppose my master would suggest this if he could see any other way?"

There was no possibility now, at any rate, of changing plans. "I never expect to see them again," declared Nicolan. He mounted his horse and turned its head toward the pass.

CHAPTER VI

1

THE HUN armies were pouring through the pass in utter confusion. Horse and foot were inextricably mixed. Towheaded Teutons marched in the company of swarthy Sarmatians. There was not a supply wagon in sight. It was Babel on foot; the air was filled with the clamor of countless tongues.

Drawing off to one side of the road, Nicolan studied the jeering procession streaming down the grade with some alarm. It had been impossible for him to carry any identification with him. The first officer he saw, fortunately, was one he knew, a slant-eyed Oriental named Monesus. The latter rode over to him, wearing a look of surprise.

"You here!" he said. "The talk around the campfires is that you are no longer in favor with the Great One."

"I am returning from a—a special mission. My report should be in the emperor's hands as soon as possible."

"You have been missed," declared the officer, in a grumbling tone. "This is the second day we've been without food. My men are scattering to forage and I can't hold up the troops behind us to wait for them. We've had only one thing in our favor since the march began. Not a drop of rain has fallen."

Nicolan waved a hand in the direction of the south. "Nor has a drop fallen on the plains. Do you count the sun an ally? Think twice, Monesus. The heat will be more deadly than a hundred legions."

The officer laughed easily. "A hundred legions? There won't be one. Don't you know they have dropped back to the shelter of their mountains? We will cross those plains so fast that nothing will matter. We won't even pause to forage."

Attila's black and white felt tent was set up on a plateau from which he could watch the endless procession of his men riding or tramping by, on their way to the descent of the unguarded pass, to spread out then like a great black fan over the plains, and finally to march triumphantly to the sack of Rome, with the feathers of the twelfth vulture in their teeth. The procession never stopped and it might have been thought that the troops were passing and repassing in a perpetual circle, for they all looked the same: black-bearded, dusty, ragged, with drums rattling, flags flapping, horses snorting, and wheels screeching. Sometimes they cheered when they saw the tent above but mostly they went heavily on, never raising their weary eyes from the trail ahead.

The tent was larger and of a more elaborate type than anything the emperor had ever used before, which made Nicolan wonder as he climbed up the steep approach. Was Attila becoming extravagant with such rich spoils within reach? Or was he finding it wise to dazzle his subjects a little so they might forget in his new grandeur the less than glorious results at Châlons? It probably was the latter, for the thickset figure of the Lord of Earth and Sky, standing in front of the pavilion, was arrayed in a glistening red and gold tunic of silk which fell well below his knees. His cap was of oriental design, his boots of shining pigskin. A youthful figure stood near him: his son Ellac, taller already than his sire, straight of leg, and with a solid bridge to his nose.

"I did not expect you so soon," said Attila, waving to Nicolan to draw closer.

"I have information for you that cannot wait."

Attila grunted. "Then you found the princess?"

"I found her, my lord. The information you had from Micca was correct. But I left as soon as I saw her safely on the Dalmatian coast. She has been taken to the sanctuary provided." He drew a document from under his belt and proffered it to the emperor. "Here is her signed agreement. She accepted every condition."

Attila did not look at the document. "Ellac," he said to his son, "there will be no Roman princess presiding over the marble palace we will use when we reach Rome."

"That is good, my father," said the youth, soberly.

"This will be cheerful hearing for the false one who gave me the information," declared the emperor, folding the document. "Half of his life has been redeemed. The other half still hangs in the balance. Ellac, listen closely to everything I say. You will learn much. You will learn how a king deals with traitors and spies."

"Yes, my father."

"And now, Togalatus, what is this information you bring me?"

Nicolan spoke slowly. "That you are here and sending your armies down into the pass makes me doubt if the reports you've had are full and honest."

Attila responded quickly. "It has been told me that the crops are not good."

"Great Tanjou, there is a drought on the land. It began in the autumn and not a drop of rain has fallen since. The fields have dried up and the livestock is dying. Your armies can't live off the parched country I have been riding through."

There was a long moment of silence. Attila's eyes had been watching the steady march of his battalions. As Nicolan spoke, however, he lost interest in everything else.

"How much of the country have you seen?"

"I have been nearly as far south as Ravenna and I have taken rides off the Via Emilia in many directions. Also I have talked to men who had been west to Genoa. They said it was the same everywhere."

"Are there not food supplies stored up in the cities?"

"Yes, my lord. But is it likely they would capitulate without destroying everything first?"

"How much stock did you see in the fields?"

"Very little. The best of it has been driven off. The roads were black with people fleeing south. Most of them had domestic stock with them."

"I have close to four hundred thousand men," declared the emperor. "How long can such an army exist on the food we will find?"

Nicolan hesitated. "I have little knowledge of supply. I can do no more than guess."

"Then guess!"

"A week."

"No more?"

"No more, O Noble Lord! In two weeks they would be killing their horses for food."

Attila scrutinized Nicolan's face with an angry intensity. "I was aware of a food shortage. But there was nothing in the reports that reached me to justify what you are saying. Why should I believe you?"

Attila began to pace about the small piece of level ground in front of the pavilion, paying no heed now to the constant drama provided by the marching files below. After several moments, he stopped in front of Nicolan.

"Why should I bestir myself to explain things to you?" he demanded, with a suggestion of anger in his tone. "You are a bright little officer with a good eye for roads and a sense of marching time. Why is it necessary for me to tell you that I have decided to go on in spite of everything? Things are not as bad as you believe, although Aetius, that man of no scruples, has been driving off the stock. Better the people starve, he thinks, if the enemy starve with them. But," he cried with a sudden gesture of his arms, "the sword is in the earth! I have driven it there and nothing must stand in the way!

"I advanced my marching time," he went on, in a tone little above a whisper, "because I found that Aetius did not intend to guard the mountain passes. This has now been confirmed by my scouts. There isn't a Roman eagle within a hundred miles of us. Is it a trap? No doubt he thinks so. And yet why should he abandon his strong defense here and allow me to lead my armies down to the Lombardy Plain where my horsemen can fight so much better? I can tell you the reason because I know what passes in the mind of this man.

"He was given credit for beating me at Châlons and it has made his pride blow up like a pig's bladder. He will take no chance of losing now, particularly as his allies in Gaul will not be with him. All through the winter he has had that fine long nose of his buried in books. He has been reading about Fabius, who delayed the Carthaginians by what he called his 'masterly inactivity.' That is what Aetius will try to imitate. Masterly inactivity! No daring, no risking of all on the throw of the dice like the warriors who are welcomed by the gods when they die. I think he intends to let the plains fall into my hands and confine his defense to the high mountains in front of Rome. I shall take this first easy prize into my two hands!"

Fire flared up in his eyes. "Ellac!" he cried. "Ellac, my son! Listen closely. A great king is subject to no laws, man-made or god-made. He makes his own laws. If the elements combine to thwart him, he laughs at them and dares them to do their worst. If obstacles arise in his way, he surmounts them. If one plan becomes impossible, he thinks of others."

His eldest son was listening with avid attention. Watching the youth, Nicolan said to himself: "He will remember every word but, if he attempts to follow this advice, he will fail. The stuff of real princes is not in him."

"Ellac! Keep your ears open, for I have more to say to you. Have you noticed how badly the march is going? How much confusion there is in the ranks? When I took my armies into Gaul, this man before me saw to it that everything went smoothly. My armies arrived on time and never once was there such confusion as we see here. But he refused to serve me further because he has a womanish dislike for bloodletting. What would you have done with him?"

The son looked sullenly at Nicolan. "I would have turned him over to the executioner," he declared.

"And you would have been wrong, my Ellac. Hearken to me! A great king never gets rid of a man who can still be of use to him. I sent him instead on a mission of some danger and delicacy. And now he is back. What am I to do with him? Set him to curing the confusion we see below us? Give him the task of getting my great armies through the neck of this mighty stone bottle?"

"Yes, my father," was the prompt response.

"And again, my Ellac, you are wrong. All this trouble I shall correct myself when we assemble on the plains. A king, my son, must be capable of doing anything that other men can do. Nay, he must do it better. If he leaves decisions to other minds and great tasks to other hands, the time will come when he will feel those other hands reaching for his scepter and those other minds coveting the crown on his head.

"And so," he added, "I have other work for this clever master of troop movements. I shall send him on another mission. He is going back into the heart of the enemy country, to demand audience of a man he once served as slave. I am sending him with a message for the ear of the dictator of Rome. None other than Aetius, my lifelong friend and most hated enemy!"

2

In the confusion of tents and wagons behind the imperial pavilion, Nicolan was halted by the sound of his own name, spoken in a hollow whisper. The voice came from one of the wagons of Micca the Mede which stood unhitched among the multiple camp carts. Over the shoulder of a guard standing in front, he saw the face of the onetime great trader, and a hand beckoning to him.

"You are back, then," said Micca, when he moved closer to the vehicle. "You saw the lady?"

"Yes. She was on the island you named."

"And did she come to terms?"

Nicolan nodded but gave no further information, not feeling free to discuss the situation.

"That is good. I am much relieved to hear of your success."

Nicolan noticed that the head which nodded to express this satisfaction was pale and gaunt and that the neck attaching it to the once well-tended and luxuriously attired body was as thin and tense as whipcord. "I cannot move closer," declared Micca, from the obscurity of his seat in the wagon, "because I am chained to the side. When I move, the sharp edges of the iron cut into my ankles. You see, O Togalatus, my fate has depended partly on your mission. Soon I hope to be free of the shadow of the sword of punishment hanging over me. But there is still another condition to be fulfilled."

Nicolan moved as close as he could get to the prisoner in the wagon. He could see then that the trader had fallen away to skin and bones. In his sunken face his nose looked longer and sharper than the beak of any kite which ever floated in the sky; a good simile, he realized, for Micca had often been called the Kite. His raiment was no longer of snowy white. It carried the dust of a month of travel and he was without any head covering.

"I am making a guess," said Nicolan, "that it was you who told the emperor about the girl and the black horse."

"That is true. There are few things that escape my notice in the course of my travels."

"The secret was held closely. I am curious to know how it came to your ears."

"A man from your own country came to see me——"

"Whose name, I think, was Ranno?"

The head of the prisoner nodded on its thin stalk of neck. "His name was Ranno. A young man of great pride and determination. It was before the armies left for Gaul and he told me he was very much in love with a lady of tender years whose hair was like spun gold. It was his desire to leave her a gift of such value that she would learn to love him while he was away at the wars. He must have loved her very much, for he bought a ring with a *diamant* as well as other precious stones. When the armies returned, he came to me again and wanted to return the ring. The lady, he said, had gone away and he might never see her again. I questioned him and he talked freely enough. The name of the beautiful girl was Ildico and she was the second daughter of Macio of the Roymarcks. She had gone away with the widow of Tergeste. This I told to Attila and he had inquiries made in your country which proved the accuracy of the story."

"Did you take back the ring?"

Even in his weakened condition, Micca could be emphatic on a point of trade. "I did not! A sale is a sale. I pointed out that he would find another wife and present the ring to her. He said no, he did not care enough for the lady who would be his second choice——"

"My poor Laudio!" said Nicolan to himself.

"—to make her such an expensive gift. He was very angry with me and made threats when I refused to return the money."

"But how did you learn of the girl's present whereabouts?"

"It is always easy to keep track of the movements of the widow of Tergeste. She is not, as you must know, like the chameleon which strives to remain unseen. Particularly when she has in her train one so very noticeable as a beautiful girl with golden hair and a great horse which throws dust in the faces of the fleetest steeds. I have correspondents everywhere and from their reports I traced the course of the party. They arrived in Constantinople in considerable state, for the widow had been winning large sums in wagers on the black horse and was inclined to spend freely.

"It so happened that my correspondent in Constantinople has

many fast horses of his own and the widow paid him a visit. They reached a distant meadow where the yearlings were kept; and there a strange sight met their eyes. The girl with the golden hair had preceded them to the meadow and they could see that all the yearlings had galloped over to greet her. They stood about her in a circle and their muzzles seemed to make a solid ring. There was so much tossing of manes and shaking of heads and much neighing that it looked—or so stated my credulous friend—as though they were gossiping with her."

"Naturally."

"You believe it?"

"Why not? Don't dogs talk to each other and don't they understand what their masters say to them?"

"But this was different. Do you suppose she was telling them about the great black horse she had ridden in so many races? My correspondent had the best of his three-year-olds race for her entertainment. The girl told them in advance which one would win. How do you account for that?"

"She had heard about it from the yearlings. Horses always know how races will end."

"When she is brought back to be the wife of Attila, I shall get my freedom," said Micca, groaning as he strove to move from his cramped position. "I have not been able to lie down since I was chained here. A full month ago. Can I survive much longer?"

3

Nicolan encountered Giso as he left the wagon where the unhappy Micca was confined. The royal attendant stopped him and motioned with his thumb in the direction of the black and white pavilion. "Have you seen him?" he asked.

"For a few minutes. I am to have a longer talk later in the day."

"He has changed," declared Giso, shaking his head doubtfully. "I thought I knew what went on in that head of his but lately I ask myself, 'Is this Attila?' I ask myself all manner of questions about him but I get no answers. My friend Togalatus, he has become a spendthrift. Did you observe his rich raiment? He has two other tunics just as fine. He has another pair of riding boots. He demands that Black Scyles find him new food for his meals.

If Selech himself was seasoning the royal pot, there would be complaints. Fruit, no less. Fresh fruit. Fish from the deep sea. I think he is preparing himself for the day when he will be the ruler of the world." The attendant paused. "And listen to this. It is very secret and you must not repeat a word of it. He is in bad health. He falls asleep in the daytime. He nods in the saddle. Sometimes he has dropped off during a council of war. He declares that he hears bells ringing in his ears. The men of medicine say he must watch himself if he is to keep the foul wings of death from brushing his shoulder. They have many reasons but there is no sense in any of them. I know the reason." Giso frowned darkly and sank his voice to a low pitch. "Too many wives!"

"Then why does he seek more?" demanded Nicolan. "He should give up this eternal search for a wife with golden hair."

"He has refused to see me for three days," said Giso, shaking his head. "Do you know why? Because I told him that. I said he should get rid of the lot of them. I said to him, when he was giving orders about finding this girl, that she would make a good wife for his son Ellac. He turned all colors. He foamed at the mouth. He got me by the throat and shook me. 'My son will have my throne someday but not the wife I have sought for so long!' He gave orders that I was to be taken out and beheaded and that Ellac was to be sent home at once. Later he changed his mind and let me live but he frowns whenever he looks at the boy."

Nicolan had been experiencing a change of feeling as he listened to the confidences of the royal attendant. "You are making me sorry for him," he said.

"Togalatus, I have been sorry for him a long time. That battle at Châlons tore his pride to shreds. He sits for hours at a time, staring at nothing, and with misery in his eyes. He talks of this wife as though she's the one desirable object in the world. He has planned a great entry for her into the city of Rome. She is to ride in a chariot made of ivory and gold. It will be drawn by the great black horse. She will wear blue and gold and purple, the colors he likes. A dead and plucked vulture will lie at her feet. A thousand prisoners of war will march in chains behind her chariot. He himself will ride behind them, very humbly, on his horse. That," finished Giso, "is the way he is planning it."

Book III

CHAPTER I

1

THE LADY EUGENIA had found this particular day one of great satisfaction. She had gone to the royal palace by express command, she had walked through the entrance hall, called the Chalké, where the golden shields and red aigrettes of a thousand scholarians had formed a picture not soon to be forgotten, she had reached the Consistorium where the Empress Pulcheria and her elderly husband Marcian sat together under a golden dome, she had received bows and smiles from each of them. Like everyone else, she had worn the stiff brocade gown provided for visitors before they were allowed to enter. It had been altogether a memorable experience; and as she made her way out to the disrobing room, she thought how foolish Ildico had been not to come with her. The empress had asked about "the girl who rides the black horse" and had seemed displeased at her non-appearance.

The day was made complete when a young man in a spotless white robe, and with red cloth bound many times around his head, approached her. She knew who he was because he had stood close to the imperial throne: a king from a corner of the desert called Davieda. He had come on a visit to Constantinople and had brought with him a string of fine-blooded Arabian horses.

He had a thin passionate face and eyes which glittered like the opulent stones in his headdress.

"Gracious lady," said the king, in perfect Latin, "I know you live close at hand. You may perhaps allow me to walk beside your litter. I have things to speak of."

The awe which the widow had felt when he presented himself faded. He was going to speak of horses, of his own string and, of course, of Harthager. Perhaps he would suggest a race. She was now completely at ease.

"It will be an honor, my lord king," she said.

It developed that Yussuff of Davieda was accompanied by a score or more of attendants. They were tall men in white, with long whiskers and long noses and smoldering eyes set in dark-skinned faces. They arranged themselves silently about the litter in two lines.

"Are you always accompanied, O King, by so many of your men?" asked the widow.

The young ruler nodded. "It is our custom. They hear and see everything, but tell nothing. And they keep assassins away."

"But aren't there times when you don't want them? Suppose you were going to see a lady and did not desire it known? Could you get away from them?"

"No, my lady. I would not try. If I see a woman under any circumstances, I am always ready to have it known. I have no interest in women. My interest," he added, "is confined to horses. I even leave affairs of state to my ministers."

It was a matter of a few minutes only to reach the widow's palace. The ruler's attendants followed him through the gate and lined up on each side of the entrance. Two of them, who had longer beards and more facial wrinkles than the rest, accompanied him through the hall with its high columns into a large square room facing the east. The king began then to discuss the matters which had brought him to see her.

"I have with me a few good horses," he said. "I brought, in fact, my favorite. Sulieman. You have heard of him?"

"Of course. Everyone has heard of Sulieman."

The man from the East adopted a more cautious tone. "He is—he is quite fast. It was an astonishment to me that the objections of two bands of the populace, composed of the lowest, poorest, and most vulgar, made it impossible for me to have my horses stabled in the Hippodrome. They are called the Greens and the Blues. You have heard of them?"

"Yes, my lord king."

"They believe the Hippodrome belongs to them and they will not allow anything but chariot racing. We would know how to deal with such loud clamor and foolish pretensions in *my* country. Here the rulers are afraid of them. What follows? My horses are at a breeding farm many miles beyond the gates. It is most inconvenient and I resent it bitterly. You must feel the same, for I am told you have a horse there also. A black stallion."

Eugenia nodded her head indifferently. "He is called Harthager."

"There have been only two horse races since you came and he has won them both."

"You will believe me, I am sure, when I tell you he ran in weak fields. Many of the Greens and Blues went to the first race. They laughed and scoffed. But there were more of them at the second. The attendance had doubled."

The Eastern king gave his head a patronizing shake. "They have been sound asleep here. About matters of state and the maintenance of armies and, it seems, about horses as well."

"It would be a great pleasure to see your Arabians in action."

"They are slender and trim and very sensitive. I am fond of them. They have good hearts and they are fast. I think well of Sulieman. Quite well."

"Perhaps it is in your mind that a match might be arranged."

The Easterner frowned. The servants had placed wine and fruit beside him and he was enjoying the coolness of the drink in his gold flagon. The wine at the Augusteon, where economies were being introduced by Marcian, had been most indifferently iced.

"The thought occurred to me. But I must explain that I am against matched races. I prefer a number of entries. It is always more exciting."

The lady from Tergeste thought this over. "It may be so," she said, with some reluctance. "I see no particular objection." She paused and studied his handsome dark face cautiously. "Is it your custom to lay wagers on your horses?"

The king gestured indifferently. "The race is what counts. To match my fine fellows against horses as fast, or faster. To see a close and hard finish. That is what provides the thrill. But when there is a desire on the part of others to make wagers, I am ready to meet them."

"I have little doubt that your Sulieman is fast enough to show his heels to Harthager but I would be disposed in spite of that to back the black. What odds would you give me?"

The king put down his flagon and turned to face her. "Odds!"

he cried. "When Sargon, King of Kings, went to war with little Samaria, did he expect odds? You have a great black stallion who has never been beaten and is the talk of all Constantinople. Yet you ask odds for him. Gentle lady, gracious lady, you demand not only the impossible but the absurd!"

The widow did not answer at once. "Well," she said, finally, "we can settle that later. I think you will come to see that the scales should be tipped in my favor. May I ask what you are prepared to wager, my lord king?"

Yussuff again displayed indifference in a gesture. "I leave that to you. I am prepared to match you evenly for any sum you care to mention."

Harthager's winnings had been colossal. Eugenia totaled them in her mind and then named the amount. It represented a fortune, even for an absolute monarch from a rich corner of the desert country. Watching her visitor closely, she observed that his color changed slightly and that his hand seemed to tremble; but in eagerness, not fear. She knew that he was pleased and excited.

"A large wager, my lady," declared the young monarch. "You must think very well indeed of your great black. Perhaps I should reconsider and ask for odds myself."

"Harthager is fast enough. And he belongs to the family of my little Ildico. I would rather lose heavily than hurt his fine reputation with a cowardly wager."

"I saw your black—at a distance. I cannot believe you will let this slender child whose name you mention take him into a race of this magnitude."

"Oh, yes." The widow spoke lightly. "Harthager was raised by her father. They get along together. Ildico will ride him as usual."

"I confess," said the king, "to a curiosity about this child who can manage such a huge and strong animal."

The widow clapped her palms together and ordered a servant to request the girl's presence in the room. Up to this point the desert ruler had been lounging in his chair while his hostess stood beside him. He sat very straight when Ildico entered in a few minutes, wearing a light green tunic and with her hair wound into braids on the top of her head. He did not rise but his eyes opened wide and from that first moment never left her face. There was a feeling of tensity, of drama, in the room.

"My lord king, I desire to present to you my ward, Ildico, daughter of Macio of the Roymarcks," said Eugenia. "Ildico, you have the honor of standing in the presence of the King of Davieda."

The girl bowed, keeping her eyes lowered in a proper manner. For several moments there was silence in the room. There was the look on the face of the imperious king of one who has unexpectedly encountered something of unimaginable beauty. He had boasted of his lack of interest in women but now his head was filled, quite obviously, with thoughts and speculations about this slender girl in green, standing so quietly before him.

"His August Majesty," said the widow, addressing Ildico, "has spoken of a match between his great Sulieman and our Harthager but he has doubts about the advisability of having you ride in such a race."

Yussuff was not listening. His mind had gone far away from the world of horses and racing. His eyes were on the face of the girl and, when he spoke finally, it was to display the intensity of the interest she had aroused in him.

"There is a brief moment each spring in my country," he began, "when the desert lands are covered with flowers of a beautiful and elusive shade of blue. Overnight the bare sands are transformed. For a few days we live with beauty all about us—and then the sun becomes so strong that the flowers fade and die. All year we live in the memory and in the expectation of more springs. . . . Your eyes, my lovely child, remind me of those moments on the desert. How perfectly they set off the gold in your hair!" He dragged his gaze away from Ildico and turned to his hostess. "My lady, you will understand now my reluctance about allowing her to race. The black is so huge and so strong! As the maker of the match, I would feel responsible if this delicate child sustained any injury."

"Harthager and I are friends," said Ildico, taking it on herself to answer. "From the moment he was foaled, he belonged to me. As a colt, he followed me everywhere. He would come and rub his ears against my arm. Anything I wanted him to do, he would understand; and off he would gallop in a hurry to obey me. Now that he has reached his top in strength and speed, he still knows what I want him to do and he is always quick to respond."

"You are planting the first doubts in my mind about the outcome of this race."

"My august lord," said Eugenia, "there will be no race if my ward does not ride him. Harthager will allow no one else on his back."

The Easterner nodded his head reluctantly. "Then we must accept the condition. But my zest in the race will be lacking. My anxiety will rob me of all pleasure in the contest."

2

The widow of Tergeste had little liking for her home in Constantinople. It stood almost in the shadow of the Column of Claudius and so was among the finest houses in the city, even being tall enough to yield over the sea wall a view of the blue surface of Marmora. But she found the grounds cramped and the fine mosaics and frescoes on the walls too minute. She had a preference for bold and solid colors.

"No purple bath!" she complained to Ildico, twisting back on her forehead a curling strand of hair. "You *must* have one if you are going to become a queen or an empress. Suppose that rich young king from the desert notices that we lack one? He'll be sure you were not born in the purple and that it's fated you are not to marry him."

"Why do you think he wants to marry me?" asked Ildico, in an indifferent tone. She was standing in a window where the steady breeze from the sea could be felt, and was thinking of Harthager. Was the king happy in the rich pastures? Or did he miss her?

"Why?" The Lady Eugenia sniffed scornfully. "He sends you a gift every day and, because he's of royal blood, insists you have nothing to do but accept. You've had a costly ruby ring, a gold necklace as old as Nebuchadnezzar, a bag coated with precious stones, and all these *wonderful* oriental perfumes. Doesn't he always write, 'Today I send you—'? That means it is going to be a habit, a daily habit." She paused and her brown eyes glistened with delight. "I wonder what it will be today? It's time for it to arrive."

It came almost immediately thereafter. Ildico read the note and opened the rich leather bag which accompanied it. Then she emitted a stifled shriek of horror and dropped the bag on the tiled floor. She continued to stare down at it as though expecting to see the head of a snake emerge from the opening.

"What is wrong?" asked the widow.

The girl moved far away from the bag. "What does he mean?" she gasped. "Is it a threat?"

Eugenia called to a servant to bring her the bag and then, with some caution, looked inside. She raised her eyebrows as she studied the gift. "No, not a threat," she commented. "I'm sure he meant them as a great compliment. There's a note inside. Shall I read it to you?"

"I won't take it out myself," declared Ildico, shuddering.

"He says these are the ears of a great king on the desert who opposed his father and lost his ears and his nose for doing so. They've brought him much luck, he says, and he hopes they will do the same for you."

Ildico crossed to the other side of the room, with the desire, no doubt, of putting as much space as possible between her and the gruesome trophies. It was a very warm day and she carried her sandals in her hand, in order to enjoy the coolness of the tiles on her feet. "I will tell Yussuff he is to take them back," she said. "I must not deprive him of such a source of luck."

"But he doesn't need them," said the widow. "He kept the nose for himself."

The donor of the dried but still bloodstained mementos of his father's triumph was announced a short time later. Ildico had to scramble to get the sandals on her feet before the king appeared in the room.

"My greetings, fair lady," he said, bowing to the chatelaine of the palace. "And to you, our lovely visitor from the sacred Mount of the Gods. You have had my gift today?"

"Yes, O King. But it would be wrong of me to rob you of so potent a talisman. I beseech you to receive it back."

The young ruler studied her face intently. "Perhaps it was ill advised. A display of too much confidence," he said. "I am going to need all the luck the gods can be persuaded to shower upon me." He turned briefly to the widow. "Gracious lady, may I have the opportunity of a few minutes alone with your fair charge?"

When the widow had withdrawn, wearing a smile from which she could not banish a sense of triumph, the young monarch began to speak with an earnest air.

"Lovely little Ildico!" he said. The gold of her hair intoxicated him. It sent forth a perfume far finer than all the varieties he had given her from the glamorous East. "Something very serious has come to pass. At first I was frightened, for it concerns you. Then I began to realize I should be happy. I could see that now you will no longer be able to dally and delay in giving me an answer. Only by marrying me can you hope to escape the danger that hangs over you." He paused, fixing his gleaming dark eyes on her face with a hungry determination. It was so silent in the room for a few moments that they could hear the faint splash as the ball fell in the water clock in the hall. It seemed as though the heat increased with every moment. Outside the sun struck fiercely on the white marble walls. "This morning," he then explained, "messengers arrived at court from Attila. It has come to his ears that you are here and he is demanding that the emperor find you and deliver you into the hands of his men. I do not understand quite what this is about. Had he selected you as a wife?"

"I don't know," whispered Ildico, whose cheeks had grown white. "He must have heard about me—and the horse. I think," she added, after a pause, "it is because of my hair. It's said he has a partiality for fair women."

The imperious young man from the desert nodded and then folded his arms with decision, the spotless sleeves falling back and revealing his fine muscles.

"This is fortunate," he said. He seemed on the point of explaining why he considered it fortunate that Ildico found herself in this dangerous situation but, reconsidering, he stopped short. After a moment he indulged in something between a laugh and a scornful snort. "This is all wrong, sweet child. I have told you my will in this matter. Should that not be enough? Is there anything you can do but bow your head in grateful assent?" Another pause. Then, with somber bitterness: "It seems there is something else you can do. You can refuse."

"I am afraid," said Ildico, "that I must."

The finely chiseled brown nostrils quivered. "It is not to be believed! I am a king. I must be obeyed. No one has ever crossed me or said no. Not even my father. Listen to me, my pretty child. I have a palace in the hills where it is cool. There is always snow and ice for the wine. There will be hundreds of servants to wait on us—none of them with a thought save of obedience. I am rich enough to cover your whole body with precious stones. It seems hard to believe but I—I have a feeling of love for you. Is it not enough that I, who never need do more than clap my hands, have made a long speech to you, giving you reasons—like a mangy court officer?"

"But—I am the daughter of the head of a proud race. My father is now an old man and not active but he too can bring servants with a mere clap of his hands."

"Then," declared the Eastern king, "I must tell you my plan. You will marry me. At once. Within the hour. Then the emperor can say to the agents of the infamous Attila, 'Yes, the Lady Ildico is here but she is the wife of Yussuff of Davieda.' That," he added, "is the only way you can be saved. Would the emperor refuse them otherwise? He wouldn't dare. He is a stout old soldier, this Marcian, but why would he let the disposal of a young woman involve him with this terrible Hun? No, he would be sensible and hand you over."

A line appeared in the middle of the girl's broad white brow. She did not doubt that what he said was true. Her presence in the city, in the company of the always conspicuous widow, was known generally. The Eastern Empire had been dancing for years to the crack of the Hun's whip. She could expect no other treatment than to be handed over to Attila's men. Marriage with this handsome young ruler from the desert would be infinitely better than to be carried off into captivity by the Huns; and yet she found it impossible to accept the alternative. Her mind was filled with doubts and strange fears. How could she face either fate?

The heat of the day was growing so intense that the thick marble walls of the palace offered small resistance. She had never experienced anything like it before. It was becoming hard to think.

"Is there a man?" The voice of Yussuff was sharp, inquisitive, demanding. "Have you some silly fancy in your head?"

"I—I am not sure."

"You must be sure. If there is a man, I must be told of him."

"I was thinking of a boy who grew up with my brother and me." Ildico was speaking in hesitant tones. "I have seen him only once since. There are reasons why I should never think of him again."

The king had taken to pacing up and down. His eyes were fixed on the intricately tiled floor and he was frowning. It was clear he was trying to adjust himself to the absurdities which the situation held for him. He stopped and drew a ring from his finger, holding it up in the light of the sun where it sparkled fabulously. Then, suddenly impatient with his purpose in displaying it, he tossed it in the air and did not look to see where it fell.

"I thought of offering it to you. The ransom of an emperor or the price of hundreds of pretty girls. Let it go. I shall offer no more bribes." He was holding himself up very straight. "I have one last thing to say to you, my stubborn daughter of the sun. We shall make a wager."

Ildico raised her eyes at this. A wager?

"This race we have been talking of holding—between the beautiful, slim horses of the desert and this great black stallion. It must be held at once. Quietly, so no one will know until it is over. Tomorrow, if that course out beyond the walls is ready. Or the day after, at the latest. If one of my horses wins the race —and I would be unfair if I did not tell you that I can conceive of no other outcome—you will marry me. If the black wins, I pledge myself to arrange your escape from the city. I pledge the lives of all the men in my train to getting you safely away; all twenty of them. Is that fair enough to suit you?"

"Why do you think you can arrange my escape?"

"I have a plan. A clever plan. If there is any danger in it, the risk is for those who remain and not for you." He glanced at her shrewdly. "Are you asking yourself, 'If this plan is so good, why does he not get me away at once?' If you *are* thinking that, my answer is that I am not generous enough. I love you too much. I must have my chance."

A feeling of relief had begun to chase the despair from her mind. She had no more doubt of the outcome of the race than he had. Harthager could not be beaten by any of the handsome but spindly horses from the desert, even though it was said they could run like the wind. She knew he would win. And because the king was equally sure that his graceful Arabians could out-run her great king, it was a fair match.

"Well?" He was regarding her with impatience. "Is it still so hard to make up your mind?"

"I accept," she said.

The weather changed early in the evening and the breeze which came in from the Sea of Marmora was strong enough to set the silver oil lamp over the table to swinging slowly back and forth on its chain.

"I have had two notes," said the widow, looking with anticipation at the fish on her plate and covering it with a garum sauce. "One was from the man who aspires to be your husband, dear child, our proud and handsome young king. He informs me that the course needs attention and that the race cannot be run for two days."

Ildico was not displaying much appetite. "I'm glad of that," she said. "I'll be able to take Harthager over it at least once again. It's rather tricky."

"How does he feel about it?"

"Who? Harthager? My dear Aunt, you are making fun of me again. You don't believe I can understand what is going on in that beautiful long head of his. Well, let me tell you this, he is as sure of winning as we are. He doesn't like the Arabians at all. They stand around together and whisper about him. They are all unfriendly. Sulieman tosses his mane. Dear Aunt, he has made up his mind to run his very best in order to beat them easily."

"I hope," said the widow, "you told him how much I stand to lose if he doesn't win."

"No, money is one of the things he does not understand."

Eugenia glanced sympathetically at her ward. "Suppose something goes wrong and he doesn't win?"

Ildico looked up with sudden gravity. "If he doesn't win, I will —I will spend the rest of my life on a hot desert as one of the wives of a proud and quick-tempered Eastern king. He has other wives, I am sure."

The Lady Eugenia reached across the table and patted her companion's hands. "Two. I have made inquiries. But he pays no attention to them. You will be his favorite, of course."

"Until he marries again. I'm afraid I shall have to wear the veil."

The widow nodded. "There will be no changes made in the customs if I have judged the young man correctly. I have watched him and I'm sure he is angry because these two old men who come with him have seen your face. It would not surprise me if he had their heads lopped off as soon as they get back."

Ildico was silent for a few moments. "Harthager must win," she said, finally. "He *must*."

"He will, dear child. Just whisper in his ear how important it is for you."

"I have done that already."

The widow had begun on her fish. "Now for the other note I received. It seems that I—that I really am a widow now."

Ildico looked up quickly. "What do you mean?"

"I mean that I was not a widow before. My third husband, who was a mean and stupid old man, disappeared and later it got around that he was dead. By that time I was beginning to see advantages in being a widow and I was quite willing to accept the news as true. But I was never sure of it. He was full of crafty tricks and I thought he might be trying to tempt me into marrying again. Then he would come back and try to recover all of the property he had transferred to me. I let people think I was a widow but I put all thoughts of marriage out of my mind."

"Are you sure that he *is* dead?"

The newly made widow nodded her head. "He's as dead as great Caesar. The letter gave full particulars. It seems he has been living a secretive existence in Antioch with only half a dozen slaves and a plump young mistress. If you ask me for my opinion, I suspect the mistress had stood as much of him as she could and put some poison in his soup." She eyed a spitted dove with a ginger dressing and decided to try it. "It's a great relief to know for certain. Now I am free to do as I please. I think perhaps I *shall* marry again."

"I hope," said Ildico, earnestly, "that you won't marry an old man with money this time."

"The man I marry," answered the widow, "must not be older than I am and he must be handsome. He must be patrician and have a little money of his own. Not too much. If he is wealthy, he will give me orders and perhaps look down on me. On the other hand, if he has no property I will get to despise him in time."

"Must he be from Rome?"

The feeling which prevailed in the provinces manifested itself in the promptness of the widow's reply. "From Rome, I trust. But he must not be in politics. I must manage to keep this one longer. To have four husbands is not wise, even if one has been the victim of circumstances. To have five would be a calamity. They would begin to tell jokes about me. People would say of a man, 'Well, at any rate he has never been married to that woman from Tergeste.'" The widow sighed. "I don't know why I married that last one. He was a scrubby little creature with a sparse red beard. Of course, he was *very* rich.

"My first husband," she went on, "was the *praefectus urbis* of Rome and you can imagine the endless opportunities he had to gather fees and make profits. My second husband was a most amusing man. He made witty and biting remarks about everyone. Unfortunately some of the ill-natured things he said about prominent men in the Senate and even in the army came back to their ears. They decided his wit was too fine a thing for this life and should be employed instead for the amusement of the gods. As he was such a very distinguished man, he was executed in the most genteel way. Which is to pour molten gold down the throat.

"My third husband was a mistake," she continued. "I knew it at the time but he gave me no peace until I said yes in desperation. You see, he was a plebe and he was always treated with scorn by the patricians. He tried so hard! I think there was always a hint of hot pipes and steam about him. He had found a way of carrying very hot water to the baths and all who used them had to pay him a certain fee each year. Can you conceive of what this meant? Think of the hundreds of public baths alone!

"And, of course, all the wealthy people wanted the hot water in their houses. They had to pay so much a year. There was one great senator who found hot baths so comforting that he fell into the habit of taking seven every day. It was said at the time of his death that too much bathing had killed him. My husband denied this bitterly. He claimed no one could take too many baths a day."

"How many did *he* take?"

"Well," she answered, "he was rather averse to bathing himself. I suppose he was so busy collecting his fees all day that he liked to put them out of his mind at home. And, of course, all the wits of Rome were having things to say about him. Calling him the Caesar of Cleanliness and suggesting he be given the right, although he was a civilian, to carry a shield with a towel stamped on it. It was this which drove him into retirement. He settled down in the East. I didn't go with him and, in fact, I had no word from him for years before his death. I did hear it said that during his last years he never took a bath. It was his way of expressing bitterness for the cause of his lack of social success." She sighed ruefully. "Now that he's dead legally, I'm afraid the Senate will refuse to pay me any of the hot-water tax."

CHAPTER II

1

IT was early on the following morning. The tall Briton, standing where the fishing boat had landed him on the stone steps, looked about him at the high peaks of Constantinople in wonder. He had expected it would be much like Rome but at his first glance as they heaved and tossed on the Sea of Marmora, he had realized how different it was. The stamp of the East was on it: the rounded domes, the minarets, the barbaric (they seemed so to him) colors. And now sounds were reaching his ears to complete the sensation of change, voices speaking in Koine, the commercial Greek which was taking the place of Latin, camels voicing their snarling complaints, a constant jingle of bells.

It was a very hot day but here again it was different from the humid heat of Rome; a constant breeze blew down the small sea and cooled his skin.

A voice from the top of the steps hailed him in a rapid tongue. He raised his hands and gave his head a shake to indicate his lack of understanding. The speaker, a stout fellow who found it unnecessary to protect his bald head from the fierce rays of the sun, was superintending the landing of netloads of fish from the vessel in which Ivar had made his crossing. After a moment the man spoke in Latin.

"Who are you?"

Ivar answered: "I was born in a country so far away you may never have heard of it. I am a Briton and my name is Ivar."

"These fellows are not allowed to take strangers. How did you get aboard?"

"I paid nothing, if that's what you mean; but if you're the owner, I'll pay you what you think fair. I spun a tale of great need which your men believed."

The stout man grunted as he assisted in the landing of a particularly well-filled net. "You might lend us a hand here," he said.

Ivar took hold of the load at which three of them had been pulling and hauling, swung it over his shoulder, and carried it up to the cart at the head of the steps. The owner watched him in wonder.

"A gladiator!" he declared. "Do you want work?"

Ivar shook his head. "I want directions. Perhaps you can help me."

"When we get all this loaded, my man."

The warehouse of the fish merchant was not far from the water front. The owner drained a mug of wine with a smack of his lips but did not offer the Briton any share of the refreshment.

"Now," he said.

Ivar spoke in low tones. "I have come in advance—I earnestly trust—of emissaries of Attila. I must warn two people to be away from here before they arrive. If not, your own emperor may face a difficult decision—and perhaps the danger of war."

A scowl had crossed the fish merchant's face at the mention of Attila. He motioned over his shoulder with a thumb covered with scales. "See that white palace. It's the Augusteon. Take your story there."

"But I'm not sure it would be wise yet. It may be your emperor would rather not know about these people I come to see. It's possible also that Attila's men have already arrived. The safest plan would be to find where my friends are and speak to them first."

The urgency in the Briton's tone seemed to carry conviction to the dealer in fish. "My name is Polotius," he said, grudgingly, as though parting with the secret of his identity was a sacrifice he did not enjoy. Then he added with a deep scowl, "The Huns wiped out the village where I come from. They drove all the people into a church and burned it to the ground. Two brothers of mine were in it." After a pause, he added, "There's someone I can send you to."

Ivar, his wonder growing with every step he took in the streets of this bizarre city, passed through three hands and finally found himself at the gate of a stone house close to the Column of Claudius. It was set in spacious grounds and bore all the outward marks of wealth. A servant with a peculiarly villainous expression scowled at him through the close pattern in an iron gate.

"Who are you?"

"I come with a message for your mistress."

"The like of you? My mistress would have me beaten if I let you in."

Ivar explained patiently. "My name is Ivar. Go and tell your mistress. She will want to see me."

"Be on your way!" ordered the servant, who had climbed up the gate to get a better look at the visitor over the top.

Ivar studied the gate and then took hold of it in both hands. Without much difficulty, he raised it off its hinges and carried it, with the servant clinging to his hold, inside the grounds.

A high and pleasant voice reached Ivar from the gardens in the rear of the palace. He heard the owner of it say, "What is this?" It was not hard for him to identify the slender girl who came into sight; nor, it seemed, for her to recognize him.

"It cannot be anyone else," she said. "Who else could be so strong?" She was looking in some wonder at his great height. "You are the one who came from Britain. Your name is Ivar."

"Yes, I am Ivar," said the Briton. "I bring a message from your father."

Ildico motioned to the servant. "Tell your mistress at once. And send as many as will be needed to put the gate back in place." The pleased excitement with which she had greeted him had died out of her face. "From my father? Is he—is he not well?"

"I saw him briefly. Because of the need for haste, I stayed less than an hour. He had been ill and it seemed to me he was still weak."

"I must go back at once. If I delay, it may be too late."

"My lady, it is to warn you not to return home that I have come." He explained what Macio had said and repeated her father's advice to proceed at once to Tergeste.

Ildico heard him through with a worried fown. "Attila's men are already here," she said. "They arrived two days ago."

The tall visitor believed there was reproof in what she said, and hurried to explain. "I came as fast as I could. But the lands I had to pass through were all strange to me. I couldn't make out a word of what anyone said. I lost time that way."

"You mustn't think I am blaming you," said the girl. "It is a miracle that you are here. Was it a very hard journey?"

"Very hot and dusty. I felt suffocated most of the time. I didn't dare drink any of the water and the innkeepers cheated me when I ordered wine."

"Did you walk the whole distance?"

The broad sun-browned face of the Briton showed a hint of a smile. "How else could I get here? You see, I am a poor rider. A horse knows it as soon as I get in the saddle and takes its own head. I soon find myself on the wrong road. And, of course, I had to come overland. It would have taken too long to come around Greece by boat."

"We had better go in now. Eugenia will want to see you. And we must talk about what's best to be done."

2

The widow was very glad to see him. She looked him up and down with a discerning eye.

"So, it *was* you," she said. "I saw you in the garden but I couldn't be sure." She had gone to considerable pains, nevertheless, to look her best. Her sand-colored palla was worn under a close-fitting gown of rich blue, a combination of colors which suited her eminently well. When she took a step it could be seen that the sandals on her small feet were gold, a luxury generally reserved for the wives of rulers. They were richly inlaid with precious stones. "Every time I see you, I have to get acquainted all over again. You keep changing. The last time you were round and as red-cheeked as a boy; and now you are as brown as an Arab chief and as thin as a shide of wood."

"I was losing weight with every step I took," explained Ivar.

"You seem to be very strong people, you black singers. Which reminds me that you never sing. At least, I have never heard you."

"I can't sing," he responded, smiling.

"Nor," she said, "have you ever been black. I was sure you had returned long ago to your native land."

Ivar frowned. "It has always been in my mind to go. But how can I get there? No ships sail to Britain since the Romans withdrew. I would have to make my way through endless forests to reach the Channel. If I got across, I would be lucky to find anyone I knew alive. I don't know what I could do to make a living. I have no trade and those who work on the land are no better than slaves."

"You are talking sense," commented the widow, approvingly. "My advice is to stay here and forget all about your savage little island."

In order to discuss what was to be done, Eugenia then drew them into a corner of the room. "I had a message this morning," she said. "From our desert friend. He says an order is being issued for special guards to be put on all the city gates. He expects also that the emperor will post men about our grounds here."

"Then the race can't be held," said Ildico. It was clear that she was relieved. She would now be free of the consequences of defeat, even though other dangers had opened up.

The widow shook her head. "The race will be held. Yussuff has seen to that. He went at once to the emperor and told him what had been planned. You remember, Ildico, the emperor was at both the races Harthager won and he went nearly mad with excitement. As soon as he heard about tomorrow, he insisted there must be no change in the plan. A company of his scholarians will be stationed around the course, to make sure we don't get away."

"Then we won't be able to escape!" cried Ildico.

"We'll escape in spite of the emperor and his scholarians. Yussuff told me not to worry. If we get to the course, nothing will prevent his plan from succeeding. But he doesn't expect to use it. He's more certain than ever that Sulieman will win."

Ildico nodded somberly. "We are going to be badly handicapped. They know Sulieman is the only one who has a chance, and the others in the race will see to it that Harthager is held back."

"The king is too honorable for that!" exclaimed the widow. "He won't try to win by foul means. I'm sure he won't let his riders conspire against us."

"It isn't the riders we have to fear," said Ildico. "It's the horses."

"Do you mean the other horses will see to it that he doesn't have a chance?" cried Eugenia.

"That is what I mean."

The widow responded to that with one word which meant something on the order of "rubbish!" People who spoke the Latin tongue had an appropriate word for it, without a doubt, but the word has long since been lost in the mists of antiquity. "Are you now going to tell me," she went on, "that you got this information from Harthager?"

"Dear Aunt, my people have been for centuries the best breeders of horses in the world. They know many things that no other race has any conception of. When I was a small girl, our head trainer taught one of our mares to count. He would say to her, 'Two and three,' and she would nod her head five times. Don't look at me like that. I am telling the truth. I saw it with my own eyes."

Eugenia repeated her expression of disbelief and derision. "You will be saying next that horses can talk."

"No," was the answer. "No horse can talk but they can convey certain things to you. They always know when there is to be a race. The trainer who taught the little mare to count used to say that they sometimes decided among themselves who was to be the winner. The Arab horses don't like the king. They think he is some kind of strange monster. They don't intend to let him win the race. Tomorrow they will do their best."

Eugenia asked in a sarcastic tone, "And the king has told you about it?"

"Not exactly. But I saw that, whenever he was in the same pasture with them, they never let him get near Sulieman. If he made a move, they would get in his way at once. It was like an army squad. Twice he came back to me in a puzzled and angry mood." She gave her head an emphatic nod. "I have no doubt whatever that tomorrow they will run him off to the side of the course and try to keep him there."

Eugenia got to her feet. "I still say it is all nonsense. I hope it is, because I stand to lose a fortune if the black isn't allowed to make his run. And you, dear child, have more reason to fear the outcome than I have. But *if* we can get to the course, and *if* the black wins, I must be ready to leave immediately with you. That means we must have all our arrangements made at once. I must get my people to work."

She sauntered in the direction of the door but came to a stop in front of Ivar. He was wearing a curious conglomeration of garments, including a tunic of as many colors as the coat of Joseph.

"Is this intended as a disguise?" she asked.

He indulged in a rather shamefaced smile. "All my clothes were stolen several nights back at a filthy little inn. I had to buy anything I could find."

His tunic was tied at the neck by a scarlet cord with tassels at both ends. Eugenia reached out and gave one of the tassels an upward flick. It struck him on the tip of his nose.

"What a time you chose to come back!" she said.

When she had passed out of the room, Ivar looked at Ildico with a puzzled frown. "What did she mean?"

Ildico was striving to suppress a smile. "Can't you guess?" she asked.

"I have no idea at all."

"It's a delicate matter to discuss when we are still strangers. But I think she was serving notice that she has selected you."

"Selected me? For what?"

"For her next husband."

The lower jaw of the tall Briton dropped in an expression of complete incredulity. He gazed blankly at his companion for a moment and then indulged in a rueful smile.

"You are laughing at me."

"No, I am not laughing at you. I am very much in earnest. You see, I know her. And I can tell that she has matrimony in her eye."

"But—but not me! I am a barbarian. An ex-slave. I have no land and no prospects. There are a few coins left in my purse and that is all I possess. This is nonsense."

"No, she means it. She's in a marrying mood. I saw how her face lighted up when she came in and found you here."

The tall visitor was not yet convinced. "Then it won't last. She'll change her mind quickly enough."

"Don't be too sure. And let me tell you this: when she makes up her mind, it is impossible to resist her. Yes, she'll get you no matter what your wishes on the question may be. If you don't want to become her fourth husband, there's just one thing to do."

"What is that?"

"Leave. At once. Not by the front entrance where you could be seen. You must go out by the gate in the garden wall. And you must never come back."

CHAPTER III

1

THE PARTY was ready to leave the next morning when Eugenia saw the tip of a bronze helmet above the stone gate. She called to Ildico: "They've come. Keep out of sight." Then she produced a length of black material and began to wind it about the girl's head until not so much as a wisp of golden hair remained in sight.

"You must not be recognized," she said.

Ildico was always uncomfortable when her head was bound up in this way. She protested that there was no need for such precautions. Attila's men knew already that she was in Constantinople.

"We can't be sure how much they know, or how little," declared the widow. "This is the largest city in the world. At court they may have been sensible enough to keep their mouths closed and, if they have, the Huns would have a fine time locating you. We must ride now from one end of the city to the other and it would be the height of folly to—to flaunt this much-talked-about hair of yours in the face of the whole population."

The captain at the front gate looked carefully at his written instructions before allowing the key to be turned. "It says two of you. And three servants. Two men and one woman. This one," glancing suspiciously at Ivar, who sat uncomfortably astride a broad-backed horse. "Is he the one who lifted this gate off its hinges yesterday? Your servants told me about it."

When she discovered that Ivar had not left, Ildico had smiled at him slyly, as though to say, "So, you are still with us after all."

"He is the one who lifted the gate," said Eugenia.

The captain studied the broad frame of Ivar. "Didn't the Jews have a fellow who carried off the gates of a city? Named Samson, I think."

"I have never heard of him," declared the widow. "This is a friend of mine and his name is not Samson. He is going with us to see a race this afternoon."

The captain nodded bitterly. "Everyone is going to see this same race. Except us. We must stand on guard here to satisfy some Huns sent by Attila." He gestured to them to start. "I am a captain in the imperial guards. Must I ask questions to satisfy a pair of bloodthirsty Huns? I have not seen this lifter of gates. Be on your way, ladies. And I hope"—winking at Ildico—"that the big black wins this afternoon."

They went at a trot past the grounds of the Library and turned on to the much-used road circling the Baths of Zeuxippes. The mighty Hippodrome loomed high above them, as impressive as any of the arenas of Rome. Not a sound reached them from within.

The widow glanced at Ildico. "No chariot races today. That captain must have been right. The secret is out and the people are going to see our race."

"The king is never disturbed by crowds," said Ildico. "I suspect he likes them."

When they turned off the Mese, the great commercial street of the city, the aspect of things changed. The quiet and emptiness gave way to noise and bustle and confusion. The thoroughfares leading to the west were filled with people, some on horseback, some in crowded carts, some walking in great haste.

No attention was paid to them until they turned on a street which skirted the Aqueduct. A man who was walking as fast as his bare feet would carry him stopped suddenly and raised a cry.

"That's her!" pointing a finger at Ildico. "That's the girl who rides the black horse."

A scoffing voice spoke from the crowd. "I can't see your sleeve but I know it carries the green stripe! Who but a Green would think that little bag of bones could ride the stallion?"

"Your words give you away more surely than the blue stripe, that badge of ignorance, on *your* sleeve!" cried the first speaker. "I swear she's the one. I can tell her by the set of her head and the way she sits that horse."

"By the iron claws of Moloch, we are all ignorant and blind, Blues and Greens alike," declared the Blue. "By running like sheep to watch this race we are doing our part to make an end of the chariots—and perhaps of Blues and Greens as well. Do you know the Hippodrome is empty today? Do you know the emperor has passed here on his way to watch this race? I tell you this is the start of something new."

"There will always be chariot races!" cried the Green.

"I would be happy if I could agree. But never have I known a Green to be right about anything!"

Hearing all this, the party started to ride as rapidly as they could through the crowded streets. Ivar, lumbering along in the rear, found it hard to keep up.

2

The course was laid out on a flat ledge of land between the hills and the Aqueduct, a distance in all of something more than a mile and less than two. Tall posts, which served as markers, carried large flags, already fluttering in the late morning breeze as though agitated in advance by the tension of the crowds lining the oval. The thick sod on which the race would be held stretched away in all directions, as green and smooth as the Elysian Fields where the gods are stirred sometimes to the matching of their winged horses. A stand had been erected on the inner side of the point where the contests began and ended. This was for the accommodation of the judges and other officials. Behind it were the horse sheds.

On the opposite side an old palace had been converted into a royal box by tearing out the marble walls in front. Here, against a background of purple velvet, Marcian was already seated, looking very stern and kingly. He was in a white silk tunic embroidered in roundels, over which was draped a mantle in purple of the type called a chlamys, a Greek innovation in costume. On his shoulder was the usual Byzantine clasp to hold everything together, a tablion, decorated with triple strings of precious stones.

The old emperor sat quietly in the midst of incessant noise and constant movement. Courtiers came and went. Guards stood in all corners, the sun glinting on their shields and drawn swords. On the level below an orchestra provided music of an oriental variety, loud, redundant, and filled with dissonance. A group of ladies sat behind the veteran basileus (the title of the emperor) and indulged in much twittering talk. On the open ground at one side of the building a series of tables had been set up with food and wine free for the public; for such as were lucky enough, at least, to get through the throngs surrounding them. There was a suggestion of meagerness about this gesture. As already stated, Marcian was not openhanded and he had proclaimed a period of retrenchment.

Already there was a solid bank of spectators on each side of the course who could not be tempted from their positions of vantage by the prospect of imperial largesse. More people were streaming through the gates in seemingly endless files.

As they rode in through the main gate, the party of three heard a voice say: "Has the basileus lost his senses? They say he's betting on the black."

Many voices were raised at once to support the judgment of the emperor. As they picked their way through the milling crowds, nevertheless, the trio heard everywhere the name of the Arabian champion, "Sulieman," "Sulieman," "Sulieman." It was clear that King Yussuff's thoroughbred had caught the public fancy.

Yussuff himself met them inside the gate, riding a glossy black mare and attired in a costume that was barbaric in its sheer splendor. His eyes glistened as they rested on Ildico with what could be translated as a proprietary gleam. Nevertheless he contented himself with a deep bow before beginning to speak to Eugenia in low tones. Then, with a lift of a jeweled hand in the air, he whisked the little mare about and was swallowed up in the crowd.

"He says we are to have no fear," said the widow. "All arrangements have been made."

"He seems confident," said Ildico, in a subdued tone. She was thinking that marriage with this resplendent potentate might offer moments of glamour but that it could be no better than slavery. They must win!

The party attracted no attention until it came to the entrance of the horse sheds. Here Borean, who was in charge of Harthager, came out to greet them. There were beads of perspiration on his brow.

"My lady, I was afraid you would not be able to get here," he said, his eyes still rolling with agitation. "They tell me the roads are so filled with people that it's impossible now to get through."

"Calm yourself," said the widow. "For here we are. How is the Great One?"

The trainer frowned and rubbed his unshaven chin. "He keeps watching. For my lady here. I've never known him to be so uneasy. He is rolling his eyes and swishing his tail."

There were a number of trainers and helpers in the end of the horse sheds which had been assigned to the Western champion. Ildico's eyes went at once to the great black bulk of Harthager in the farthest corner and it seemed to her that he was in a state of nerves to justify the uneasiness of Borean. If anyone tried to get near him, a heel would lash out and he would trumpet his displeasure. He gave her no sign of recognition.

"Has to depend on his eyes at this distance," whispered Borean. "I guess that black thing on your head puzzles him. Don't go near him until he's certain it's you."

But Ildico had no fears. "O King!" she cried. "My fine one, I am here."

Without hesitation she walked up to the stallion and laid a caressing hand on his silky mane. "Didn't you know me? Ah, my great one, I must wear this hideous thing on my head but I don't like it any more than you did when they painted a star on your beautiful black nose and made you wear the blanket of a common pack horse."

Harthager's uneasiness had already left him. He shook his head and stamped with excited hoofs, emitting at the same time a whinny of welcome.

"King," whispered Ildico, "today we must ride as we have never ridden before. We must be fast enough to catch that wind we have chased so often in the hills but have never caught. These little horses from the desert are fast, my great king, but you—you should have no trouble with them."

A trumpet sounded from the judges' stand outside. A slight shiver seemed to pass over the taut frame of the great horse. Then he raised his head and prepared to turn about. He knew what the trumpet note meant.

Ildico removed the robe she had worn on the ride down and stood in silence for several moments, her eyes fixed on a part of the course visible through a window. She looked very slender and young in a white tunic which fitted her shoulders and waist snugly and a skirt loose enough to divide like trousers and thus allow her to ride astride. She looked down doubtfully at her riding boots. They were masculine, nothing suitable of the kind having yet been devised for feminine use; and so, although they were the smallest to be found, they were still loose and not secure on her small feet. "They will fall off," she thought. "They always do. And people will scramble and fight for them. Why can't I discard them now and be comfortable?" But on second thought she decided to wear them. There had been enough criticism already of a lady riding thus in public.

She laid a hand on the shoulder of the black and, without any assistance, vaulted to his back. Borean unsnapped the chains. There was a loud clatter of hoofs as Harthager backed out from his stall. He tossed his head high and emitted a shrill note of challenge.

"He knows!" cried the trainer.

Ildico leaned down so that her lips were close to his ear. "My king," she whispered, her voice tense and her eyes brimming with tears, "you must win today or I will be in very great trouble. I will be taken far off. To a country where they have nothing but Arabian horses. I will never see you again. I will never see any of the ones I love. And, O King, I love them so much, so very much! I will soon pine away. Today you must do your best for your poor lady!"

The eyes of Borean took in the magnificent lines of the black. "He will run his best!" he cried, his confidence fully restored.

But the grooms and handlers stood about in glum groups. "The odds favor the Arab," she heard one of them say, as she patted a shiny left ear and rode out into the fierce sunlight.

Ildico gave one hurried glance at the imperial box. She saw the stocky form of the emperor straighten up in taut anticipation. She saw the musicians on the lower level sawing away at the strings and blowing lustily into their pipes. On a bench some short distance from the orchestra, she saw three dark-visaged guests who wore the peaked round hats with red tufts of the Hun army. She was glad now of the dark headdress and fingered it anxiously. It must not be allowed to tear loose in the violence of the race.

A silence fell on the great crowd as she guided the black to the starting point.

3

The Arabian horses were streaming out from the other end of the sheds. There were five of them, Sulieman in the lead. This was an assumption on Ildico's part, for she had never seen Sulieman. But the rider had a purple headdress and wide purple bands on his sleeves and that seemed conclusive enough.

Ildico did not like the look of things at all. It had already been announced that Sulieman was to have the inside position (for, after all, he had a royal master) and two outside entries were next, a Turcoman and a Scythian mare. The remaining Arabians would have Harthager in a pocket, two on each side.

"I protested," Eugenia had said on the ride through the city, "but Yussuff contended there was no unfairness about it. With more than a quarter mile to the first turn, a fast entry could gain the lead, no matter what position he held."

A boy had been maneuvering about inside the sheds, a small specimen in shapeless and grubby white, with eyes as sharp as a monkey's; asking questions, trying to be useful, and full to overflowing about the race. He was the son of someone connected obscurely with the grounds. Now he came up to Harthager's side and squinted at Ildico.

"Lady," he said, "my honorable father is wrong. So are all these other honorable fathers who are afraid of the Arab. Lady, the black is going to win. He let me edge in beside him this morning. Just for a minute, lady. I knew he was angry because there were only strangers around him and he was lonely for you. It wasn't because he was afraid of the race. He has taken on the edge, lady. Oh, what a fine edge!"

"What is your name, boy?"

"Malhudi, lady."

"You make me feel better, Malhudi."

"But, lady," said the boy, earnestly, "you won't win if you keep that thing on your head. You've always let your hair loose before.

I don't know just what about it but I think it means something."

"Perhaps you are right, Malhudi."

The horses fell into line and paraded up the track for the emperor to look them over, Sulieman in the lead and Harthager in sixth position. When they were brought into line, Ildico looked at the riders on either side of her and became somewhat reassured. There was no hint of slyness or villainy about them. They smiled at her, displaying rows of the finest white teeth. One of them said something in his native tongue and the other translated in halting Latin.

"He says, 'It will be a fine race, fairest lady.'"

But when the clashing of cymbals from the stand raised a mighty roar from the spectators and threw the line into furious action, her worst fears were instantly confirmed. The horse on her right had veered in so close that the leg of the rider pinned her to Harthager's flank. At the same instant the Arabian on her left had been brought a full stride ahead, so that the pair of them formed a triangle. She tapped Harthager's ear and in response he eased his pace with the intention of cutting in toward the center. It was apparent instantly that this maneuver could not succeed. The second horse on her left had fallen back a stride also and barred all chance of escape there. Two horses on each side, determined to hold her in confinement! Already Sulieman was out in front. Well out and running free.

Ildico realized that whatever she did to escape this encirclement must be done at once. Deciding on her course, therefore, she tapped the right flank of the black and brought him almost to a walk. The others could not check their speed in time and she was able to turn sharply out to the extreme right of the course.

"Fast, fast, fast!" she cried.

She knew that the ground along the outer edge was rough and that a drainage ditch about four feet wide added to the difficulty of passing there. But she had not realized the full extent of the handicap she had assumed. The black had to proceed gingerly and set his feet down at each stride with great caution. A hostile formation, running slantwise across the track, made it impossible for her to get back.

Deciding on a mad effort, she waved frantically to the spectators to stand back from the side of the course. It took many precious seconds for them to understand what she meant and then they seemed to respond doubtfully. In sheer desperation she took a chance, turning Harthager into the first gap that seemed wide enough to admit them. The spectators, shouting in wild alarm, scattered like pigeons before the swoop of a hawk. It was necessary to ride slowly at first to avoid running any of them down and the golden seconds passed inexorably away before she saw a clear path ahead.

"Now, King, now!"

Word of what had happened sped ahead of them and the path was opened wider by the urge of self-preservation. The sod was level here and soon the black was pounding along with great strides of his long legs. On the track the delaying squadron, which had slowed along the edge of the ditch to block any attempt at return, now found themselves compelled to desperate speed to keep pace with the flying Harthager.

At the turn into the wide curve of the course, she saw that a short gap had opened between her and the pursuing Arabians. Was it wide enough to get back into action with no danger of further interference? She decided to try.

"In!" she cried.

The black cleared the ditch at one bound and fell into his even stride again. The nearest of the opposition was a full length behind.

"We are free of them!" For an exultant instant in time, Ildico was filled with pride over the success of her maneuver. Harthager was in the clear and there would be no more interference.

4

Eugenia stood in the enclosure in front of the imperial box and wept openly. The crowd was so thick in front of her that she could not see the course; but Ivar, standing high up like a flesh-and-blood tower, had been able to follow what was happening and report to her.

"We've lost," she said, in a piteous tone. "Why did she take the black into the crowd like that? Oh, I know they had her crowded but that has happened before. Why didn't she wait for a chance to break out!"

"I don't know anything about racing," said the tall Briton, "but it seemed to me they had her in a vise. And Sulieman was almost out of sight."

Suddenly there was a roar from the spectators massed along both sides of the course. People shouted in violent excitement, waving their arms, jumping up and down. Eugenia seized Ivar's nearest arm.

"What is it? What has happened?"

The Briton said something in answer but the din about them was so great that she could not hear a word. "Speak louder!" she cried, her grip on his arm tightening.

He leaned down until his face almost touched hers. "She's clear!" he cried.

"She's clear? What a wonderful feat of riding! Ildico, my brave child, why did I ever doubt you?"

"Harthager came out with a bound and sailed across the ditch magnificently. He's on the track again and running like mad."

"And I missed it! Ah, this absurd, back-country track where no one can see what goes on! Why did I agree to hold the race in this miserable trap? And why, oh, why did I let that smooth, smiling son of Satan talk me into making it an open race?"

The spectators continued to shout in amazement at the sudden change in the situation. Someone rushed up to the stand where the white-haired trio of judges sat and began to address them vehemently. "I know what that's about," commented Eugenia, bitterly. The heads of the judges were about all she could see. "He wants the king ruled off for leaving the track." People who had laid their wagers on Harthager and had been brought back from the tomb of their hopes to a new span of life saw danger in the colloquy on the stand. They began to hiss and boo and scream in fury. Those who had bet on Sulieman were crying out in righteous wrath that the black must be barred.

"Ivar, Ivar!" cried Eugenia. "Have we a chance?"

He surveyed the field with an intent and rather dubious eye. "It's too soon to say. But—but the other horse has a great lead. We mustn't get our hopes too high."

The veteran race-lover in Eugenia asserted itself. "You are never beaten until they drop the flag."

The owner of Sulieman, so recently and bitterly characterized as a smooth, smiling son of Satan, came toward them, elbowing his way through the milling and noisy throng. He might be a king in Davieda but at this moment he was just another troublesome human being to the excited watchers. His face carried an air of triumph.

"The race is won," he said to the widow. "Of course our fair lady is of fighting stock and will make some kind of contest of it."

"The black is gaining," declared Ivar, not taking his eyes from the distant stretch where, it seemed, toy horses were moving on leaden feet.

"There will be no miracle," asserted the king. "It may be that the judges will bar your horse for leaving the track."

"There is no rule against it!" cried the widow. "Let me up there and I'll lay down the whole scroll of the law to them!"

The face of Yussuff lost its look of elation and became grave. "No matter what they say or do," he declared, "it will not change our understanding. I shall stand by my pledge."

Another outburst of wild applause arose from the lucky spectators who were close enough to see what was going on.

"What is it?" asked the king, with sudden anxiety.

Ivar's superior height still made it possible for him to follow developments. "The black has passed one of the others. I think the one called the Scythian."

"Is that all?" Yussuff showed an immediate relief. "Gentle lady, I am afraid your ward cannot win now but we must be ready if—if such a miracle does happen. To carry out my plan, you must get to horse at once."

"Must I go before it is over?" The widow asked the question with an almost pathetic air of entreaty.

"Yes. At once. One of my men will be ready for you at the horse lines."

"If I could have one glimpse!" Eugenia looked about her. In the crowded space where they stood men were lifting children up in their arms and a few were breaking convention by doing the same for the ladies with them. The excitement was so great that no one knew or cared what others were doing. Eugenia looked up at the Briton who towered above her.

"Are you strong enough?" she asked.

He seemed puzzled for a moment, then stooped and lifted her

in his arms until her head was well above his. To steady herself she gripped a lock of his hair, but was careful not to tug too hard.

"I didn't realize how large the track is. I can hardly see the horses." Then she began to wave her free arm with excitement. "I see her! There, she's passed the Turcoman! Only the Arab is ahead now. And I think—I think—she's gaining! She's gaining!"

"You must get away at once," protested Yussuff. He did not seem pleased with the developments on the track.

Ivar lowered his burden to the ground. She looked up at him and smiled. "Thank you!" she said. "Ah, how very strong you are!"

5

The feeling of relief and pride which filled Ildico when she succeeded in bringing Harthager out on the track again was of short duration. They were in the clear and there would be no more interference; but in front, so far that horse and rider seemed almost tiny, was the fast-racing Sulieman.

"We can never make it up! Never! Never!" she thought, despairingly. Tears began to stream down her cheeks. Was there anything she could have done? Should she have forced the black into the interference on their left and so have broken a path to the center of the track? This, of course, might have resulted in a general spill and some loss of life. Should she have slowed down at once and demanded of the judges a new start? She doubted if this would have done her any good. Horse racing was still a confused form of competition with few established rules. The only instruction the presiding judge had given them was, "Start with the sound of the cymbals and ride your best." She feared she would have had no more satisfaction from the officers than a sharp admonition to stay out of a man's sport if she lacked the strength to protect herself.

While these thoughts filled her mind, Ildico had been conscious that Harthager had settled instantly into his fastest stride. It seemed no time at all until the spirited little mare from Scythia came into full view on her left and then slowly receded and disappeared. By the time they had completed the arch of the course, they had passed with equal ease the laboring Turcoman, and the fast-flying black was free to take for himself the path closest to the marking posts. All that remained now was to overtake Sulieman.

With a sudden surge of hope she realized that the distance between them was not as great as she had thought. She could even make out the detail of the rider's purple-striped robe and the tightly wrapped bands of his headdress. When he turned on to the lower arch, the rider swung his head around to look back at them and it was clear from his expression that he had suffered an unpleasant surprise. When they turned into the stretch, she estimated they were not more than half a dozen lengths behind.

Would the handicap prove too great? Could Harthager maintain to the end the tremendous burst of speed with which he had been closing the gap? Was his great heart equal to the strain?

What she had been expecting from the start happened as they made the turn. The pressure of the air caused the bands of her headdress to loosen and suddenly they were torn away. Her hair, as though happy to be released from such unusual restraint, streamed out behind her. She was not alarmed that this proof of her identity had been provided for the emissaries of Attila; they had known without a doubt before the race started. Another thought caused her a brief moment of amusement. "That funny little boy! Perhaps he was right after all. It may be that now we have a chance to win!"

The freeing of her hair brought consciousness to her, for the first time, that her feet also were free. Had this occurred when the black launched himself so magnificently across the ditch and regained his footing on the track? They had been handsome boots, with gold figures stamped into the green leather. It was too bad that she would never see them again.

The rider on Sulieman, shaken into real alarm by their closeness, had taken to his whip. Ildico heard his voice, high-pitched and tense, crying for speed and more speed, and she saw a welt on the flank of the gallantly striving Arabian. Sulieman, like the thoroughbred he was, did not falter. He responded with even greater efforts.

Ildico leaned still farther forward and patted the heated neck of her mount. She began to talk to him. "It's now, King!" she said. "Now or never! Can you pass him? Oh, great King, you must save me!"

It seemed to her that the steady rhythm of his stride became

faster. How wonderful he was! Her father had made no mistake
when he judged the young black fit to succeed the kings of the
past. But would his heart continue to withstand this almost unbearable strain?

There *was* a chance now. She realized that they had drawn
up so close that she could almost have reached out and touched
the sleeve of the Arabian rider. He was crying madly to the
strange gods of the desert people and plying his whip. They continued to gain. Inch by inch. This was too slow, they would never
close the gap in time. The finishing line seemed just ahead. Inch
by inch. She cried, "King, O King!" and shut her eyes, fearing to
watch through the tense seconds which remained. She felt her
bare feet curl up involuntarily.

A roar rose from the spectators. She opened her eyes. They
had crossed the line. Harthager was a full head in advance of
Sulieman but had it been that way when they flashed by the keen
eyes of the judges on the stand?

It had been close certainly. Her heart had seemed to stand still
but now it began to beat again. She could at least hope. Auto-
matically she touched the flank of her mount and said: "Easy,
King. It is over now."

They fell into a slower pace with Sulieman some lengths behind. She dreaded swinging about for the return to the judges'
stand, fearing that the verdict might be against her after all. Then
she became aware that another horse was following close behind
her and that it was not Sulieman.

"Don't stop," said a voice which she recognized as that of Yussuff. "Don't turn your head. You must not be seen speaking to
me." There was a tense pause and then he said: "You won. Did
you know?"

"I hoped so," she said, in a whisper. "But I couldn't be sure."

"Say nothing more. Listen closely. Every second counts now."
There was a pause and then the man from the desert continued
in a quiet voice. "I have lost you. I am not happy about it. At
first I thought of doing away with Sulieman, who had failed to
win you for me, but I was sure you would think ill of me if I did."

"He ran such a gallant race!"

"The rider used the whip too much. I am not forgiving enough
to let him go without a touch of the same whip on his ribs——

Look ahead of you. Do you see that break in the line of trees to your right? Turn in there. There's a road which runs off into a thick wood. Follow it. You'll find your friends waiting. There will be another horse for you to take. Ride fast. You must all be well on the road to the west before they discover that you have disappeared. My men will look after the black. He will be cooled off and rubbed down and will be taken on to join you during the night. All these details have been arranged."

There was another, a pregnant pause. "Now look at me. A quick glance. Ah, how beautiful you are—and I shall never see you again!"

CHAPTER IV

1

NICOLAN had expected an audience alone with Aetius. But when he was shown into a long room with marble walls and a raised section at one end, he discovered that the Roman leader had gathered a large group about him. There were soldiers whose use of fine material in their tunics and whose addiction to elegance in the handles of their short Spanish swords marked them as tribunes in the army. There were men whose nobility of forehead was in contrast to the harshness of their other features; and who quite unmistakably, from the purple borders on their togas, were in political posts. They were all stationed on the raised portion of the floor and each pair of eyes was fixed with hostility on Nicolan as he crossed the room.

An official, standing on the steps, indicated that the emissary was to remain below.

"Your name?" demanded the official.

"Nicolan of the Ildeburghs."

"What brings you here?"

"I bear a message from Attila, Emperor of the World and Supreme Lord of the Waters and the Skies."

The official shook his head sternly. "He is not known."

Nicolan used, then, the title which he had reason to believe was preferred by Attila himself to all others.

"I come from Attila, the Scourge of God, who is at war with the empire of Rome."

The official, receiving a nod from above, bowed in turn to Nicolan. "He is known. What is the message?"

"I have been instructed to speak to the commander of the Roman armies."

At this point Aetius detached himself from the rest of the group and descended several of the steps until he was facing the visitor.

"I am Aetius."

They faced each other for a brief moment. "So! You are the aide of Attila's of whom we have heard so much. It is a matter for surprise that he has allowed one as valuable as you to place himself in my power." The stern and handsome features of the Roman leader became more set and hard. "It is hard to believe that a man of your condition and years could rise so quickly. Perhaps the ruler of the Huns has sent you, my former slave, as an expression of his contempt."

"I am acting on his orders, my lord Aetius."

"Have you no fear of the consequences? It is my right to have you taken out and nailed to a cross as an escaped slave."

"I am aware, my lord, of the danger in which I stand. But I come with papers of safe-conduct."

Aetius glanced back at the members of his entourage. He frowned doubtfully. "You display courage. Speak, then."

"The injunction has been placed upon me, my lord Aetius, to state that the supreme head of the invading armies is aware of the nature of the defense he will encounter. You have left the plains of Lombardy open to him but you have stripped the land of livestock. You have destroyed much of the grain in the hope that no army may live off the land. The garrisons of the cities will fight desperately behind their stone walls. There is nothing new in this method. It has been employed before. Even in the defense of Rome."

He was aware as he spoke of the hatred in every pair of eyes. It astonished him how much alike they all seemed, these masters of civilization, their eyes cruel and hard, their faces revealing no vestige of weakness and no sense of fairness. Would his safe-conduct protect him from their malice? For the first time the coldness of fear took hold of him.

"But," he continued, after a moment of silence, forcing himself to put aside this feeling of panic, "it is the desire of Attila that you realize the nature of the price he will exact from you. It is his purpose to burn the forests, to poison the lands, to foul the rivers and the lakes, until the smoke of a dying land will be seen from the highest walls of the city on the seven hills. He will capture the cities and destroy the buildings until not one stone stands on another. The destruction of these proud cities will be so complete that in future ages it will be impossible to find where they stood.

"He will put to the sword every man, woman, and child with a ruthlessness never before practiced on the face of the earth. The cries of the victims, left to this terrible fate, will fill your ears as you sit in these hills and wait in imitation of the Roman Fabius. The cries will reach the ears of the world and will raise wonder and, perhaps, feelings of scorn.

"Will it be of any avail to save Rome and at the same time deliver to utter destruction the fertile lands which feed your proud city? Can discretion save a great empire which was built on courage and daring?"

"These are strong words," said Aetius.

"It is my lord Attila's will that you realize the extremes to which he is prepared to go. These fertile provinces will be destroyed with a savagery of which the human mind has had no conception. Pride will shrivel and great reputations will die as the cries of the victims rise above the clamor and the roar of the flames."

The face of Aetius, which had flushed with anger as the first words of the message were delivered, had now changed to a set pallor. He returned up the steps to confer with his people, and then stepped back after a few moments.

"I have known from the first," he said, "that to leave the passes open would lead to the situation which confronts us. I made this clear to all of you." His eyes went from face to face, finding many of them cold and hostile. "I am aware that among you are some who disagree with me. Because of the course I am following, I may go down in history as a coward who stood by and watched while whole populations perished. But I know that the course I am taking is the only way to save Rome."

A voice, filled with bitter dissent and deep with passion, spoke from the group. "You could have destroyed the Hun at Châlons. But you stood by and let him escape."

Aetius turned on the speaker. "You did not fight at Châlons, Quintus Cassius," he said. "You are not a soldier. You have never seen action. If you had been at Châlons, you would have seen why we were powerless to do more. It was not uncommon in the arena for two gladiators to fight so furiously that both would sink to the ground, too badly wounded to raise a weapon again. That was how it was at Châlons."

He moved back toward the steps and raised a hand in the direction of Nicolan. "We have heard you. There is no answer. You may retire."

As soon as Nicolan had been escorted from the room, Aetius turned to his advisers. He smiled bleakly.

"This is Attila's last word. It is clear to me that his desperation shows in every part of it."

"He means what he says," declared the man Quintus Cassius. "He will destroy the country of the plains."

"Yes," responded Aetius, "and if we venture out to fight him, he will destroy Rome."

"We defeated him at Châlons! Why can't we do it again?"

"I will tell you why I can't defeat him again as I did at Châlons." Aetius was keeping his feelings under control with difficulty. "We lost the pick of our men in that battle and they have been replaced by raw levies. We lack today the allies who fought beside us there. We are seriously outnumbered. In a pitched battle the Hun horsemen would outflank us without opposition. It would be a disaster." Suddenly his face became livid with rage. He cried in a loud voice: "I saved civilization at Châlons! And what thanks have I had? The criticism of little men who have never stained a sword in defense of the empire. The carping of politicians who resent the power which has come into my hands. I have one thing only to say to you, my fine citizens, who live soft and sleep easy of nights. I am prepared to step down and let you assume the responsibilities and the burdens of defense. I shall be well content if you can find another general to win you a second great victory."

It became apparent at once that this was not what they wanted. The glory of Châlons still clung about the victor. They wanted to control the policy of defense but they could not dispense with the man who had saved them once.

"But," declared a senator, "the victims of the savagery of this wild beast will cry out against us from the blood-soaked ground! Can we stand idly by and see a large part of our population wiped out?"

"You are repeating what was said in the days of Fabius," said

Aetius. "Yet he saved the empire. If you leave this decision in my hands, I will save Rome. For the second time."

2

Nicolan was summoned back for a second audience with the dictator of Rome. Aetius had recovered from the emotional scenes in the council room. Seated at a desk, which was piled high with work, he seemed composed again and completely absorbed in detail. This was the cool and hard-working Aetius that Nicolan remembered from his days in Rome.

"Sit down," said the Roman leader, not looking up.

After several moments of absorbed attention to the documents in front of him, Aetius raised his eyes.

"What other message have you for me from—from your new master?"

"It is true," responded Nicolan, "that he had other points which I was instructed to raise. But they were for your ears only."

"Naturally."

Aetius leaned back in his chair and watched his visitor with his cool, hard eyes. Back of him the wall was covered with standards which had been captured at Châlons, grouped around a sword; probably the weapon he had carried that day.

"My message is this. Attila would consider a peace by negotiation. If it could be settled at once. His terms, my lord Aetius, are not light. He demands certain territorial concessions which I am at liberty to name. A heavy subsidy in gold must be paid him on a yearly basis until such time as new terms are reached."

The Roman dictator gave his head a backward toss and smiled scornfully. "Does he expect to reap the rewards of victory without striking a blow?"

"The northern provinces of Italy and the great Lombardy Plain are at his feet. He will leave everything untouched. The fine and prosperous cities will be left standing and not one drop of blood will be spilled. That, my lord, is what he offers you for the concessions he will demand."

"I have no authority, and no desire, to give away a single foot of the land won by the might of Rome. We did not beat Attila at Châlons to throw away any of the fruits of that victory."

Nicolan considered his next words carefully. "Something has occurred which might serve as a basis for the terms of settlement. It may not have come to your ears that the Princess Honoria is at liberty and has cast in her lot with Attila."

Aetius answered in dry tones. "We make it a rule to know everything that happens," he declared. "We learned of the escape of the princess immediately after it took place. We knew," he added, giving his visitor a cold stare, "that the escape was of your contrivance."

Nicolan leaned forward and spoke in lowered tones. "May I say to you, my lord Aetius, that I was not guilty of the offense for which you had me punished. It is true that I knew of your desire to marry the princess but no word of it passed my lips."

Aetius indulged in a somewhat careless gesture. "I became convinced of your innocence."

"It is in Attila's mind that you might desire to renew your suit. As the husband of the princess you would have control of such possessions as might be awarded her in the treaty settlements. You would then have an even stronger measure of control in the imperial family than is now possible."

The hint of a smile began with the tight lips of the dictator and spread slowly up as far as his eyes. Here it struggled briefly for control before abandoning the effort.

"Your sources of information," he said, "cannot be as quick and reliable as ours. Is it not known to you that the princess has disappeared from the household in which she was placed after being removed from the island?"

Nicolan's face made it clear that he had been taken completely by surprise.

"I see you had not heard. It occurred two weeks ago. It is believed she disappeared in the company of a slave belonging to Micca the Mede. There was some talk that this slave was the son of an Arab ruler. Whatever the truth of that, they were taken on board a trading vessel which was leaving for the East." There was a moment's silence. "It seems to me highly improbable that the princess will ever be heard of again.

"As to the possibility of a negotiated peace," went on the Roman, "I shall give it consideration. I must tell you that great difficulties suggest themselves to me at once. We might make peace now and have Attila come back in greater force another year. Treaties are not sacred to him. They are made to be torn up. There is this also: the health of your leader is not good. There is no one else capable of holding all the conquered races together. When he dies, his empire will burst like a soap bubble. Time," concluded the Roman, "is our handmaiden."

"But he will carry destruction over the northern provinces in the meantime," warned Nicolan. "It is not an idle threat. Every man, woman, and child will perish."

"They will die to save Rome," declared Aetius. "Could they ask a better fate?

"As for you," he went on, after a moment, "my mind is not made up. My kindly advisers are clamoring for your life. They do not remember, as I do, that Attila has many of our people in his hands and would exact a tenfold return in blood if we killed you. You will probably be allowed to live but you have seen and heard too much to be sent back. You will remain here under guard until the situation resolves itself."

He clapped his hands and a tall young officer appeared in the doorway.

"Lutatius Rufus," said Aetius, "I place in your hands this emissary from Attila the Hun. You will be held responsible if he makes his escape. Or if any harm befalls him."

The officer looked at Nicolan in a somewhat startled manner. He lacked completely the mark of the typical Roman soldier, the hard eye, the resolute jaw, the overweening nose. He was, in fact, of a somewhat bland cast of countenance; a patrician, clearly, and a sharer in high privilege.

"I have heard your orders, my lord Aetius," said the officer.

3

Nicolan realized quickly that he was to be treated well but that he would not be allowed to escape. The room to which he was taken was at the end of a long narrow *aula* and had securely barred windows which looked out to the north and east. The door closed with the hollow sound which warns that only a jailer's key will open it again. There was a large bed and in one corner a bath. He felt that he had reason to be content because he had come expecting summary treatment. His one regret now was that he would be unable to reach the country where the party of the widow of Tergeste might be expected to put in an appearance, if they had not already emerged from the difficulties and perils of the tunnel under the mountain.

He stood at a side window which looked to the east and tried to picture Ildico perched on the broad back of Harthager, her telltale hair concealed under some kind of heavy headdress, her eyes dancing with excitement. Thinking back over the years, he could not recall a single occasion when he had seen her in repose. She rode, she danced, she sang, she laughed! How wonderful she was! Had he any right to hope that someday he could capture her and cage her with selfish bonds? She had given him little enough reason to expect her favor: a glance or two when they rode together up into the hills, a few friendly words, a hint that she understood his reason for serving Attila. This did not give him much substance to build upon.

"I should be there to greet her," he thought. "I must have the chance to serve her greatly if I hope to win her lasting favor."

He could not dismiss his fear that the party had already reached the Dalmatian estates of the widow and that they had seen in the absence of Attila on his military gamble the opportunity to return Ildico to her anxious father. "Surely Ivar would convince them of the danger of doing that," he thought. But he could not be sure that Ivar had succeeded in joining them. The tall Briton had ventured into strange territory and he could easily have failed to find them.

Other thoughts came at intervals to occupy his mind and give him momentary relief from his fears. The gardens outside his window had been converted into an armed camp. The tents had been pitched with the same thoroughness shown on a campaign, with a ditch and rampart about them and each covered with leather extensions. There was a *draco* floating in the air, which was seldom the rule except when the legions were in alien territory; but it was hanging limply as though the large silver jaws of the dragon were too heavy, and the breeze was not sufficient to inflate the body. He heard a *decanus* (the equivalent of a corporal) drilling a squad of new recruits and here and there about the camp were soldiers of the legion in marching order, with helmets suspended over the right shoulder and kits carried in a bundle and slung on a pole over the left. Aetius might have no intention of marching out against the Huns but he was seeing to it that his troops were ready to go in case of necessity.

Beyond the tops of the tents he saw the tall banks made after centuries of toil by the waters of the river Po. There the camp ended; there was nothing beyond. "Aetius," thought Nicolan, "is allowing himself a safe line of retreat if the Huns come this far."

The officer, Lutatius Rufus, put in an appearance with the first meal served the prisoner. He sprawled out in a chair so low that his knees came surprisingly close to his chin.

"You have thrown things into a turmoil here," he said. "Opinion was divided enough before. Now it's split open. The soldiers back Aetius. The politicians, who won't have to fight, are crying out for immediate action." He sighed as though he had little stomach for such matters. "Aetius, of course, is right."

The food had been good enough but the wine was new and quite obviously cheap. Remembering the strict parsimony in the household of the dictator, Nicolan took no more than a sip.

"Do you believe you can win another victory like Châlons?" he asked.

"Never!" declared the officer. "My good ex-slave and bold emissary, you must see how things are. Rome has gone soft. Look at me. I belong to one of the oldest families and I am only in the army because it seems to be expected of us. I have no intention of fighting. I'm not going to march all day in a broiling sun and freeze at night, and be hacked to pieces by hulking barbarians. There are ways of getting out of it. Ways. Yes, and means. I know them. My great regret is that I wasn't born centuries ago before these wretched barbarians came pouring out of the woods. It could all have been avoided if Aetius had been ready to take the easy way by buying them off. That's how they do it in Constantinople and we could have kept the peace too if Aetius hadn't forced himself on us and decided to do it his way."

"Does that mean," asked Nicolan, "that his rise to power was not due to a popular demand for him?"

"What a fantastic idea! Of course there was no demand for him. Why, his father was a barbarian. In Moesia, moreover. A vulgar province. Aetius connived to get himself into power. Both the emperor and the old woman hated him. Didn't you know? He's an able general, of course. It needed an energetic campaign of whispering and lying to keep the howling population from turning him into a god after Châlons. But we succeeded. And now things are being reversed. The people will clamor for his head if he doesn't lead the army out to fight Attila."

Lutatius Rufus then began to display a weakness for gossip. He doubled up his long calves under him and gave Nicolan the benefit of an amiable smile.

"The court was furious because Honoria got away," he confided. "I'm glad she gave them the slip. There was a time," he grinned self-consciously, "when Honoria had a fancy for me. For once in my life I was sensible. I took to my heels. I went on a tour—Tunis, Cairo, Antioch, Constantinople. When I got back she was scattering her favors. I hear she even fluttered her beautiful lashes at you. When you were a slave in the household of Aetius."

"How did you hear about that?"

"I have a gift for hearing things. Ways. And means, you know. I get all the gossip."

Nicolan shot a conversational arrow into the air. "Have you heard of the widow of Tergeste?"

"I know *everything* about the widow. I can tell you the exact size of her girdle and the kind of dye she uses on her hair. I know where she comes from. She says her father was governor of a province—but what province she doesn't say—and that she was a fourth daughter, which makes her full name Eugenia Quartilla. But I know the real story. Her father was a poverty-struck divinator, a *sortilegus* who predicts the future by natural things. You know, the moss on a rock, the ruff of a wolf, the teeth of a dog, and all that kind of nonsense."

"You don't believe in it?"

"In divination? Listen to me, my friend. I am a poor enough specimen of a man and I've wasted my life in foolish pastimes. I even suspect that I'm a coward. But I am *not* weak enough to think you can tell the future from the bowels of a slain animal or to read prophecy in the rustling of the oak leaves at Dodona."

"Is the widow very wealthy?"

"The wealthiest woman in the world. If you go to a money-lender, all you have to say is that you expect to marry her. All

her husbands were old, rich, and doting. She's found some way
of keeping the hands of the law off what they leave her."

"They say she travels much."

The face of the officer beamed with the pleasure of the rac-
onteur. "She never stops. It's my opinion she's always on the hunt
for husbands. Here's a story that will interest you. Right now she
has a pretty little creature in her train. Fair, blue-eyed, slender."
He blew a kiss into the air. "Exactly the kind I like. But now
that the widow's free again, this girl will be in the way. Can the
widow find a husband for herself with this lovely detriment beside her? First she'll have to find one for the girl."

"How do you happen to know all this?"

"Didn't I tell you? I have ways. So, the widow found a
real catch for her somewhere over there: rich, young, not repul-
sive. The girl said no, she was already in love. 'Love!' cried the
widow. 'What do you know about love at your age? Wait until
you get as old as I am. Who is this fellow?' 'It's someone I've
known all my life.' 'Absurd!' cried the widow. 'Some hairy savage, with greasy locks and uncombed beard and a body fashioned
like a bear.' The girl protested that he was the handsomest man
in the world."

"Then she wasn't meaning me," thought Nicolan.

"Well, the girl wouldn't change her mind," went on the officer.
"So all the men who came around had eyes only for her. It's even
said that Attila knows about her and would like to add her to his
harem."

Nicolan decided to change the subject. "I have been wondering," he said, "if there are ways and means of getting out of a
place like this."

Lutatius Rufus got to his feet at once. His manner had developed a wary note. "As to that," he declared, "I am able to be
quite definite. No, there is no way."

4

Early one morning soon thereafter Nicolan stood at a window
in his room which gave him a view of the north. He realized
that something had happened which was agitating the whole
camp. The soldiers of the legions, which Aetius was holding at

this strategic spot, stood about in noisy groups and talked wildly among themselves. There were priests on the paved court from which the council room opened, their eyes peering out with grimness and fear from under the cucullus that each of them wore. Footsteps passed and repassed outside his door. Several times Nicolan heard sounds of weeping.

Rufus brought him the answer. That doughty officer came in slowly, looking pale and shaken.

"Aquileia has fallen," he announced. "The garrison fought stoutly but the Huns were like the sands of the desert." He swallowed hard. "The city has been destroyed and the people butchered without mercy or discrimination. The men were herded into the market place and literally chopped to pieces. The dead bodies were mutilated. Every Hun will ride now with a rotting head on the point of his spear. The women were spared the first day while the Huns feasted on the food supplies and enjoyed themselves, then they were all beheaded. It took the better part of the day to get rid of them all. The children had been killed first by dashing their heads against the walls."

"They were so confident the walls couldn't be stormed," said Nicolan, feeling stunned by the horror of the story.

"The same thing will happen to the other cities," declared Rufus, in a strained voice. "They are all in easy reach. Alimium, Concordia, Padua, Vicenza, Verona, Bergamo. Perhaps even Milan and Pavia. There's no safety anywhere with this fiend loose in the world."

Realizing how this disaster might affect his own fate, Nicolan walked to a window and stared to the north. It was a beautiful day. Birds sang along the banks of the great river and cheerful sounds of neighing came from the horse lines. The sky was bright and benign; but beneath it, not many miles away, these incredible things were happening.

"There will be no getting out of it." Rufus seemed on the point of whimpering. "No possibility of staying home now. I'll have to go. And I won't come back. I'll die a miserable death."

"No, there will be no fighting," declared Nicolan. "I know Aetius. He won't change his mind. He will sit here and let Attila destroy one city after another."

"If that is true," said the officer, "you are in a bad position yourself. The people will demand the chance to retaliate. *You*, my poor friend, will be one of the first victims. In fact, I heard talk about it this morning."

Nicolan nodded his head grimly. "I know. I sensed it this morning when I looked out and saw those grim faces. I've been expecting it."

"You seem to take it calmly," said Rufus, regarding him curiously.

"If I seem calm, it's not because I am reconciled to such an end. I've known myself to be under sentence of death ever since I refused to serve any longer in Attila's armies. You get to a numbed state of acceptance after a time."

"But why did you refuse to serve?"

"I became concerned about the state of my soul. You see, I had been converted to the Christian view of things."

"I'm a Christian myself," affirmed the officer. "But I'm not one of the kind who take such things seriously."

"Attila threatened to have me executed and then began instead to find missions for me. Each time I face death if caught."

"But"—in a puzzled tone—"you've had chances to run away. Why did you come here?"

"What chance is there to escape? These two empires have the earth divided between them. Sooner or later you are caught. I thought there was a chance this way at least. But now the chance is gone." After a moment's silence, he asked, "What brings so many priests here?"

"Pope Leo is coming from Rome. As a last resort."

Nicolan frowned uncertainly. "What can he do? Save Rome by a miracle? Can he command the waters of the Adriatic to roll in and destroy the invaders, like the Red Sea swallowing the Egyptians?"

Rufus seemed to share his doubts. "Is the pope of Rome a god or a mere man? Anyway it's too late for miracles now."

Nicolan had seated himself on a marble bench beside the bath, which was filled with water.

"They say Leo is a strong pope," said Rufus. "He and Aetius are the only leaders we have. The emperor is a weak idiot." The young officer began to pace up and down the room with lack of spirit in every line of his tall limp frame. "We are going to be cut off in the flower of our youth, you and I. Why not make it as easy for yourself as possible by stretching out in that bath and quietly drowning yourself?"

Nicolan shook his head. "No, friend Rufus. I prefer to face the issue. Suicide is the most doubtful road to choose if you hope to reach the kingdom of heaven."

Rufus frowned doubtfully. "Is that what the Christians preach? My grandfather changed over when it became the state religion but only because everyone did. None of us has gone into it seriously."

The symptoms of suppressed excitement were noticeable at all hours of the day. Nicolan stood at his window and watched, expecting to be summoned at any moment. When the sun went down, he thought desperately, "I will never see it again."

It had become dark when footsteps were heard in the hall, coming to a stop at his door. Nicolan rose. "This is the word," he said aloud.

Aetius entered the room, followed by a servant with a lighted lamp. The illumination thus provided gave Nicolan a chance to study the dictator's face. It seemed quite calm and collected.

"Have you heard?" asked Aetius.

"I have been told of the capture of Aquileia."

"Your master was as thorough in his extermination of the townspeople as you declared he would be. I haven't changed my mind, nor do I intend to, even if he destroys city after city. But the people are smoldering and demanding retaliation. You are the first victim they want." He paused and then said in even tones, "I am not going to deliver you over to them."

When Nicolan started to speak, to voice his gratitude, the Roman leader silenced him with an impatient gesture. "You must not think I do this because of any concern for you. I am doing it for my own peace of mind. I made you the victim of a great injustice once. Perhaps this will erase from your mind any feeling you may be holding against me. And there is another point." His voice suddenly became almost explosive in its violence. "I am still the master of Rome! Why should I yield to the demands of hypocritical senators and weak-spined generals? I have told them they may go as individuals and help in the defense of the cities which remain if they feel the situation so keenly. Instead they want to stay safely here and wallow in the blood of helpless victims.

"I can spare a few moments only," he went on, his voice sinking to a normal tone, "so listen carefully. This end of the palace has been cleared. I will not lock the door when I leave. Follow soon after me, closing the door and turning to the right. One of my servants is stationed at the end of the *aula*. Follow him to the horse lines. Your horse is saddled and ready. There are supplies for a week in the saddlebags."

"What of the members of my party?" asked Nicolan.

Aetius gave an indifferent gesture. "They will be turned loose later. You don't need to feel concern about them." He gave Nicolan a curious glance before starting back to the door. "Do you think it a sign of weakness that I am disturbed over the verdict of future generations? I am sure of this: that I, who will save the empire by my prudence as surely as the sun will continue to shine on the eagles flying over Rome, will be set down in the pages of history as a coward. What is more the great Roman public, the unwashed multitude who bellow and scream over things they do not understand, will never believe I am taking the only way of saving them. They will not give me credit when Attila retreats with his starving army. They will probably clamor to have me punished. I have no illusions." He paused for a moment at the door. "Now, at least, I won't be charged in history with the murder of military envoys."

He turned after a few steps in the direction of the door.

"Do you still hope to see the Huns in possession of Rome?"

"No, my lord Aetius."

"But you felt that way once."

"That is true."

"I believe you were the only one of your nation to feel that way. The rest retained their allegiance to Rome."

"No, my lord. They preferred Rome to Attila; but it was nothing more than a choice of evils. When a conquered nation is strong of heart, the allegiance of the people is to their own traditions and memories. My people, my lord, are strong."

Aetius paused, rubbing a hand over his chin, which was like finely carved marble. "When I said you were to go free, I should have added that I must make two conditions. First. You are not to return to the service of Attila."

"I pledge you my word."

"Your eyes are sharp and shrewd. You have seen much while here which would be useful to him. If you should fall into his hands, you must tell him nothing. No matter what form of persuasion he may use."

"I swear, my lord, to say nothing."

"Second. Go first to Ravenna. It will not be an easy route. The highway through the marshlands to Ravenna has become the Road of Cowards. All good Romans who have the fear of the Hun in their hearts and heels are racing down it, hoping to reach the sea. They are in such a hurry that there is danger in joining such a mad scramble. Nevertheless, I am instructing you to go that way and cross to Tergeste as soon as possible. There is a letter I desire placed in the hands of a man in that city. It may not surprise you to know that there is a conspiracy on foot among my enemies to have me removed from the command and charged with treason. My safety may depend on the delivery of this letter. Are you prepared to take it?"

"Yes, my lord."

"I trust you," said the Roman commander. He handed the letter to Nicolan. "Be discreet in everything. No one must know you are acting for me. It is a matter of such importance that I dare not entrust it to anyone about me." He walked to the door, saying over his shoulder, "There is not a moment to be lost."

CHAPTER V

1

NICOLAN was escorted through a dilapidated entrance, along a maze of halls, which reeked of oil and tar and strange smells of the East, up and down steps and around many turns; and finally reached a small room where a clear view of the harbor was possible. It was a room of mean proportions and the same might be said of the occupant, a dried-up little man with features of ferret-like sharpness.

His name, he conceded, was Q. Caius Roscius, and he read the communication from Aetius twice, grunting to himself as he did so and allowing Nicolan to remain standing. "He says you are to be trusted," he declared, finally. His face had taken on an angry flush. "It is a disgrace that the man who saved the world from the barbarians at Châlons should find it necessary to plot —yea, *plot!*—for his own welfare and even his safety when the fighting is over! These politicians at Rome, these designing men with soft bellies and fat purses! I spit with the scorn I feel for them!"

For several moments the deep-set eyes of the master merchant of Tergeste were fixed on the gray outline of the Karst hills. Then he swung back to his visitor.

"What have you noticed about this great city?" he asked.

"There are holes in the walls through which six Hun horsemen could ride abreast."

"What else?"

"I saw no armed men."

"All the legions in Illyria were withdrawn when Aetius was assembling his army. It was a necessary step. I am not a soldier but it was clear even to me that the defense of Rome came first. What else?"

"I saw no sentries, either at the gates or on the walls."

"Did you have an eye to the conditions in the province?"

"The country is green and the crops seem bountiful. And yet across the head of the sea the country is yellow and bare. Attila's army will starve."

"You have an observant eye, young man. How long do you think Attila can remain on the Lombardy Plain?"

"Until he has captured all the northern cities and has used up their stores of food. Not a day longer."

"Word reached us that all the cities of northern Italy are now in his hands." Q. Caius Roscius was regarding his visitor with a smoldering eye. "Our governor is an open enemy of Aetius," he went on. "He complained to the Senate when the legions were taken away. It is whispered about that he scraped every coin out of the treasury here in Tergeste and sent a heavy subsidy to Attila in return for a promise to pass us by. It was an act of treachery and, of course, he denies it. But since Attila swung his forces down against Aquileia, this smug fool struts about and smiles as though to say, 'I did it. I saved the city.' But will Attila continue to keep his promise?"

"Only as long as he can afford to do so," declared Nicolan, with an emphatic shake of his head. "He will keep his word until all his food supplies are exhausted."

"And then?"

"Then you will see dust on the northern horizon and the horsemen of Attila swooping down to destroy this province."

The shipping merchant nodded in agreement. "I have tried to convince the men of Tergeste that this will happen. They will not believe it. They should be repairing the walls and arming themselves for a siege. But instead they laugh. I say to them: 'Where is Aquileia today? Where will Tergeste be tomorrow?' It does no good. They are fat and content with things as they are." He tore the communication into small pieces and set them afire in a brazier in one corner of the room. "Why is it, young man, that stupidity feeds on success? We are prosperous here in Tergeste and our wealth makes us blind. And now may I ask what your plans are?"

Nicolan decided to give a frank answer in the hope of gleaning some needed information. "I may go farther south. I am seeking the widow of Tergeste."

The old merchant snorted. "The widow of Tergeste! Don't you know she wasn't a widow until a few weeks ago? Her third husband ran away from her. He was a dull, grasping fellow. Perhaps he couldn't stand her tempers. Whatever it was, he disappeared and after a time it was assumed he had died. He was in the East, it has come out, and he has finally dropped his lids. Now that she is legally free, she will be much sought after. Her wealth is almost beyond belief and she owns much property here in Tergeste." He paused and permitted some relaxation of the perpetual scowl into which his features were drawn. "If I could take ten years off my life, I would marry her myself."

Nicolan bowed and began to back in the direction of the door. "If you have no commands, I should be on my way," he said.

The communication he had brought had turned to charred wisps in the brazier. Roscius stirred the ashes with a questing finger.

"I think it would be well to stay over the night," he said, looking up at Nicolan. "A teller of tales is here and they say he has something strange for our ears."

2

Nicolan acted on this hint and, when the sun began to sink and darkness settled over the ruinous fortifications of the city, he made his way in company with most of the men of Tergeste to one of the largest breaches in the outer masonry. There was an adequate cleared space immediately inside the walls at this point and the storyteller had elected to gather his audience here. He was a little man, wearing a curious round felt hat and with an undertunic of sharply contrasting colors showing at intervals under the pale gray of his outer robe. Torches on long poles had been set up in the breach and the entertainer had stationed himself between them, so that his face was plainly visible to the crowds below. When he took off his hat it was seen that his round head was as completely bald as the egg of some huge extinct bird. His eyes, under hairless brows, were singularly alert.

"Citizens of Tergeste," he began, and it caused much wonder that such a slight frame could contain so deep and resonant a voice, "you are all of the Christian Church. I am not. I come from a land beyond where the sun rises and so the humble carpenter who has inspired your faith has never been heard of there. We have a faith of our own. An old one. So very old that my people live by it and die by it in an easy content."

He let his deep-set eyes wander over the people standing close-packed beneath him. "Look at the shape of my nose, the line of my brow, the color of my skin. Care you to guess from where I come?" He directed another glance about him and, when no voice was raised in response, his aged face revealed an infinity of new wrinkles in an attempt to smile. "The land from which I come is far beyond the great rivers and the high mountains and my people have many strange legends which I could tell you. But, my good friends, it so happens that I have a wondrous tale to relate which transcends anything I have heard in the land of my birth.

"Listen to me. Listen carefully. I, Tarmanza, a humble teller of tales, stood close to Attila and the great father from Rome, who is called the pope, when they met on the banks of the Mincius. How did it come about that a footloose alien was allowed to see and listen at this great moment? I will tell you. When it became known that the great father from Rome would ride to meet Attila without a single armed guard, there were some among those selected to go who said to themselves, 'Truly, I am not feeling well enough for such a long ride, nor do I think my head would make a suitable ornament for the tip of a Hun lance.' Now I am an old man and I shall have very little further use for this head of mine, so I went to one of these dubious priests and said I would wear his robe and go in his place, and that I would keep the cowl down low over my face, so none would know the difference. It was agreed.

"When we came to the crossing of the Mincius and we saw the Hun forces on the other side, the pace of my fellows grew slower and slower. No one protested when I passed, and gradually I progressed from my humble place in the rear until I stood close to the shoulder of supreme holiness.

"The waters of the river ran sluggish and thin, for there still had been no rain. I could see that the tents of the Huns were as many as the sands of the riverbank and that the sky was red with their banners. But I could see also that their bellies were hollow and that the ribs of their horses could be counted. Behind us there was nothing but a grim and fearsome emptiness. No Roman eagle flew there to give us courage."

There was a pause of several moments and then the voice of the narrator rose to a higher note as he propounded a question. "Of whom shall I speak first? Of Attila, the Scourge of God? Or of Pope Leo, who rode without fear to tell the Hun that he must never set foot in Rome?"

The response was immediate and unanimous. Voices rose from all corners of the cleared space. "Attila! Attila! Tell us of the Scourge of God!"

The narrator smiled bleakly. "It is always so. It is the villain of a story who commands attention. Never the kind, the godly, the brave. It shall be as you say, good friends of Tergeste, I shall tell you first of Attila.

"Peering out from under my cowl," he went on, "I could see these two great men more clearly than I see any of you below me tonight. I saw at once that the body of Attila was old. His back was bent as he sat his horse in front of the clump of advisers and guards. But his eyes were not old! I could see them glitter as he studied the face of the pope. It came to me as I watched that here was a man who would set loose all the evil in the world to accomplish his ends and still believe that the end was good. I saw him then as a man filled with contrast. There was death in the fierceness of his glance but to the observant eye a hint of compassion in his hands. He wore precious stones of a value beyond compare but the tunic on which they clustered was old and stained. The men behind him were ready to spring at the throats of the priests but they fell silent and still when Attila moved a finger. They carried rotting human heads on the tips of their lances but he had about him no trophy of the wars.

"The pope was also a man of contrasts," he continued. "He was a Roman of Romans, with the high courage, the pride, and the arrogance of his race in the curve of his nose and the set of his jaw. And yet there was gentleness and compassion to be read in him also, and a faith that nothing could shake. He wore the rich vestments of his office but only to impress the barbarian foe. Looking at them, listening to the words they spoke, it came to me that the priest on his plainly caparisoned mule would be the harder man to convince and the slower to change.

"The pope reached out a hand to the Hun leader. Attila edged his horse a pace or two nearer and bowed over it. He did not kiss it as the pope had expected. The Hun leader said: 'This salute is not for you, who have great power in Rome which you use against me, but is in honor of the God you serve. Of whom I have heard good things said.'

"The pope's eyes grew even more stern and he said in a threatening voice: 'Form no hasty opinion of the God I serve, O Attila. He is a stern God. He will strike you down if you set foot in His holy city of Rome, even as He did the savage Alaric.'

"They talked for a long time. At least, Pope Leo talked. Attila said little. The Huns who sat their sturdy little beasts behind him could not understand what was being said; but they fingered the handles of their swords, to make it clear that this was the only argument they knew."

There was another pause. Then the teller of tales began to speak in a voice which made it clear that the bemusement into which he had been plunged at the time still had him in its grip.

"Listen now to what befell. The pope raised an arm in the air and cried out in a voice that could be heard up and down the bare banks of the Mincius for great distances. 'Take not my word for the punishment which the God of Israel will mete out to you if you set your heathen foot on the holy stones of Rome. I beseech Him now to send messengers of His own to warn you of your fate. I beg, O God on high, the aid of St. Peter and St. Paul in this hour of great moment!'

"As he spoke, the skies seemed to open and two nebulous figures appeared through the cleft clouds and came flying down to earth on swift wings. I saw them with my own eyes, even though the light was so great that it came near to blinding me. They were tall, these spirits who came at the call of the pope, and they wore circlets of light above their heads and the wings on their backs were as white as fleece. When they came to earth, I could not gaze on their faces, so fierce was the light surrounding them. I covered my face with my hands. But I could hear their voices, even though I could not tell what they said."

The narrator paused. "I have already told you that I am not of the Christian faith. And yet I say to you now that what I saw was not due to any conjuring or magic trickery. I saw the skies open and I saw those two awesome figures come down on their great wings through the path which had opened for them like a stairway of gold. I saw their feet touch earth and I knew they came in the guise of men but that no mortal man who ever strode this earth was such as they.

"I kept my eyes closed until the sound of their wings began again. I looked up then and they were gone. The clouds had closed and there was no trace left of these strange visitors. And then I saw that all of Attila's men had disappeared too. What I had mistaken for the rolling of thunder had been the beat of their horses' hoofs as they rode away in a panic. Attila alone had not moved. He had reined in his horse to keep it from following the others and now had it under control. There was the hint of a smile on his face.

" 'My men,' he said, 'have seen enough of your angels, O Pope.'

"The panic had not been confined to the followers of Attila. The three priests who had carried a tall cross before the pope had let it fall from their hands and they were still on their knees, with their cowls pulled down over their faces. 'It is not strange that you stand alone, O Attila,' said the pope. 'The light from heaven is too fierce for mortal eyes.' 'I shall ask no questions,' declared the Hun leader, 'although I have been told that one Simon Magus could cause figures to appear and disappear at his will. I do not speak of this in mockery nor to cast doubt on the powers of your God. I have seen Him spread famine before my advancing horsemen and so cause them to halt. And this is something the legions of Rome could not do.' After a long and pregnant moment, Attila added, 'I shall give thought to what I have seen and heard.' "

The teller of tales extinguished one of the torches beside him and stepped down to the level of the ground. He placed a large bowl of base silver on one of the upturned stones.

"I have one word to add. An hour after the train of the pope turned back across the Mincius, there was a sound of great preparations in the camp of the Huns. The tents were lowered, the horse lines were emptied, the clatter of receding hoofs filled the night air. By morning the camp of the enemy had been deserted."

Nicolan set a good example by depositing in the bowl a coin which gave out a solid ring. The man from the East, standing beside the bowl, gave him a smile of approving thanks. Tellers of stories are always poor men and there was reason to think, in this instance, that a good reward had been earned.

Nicolan, accepting an invitation from Roscius to pay him a second call, found the old merchant in another tiny room in the countinghouse overlooking the harbor. The latter was enjoying a sparse supper, in which Nicolan refused to join, alleging lack of appetite. It consisted of a jug of wine and a few shellfish which Roscius picked out with the point of his pen.

"Are you surprised at the success of the pope?" asked the merchant.

Nicolan pondered over his reply. "The story that little man told keeps going around and around in my head," he said. "It is not hard for me to believe that the spirits of the two great saints came back to earth again. If the God of Israel felt that the feet of the barbarian should be stayed, He could destroy the whole Hun army at a nod. Perhaps, instead, He chose to listen to the voice of Leo. And yet there is this to be considered. It is impossible for me to believe Attila was frightened into returning. He was in a desperate position. His men were starving. Aetius refused to be drawn out to fight a decisive battle. What would men say of a leader who led his army into such a hopeless position? To retreat would be to acknowledge the enormity of his mistake. But here an excuse was offered him. Do you suppose he said to his generals, as soon as he could overtake them, 'We could have crushed the Roman army but we cannot stand before the wrath of this mighty God of the Christians'?"

Through the open windows they could hear the shouts of the townspeople, exulting over the retreat of the Hun armies. The whole city was filled with the sound.

"This wonderful news," said the old merchant, "has not yet reached Rome. Ah, how they will rejoice when they hear! The people will flock to the public squares and arenas. Every Hun prisoner, unlucky enough to be held there in prison, will be dragged out and butchered in the streets. Ah, how I wish I could see it!"

Nicolan rose to his feet. "What I have heard tonight makes it necessary for me to change my plans. I had intended to go south along the coast to where the widow lives." He looked sharply at the merchant, wondering how much he dared tell. "The retreat of the Huns will mean the end of the war. Attila thinks he can collect another army and march against Rome. But he's wrong. He won't be able to keep his divisions together. Nothing he can say or do will prevent them from returning to the countries from which they come. It's even possible the Hun empire will fall to pieces."

"It's more than possible," declared Q. Caius Roscius, in a quiet voice. "It's as certain as the rising and setting of the sun."

"My countrymen," went on Nicolan, "will have the chance at last to regain their freedom. I must be there. Macio is very old and very sick. Did you know that?"

The merchant smiled slyly. "I know everything about Macio. He has written me every week for many years. You see, young man, I have been his agent. I sell his horses in the markets of Rome and Constantinople. You did not know that?"

"No," affirmed Nicolan. "I did not know that."

"I will tell you the latest word I have had about him. He is dying. He may be dead, even as we speak together here tonight. The flames of his funeral pyre may be lighting up the skies."

Nicolan shook his head despairingly. "I must get home before he dies. You, who know so much, must be aware that his only son was killed at Châlons. Nearly all the sons of the leading families died there. The only one of them alive today is Ranno of the Finninalders."

"Ranno," declared the old man, in bitter tones, "is a traitor, a coward, a liar, and a thief! It will be a sad thing for this country of yours if he becomes leader."

"That's why I must go back. It isn't going to be easy. I shall have to ride fast to get through the pass before it's filled with the retreating armies. I must start at once. Can you give me a fresh horse? And well-filled saddlebags?"

"I can give you everything you need. For, young man, I'm as anxious to have you back as you are to be there. I want to see your country prosperous again, so there will always be plenty of your fine horses for me to sell."

Nicolan had been aware for some minutes of activity throughout the dilapidated building, a closing of doors and slamming of bolts, of the calling of voices from one part to another. An interruption was now provided by the arrival of a wizened man in a far from clean tunic, carrying a metal lamp of curious design in one hand.

"Master," said the new arrival, "all the doors are locked. The guards are in their places."

"Are the doors to the wharfs double-locked? Are they bolted from within?"

"Yes, master. I made the rounds and questioned each man on duty."

"Did you inspect the food laid out for their supper?"

"Yes, master."

"Are there still any complaints from them?"

The man took enough time to scratch himself under both arms before replying. "They complain still. They complain about everything. They say there are bugs in their bedding."

"Who are they to complain of such things?" cried the merchant in a tone of exasperation. "There are bugs in my bedding. Do I complain? Are the lights out?"

"All, master, save this one you are using." As he spoke the servant raised the candle and set a light going in the lamp he had brought. It gave out such a feeble illumination that he took it up and shook it impatiently, muttering to himself: "They are no good, these lamps. They are made for appearances only. That cheat in Antioch who peddles them should be told what we think."

"He sells them to us cheap!" snapped Q. Caius Roscius. He smiled in mild apology to Nicolan. "One has to be careful, for there are thieves everywhere. This has been a wearisome day and I must now get to my rest."

There were two small cots in the room. The grumbling servant had already stretched himself out on one of them.

"Get up, you wallowing hog!" exclaimed the master. "I pay you to watch over me and not to sleep yourself. Take this man to the main gate and turn him over to Carlac." He had been scribbling a note which he now handed to his guest. "This will get you what supplies you need. Carlac will see to it."

"May I ask a favor? If the widow arrives back safely from the East, send her word of me. And if anything is seen in the city of a very tall and strong man who goes by the name of Ivar, have him brought to you. He will be seeking word of me. Tell him of my plans."

Q. Caius Roscius had already stretched himself out on his meager bed. "It shall be done," he promised, closing his eyes.

CHAPTER VI

1

THE STREETS of Tergeste were littered next morning with broached wine casks and broken flagons as well as the inert forms of snoring citizens, stretched out drunkenly in the mud, after celebrating the retreat of the Huns. Nicolan had to pick his way carefully in seeking again the warehouses of Q. Caius Roscius.

"I leave for the north at once," he informed that most influential of citizens. "The passes will soon be filled with Attila's men, so I must go in disguise."

The merchant sent out for a man from the East to attend to this need. He proved to be small with a dark skin and a huge nose which seemed heavy enough to keep his head bent forward. After looking Nicolan over, he untied a bundle and produced a variety of tiny containers. These were filled with dyes and secret concoctions from the East. It took a very short time to stain the traveler's head and neck, and his arms and hands and legs, to a soft brown which glowed in the light. Then his hair and eyebrows were changed to solid black. With a skilled forefinger the man of disguises made lines on his skin which started at the nostrils and circled down around the corners of his mouth.

"It is good?" asked the changer of faces, stepping back to inspect his work.

"It is good," agreed the merchant.

Nicolan studied himself in a small mirror and saw the face of a complete stranger, at least twenty years older, staring back at him.

The discussion then turned to the occupation he was to assume. Roscius thought he should carry a bundle of trade goods and pose as an itinerant merchant. Nicolan shook his head in dissent. "If you carry goods for sale and never try to sell them, people get suspicious. It will be better to go as a Christian missionary."

"To what country?"

Nicolan pointed due north. "To the lands of the Alamanni. That way takes me first to my own country. I may find this disguise necessary there. It lies, as you must know, in a corner between Noricum and the great river."

He started out, therefore, on a staid horse and wearing a cross on the sad gray of a threadbare tunic. The passage of the mountains offered no difficulty, for the retreating armies were as yet represented only by food commissioners who were stripping the land of food and building up depots for the use of the troops following them. Turning due north, he found himself on the roads to Noricum and thus avoided the fertile Pannonian plains which had been Hun headquarters for two generations.

Wherever he stopped, he asked the same question: "Have you seen aught of the widow of Tergeste? She travels north with a long train. Many horses and tents of silk and carts loaded with food."

On the third night out from the pass, the keeper of a small inn nodded his head in response. "Widow T'gest pass this morning," he said, in a broken mixture of tongues. "But no longer widow. She wife. Find new husband."

"Again!" cried the supposed missionary. On second thoughts, however, he did not consider this information surprising, in view of what he had heard while a prisoner in the hands of Aetius. "She can afford many husbands, for she is a fine woman and the possessor of much wealth," he commented.

The publican nodded in agreement. "She have much of everything. Land and houses and horses and cattle. And slaves. Also much of high temper." He giggled. "Ah, what temper! But under everything much kindness of heart."

"What direction did they take?"

The innkeeper pointed into the north. "To land of fine horses," he said.

"Was there another lady with her? Young and beautiful?"

After rubbing his nose in reflection, the owner of the inn nodded. "Small," he said. "Nice in thin way."

"With golden hair?"

The owner made a circular motion around his head. "Wrapped in black," he said. "Hair not show."

2

Pleased beyond measure by the information he had received, Nicolan stirred his patient steed into action and overtook his friends as they were setting up camp for the night. Tents were being put up and the horses were being staked out while a most enticing odor of food radiated from the campfires. He was amazed to see a tall and commanding figure in white, with a heavy gold chain around his neck and silk cords on his sandals, and to recognize this spectacle of magnificence as Ivar. The tall Briton was superintending the work of the camp with great briskness. The widow (for he could not yet call her anything else) was seated in comfort in a chair. A slender and travel-weary figure crouched on the ground beside her. Nicolan's heart turned over with joy. If he had seriously entertained doubts as to his love for Ildico, they flew away into the rapidly darkening sky. He wanted to pick the tired figure up and cradle her head on his shoulder.

Nicolan turned his horse in toward the camp. "There is much danger on these roads for solitary travelers," he said. "Might a humble servant of the Lord set up his tent on the edge of your camp for the protection it will give?"

Ivar came forward and gave him a glance of inspection. "We will be happy if you join us, Father," he said. "You will be welcome to share in the supper which is being prepared."

"Your kindness is far beyond my deserts. But I have not broken fast since morning and I confess to an appetite."

The slender figure beside the widow had risen and walked over to take part in the discussion. She stationed herself close by the head of his horse and stared up at him with close interest.

"Take the pebble from under your tongue, Nicolan of the Ildeburghs," she said.

Nicolan, completely taken aback, stared down at her, while the light of recognition grew in her face. She gave a laugh of sheer delight and relief. "You are back!" she said. "You are safe. How kind the Lord has been to you. And to all of us."

Ivar had been watching with an incredulous frown. "Are you mad, Ildico?" he asked. "This is an old man. I see no resemblance in him at all."

Eugenia left her chair and joined the group, passing an arm under Ivar's elbow and leaning her head against his shoulder. She also studied the dark and deeply lined face of the stranger on the passive horse.

"It's an old face," she said. "And yet—and yet——"

"I knew his voice at once!" cried Ildico. "And now I see behind that clever mask someone who—who has been much in my thoughts."

Ildico had been right about the pebble. Nicolan removed it from his mouth and sprang down to the ground. He reached out and claimed both of her hands.

"I have been in your thoughts!" he cried. "How happy that makes me! I am proud that you recognized me."

They were so concerned with one another that they were paying no attention to the others. Ivar, who had recognized him as soon as he resumed his own voice, was dismayed over the slowness with which he had identified his friend. Eugenia murmured to him: "Be not concerned, my husband. It is right they should think of each other first."

Nicolan, refusing to release her hands, was saying to Ildico: "I would never fail to recognize you because I have always been able to keep a full picture of you in my mind. Once when I sat in the inner cabinet of Aetius, an artist paid him a visit. I heard him say that there is in every face one feature so distinctive that it serves as a sure root of recognition. If you can keep that one point clearly in your mind, the whole face stays with you and never fades away."

She asked, "And what is there in my face?"

"Chiefly the line of your brows. Instead of being straight or tilting up at the ends, they turn down. Whenever I think of the sweetness of expression this gives you, I can see your whole face as clearly as though you are with me. In addition"—he released one hand to lay a finger on his nostril—"there is the beauty with which the divine sculptor fashioned the tip of your nose."

"We also are glad to see you, dear Nicolan," said the new bride.

He walked over and took a hand of each in his. "It is not hard to reach the conclusion you are married. I passed an inn early this morning where the owner told me you had ceased to be a widow. But I had no suspicion that the man you had selected was this Goliath from the islands." He turned to Ivar. "My old friend! I am pleased beyond words. The impression grows in me that you are both going to be very happy."

Ivar, who seldom smiled, indulged in a somewhat self-conscious grin. "Yes, I am happy. And proud. And now I am doubly happy because you have returned safely."

"It is true," said the bride, with a slight toss of the head, "that I selected him. I could see it was the only way. I went about nine tenths of the distance and then my pride compelled me to stop. I waited. He came the rest of the way, stumbling and hesitating and hardly able to speak. But now we are married. I have him, my strong, my fourth, my last husband. He is worth more than all the others put together."

"I had made up my mind from the beginning," protested Ivar. "I had seen the sweetness in your eyes."

The wife turned to look at Ildico and Nicolan, with eyes which had opened wide. "I swear this is the nicest thing he has ever said about me!" she declared.

Ivar became quite loquacious. "I am being given a free hand to guide our lives in everything that counts."

"Well . . ." began Eugenia. Then she smiled. "Go on and tell them about it."

"My wife accepts my beliefs, my views of life, my opinions. I decide where we are to go, and when. I even take it on myself at times to decide what my wife is to wear."

"But," said Eugenia, "he never shows any interest in what lands I own and the horses and cattle I have. He has never asked how much gold I have laid away. As long as he does not bother me about such matters, I am content to have him control these other trifles which he thinks are so important. So, it may be that our marriage will prove a perfect one."

Nicolan had heard much of the luxury which prevailed at the tables of the great families of Rome but he was not prepared for the succession of dishes which the cooks, laboring over the blazing campfires, had been able to prepare and which were now served on a commodious table set up for them. The ladies had changed to more suitable clothes, Ildico a light blue robe and Eugenia a tunica of modest white and a palla worn over it of a quiet green without a single jewel and no more than a modest showing of embroidery. Nicolan asked himself in wonder when he saw her, "Did Ivar have a hand in choosing this most becoming costume?"

The meal began with a white fish caught that morning in a lake they had passed. Roast shoulder of hare followed, which caused the hostess to smile at her husband. "My dear Fourth," she said, "this is supposed to enhance one's charms. Perhaps I should take a large portion."

"No," said Ivar, firmly. "It is more likely to enhance your waistline."

The main dish was white sausages nestling in mounds of white meal, with sliced figs. With each course a light and sparkling wine was served.

3

"And now," said Nicolan, when the meal was over and only a flagon of the wine was left on the table, "I have a preference to declare. I want to hear all that has happened to you before I tell you anything of the rather sorry adventures I have encountered."

So he was told how Ivar had found them in Constantinople, with special emphasis on his emulation of the great Samson, how Ildico won the race, how generous the desert king had been, and how the wedding ceremony was performed in a small Christian chapel on the banks of the Danube. It developed that Ivar had worn for the occasion a tunic of cloth of gold with a belt of the deepest blue, his own selection.

Ivar began then to tell of their journey back from Constantinople. "We found that Macio had been right. There was too much danger on the regular routes to Rome. The mountain passes were closely watched. So we had to come through the Garizonda."

"The tunnel under the mountain?"

Ivar nodded. "I had my doubts about trying it, with two such lovely ladies. But they wouldn't listen to any other plan. Ildico even offered to take a pair of our men and make a trial venture into it. I wouldn't agree to that, so finally we provided ourselves with plenty of torches and saddlebags well stocked with food—in case the getting out didn't prove as easy as the going in—and down into it we went.

"It was a great adventure," he went on. "The floor of stone had been worn level and smooth during the centuries that the water flowed over it. It was slippery also and we had to keep our horses on a tight rein. I rode first and I promise you we went at a sedate pace."

"Did you encounter anything alive?" asked Nicolan, recalling the stories he had heard about the passage.

"There were snakes near the entrance. But after that—nothing. Nothing but continuous sound. Each hoofbeat was taken up and echoed through the caverns in the rock above us. When one of us spoke, the words were repeated over and over until they died away in a mere whisper. Ildico sang and shouted for the pleasure of hearing her voice come back from all around us."

"What did you see?"

"Nothing but the light of the torches. There were twenty of us and each carried a torch. When I looked back, it was like a long line of large fireflies in the dark. Ildico's eagerness not to miss anything had brought her up beside me and she insisted she could see things. She said there were inscriptions on the walls. Ancient letters and rough sketches of men and animals. She has rare powers of sight and sometimes we called her Little Mistress with the Eyes of a Cat. But when she began talking about the inscriptions, we laughed at her and said she was imagining it. But perhaps she was right. She gave us one proof before we reached the other end of the tunnel."

Nicolan's interest had been roused to a high point. He said, "Tell me all about it and what she really saw."

"She said that there was a deeper channel at one side and that she had seen the body of a man lying at the bottom of it. When I got off my horse to investigate, she was determined to go with me but I insisted she stay where she was. Well, it turned out she was right. There was a deeper channel and there *was* a body in it. But it had been there a long time. Only a skeleton was left."

"Did you find anything to show what kind of man he had been?"

Ivar shook his head. "He had been there so long that even the bones were crumbling to dust."

4

Nicolan's recital of his two missions into Roman territory took a long time, for his friends were eager to hear everything. Eugenia laughed when he mentioned Lutatius Rufus. "That foolish fellow, that great piping loon!" she said. "Will you believe that I considered him once as a possible husband? Because his blood was of the purest patrician strain. But he was younger than I—well, a year or so, perhaps—and he babbled all the time. I quickly gave up the idea."

"He told me," said Nicolan, "that the Princess Honoria had her eye on him once."

Ildico sat up straight at the mention of the princess. She plied him with a score of questions which he answered briefly and without any embellishment. Was she beautiful? Yes. Did he like her? Well—yes. Did she like him? Yes. The affirmative nature of his responses finally reduced her to silence, after an explosive summing up: "I think everything they say about her is true. And I feel very sorry for that handsome slave from the East. She will treat him badly."

When the newly married pair had retired to the silken pavilion, with which the Lady Eugenia had hallmarked her wealth and prominence, Ildico removed the black bands which covered her hair. She ran her fingers through the long golden tresses and sighed with relief.

"And now," she said, "we have much to talk about. Particularly your reason for going home. You know, of course, the danger you will face?"

Nicolan nodded his head. "We'll undoubtedly find that Ranno of the Finninalders has established himself in a position of power. I'm sure he has been spreading lies about the part I played in the battle of Châlons. Sooner or later I expect to be summoned before the Ferma. For that reason, I'm going to keep this disguise until I feel it safe to come out into the open."

"But why return now?" She hesitated before continuing. "Suppose the verdict of the Ferma went against you? Ranno is clever as well as sly. He'll stop at nothing to destroy you."

"He has many reasons for hating me. For one thing he still

holds the lands which belong to me." Thinking how large and lovely her eyes were in the fading light from the campfires, he added to himself: "But chiefly he hates me because of you. He's afraid you may have retained some of the liking you had for me once."

"But you haven't said why you feel you must go back," said Ildico, wrapping her hands about her knees and leaning closer. "Do you think there's a possibility that our people can strike for their independence now?"

"Attila is retreating from the plains," answered Nicolan. "It may lead to the breaking up of the Hun empire. If that comes about"—he paused and his eyes began to glow—"I must be there to help. I've learned something of army organization which would be useful." After a moment's silence he added, "I happen to know that Attila is a sick man."

"My father's too old to command any more," said the girl, in a despairing voice, "and my brother is dead. The Roymarcks will have no part in the great day. How fine it would be if you could lead us when the time comes!" She was silent again and he could see that anxiety had taken possession of her thoughts. While he waited to hear what more she had to say, a loud neigh reached them from the direction of the horse lines. Her face lighted up. "That is the king. He is wishing me good night." Another thought had crossed her mind, apparently, for she seemed to be considering some course of action. "Nicolan, something seems to tell me a time may come when you will need a horse to carry you far and fast. I wonder if—well, why not try? The king might take it into that haughty head of his to like you. He might let you ride him. Let us get up with the dawn and see how he will respond."

Harthager lifted his head and trumpeted a greeting. He reared up on his hind legs and pawed at the air in his pleasure at seeing his mistress.

"Ah, my fine one!" said Ildico. "You have missed me, then, O King?"

From a proper distance, Nicolan gave full rein to the delight he felt in watching her. She had matured since that morning when he had seen her ride away in the widow's train. The slight hollows of youth under her cheekbones had filled out and the slender lines of her early years had merged into a more rounded figure. Her carriage, as a result, was surer and more graceful. Even her golden hair seemed to shine with a more vital glint in the morning sun.

Constantinople had left its mark on her. Her dress was red and cut straight across the neck but with a V in the back. There was an arrow embroidered in gold thread on each shoulder, pointing outward. Her belt was of leather and richly encrusted with silver. Styles were much simpler in the plateau country but he realized how very much the costume became her.

The affinity between the girl and the great black race horse was a surprising thing to see. Harthager was as gentle as a colt. He stood at ease as she spoke into his ear and occasionally he would raise his head as though affirming what she was saying. It seemed to the watcher that something of the origin of their race could be learned from this handsome specimen. It was clear enough that he owed much to the Arabian strain, his glossy skin and his speed, but his length and the smallness of his head suggested that he had something of the Turcoman in him as well. It might even be that his obvious strength of bone came from the rugged horses of the Eastern steppes. Had the race come originally from the cold barrens?

After a few moments, Ildico turned her head. "I am telling the king that you are a friend. That he can trust you and that someday soon you may ride on his back. Have you seen how he watches you? He has a mind of his own, you know, and it is usual for him to make it up quickly. Sometimes it is instant. There's a spark, a flash in his eye. He will show his likes or dislikes as quickly as that. I have seen him take the most violent dislike, a hate almost, and when that happens it is well for whoever it is to stay at a distance. I can't be sure about him now, for he seems to be taking his time. But I think he's going to like you."

"I haven't noticed any trace of antagonism," said Nicolan.

"Well, you are one of us and he knows it. The only point is whether he will like you well enough to let you ride him. I'm the only one he has allowed on his back since we left home. He knows he's the king and he won't permit liberties.

"He's getting a little out of temper lately," she went on. "I think he wants to go home. I've seen him many times, standing very still and gazing into the north. I think he's homesick for the coolness in the air and the richness of the grass, and the brothers he left in the Roymarck pastures. Sometimes I believe he thinks of Roric. You know, he and my brother were great friends. Do you suppose he knows that Roric is dead?"

"Yes, he would know," said Nicolan. "If Roric *is* dead."

Ildico left her position at the horse's head and ran a few steps toward him, her hands outstretched. "*If* he is dead!" she cried. "Nicolan, what do you mean? Is there any doubt? Do you know something you haven't told me? You mustn't hold it back if there is any reason at all to hope."

"It's cruel to rouse false hopes, so I haven't said anything to you. But, Ildico, his body was never found. The slope of the hill was searched from top to bottom, so I was told, because it would have been to Ranno's advantage to display the body. It was not there. Early the next morning, before leaving with the rear guard, I went all over that part of the battlefield. Many bodies were still on the ground but not Roric's."

"But, Nicolan!" cried the girl, in a voice breaking with emotion. "If he wasn't dead, what became of him? And he was so terribly wounded. An arrow in his eye!" She shuddered with the horror this aroused in her. "Had he been carried off? Who could have done it?"

"I have asked myself those questions a thousand times. And I have never been able to see any light."

"If he is alive, where has he been all this time? Why haven't we heard from him? It's a terrifying thought! Was he taken prisoner? By those savage people who were holding the top of the hill? Has he been sold as a slave?"

"I am sorry now that I spoke. I have raised these questions in your mind and you won't be able to put them aside."

"I know that the chance is so very, very small. And yet it is sweet to have hope."

She turned back to Harthager, who had continued to stand quietly by. She laid a gentle hand on his muzzle. "Do you remember Roric?" she asked. "Of course you do. You were friends, you and my dear Roric. He was the first to ride on your back. He rode you that morning when you ran so fast and my father selected you as the new king."

Nicolan was watching the black. When Ildico stepped aside, he took her place at the horse's head.

"Harthager," he said, "you are a king in your own right. You can choose the few on whom you bestow your favors. I may not be one of them. But a lady for whom we both have a very great affection hopes that we can be friends. Perhaps you will accept me for her sake."

He laid a hand on the horse's withers. Harthager remained perfectly still. His skin did not shrink from the alien touch.

"It is a grand day for a gallop in the hills." Nicolan moved closer slowly and then, tightening his grip, sprang up on the horse's back. Harthager tossed his head and lifted his front feet from the ground as though to rid himself of this sudden burden. For a moment it was touch and go; he might give in or he might exert his great strength to remove this presumptuous human from his back. Nicolan waited and then exerted the pressure of his right knee on the heaving flank. Harthager turned instinctively and began to gallop up the road.

"Faster," said Nicolan, in a tone free of all incitement or urgency. "Lengthen your stride, O King. The wind will fill our lungs. It is a day when the sound of your hoofbeat should come down from the hills like a rumble of distant thunder."

In a very short space of time, Ildico, listening and watching eagerly, heard a sound like the coming of a storm from the road winding up above her.

CHAPTER VII

1

IT WAS around midnight when the party reached the long and rambling house of the Roymarcks. The gate in the palisade was strongly barred against the Devil or other nocturnal visitors of ill intent, and not a light was showing. The leader of the horse troop sounded a high note on a shell trumpet but had to repeat it twice before a voice behind the sharply pointed logs demanded to know who was there. A quaver in the tone indicated that the worst was feared.

"It's Bustato!" said Ildico to Nicolan, in a delighted whisper. "Being disturbed at night doesn't please him at all. I expect he's twitching his nose as a cat does its tail."

Old Blurki, the clown and jack-of-all-trades, was holding a torch behind Bustato and, by the light it cast, it was easy to see that the major-domo was indeed in a bad humor. "Who is it, who is it?" he asked in a querulous voice. "Is this a time for decent people to be demanding shelter?"

"A fine welcome you're giving me, Bustato!" cried Ildico, stepping forward into the circle of light.

The ancient servant peered out incredulously. Then he recognized her and raised his voice in a welcoming screech. "It is the Lady Ildico! Get everyone up, Blurki, and have food prepared at once. Let the Lady Laudio know, Brynno. The daughter of the house has returned!"

The clown indulged in a grotesque step which was supposed to express delight and then vanished into the darkness of the house, shouting in hoarse tones: "Up, knuckleheads! Get the sleep out of your eyes, stinking sons of swine!"

All members of the party had entered the courtyard when the older daughter of the house appeared. Laudio had hastily wrapped a blue robe about her and it was clear from the slightly disheveled state of her fine dark hair that she had been sleeping. She gave a questing glance at Ildico and then said, without much warmth in her voice: "So, it is you at last, my sister. You have been long away."

The younger daughter ran forward and threw herself into her sister's arms. "Laudio!" she cried. "How happy I am to see you. Are you well? And content?"

Laudio's welcome took the form of a cool kiss on one cheek. "I am quite well. But I've had little reason to be content."

Ildico drew back far enough to study her sister's face. "Laudio, my father! Is he—is he . . . ?"

"He's still alive if that is what you are asking, but we can't expect much. It's a matter of time now. Of days. Perhaps of hours."

"Oh, God, I thank Thee that I have arrived in time to see him," said Ildico, stifling her tears.

She proceeded after a moment of intense silence to introduce the members of the party. Laudio had undoubtedly expected to hear that the lady muffled up in a light blue cloak of the richest material from the East was Eugenia of Tergeste. The fame of the once fabulous widow was widespread. Despite the tension created by Ildico's grief over her father's condition, the deep brown eyes of the older sister made a thorough survey of the becoming apparel of the guest from the south. She then looked at the huge form of Ivar with a suggestion of recognition but did no more than bow to him.

"My new husband," said Eugenia. "The fourth."

The voice of Blurki was heard to mutter in the background, "Who can say it doesn't pay to travel?"

"There are sixteen of us in all," explained Ildico. "Can you find room for us?"

"Certainly," declared Laudio, proudly. "Are there limits to the hospitality of the Roymarcks? Have you been so long away that you have forgotten your home?"

Servants were pouring out through the main door of the house, their eyes heavy with sleep but their delight in the return of the younger sister manifest in the fervor with which they came forward to kneel before her and kiss her hand. Old Blurki was still rousing the laggards, for they could hear him declaiming from within about malt-horses and gig-geese and slobberchops.

"I will tell Father that you have arrived, Ildico," said Laudio. "Perhaps he will feel well enough to see you. He is in a weakened condition."

The younger sister was a picture of surprise and dismay. "But, Laudio, I will go with you!" she exclaimed. "Am I not a daughter of the house also? I can't wait a moment to see my beloved father."

"As you wish. But it may prove too much for him."

Nicolan was thinking to himself, "If this woman marries Ranno, they will be a well-matched pair!"

2

Nicolan had been one of the last to enter the courtyard and he had kept himself inconspicuously in the rear. But standing a full head above everyone in the crowded yard, over which two torches had been raised on the points of spears, Ivar was the cause of much comment. Was he not the tall man who had come once before in the company of Nicolan of the Ildeburghs? If so, where was Nicolan? Was he again with the armies of Attila?

Food was laid out in the hall, which monopolized most of the space on the ground floor, and there was a subdued clatter as the travelers applied themselves to cold meat and the rich red barley beer. Nicolan excused himself from joining the company by raising the cross from his breast as a sign that he was fasting. He was waiting anxiously for Ildico's return and the report she would bring of her father's condition. Standing wearily in the vestibule, he was rewarded finally by the sound of her voice from somewhere back in the shadows of the house. If her tone lacked hope, it did not suggest that a crisis had been reached. Macio, then, was still alive.

Retreating still farther back in the shadows, he saw her emerge from the room where her father lay. She looked, he thought, like the bud of a flower which has been carelessly crushed; but there was on her features, in spite of this, the merest hint of a smile. He heard her say to her sister, "How fortunate that I have come in time," and Laudio's composed rejoinder, "We have carried a heavy burden since you went away."

The two sisters faced each other in silence for several moments. It was as though they were seeking to understand the terms on which they might stand. Nicolan read this in the stiffness with which they held themselves and in the intentness of their eyes. He said to himself: "My poor Ildico! She was expecting so much happiness in being with Laudio again. She's puzzled, that lovely child, and very unhappy."

The conversation which followed was conducted in such low tones that he could not hear any of it at first. Laudio's features never changed and her eyes, cool and removed, did not leave her sister's face. Ildico was close to the point of tears.

Finally he heard the latter ask about their brother. "You have told me nothing of Roric," she said. "That means, I fear, that no word has been heard of him."

Laudio shook her head. "Roric is dead. We have been reconciled to that for a long time. All we can hope for now is to establish in the Ferma the guilt of those who were responsible for his death. And to see them punished."

"Who will take Father's place?"

Laudio turned her cold and set face toward her sister. "Who else but Ranno? Why should it be necessary for you to ask? He is the only son of the first families to survive that terrible battle."

"Has it been voted on, then?"

"There has been no meeting called. When there is only Ranno, why should the Ferma be summoned to vote?"

"But, Sister, it has always been done by the vote of the people. Have you forgotten the story of how the head of our family was chosen centuries ago? A meeting was held on the banks of the Volga and it took a full day to reach a decision. There has been a Roymarck at the head of the Ferma ever since."

Laudio said stiffly, "Times have changed since then."

Ildico hesitated. "Will you marry Ranno soon?"

A flush took possession of the older sister's face. "Why do you think I would know? My marriage is in my father's hands. He has told me nothing. It's not his way to let me share his confidence. That privilege has always been reserved for you. Perhaps" —with a hint of bitter antagonism in her voice—"he will tell you what plans he has for *me*."

"Dear Sister, you are so cold and hard," exclaimed Ildico. "I have always loved you so much! I was hoping you would be glad to see me but now it's clear you are not."

"You didn't come back to see me. But as you are here, I have a word of advice for you. Keep your hair under that black wrap. Our men will be less concerned about you if you don't flaunt your yellow tresses in their faces. And you must know that the armies of Attila are retreating. You may have delivered yourself into his hands by coming back like this."

With a gesture which said, I have been letting you have the benefit of the truth, Laudio turned and walked through the vestibule where Nicolan was standing. She frowned as though she had just realized something about him, and paused to stare for a moment. Then she passed on.

"I'm afraid she's beginning to suspect who I am," thought Nicolan.

Bustato sought him out to explain that it would be necessary for him, in spite of his cloth, to share one of the small cubicles which stretched across the rear of the house, with two other members of the Lady Eugenia's train.

"The Abbot of Furle arrived early in the evening with eight in his party," explained the major-domo. "Ten of our own people will have to sleep under the table. The maids may go to the stables and sleep in the hay."

Bustato watched Nicolan closely as he talked and it seemed possible he had some inkling of the latter's identity. If he had, he was keeping the knowledge to himself. Perhaps Ildico had warned him.

The two horsemen with whom he was to share one of the tiny sleeping rooms were already curled up on the reed-strewn floor, and were filling the place with the rhythm of their snoring. A length of tree trunk had been provided for a pillow. He lay down but for a long time was forbidden the solace of sleep.

3

A lane led back from the pasture lands which, after a steep climb, ended in a clump of high trees. Nicolan had been perched on a limb of the tallest of the trees since dawn. From where he sat he could see much of the land which was rightfully his and his eyes had shone as they rested on the green of the low hills and the sweetness of the fields where the Ildeburgh horses had once grazed. "I'll never get it back unless I take the bold course," was the thought which ran through his mind. "Why have I returned home disguised, like a thief in the night?"

Bracing one leg around the trunk of the tree, he drew a small bottle from his belt. It had been given him as a means of removing the stain and he proceeded to apply the contents to his face and neck with a rough vigor. By the time he exhausted the lotion, the soft rain, which had been falling for hours, had turned into a cold and ice-tipped downpour. The canopy of the clouds changed from a black as opaque as a panther's coat to a sodden gray, and the tops of the trees pitched and tossed and threatened to precipitate him to the ground.

He became aware at this point that a slender figure, muffled to the neck in a dark blue cloak and wearing one of the rough cloth caps which peasants used in the fields, was hurrying up the slope. A second glance revealed that it was Ildico.

The girl paused breathlessly in the far from adequate cover of the trees and glanced up at him. "I thought you might be here," she said.

Nicolan was taken by surprise. "There wasn't a sound in the house when I left except a footstep in the kitchens. How did you guess?"

Her eyes followed the flight of some bedraggled crows on their way to the Ildeburgh woods. "When I was a small girl I used to climb that tree often. I would sit there and pray that someday you would escape and come back. Then I would go home and beg my father to buy your freedom. But he said no one knew where you were." Then she cried out in amazement. "You've removed that ugly stain! I'm glad, although it may betray you to Ranno." She continued to stare up at him. "I'm happy to see you haven't really changed at all from the long-lost friend who came back that one day and thought he could catch me when I was riding Harthager. From the way you were disguised, I couldn't be sure." She indulged in a light laugh. "You looked like a sad and lonely monkey, pining for the jungles!"

Nicolan descended to the ground by swinging himself from limb to limb, after the order of the hairy tribe she had said he resembled. He faced her for a moment in a tense silence.

"I have loved you all my life!" he declared.

Ildico displayed her surprise at the unexpectedness of this declaration. A pink flush spread over her cheeks and brow.

"It began the first time I saw you," he went on. "That was when you were so young that you couldn't possibly remember."

"But I do," she insisted.

"My father took me along on a visit he was paying to *your* father. I was quite young myself and he was sure I was the best rider for my age that ever sat a horse. He was planning to have me show what I could do. But when we rode down this slope and came out on the flatlands, we saw a very small figure riding a black colt."

Ildico nodded her head, with excited recollections. "That was the king's grandsire. We thought he would become king but it was soon clear that he hadn't the speed."

"My father said to me, 'That must be the second daughter.' Then he drew in his horse to watch. You couldn't have been more than five years old and yet you were performing feats I had never dreamed of trying. You were taking the high hurdles and not hesitating at any of the ditches. My father said, 'She's hardly out of the cradle.' Then he turned to me with a black look on his face. 'My son,' he said, 'when we arrive, you will get off your horse and not mount again until we are ready to leave. When we get home, I shall take your training in hand myself.' I wasn't too young to realize that he was deeply mortified. 'There will always be a whip in my hands. You are going to learn to ride.' Between my father and his whip, I *did* learn." He paused. "You don't remember anything of this."

"Yes, I do. I remember everything. I saw you coming in the distance and I decided to show you I was worth some attention, even if I was so small. I remember thinking, 'It's the Ildeburgh boy. Does he think he can ride like a Roymarck?' But you looked very big and grown up to me. *How* you must have hated me!"

"No!" cried Nicolan. "I had never seen a girl with golden hair before. And you were wearing red shoes and they were small enough for a kitten. You have no idea how easy it was for me to fall in love with you.

"From that time on," he continued, "you were never out of my mind. I thought of you all day and I dreamed about you at night. Are you interested in all this?"

"Oh, I am! I am very much interested. I want to hear everything."

"When you were not in my dreams, they were vague and meaningless and soon forgotten. But I remember everything that happened when you came into them. Do you ever dream in color?"

Ildico frowned uncertainly. "In color? I don't know. I've never thought about it. As far as I can tell, my dreams are always gray in tone and not very clear."

"I heard the point discussed in Rome many times. The young patricians, looking for favors, would come to the cabinet of Aetius and try to impress him with their learning. Sitting in my corner, I heard everything they said. This was one of their favorite topics and they all seemed to think that it was due to sleeping late—all Romans slept late except Aetius—and having the sunshine on their faces. I knew they were wrong because I dreamed of you constantly and you always appeared in the most gorgeous of colors. I tried to write poems about it but I only succeeded in getting one line: 'Your hair is like the dust of fire opals.' That convinced me that I would never be able to finish a verse."

"But it was *good*," she insisted.

"In the summer, you would get a few freckles on the bridge of your nose. That delighted me because it proved you were human after all. One night I saw you much more clearly than I had ever been able to do in sunlight, and I counted them. The next day I asked you to take a mirror and count them yourself. You answered——"

"Seven," responded Ildico, promptly.

"And that was the number I had seen in my dream." He paused for a moment. "Even then I realized how presumptuous it was of me to fall in love with you. And now—well, you have rejected the hand of an Eastern king and you've been running away for years from the prospect of becoming the empress of the Huns."

"One in forty," she reminded him. "Doesn't it occur to you that there may be someone else I prefer?"

The rain was gaining in volume with each passing moment. They huddled close to the trunk of the tree for shelter and he saw that her cloak had been a poor protection against the downpour. He wrapped a veil about her throat, his fingers trembling when they came near the dimple in her cheek or touched her small chin. To break the spell, she reminded him that he had not told her why he had thrown away so soon the protection of his disguise.

"For many reasons. How could I expect to win any favor in your eyes while I looked like that sad-faced monkey from Africa? Could I hope to play any part in the preparations we should be making for the day when the Hun empire breaks up? There must be no delay about that because we can't leave the leadership in the incompetent hands of Ranno. How could I wait any longer in removing the stain from my honor by proving I had no part in the plot which sent your brother to his death?"

She looked up quickly at that. "I never believed you did! Never!"

Nicolan took possession of her hands and pressed them with a fervor which could be traced in only a small degree to gratitude. "I didn't intend to declare my love so soon," he said. "But, presumptuous or not, I found I couldn't be silent about it any longer."

"But are you being fair? A woman prefers to hear a declaration of love when she looks her best. She must be wearing the finest of silk which rustles with every move she makes. Her hair must be beautifully tired. She must be pomaded and perfumed. Certainly she must not look as I do at this moment—like a poor little half-drowned mouse."

"You look more beautiful as you are than Cleopatra in her cloth of gold and all the royal jewels of Egypt in her hair."

This won a flashing smile from her. "What a gallant speech! I shall never forget it. But, please, let me tell you first of my reason for following you here." She was able to find a dry spot close to the trunk of the tree and, seating herself there, began to speak in a low tone of voice which indicated a sudden drop of spirits. "I am certain many things are going to happen. Strange and perhaps dreadful things. I came here to meet you because I thought we should talk alone about what we are to do."

Nicolan seated himself beside her. The rain had become almost autumnal in its fury. It was as though the spirits of the air had opened all the spigots from the celestial cisterns which held the supplies stored up for winter use.

"That day at Epirus," she said, "when I rode Harthager back from the race, I found a little black man sitting against the woven fence of the enclosure, tossing gold coins in his hands. He was incredibly ugly and wicked-looking. But, when he spoke to me, it was in a friendly and persuasive voice. He said he had won the gold by betting on me and the black, and he wanted to repay me with a word of advice.

"It seems he was from Africa and was in some small way a trainer of racing horses, so that he came in touch with all manner of people. He had heard much talk. 'Go away,' he said. 'Go away at once. That Attila, that bad man, he has spies here. They will lose no time in letting him know about you.' I said to him that Attila couldn't do me any harm so far away from his borders but the little black man shook his head. 'He will catch all your people and your friends and he will threaten to kill them by slow torture unless you go to him. But he can't do that if you vanish from sight. Listen to me, my lady. Go over to Athens. Take boat there for the East. Go as far as Cathay. There only will you be safe from this very bad man.'

"I told the widow about it. She knew the trainer. 'He's an honest little whipster,' she said. 'If he says Attila has agents here, then it's the truth he's telling. We had better leave at once.' So we left that night when it was dark. The little man came to see us go. He told me, 'Agent of bad man has had picture of you painted to send to him. You better ride fast.' We rode fast until we reached Athens but we didn't take ship there. As you know, we rode north to Constantinople instead.

"I talked to my father last night," she continued, "and he gave me the same advice as my little friend from Africa. We must all leave at once. The only safe plan would be to cross into Gaul by the route north of the great mountains and take ship for the East from Marseilles. He said Eugenia and Ivar must go with me, and Laudio, if she could be persuaded to leave."

"Did he know about me?" asked Nicolan.

"I told him you were with us. He sank into a long silence and then said, 'He will be needed here when Attila's empire breaks into pieces like a ripe nut under a blacksmith's hammer.' I said that was your reason for taking the risk of coming back, and he said, 'He will fill the place of my poor Roric.' I told him then that I did not intend to run away."

"But you must!" said Nicolan, vehemently.

Ildico kept her eyes fixed on the path which had been baked so hard that the rain rebounded when it struck the earth.

"No," she said. "I will persuade the others to go. There is no reason for them to risk their lives. But my place is here."

"What did my lord Macio say to that?"

"He asked me if it was because of you that I wanted to stay. I said——" She seemed to find it impossible to go on. Her face, which had been pale and tense, was suffused suddenly with color.

"Please. Tell me the answer you gave him."

She looked up then and her lips quivered slightly as she said, "I told him, 'Yes.'"

They looked steadily into each other's eyes for some moments without saying anything more. Words were no longer necessary. He had received his answer and a great wave of joy swept over him, even though he knew that the future held out small hope of happiness for them.

Finally he said, leaning forward and gathering her hands into his, "Do you agree that it's my duty to remain?"

She did not hesitate. "We will probably lose our lives. But there is no other course."

Nicolan nodded somberly. "Ranno will lose no time in laying charges against me in the Ferma. It's just as certain that Attila has spies who will get word to him that you are here. Do you still want to face the risk?"

"I will stay with you."

"Then," said Nicolan, "we must take such precautions as we may. I will see Father Simon at once and ask him to marry us. Perhaps he will agree to share the sanctuary of his cave in the Belden Hill."

"As long as my father remains alive, I must stay with him. Then—if nothing has come about to prevent it—I will join you. There will be room for both of us in the cave. Father Simon told me once it was large and not *very* damp."

Nicolan shook his head with grave misgivings. "I've brought you to a sorry pass. To have refused two thrones and then come to *this!*"

The tendency her eyes had to crinkle slightly at the corners when she smiled showed itself for a moment. "I am content," she said. "I think we should go back now. I haven't seen my father this morning and he may be asking for me."

She stooped to remove her shoes. "I'll go barefooted on the grass," she decided. The shoes were so small that they seemed to have no weight when Nicolan held them in his hand. He put them in an inside pocket of his thoroughly soaked tunic. Then he placed a hand on each of her shoulders and drew her around to face him. "Our great Lord on high, by whose command all things are done, was not fair when He decided to have you cast in such a beautiful form. Not fair, I mean, to other women, and to the unfortunate men who see you and fall madly and hopelessly in love." He drew her close to him and kissed her for the first time. It was a fervid kiss and it seemed as though he meant it to last forever. If such were his intent, she gave no hint of dissent but nestled happily into the support of his shoulder. "I can believe now that you really belong to me. And I am the happiest mortal on earth!"

As they stepped out, hand in hand, from the shelter of the trees, the rain seemed to be diminishing in volume. The sky grew less dark and forbidding. They began to run nevertheless on the wet grass, paying no heed to the pools of water through which they splashed. Before they reached the level ground, it was clear that the storm had passed. A cold wind reached them from the north and the clouds began to break into fantastic shapes. Shafts of light appeared dramatically through the rents in the black canopy above.

Nicolan pressed the hand she had confided to his care when they began their return. "I believe you can run as fast as I can," he said. "And yet I saw no trace of wings on your ankles."

Ildico stopped when they reached the hedge which marked off the pasture grounds, although she was trembling from the discomfort of her wet garments.

"This will be worth seeing," she said to him. "I am curious to find if—if the kingship of Harthager is still recognized."

All the horses had sought shelter in the sheds but, as soon as it was clear that the downpour was over, a black muzzle appeared in the opening. Its owner, apparently, was giving the situation a careful appraisal, for it was a minute before the full head could be seen.

"I knew it!" cried Ildico, in a voice filled with delight. "They've waited for him to give them the word of command. Now watch."

Harthager emerged slowly from the shed. He walked a little distance into the open space, then stopped and raised his head to study the clouds above him. A swish of his tail seemed to be intended as a signal, for the rest of the horses began at once to follow him out, the older ones coming first. They were careful to remain in a close group behind him, the effect being of a general surveying a field of battle with his staff remaining respectfully in the rear. The youngsters then ventured out, the "baws" and the two-year-olds. They dashed madly for the far reaches of the pasture, where they frisked and caracoled and kicked their heels, racing in small groups in an exhibition of wild spirits.

Ildico crouched down below the level of the hedge and motioned to Nicolan to do the same. "I mustn't disappoint him," she said, in a low tone. "I have nothing for him and he'll be expecting apples and lumps of saccharum. I think we should get away at once."

They began to follow the hedge in the direction of the house. "You rate the powers of the great Harthager very high," said Nicolan. "Sometimes it seems you think him born with human intelligence."

It was hard to believe that anything resembling the unmannerly sound generally described as a snort could issue from a nose as delicately made as Ildico's. But her response to his remark fell most certainly into some such category.

"He's wiser than most people," she declared. "He always knows how to conduct himself and what to do. He keeps himself in good condition and never eats too much. He commands respect and holds his followers in their places. And what a wonderful heart he has!"

"You know much more about horses than I do," conceded Nicolan, humbly.

"My dear one, you've lacked the chance. You were so young when the slavers took you away. Besides, your father and most of the other large landowners had cattle and sheep as well as horses.

The Roymarcks have confined themselves to breeding horses for generations and generations. Perhaps for centuries. I'm sure we've learned things about them that isn't known to anyone else." After a thoughtful pause she added, "I'm afraid there will be a break in the family line someday and that all the things we know will be lost and forgotten forever."

"You believe they know what you say?"

"In a way. Oh, they don't know the meaning of many words but they can read the tones of your voice. They know if you are pleased or angry. They can tell when you are happy and when you are sad. They watch you out of the corners of their eyes and can tell what you intend to do." She paused. "Did you talk to your horses much?"

"No. Not much."

"But you should. They love it more than anything else. Make no mistake, horses don't like to be left alone and they are happiest when someone is working around them and *talking*. Let me tell you a story about Harthager. In the race at Constantinople, when we came back on the course, I knew it was almost impossible to make up the lost ground. There were two other horses ahead of us as well as the Arab who was far in front. I leaned close to the king's ear and talked about how necessary it was to beat that fast little fellow. I beseeched him to do his best, over and over, because the thunder of the hoofs made it hard for him to hear. But finally he seemed to understand. Nicolan, he nodded! A cool, matter-of-fact shake of his handsome head. And immediately he lengthened his stride. He took charge of the race from that moment on and I was happy to leave it all to him.

"Well, when we flashed by the post so close to the Arab that I wasn't certain we had won, Harthager turned his head. For the briefest moment. He looked back at me and caught my eye. He gave me a deliberate nod. It was as though he said to me: 'You asked me to beat him, my lady. And I've done so.'

"But I wasn't sure. It had been so close that the judges might give the victory to the Arab. I said: 'Oh, King, are you sure? Were we really ahead? Did we win?' He turned again. There was just a hint of amusement for human frailties, a trace of impatience even in the lift of his head. I felt he was chiding me, as though he were saying, 'You should take my word for it. I *know* when I have won.'"

A voice reached them from the direction of the house. They could not see the owner of it but it was evident that extreme urgency was back of the summons. Ildico straightened up.

"It's for me!" she said, in a tone breathless with apprehension. "It must be about Father. Nicolan, I'm afraid! We must lose no time."

She did not pause to replace her shoes but began to run down the road. It was rough and deeply rutted and must have pained her bare feet. But, with fear lending her speed, she was able to keep pace with Nicolan's long legs.

She said, when they reached the entrance, "This may be the first of the blows of fate I have been expecting!"

4

The summons, it developed, was for Nicolan and not for Ildico. The crotchety Bustato took one look at him and said to himself, "It is as I thought," before leading the way through the curtains of rough cloth which served as door to Macio's bedroom. The major-domo threw open the wooden shutters which kept the darkness in and the Devil out.

The room was bare of furnishings, save for the bed, which had the rare distinction of being raised from the floor on legs. There was a crucifix on one wall and the sword of the old warrior stood in a corner.

The eyes of the dying man, feverishly large in his wasted face, turned to the visitor. "You are Nicolan, son of Saladar of the Ildeburghs," he said in a slow whisper. "I have something for your ears alone."

Nicolan knelt on one knee beside the couch. "I am at your service, my lord Macio."

Each word spoken by the old man had left him breathless. Now, however, he seemed to call on some reserve of strength, for he began to talk without any hesitations or delays. "I can trust you. My son Roric, once your friend, is not dead. He is alive and on his way here. But he was sorely wounded and he has not yet much strength."

"God be praised!" said Nicolan, fervently. "This is what I have prayed for so often. It will be the answer to all our difficulties and our troubles." He added after a moment, "I think we were as close as David and Jonathan."

The head of Macio, over which the skin was stretched so tautly that it resembled a skull, turned slowly in the cane frame which served him as a pillow. "Son of my old friend," he whispered, "believe what I am going to tell you. I saw Roric and talked with him during the night. It was in a dream and yet I know that what I saw and heard was real."

The old man proceeded to tell his story in low whispers and with long pauses for rest between sentences. It was clear to him that he had remained in his own bed, because he could see the glint of moonlight on the handle of his sword. The side of the room which faced him, however, had been removed so that he could stare out into open space without moving. The extraordinary thing was that his tired eyes had not rested on the ground about the house. What he saw was foreign terrain which, although strange in most respects, still impressed him with a sense of familiarity. There was a ridge of hills in the background, the peaks standing up tall and gaunt against the sky. A stream issued out from this rocky curtain and meandered slowly across the flat land, coming close to the open end of the room before swinging abruptly and vanishing from sight. On the far side of the water stood a circular stone house of considerable size. From somewhere in the distance came a continuous and mournful sound which he identified as the lowing of cattle.

It was as though the bedroom had been lifted up on magic wings and transported to a far country before being set down so that he could look out over the new scene like a spectator at a play.

Then he heard his son's voice say, "You have come at last, my father."

"Have you been expecting me, Roric?"

"Yes, my father. I have needed you."

Macio was certain at this point that he had died and that his son had come to greet him and help him on his way over the mountains and on his path far up into the skies. This impression, however, was not of long duration. Roric, he perceived, had been so badly wounded that an ugly scar had taken the place of one eye. He was very weak and seemed to have found the few steps it had been necessary for him to take a drain on his small store of strength. Macio knew that men do not take their mutilations with them when they climb up to the kingdom of heaven and that all their physical infirmities vanish when their souls take wing. He was sure, therefore, that it was Roric in the flesh who came into the room and stationed himself beside the couch.

The talk between father and son had not been a protracted one. Roric explained how he had remained alive after being so badly wounded in the great battle. Another survivor had carried him off the field and for several months he had existed in constant pain and distress in the hut of a Frankish peasant. Finally he had gained enough strength to begin the long journey homeward. He had traveled alone and had found it necessary to take long periods of rest, depending on the charity of the poor people in the lands through which he was making his way.

There was complete understanding between father and son. Each was capable of reading what was in the mind of the other. Roric knew how close his father lay to death. He was aware also that Ildico had returned and that Nicolan had come with her.

"I will not get back in time unless I have help," Roric repeated several times. His father realized that he was referring to the peril which hung over his sister and his friend. "Send Nicolan to me here. At once."

At this point in his story the old man was so exhausted that Nicolan saw the heavy lids close over his eyes and realized he lacked the power to continue. After several moments of anxious watching, he asked, "Where must I go to find him?"

Not for a moment had he doubted what he had been told. The land of dreams was a dim and mysterious region where things came to pass which soothsayers alone could understand, or perhaps the Selloi who slept under the whispering branches of Dodona. It was easy for him to believe that the minds of father and son had been brought together in this strange way.

It was some time before Macio answered. "I—I cannot tell. My mind refuses to guide my tongue."

Nicolan had been recalling, as the old man spoke, that during his boyhood his own father had often journeyed into Raetia, which lay just beyond the borders of the small corner of Noricum where the plateau people lived. He remembered also his sire's report of that province as a place of high foothills where the people devoted themselves to the raising of cattle.

"Is he in Raetia?" he asked.

Macio's eyes opened again at this point but it was clear to Nicolan that now the vision of the chain of hills against the sky had left him and that all he saw was the bare wall of the room and the one window with its opened shutters.

"Raetia," the old man repeated in a whisper. He moved painfully on his couch and the cane rest creaked under his head. "I cannot remember."

"It lies in the path Roric would take in coming home," said Nicolan. "He would strike south between the mountains and the great river and so his path would lead through Raetia. But it's large and thinly settled."

The sick man succeeded in shaking his head with a suggestion of impatience with his own weakness. "Names have left me. A woman came after I wakened. She said she was my daughter."

"Was it Laudio?"

The name apparently meant nothing. "She was a stranger."

Nicolan began to question the old man with a sense of desperation. He was now taking it for granted that Roric's temporary sanctuary was in Raetia. He phrased his queries slowly and carefully. Was it far away? Was it close to the river? By which spur of the foothills was it located? By which road could it be reached? Macio, it was clear, was striving just as desperately to draw together the faint wisps of recollection which were left to him but with little success. The only clue he could give was a word which conveyed no meaning at first to his questioner. "Rukh," he whispered. He repeated it several times before sinking into a state of partial coma.

"Rukh?" said Nicolan, to himself. The word seemed to stir some recollection in him but it was so vague that it kept eluding him. Finally he gave up the effort.

Macio's breathing had become light and fitful. The hand of Bustato touched Nicolan's arm. "Come," said the major-domo, looking down at the face of his master. "It will be of no use to ask more questions now. Perhaps when he has rested he will be able to talk. But I don't know. He may never rouse now."

As they left the room Nicolan asked, "Did your master go often to Raetia?"

"Not of recent years, my lord. There was a time when he went frequently. To buy cattle. Or to trade horses for cows."

"Did you go with him?"

"Never. My duties kept me here. My lord Roric often rode with his father and half a dozen of his best horsemen always went. The border between this country and Raetia was full of bandits."

"Did he deal with more than one breeder of cattle?"

"I think not, my lord."

"Can you tell me the dealer's name?"

Bustato frowned in concentration and then gave his head a shake. "I knew it once. I think he must have come from the Alamanni, for it was a heathenish name. Perhaps it will come back to me but at the moment it has gone out of my mind."

"I could get the information from one of the horsemen who served as guards."

But Bustato gave his head a second shake. "No, my lord. They were all killed in the great battle."

The wide-spreading red house of the Roymarcks was lacking in many respects; but above all else it lacked privacy. It swarmed with people of high and low degree at all times of the day. They filled the halls, they squatted in corners, they talked and disputed and declaimed. When Nicolan emerged from the room of the head of the household, he found that the space between the main entrance and the high wooden framework closing off the great hall was pre-empted by Ildico, supported by the Lady Eugenia and surrounded by the female servants of the establishment. Having no better place to go, they had gathered here. The floor was heaped high with feminine attire, all in the multicolored magnificence of Byzantium, and articles of oriental derivation. There was much talk going on and exclamations of wonder and even some laughter.

Ildico, quite clearly, had received a good report of her father's condition from Bustato, for there was no trace of immediate strain on her face. She had changed from her wet clothes to something graceful and becoming in green and yellow, with a portrait of her father done with golden thread and small semiprecious stones on the tablion which drew her tunica in snugly at the waist. Her old dog Bozark lay at her feet, or more properly under her feet, and was snoring happily. In her arms she held a silver-toned kitten with long hair and a very bushy tail.

The servants scattered on noiseless feet when Nicolan appeared in the hall, taking with them the presents which the daughter of the house had brought with her. The purpose of the gathering, apparently, had been to distribute them.

Eugenia looked up at him and then glanced quickly at Ildico. This transfer of her interest was repeated several times and then she began to smile. "How wise of you, Nicolan," she said, "to get rid of that absurd disguise! It has come about at last. Ah, the sweetness of young love! It is written all over your faces. And I am reminded that my presence here is no longer necessary or desirable. I shall join my husband and the good churchmen who are breaking their fast on boiled mutton and duck's eggs. A rather more substantial meal than I seem to require at the moment."

Ildico's hair was hanging down her back and overflowing on the oak bench where she sat. One of the maids had been combing it, and several toilet articles, of purpose unknown to Nicolan, still lay at one end of the seat.

Not once during the days that they journeyed together had he seen her without a dark covering on her head, and her face had not escaped its due share of the dust of the road. Now this glorious creature took his breath away. Even his capacity for vivid recollection had failed to supply him with any indication of the burnished beauty of her hair. In the richly colored robes from Constantinople, she had seemed a little more mature and her face had carried a faint hint of bronze from the sun; but this girl who smiled up at him was slender and white, her eyes a dazzling blue, her nose and brows of such beauty that the finest sculptor in the years of Grecian glory would have thrown his chisels down in despair.

"Now I *know* it was a dream!" said Nicolan.

"A dream? What are you talking about in that most doleful voice?"

"What happened out there in the rain."

"No," she said, smiling at him. "It was not a dream. You told me you loved me. And I, with a proper degree of maidenly reserve, I trust, made it clear that I—that I felt the same way about you. We decided, in fact, to be married. And I have no intention of allowing all this to be considered a dream."

While he continued to study her with worshipful eyes, she raised her skirt a few inches to show that the feet which rested on the furry back of Bozark were bare. "Perhaps you will be good enough," she said, "to restore my shoes."

Nicolan drew them hastily from a pocket in his tunic. They were so completely Grecian and different that, even in his bemused condition, he gave them a moment's study. In Rome the sandal was still worn almost exclusively but these were of the variety known as *calcei*, made of very soft skin, with a thin reinforcement on the soles and with tops which were bound with silk cords to cover the ankles.

He allowed the delicate green footwear to fall on the floor and looked up with sudden gravity.

"The sight of you has driven everything out of my mind," he declared. "Your father told me that Roric is alive."

Ildico was at first overcome with astonishment. Then her face lighted up in a manifestation of uncontrollable joy. "O, Nicolan, Nicolan! Do you mean it? Are you sure you heard him aright? It seems too wonderful to be true!" She leaned forward then and it was apparent that she was experiencing some doubts, for she began to pour out questions without waiting for answers. "When did the word come? It must have been this morning because I was with my father late last night and he said nothing of it. Why was I not told? What messenger brought the word?"

"The messenger," he said, "was too lacking in substance to be visible to the human eye." He proceeded to report in full detail what Macio had told him. Ildico listened in a state of changing moods, determined to believe the story yet afraid to accept it, lifted up with hopes but cast down quickly by the doubts which refused to be put aside.

By the time he was through, she seemed to have been convinced. "The power is often given to see into the future when one stands close on the threshold of death," she declared. "What is your feeling?"

"I think I should begin to search for him at once, whether I believe it or not."

"But where will you go? Where will you begin to look?"

"I'll cross the border into Raetia. From what your father said, I am certain he is somewhere in that province. But Raetia is large and it has few roads."

"Did he say why he was telling you?"

"Because he wants me to lead a party in to find Roric. It may prove a tough adventure, with hard riding and some riffling with the sword. If Ranno hears a whisper of what is afoot, he will do everything in his power to prevent your brother from getting through. Roric holds the fate of that coward and traitor in his hands." He paused for a moment. "Laudio was in to see your father this morning. She seems to have been questioning him."

Ildico's face displayed alarm. "She left early this morning and no one knows where she has gone."

"I think it's clear enough she has gone to see Ranno. She looked at me closely last night and I felt sure she recognized me."

"That means Ranno will proceed at once to lay charges before the Ferma. He will see the need to get a decision before Roric can get back. You must go to Oslaw at once and tell him everything."

"Oslaw! Is he still alive?"

"Fortunately, yes. Alive and active. He still conducts all trials before the Ferma."

The strained look on Nicolan's face was replaced by one of hope. "Oslaw has always been fair. I can depend on a thorough hearing with him in charge. But the first thing is to locate Roric and bring him home. I have one small clue. Your father repeated a word several times as though he hoped it would help me. Do you recall a gift someone brought you from the East, a collection of figures carved out of ivory? It was when you were very young. I saw it once and I thought the figures were most beautifully wrought."

"It was a game," said Ildico, thoughtfully. "I haven't seen it for years so I suppose it was put away. I will ask Bustato." Then she changed her mind. "No, his memory is getting very short. I'll ask old Blurki."

Old Blurki, accordingly, was summoned. He nodded his head, vanished for a few minutes, and then returned with a low table of teakwood on which stood a variety of pieces most elaborately carved out of ivory.

"The sport of kings and wise men," said the old jester. "But sometimes fools usurp the functions of the great. I, for instance, the most ignorant of all fools, can play the game. I have never played against a king but I've caused the faces of bishops and abbots and learned men of the law to burn with mortification on some occasions."

Nicolan was studying the exquisitely designed pieces with a thoughtful air. Finally he reached out and lifted one which resembled a slender tower with turrets. "What is this one called?" he asked.

"The rukh," replied Blurki.

"That's it!" cried Nicolan, starting up so abruptly that he overturned the table and sent the pieces rolling in all directions. "That's the word your father repeated. What he wanted me to take from it was that this cattle breeder has always used a sign on his stock which resembles a tower. The rukh. That's the key!" He asked the clown who was down on his knees collecting the pieces, "What breeder in Raetia burns the sign of a tower on his cattle so they can't be stolen or claimed?"

"Victorex of the Foothills."

"Victorex!" exclaimed Nicolan, triumphantly. "That's the name I've been trying to remember."

Old Blurki left and Ildico rose to her feet. With a deft movement of one arm she caught her hair up and wound it around her head.

"Now we know what we must do," she said. "If Roric is alive—and somehow I am certain he is!—we must get to him at once. First, you must see Oslaw and tell him your story. I want to be with you when you do. How far are the lands of Victorex from here?"

"Something over one hundred miles. Six days, there and back. Perhaps it can be done before the crisis. Do you mean that you intend to go with me?"

"Of course! I shall speak to my father first. But I'm certain he counts on the return of Roric above everything else."

Neither of them had given any thought, it was clear, to the question of personal safety. In less than an hour's time Ildico could be off in the train of Eugenia and on the road which would take her north of the Alps and free for all time of the danger from Attila. Two brisk days in the saddle would carry Nicolan far beyond any trouble from the machinations of Ranno. But they were both convinced that they must bring Roric back and then face the charges which Ranno would lay before the Ferma.

Ildico, after pressing his hand with a sudden fierce possessiveness, left him to visit her father. It was half an hour before she returned and the pallor of her face told him the story.

"He is dead!" she said. "He knew me at the end but he could not speak. Come, my love, we must be on our way."

CHAPTER VIII

1

IN THE plateau country, where men loved the sunshine, there were no prisons. It was customary for those against whom charges were laid to remain, pending the hearings, in a small building at the center of the space set for the sessions of the Ferma. Here, under the eye of the Orator of that body, they were allowed a certain degree of freedom. They could receive their families and friends and they could go where they pleased within a radius of five miles. They were under oath to remain and to abide by the decisions of the court, even when the death penalty was involved. This attitude had become ingrained in the people of the plateau by continuous application of the rule and by centuries of tradition. Not once within the memory of the oldest inhabitant had a defendant taken advantage of this partial freedom to run away.

When the two lovers came within sight of the bowl in the foothills, they reined in and considered the prospect. Ildico, who had wept at intervals during the ride, applied a square of linen firmly to her eyes and said, "I must keep my grief to myself now."

"My father talked of bringing me here," said Nicolan, studying the space within the bowl, which seemed because of its geometrical accuracy to have been scooped out by the hand of man. "But he never did."

"I was brought to see a trial once. It took my breath away. The slopes were filled with people, sitting close together. I don't remember much about the case except that it had to do with a murder. When the verdict was announced, everyone stood up with their right arms extended. A sign of their agreement with the decision of the court."

"Was he found guilty?"

"Yes." Her manner had suddenly become subdued. "But it wasn't a man. It was a woman."

"Was she put to death?"

Ildico nodded silently. For several moments nothing more was said, then she sighed deeply. "I've been trying to keep that part of it out of my mind."

"I wouldn't dare look you in the face if I took the easy way."

"It keeps going around and around in my head. Deep down inside me, I know that there is only one course for us. You are an Ildeburgh and I am of the Roymarcks. We can do nothing else. But I can't help thinking of—of consequences." She pressed his hand suddenly and then smiled. "It can't happen. Not to you. Your innocence will be so—so apparent. If the verdict should be wrong, the people will show their disapproval. They won't raise a hand. It happened once that way."

"What did the judges do?"

"They didn't change the verdict but they made the sentence a mild one. It was found later that he was innocent."

"But in my case, the voice of the people will be against me. Ranno has seen to that." He paused and allowed his gaze to roam over the natural amphitheater beneath them. "You said, my sweet and beautiful one, that when you saw that trial the people filled all the slopes. How could they hear?"

"Do you see those small raised platforms at regular intervals? Announcers stand on each of them. The Orator has a staff of clerks who write down the important questions and answers and send them up to the men on the platforms to be read aloud."

In the center of the bowl there was a small level space (at least it seemed small from where they were), containing on one side a rather pretentious building and on the other a raised row of seats for the members of the Ferma. It was on the space between that the trials were enacted. They turned their horses onto one of four paths which led downward, Nicolan riding first. He looked back over his shoulder and saw that her courage had returned in full measure. Her eyes were shining.

"My brave one," he said.

An elderly man met them on the level space below. He was dressed plainly in a gray tunic with a cord around his waist, from which were suspended two keys of ancient design. He came forward as soon as his eyes rested on Ildico and laid a hand on the mane of her horse.

"I heard of your return," he said. "How happy a chance that you came in time to see your father alive."

Nicolan said to himself: "Ranno has been here already. The news could not have been had in any other way." He could not avoid a sense of alarm. Ranno was moving fast.

"There is sorrow in your eyes, my child," the Orator was saying. "Does it mean he has gone at last, my good old friend?"

"Yes, my lord Oslaw. He died this morning."

The dark eyes of the old man, under the heavy white thatch of his brows, showed how deeply he felt. "We must all go when our time comes. But this is a grievous blow. How shall we get along without him? He and I faced many troubles together. He was brave and wise, and as firm as a rock. We stood out many times against the clamor of the people and it was always found later that we were right. I have missed him sadly since the ills of old age have been upon him."

He shifted his gaze to Nicolan. "I heard at the same time of your return. Ranno has just left. He rode over in a great lather, having been told the news himself this morning." The manner of the old man displayed an increased gravity. "Your father was one of my best friends and so I am deeply concerned. Ranno has laid charges against you and is demanding an immediate hearing before the Ferma. Had you any reason for suspecting this?"

Nicolan nodded his head. "I've known of his activities. It was partly to clear my name of the lies he has been spreading that I came."

"It is treason he lays at your door. And a conspiracy which resulted in the deaths of so many of our young men."

"There *was* a conspiracy," declared Nicolan. "If I can get my witnesses here, I am prepared to lay countercharges. Placing the blame for the tragedy at Châlons where it belongs: on Ranno's own shoulders."

"We have reason to believe," said Ildico, "that my brother is alive."

The old man turned back to her with an eagerness of manner which indicated where his personal sympathies lay.

"Roric is alive! Ah, what a stroke of good fortune! To have him return, seemingly from the grave, and at such an opportune moment! When did this most welcome word reach you?"

"Perhaps," said Ildico, "we are too prone to believe the story. My father saw him in his dreams last night and talked with him."

Oslaw looked up with openly sharpened interest. "He appeared to his father in a dream? I am an old man, my child, but never have the dead come to me in my sleep and talked with me. It is against the laws of nature. I think this may mean that Roric is indeed alive." He frowned uneasily. "How far away is he supposed to be?"

"In Raetia. With Victorex, the cattle breeder. To get there and back will take a week."

The old man turned to Nicolan. "You know the laws of the Ferma. Since charges have been laid against you, you may not go farther away than five miles. But it is part of my responsibility to see that the witnesses for both sides are in attendance. I'm prepared to send out a party of horsemen in search of Roric."

"It was my father's wish to have Nicolan lead the party," declared Ildico.

Oslaw shook his head firmly. "I am sorry. But this rule is one that cannot be broken."

"My brother is still suffering from his wound. Someone he will recognize and trust must be with the party. If Nicolan cannot go, I shall take his place."

Oslaw gave the matter several moments of close consideration. "This must be handled with the greatest secrecy. Ranno will go to any lengths to prevent Roric from appearing at the trial. If he gets wind of what is afoot, he will not stop at anything. At least half a dozen good horsemen will be needed, honest fellows, ready to risk their skins in a rough and perhaps desperate adventure. Is it necessary, my child, for you to take a share in such risks?"

"I am sure it would be my father's wish if he were alive." Her eyes, which had been so filled with doubt and distress, had suddenly come to life. To Nicolan they seemed more vividly blue than he had ever seen them. "I am certain that Roric is alive. I must not lose a moment in setting out to find him."

An hour later a party of eight took off on the road to Raetia. Riding in the midst of the horsemen, in a robe of the roughest cloth, Ildico was sufficiently well disguised to escape recognition.

Nicolan walked his horse beside her on the climb to the top of the slope.

"If we had been a half hour earlier!" he said. "We would have been off to find Roric before Ranno could lay his charges. If we were lucky enough to bring your brother back with us, Ranno would have been in a sorry position; for Roric's evidence would destroy him."

"We will ride like the wind!" declared Ildico. She reached out and drew him near enough for her head to rest against his shoulder. "Roric is alive. Something inside me says that it is so. . . ."

"You must promise me to be discreet, my loved one. See that the utmost care is taken on the journey back. Word of what you are doing will reach Ranno and he will have the roads watched. Ride as much as possible at night."

They paused on the crest for a brief moment. "I don't consider myself the victim of ill luck," he said. "This morning you said that you love me. What more can a man ask of life? I shall be happy if you bring Roric back. But come home safely yourself."

2

Oslaw led the way to a room in the house which faced the stand of the judges. Here he had lived for the forty years during which he had held the post of Orator. Here also during that period the defendants had been lodged, pending the hearing of their cases.

When they were seated, the old man knitted his thin scholarly fingers back of his head as he settled himself to listen. There was an autumnal nip in the air following the heavy downpour, and the position he assumed revealed the fact that he had already donned the long woolen garments that Roman soldiers wore when campaigning in cold climates.

"Your father was a brave man," he said. "Too brave for his own good. You have given evidence of an equal share of courage. And of unusual capacity. Now we must get to the core of things and determine how wise you have been in the matters which must be discussed before the judges."

Nicolan had found his attention drawn to the old man's hands, which he employed to accent what he said. If fingers can be eloquent, these spoke in Ciceronian measures. Later it would be demonstrated how dramatically they could be used to drive a point home.

"I have a sincere desire," continued Oslaw, "to be helpful to you within the bounds of my official duties. I must have the whole truth. There must be no hiding of facts, no juggling with words. I promise that I shall use every resource to extract the truth also from those who will testify against you. That, as you know, is my function."

Nicolan told his story in full detail, beginning with the tour he had made on the evening before the battle to study the slopes of the hill occupied by the Goths. He explained the report he had carried back to Attila, recommending an attack by foot troops on the eastern face; of the visit Roric had paid him during the night and the things they had said; of the station he had been assigned on the morning of the battle and how he had directed the work of the dispatch riders; of his efforts to countermand the orders of Prince Tallimundi which had sent Roric with his horsemen up the steep northern slope; and finally of his meeting with Ranno in the closing phases of the battle.

Oslaw of the Solvars listened with deep absorption. Once or twice he nodded and at intervals he interjected questions. At the finish he remained in thought for several moments.

"You have given me a clear picture of the battle," he said.

With the unsteadiness of ancient muscles, Oslaw shuffled to a window. Resting one knee on a marble bench, he gazed out in the direction that Ildico's party had taken. He began to speak in low tones. "I have not been content with the explanations Ranno has made to me," he said. "As each of you is the sole surviving member of a leading family, it will become a case of one man's word against the other; and I may tell you that Ranno has worked day and night to poison the people against you. If Roric is alive, his word should be sufficient to dictate the decision. But let us suppose he is not alive. What I said to his sister may not apply in this case, for it is also true that in the last extremity men are like to become vague and confused in their minds, to talk wildly and without sense or substance. If there is no help to be obtained from Roric, then we must depend on other evidence. What witnesses can you bring?"

"The Huns are already streaming up through the passes," said

THE DARKNESS AND THE DAWN

Nicolan. "Attila will probably disband at once. If I could be on hand, it might be possible to bring Prince Tallimundi back with me or, at the worst, a statement from him. There are also the two dispatch riders who carried the messages back and forth. Somutu and Passilis. They were bitterly concerned over the mistake made in sending our troops up the slope and they promised to support me if it came to a hearing later."

"As I have already explained, the law prevents you from going. Could anyone act in your behalf?"

"My friend, Ivar the Briton. He was with me all day at Châlons and was familiar with the dispatches which were exchanged. We might send him to headquarters to find Somutu and Passilis."

"There will be time enough," declared the old man, after a mental calculation. "Where is the Briton to be found?"

"He is married to the lady once called the widow of Tergeste and is with her at the house of the Roymarcks."

A smile brought a host of wrinkles around the shrewd eyes of the Orator. "It is generally the case that the evidence of an alien does little to convince our judges," he said. "Still, as the husband of the wealthiest woman in the world, his word may carry some weight. I will send him out at once. If he fails to find any of your friends, he must come back in great haste, for what he knows will prove of some help to us."

The discussion between them went on for another hour. Nicolan was encouraged to talk about his reasons for the course he had followed, in particular of his service on Attila's staff. While he talked, the Orator got to his feet again and paced about the room. Sometimes he would halt and ask an abrupt question. On a few occasions, he prefaced a query by raising his hand and pointing a long index finger at the testator. Whenever he did this, Nicolan felt an impact as though a current had been projected from the tip in his direction. On points of special importance, they went over the ground again and again, seeking further light or striving for information not previously recalled.

At the end, Nicolan was exhausted. His appearance must have made this evident, for the elderly inquisitor, who seemed still quite fresh, paused in his questioning. He walked to the chair where the younger man sat and laid a hand on his shoulder.

"I am convinced," he said, "that you have been striving to tell me everything you remember. In the matter of veracity—well, I must say nothing about that. But I feel I should leave you with a word of warning. Son of my old friend, the case against you is strong. Ranno is leaving nothing undone to get a conviction against you. He is clever and he has friends, and much influence. He has unseated some of the older members of the Ferma and replaced them with younger men, all his own adherents.

"Do not allow yourself," he went on, earnestly, "to feel too confident of the outcome. Unless you can bring the witnesses you have named, it may be hard for you to contest the testimony of Ranno and those who will come forward to support him. I am a Christian and I believe that truth will win if God in His wisdom so wills. And yet I must add that I have served as Orator for many long years and I have known cases where, because too little was known of the circumstances, the truth did not prevail.

"Bear this in mind also," he concluded. "I am well disposed to you personally but duty imposes a strict impartiality on me. I must do everything possible to obtain for the members of the Ferma a convincing picture of the case. And in the end the decision rests with them."

CHAPTER IX

1

NICOLAN looked up at the sky where a few stars showed. Well above the dark shadow of hill and forest, the clouds were lighted with a reddish glow. He knew what this meant and he wished it had been possible for him to look once again on the face of Macio of the Roymarcks before they wrapped his body in its velvet robes and committed it to the flames.

The next morning the guard, who shadowed his movements when he left the grounds, brought out one of the light but deadly whips used in dueling. He gave it a preliminary swish. "More practice today?" he asked.

Nicolan took the whip into his hands. "I have been improving," he said.

"Yes, you are better," conceded the guard, whose name was Jackla. "But I hear Ranno always has a whip in his hands these days. What do you suppose he's planning to do? Challenge you if you win the verdict?"

"I was never afraid of Ranno. When we were boys, I was sure I could beat him at anything. I still feel that way. He can practice as much as he likes." Nicolan returned the whip. "In the meantime I must see some of the older families today. I'm going to need all the support they can give me."

"Few of them left," answered the guard, who seemed to take a friendly interest in his welfare. "The old ones are dying. Many of the young are gone too. Wiped out in the battle."

"Well, Jackla, I must see those who remember my father and mother. Particularly those who will recall how the Finninalders stole our land after my father was killed."

Jackla pulled reflectively at the end of his long red nose. "Most of them dead now. Do you want a word of advice? Have a care about that word 'steal.' Young Ranno's been working hard to get feeling on his side. Far as I'm concerned, it's the word to use but—you've got enough to stand against as it is." An expression of deep dislike had settled on Jackla's face. "Young Ranno! He got me ten lashes once with his lying tongue when I was a boy. He seems to think I don't remember it and expects me to act as a spy for him. He gets me aside when you're not looking and asks me questions. Where have you been and who have you seen? What did you ask? What were you told? What did this one say and what did that one tell you? Are any of them friendly to you? He's a sneaking hound, that Ranno!"

Nicolan encountered many disappointments during the hours which followed but the result was as favorable, perhaps, as he might have anticipated. The feeling in the plateau country did not run wholly against him. A few of the old friends of his parents had even promised to appear in his behalf before the Ferma.

He was silent, however, when he reached his room in the council house that night. Too many women had rushed out as he passed to cry that the blood of their husbands and brothers was on his hands. Some had taken to throwing stones. One old crone had hidden herself in the brush and had sprung at him with a knife in her hand, screaming maledictions on his head as the murderer of her son.

"Ranno has been thorough," he said to Jackla. "The Finninalders were never well liked in the old days. Why do so many people take his word now?"

"There has been another change in the Ferma," said Jackla, giving his head a shake. "That Ranno, he is a cunning one! He has persuaded old Furla of the Manderecks to give his seat to his son, young Furla, who is a friend of Ranno's."

Nicolan's forehead drew into new wrinkles of apprehension. His enemy was leaving nothing to chance. As a boy young Furla had tagged at Ranno's heels and had done his bidding in all things. There could be no question at all about the stand he would take. He would vote at Ranno's nod.

"Only four of the old ones left now," said the guard. "The other five are young. I know little of any of them, except that I'm sure Ranno has selected them carefully." He named the new members one by one and shook his head doubtfully at each. The last was Hasca, who owned lands on the great river, where the hillsides offered pasturage for sheep. Hasca owned few horses and was considered almost an alien.

"What of Hasca?" asked Nicolan.

Jackla's forehead wrinkled up in thought. "I hear he's a sulky fellow. He makes no friends. But Ranno has been north to see him. Master, I would not count on Hasca."

"If the older men are favorable, it will be five to four against me; and a majority is all that Ranno needs," thought Nicolan. "And I can't even be sure of the four."

He went to the window and cast an eye down the road by which Ivar would return. There was no one in sight on it—no horseman urging a tired steed, no cloud of dust in the distance.

Hearing his name called in a cautious undertone, Nicolan turned to the window and saw a shadowy face staring in at him. A week had passed since the visit of Oslaw, during which time nothing had happened, and his first thought was that it might be Ivar. On brushing aside the insect curtain, however, he found it was one of the Lady Eugenia's servants.

"Master, is your man asleep?" asked the visitor.

Nicolan looked back over his shoulder at the inert figure of Jackla stretched out on a low couch at the foot of his bed. A steady snoring filled the room.

"He won't waken until the morning sun strikes his face," he said.

"Then come with me, if you please, master. My mistress is waiting for you."

Eugenia wasted no time in preliminaries but came straight to the point of her visit.

"Nicolan," she said, in a cautious but intense whisper, "you must not stay for the trial. The horses are ready. You can start at once and ride all night. By the morning you will be safely beyond their reach."

"But I have sworn not to leave. I can't be guilty of breaking a vow."

"That has been said to me so often," declared Eugenia, in grim tones, "that I am sick to death of the silly sentiment back of it. If you don't come now, they will cut off your head or kill you in some other terrible way. Now listen to me. There's a conspiracy to deny you a fair trial. I heard all about it today. Straight from the lips of the base rascal who has planned it, this black Ranno, with blood on his hands and murder in his heart. He came to see us. He was so sure of himself that he boasted about the success of his conniving. Oh, you'll be chained to the chariot, if you stay here! The old men on the Council have been shoved aside and their places taken by sons. All of them friends of Ranno's. And that's not all. He took me aside and whispered that it's not Laudio he intends to marry but Ildico. He said that Macio had agreed."

Nicolan made no comment for several moments. He looked about him and felt for the first time that the dark trees, which had always seemed friendly, now held menace and a whisper of danger in the rustle of their leaves. He did not want to die on false charges trumped up against him by his worst enemy. But he had taken the customary vow and there had never been a prisoner, held in open custody, who had run away.

Eugenia sensed what was running through his mind. "When a hyena in the guise of a man has you in his power, is it any time to think of honor? Don't you see any advantage in keeping a head on your shoulders? A head to plan for others, to find ways of meeting this conspiracy? My dear little man, don't let this nonsense make you selfish. Do you want all your friends to suffer? Remember this. One terrible moment and it's all over for you; you will be dead and free of everything. But your friends will suffer grief all the rest of their lives."

"If I run away, I will have no friends left."

"We will respect you for your courage and good sense," she protested.

"The time would come when no one would remember anything about me, except that I broke my word."

"Perhaps it takes a higher kind of courage to do that than to stay here and submit to Ranno's will. The truth will come out sooner or later and you will be vindicated."

2

As the first shadows of night began to fall there was a loud rap on the door. Nicolan had been making an effort to eat his evening meal but finding that he lacked all appetite. A steaming joint of venison, almost untouched, lay on a platter in front of him.

Jackla went to the door and ushered in Lonado, the clerk of the Ferma. The latter gave Nicolan a stiff inclination of the head.

"Your friend, the Briton, has returned," he said. "He asks leave to see you."

Nicolan got to his feet, a wave of exultation sweeping over him. Things could not be so black with Ivar beside him. "I thank Thee, O Lord!" he said to himself. "Thou hast seen the greatness of my need and sent my friend to stand beside me."

"I can admit no one, save with the sanction of a member of the Council," said Lonado, in a crisp tone which gave no indication of friendliness. "They have gone for the night, all save Hasca. He was not at all sure your friend should be admitted to see you. He grumbled and shook his head. Then he said, 'After all, why not? It can have no bearing on what will happen tomorrow.' So he has given his consent. But only the Briton may be admitted. The other, who has come with him, must remain without."

"He is a witness, the other one!" cried Nicolan. "I am allowed one talk with each of my witnesses. It is the rule."

"It is the rule," admitted Lonado. "But how am I to judge about this stranger?"

"Bring him as far as the door. I will be able to convince you then of my right to see him."

Ivar came in, looking dusty and very weary, for he was not yet at ease in the saddle. He beamed at Nicolan and said: "We have ridden hard to get here. It is lucky we did, for I heard, as I came up the road, that the hearing starts tomorrow."

"No man ever had greater need of a friend than I have of you!" cried Nicolan.

"I bring Somutu with me," said Ivar.

The dispatch rider appeared in the door, his flat cap in his hands and a smile on his face. He bowed several times to Nicolan.

"Somutu, you are thrice welcome," said Nicolan. "Tell this officer who you are."

"I am a rider on the staff of Attila, Lord of the Earth and the Seas," declared Somutu, bowing deeply. "I have come to tell what I know of the great battle when the dead lay in heaps on the ground and three horses were killed under me with arrows in their flanks. It was a bloody day and few of us were left at the finish. Over thirty of Attila's dispatch riders were killed. I was lucky to live."

Nicolan looked at Lonado. The latter nodded his head and said: "A quarter hour. No more. It is the rule."

When the clerk had withdrawn, Nicolan invited the new arrivals to share the supper he had left untouched. The conversation among the trio, therefore, was carried on to the accompaniment of a hungry chomping of jaws and long, thirsty pulls at the flagon of wine.

Somutu, who was of a deep chocolate color, his face enlivened with a pair of deep black eyes, looked at Nicolan over the bone he was stripping of its meat and smiled cordially.

"My lord, I am happy to be here," he said. "And to be of service."

"With you here, I will no longer be standing alone against lies and inventions." Nicolan turned to Ivar. "What of the others?"

Ivar spread his hands in a gesture of futility. "Only Somutu could come. There had been a rebellion in the country of the three princes. The people, it seems, were tired of the drunkenness and cruelty of the brothers. Two of the princes got away. One was taken. Tallimundi. They turned him over to the women, who beat him to death with sticks. Very slowly. And so, being well dead indeed, Tallimundi could neither be seen nor brought to give testimony."

"And the others?"

"Allagrin went foraging after the capture of Concordia. The peasantry were in an ugly mood. One great strong fellow killed Allagrin with a pitchfork."

"And Passilis?"

"I talked with Passilis and he was ready to come with us. But the day before we left, he took some little disease. It was a child's disease, I think; but his jaws swelled up and his face became red and he was too weak to get up. I was much disturbed about time and did not think it wise to wait any longer. We left him groaning in his hammock, and came."

Nicolan had not forgotten what Oslaw had said about the small value of alien testimony. If it had been possible to bring all four witnesses, the members of the Ferma might have been convinced. But would they pay much attention to the evidence of one only? He had little hopes of that. Still, it was the best they could do and his case looked better now than it had earlier in the day.

ALL THROUGH the night Nicolan had been aware of activities on the outside: the neighing of horses, the tramping of feet, the clack of tongues raised in greeting or dispute. When dawn came he went to a window and was amazed at what he saw. The amphitheater was already filled with humanity from base to crest. The spectators, who had gathered this early to witness his ordeal, sat chockablock on the ground, knee to knee, shoulder to shoulder; men, women, and children, in their best attire, fashioned in the rich colors which the plateau people had brought with them from the East so long before. They were already beginning to finger the contents of the baskets of food and even to sample the stout bread, the cold meats, the rich cakes dripping with honey. Between the crest and the fringe of trees back of it many hundreds of horses were tethered, the fine spirited stock of the plateau, alert and interested, their tails swishing, their ears perked up.

Nicolan felt a deep sense of oppression take possession of him. "Most of these people, these heads of sheep, believe the lies that Ranno has spread," he thought. "They are here, hoping to see me convicted, sentenced, and put to death."

It was going to be a beautiful day. The sky was cloudless, the air still. The heads of sheep would sit there all day in perfect comfort.

Jackla, bringing in some breakfast dishes, said: "The equal of this"—thumbing back over his shoulder—"has never been seen. The plateau must be as bare as a beggar's dish."

"Have you heard any news?" Nicolan asked.

"Nothing much," was the answer, delivered with more cheerfulness than the circumstances seemed to warrant. "Nought has been seen or heard of your lady—though there is a rumor spreading around. Ranno has just arrived. He looks black and he has been snarling at everyone. He has had some hot words with my lord Oslaw. Perhaps he's heard this rumor."

"What is it?"

Jackla had been arranging the dishes as he talked. He now motioned to Nicolan to take his place but received a negative shake of the head.

"This is what is being whispered: that Roric is alive and is to be produced as a witness. They're talking of nothing else up there on the slopes."

Nicolan felt his spirits rise. More cheerful thoughts began to race through his head. Could it be that Macio's dream was coming true? He had tried to believe in it but doubts had persisted in the back of his mind. A full week had passed since Ildico had set out. This, he had been forced to conclude, was proof that she had not been able to find her brother. Still, why was the rumor spreading now?

Some minutes later Ivar was admitted. He looked glum and unhappy as he confirmed what Jackla had said. It was apparent that he had lost faith in Ildico's mission. In one hand he carried a sword which he tendered to Nicolan.

"This was your father's," he said.

Nicolan took it into his hands with eagerness. It was a short-bladed weapon with a jeweled handle of curious design. His eyes rested on the sign of the Ildeburghs stamped on the hilt, a tree with spreading branches. The minute workmanship of the East showed in every detail.

Nicolan nodded. "It was my father's most prized possession. It has been in the family for many generations. How did you get it?"

"A sympathizer brought it in. He was a neighbor at the time when your father was killed. He didn't explain how he got it but he thought you would like to have it now."

Nicolan attached the sword to his belt with unsteady fingers. "The feel of it against my thigh will bolster my courage," he said. "If you see this neighbor again, convey my thanks to him."

Ivar took him to one side. "Because of this story that's going around, Ranno is determined to rush the hearings through," he whispered. "I spoke to Oslaw and he said, 'The conduct of the case is in *my* hands.'"

As he spoke, the Orator of the Ferma entered the room. He had donned the costume of his office, an outer garment of reddish brown which resembled the Roman *tunica talaris* rather than the toga. It fitted closely at the neck, the sleeves, which were long and full, were embroidered elaborately in gold and blue. In the front of the belt was a large tablion containing a horse's head modeled in gold.

He was an imposing figure with his bare head and his white hair falling in profusion to his shoulders.

"My son," he said, "we must begin in a few minutes. Have you any final words for me?"

Nicolan was overtaken suddenly by a wave of angry emotions. "I have much to say, my lord Oslaw. Why do these people out there, my own people, hold so much hatred for me? On that black morning when my father was murdered they did not come to our aid. They made no effort to trace what had happened to my mother and me. One of our neighbors made a bargain with the murderers which brought our lands into his possession. His infamous son still holds the land but not the smallest copper coin has found its way into my hands. The other neighbors seem to have shared our household goods between them."

"Yes," said Oslaw, with a grave nod. "All this is true."

"And now," went on the defendant, his voice rising, "they have come in their thousands to hear me charged with foul, black lies which have been spread by one ambitious and cowardly man. The same man who holds my lands. They believe what he says and they have come in the hope of seeing me convicted."

There was a moment's silence. "Nicolan of the Ildeburghs," said the Orator, "it has been in my mind that all this should be made clear today. I shall so devise my questions that you will have a chance to say to them what you have said to me. But a word of advice, son of my old friend. Do not gird at them with too much bitterness. Say what you have to say with dignity and conviction rather than rancor."

"Your advice is good," agreed Nicolan, after some thought. "And I have a question to ask. I know that the penalty of guilt is death. If the decision is against me, have I any choice as to the—the means?"

The old man's expression became even more grave. "In that

event," he replied, "you have the right to fall upon the point of your sword."

A bell, located on the roof, struck once loudly. Nicolan straightened and took a step forward. "I am ready," he said.

A dramatic silence fell over the crowded slopes as Nicolan followed Oslaw out into the sunlight. Then, simultaneously, everyone began to speak. The sound came down to the main characters like the beating waves of an unruly sea.

Nicolan looked about him. In the center of the open space was a small round table with a single chair beside it. This, obviously, was for the use of the Orator. Beside it was a long bench at which a score of clerks sat with reed pens in their hands and an air of expectancy about them. There was another bench behind the inscribers of notes, with a chair; this might be for his use.

The seats of the judges were raised about six feet above the level, with one in the center which was more ornate than the others. Here Macio had sat year after year, dispensing honest judgment, until Ranno had usurped his place. All the judges wore robes of ermine with deep red collars. The recent additions, who had taken over their fathers' right to vote, seemed to shrink a little within these majestic trappings, and to feel, perhaps, out of place. None of them seemed willing, at least, to look the defendant in the eye.

On the table before Ranno was a gavel with a gold handle.

Nicolan's eyes went at once, however, to a grim reminder of the possible outcome. At one side a block, about two feet in cubic measurement, had been placed on the sod. Beside it stood a tall figure, brown and sinewy and sinister, naked except for a loincloth. A black mask covered the upper part of his face and in his hands was a sword of extraordinary proportions. The blade was at least six feet long. The grinding to which it had been subjected by the long succession of insensitive executioners who had wielded it had worn the steel down to a width of less than three inches. Nicolan had never seen this instrument of official punishment before but he knew it was called the Stroke of Expiation.

Looking at the taut dark hand clutching the handle and at the bend of the thin figure, which suggested a degree of eagerness, he could not help wondering how many unwilling necks had been severed with one expiatory blow on orders from judges who had filled these carved and gilded chairs.

His fingers sought the handle of his father's sword. It was like encountering the hand of a friend.

2

After studying the setting in which he must wage his desperate fight for life, Nicolan turned to study the new judges. He knew them well and had a poor opinion of each man there. They had been weaklings when they were boys and now in manhood they seemed to show the same lack of strength and integrity. He was surprised to observe a marked change in Ranno. The latter was heavier in figure and somewhat red and puffy of face. When their eyes happened to meet, it was Ranno who turned away.

Oslaw in the meantime had stepped into the center of the open space and was addressing himself to the spectators. The clerks were putting his statements down with flying quills.

"The theory of justice in which we of the plateau people believe," he declared, in a voice which carried far, "has been evolved gradually over the centuries and it is different in form and usage from that of all other lands. It is based on the belief that justice is the concern of everyone and that trials should be held in the hearing of all and not in small rooms by cruel old men in black cloaks. As the human voice is incapable of reaching all of you who make up this large audience, our system for the relaying of questions and answers will be followed more fully than perhaps ever before. This will cause a certain amount of delay and I must ask you to assist us by saving us any interruptions and other evidences of impatience."

The Orator then returned to his table and spoke to the defendant. "Nicolan of the Ildeburghs, is there anything you desire to say before the hearing begins?"

Nicolan advanced a step into the open space. "There is something which disturbs me deeply," he said, and was pleased to find that his voice was steady and natural. "I am surprised at the composition of the Ferma. The nine chairs have been, from time immemorial, occupied by the heads of the nine leading families. No limit has ever been placed on the time a man may serve; nay, it has been understood that each occupant acts for the period of his lifetime and is succeeded on his death by his eldest son. And yet I see that some of the chairs are occupied today by young men. I suppose it is understood they are acting for their sires. But, my lord Orator, all of the legal occupants are alive and well able to continue their duties. May I ask the reason for this arbitrary change?"

Oslaw considered his answer carefully. "I am informed that the changes have been made in each case with the consent of the member who has retired."

"But, my lord, it must be well known to you that any change is made in open meeting and that anyone who attends is free to express an opinion. This clearly has not been done. Are we departing from the customs, sanctioned and hallowed by time, which our forefathers evolved?" When no response was made, Nicolan addressed another question to the Orator. "You, my lord, have performed the duties of your office for a great many years, I believe."

"For forty years."

"In all that time have you known of any other case where the rightful occupant of a chair surrendered his place before being summoned by death to a higher court?"

Oslaw shook his head. "There have been no other resignations in my time."

"Is there any record of resignations at any time in the past?"

"Not that I know of, Nicolan of the Ildeburghs."

"For many generations the post of chief judge has been held by the head of the family of the Roymarcks. It has been handed down from father to son and I am sure all in this gathering will agree that they have proven themselves worthy of that trust. It now seems to have been taken over by Ranno of the Finninalders. May I ask how this change came about?"

A deep silence had fallen over the thickly packed slopes. A hasty glance about him made it clear to Nicolan that the spectators were leaning forward and following the proceedings with an intensity of interest. Most of them had transferred their gaze to Ranno. The latter seemed little concerned.

"Macio is dead," said Oslaw. "His only son is believed to have been killed in the battle at Châlons."

Nicolan's voice rose to a peremptory pitch. "And who made this most important of all decisions?"

"It was discussed among the other members and a decision reached."

"Were the people of the plateau consulted first? Was a vote taken?"

"It may have been that an expression of opinion was secured from a certain number of individuals. But no vote was taken."

"I was told by my father, long since dead under tragic circumstances familiar to everyone here, that the first Roymarck to occupy the post was selected at a meeting in the open on the banks of the Volga River. It was by the voice of the people that he was elevated to the chair. It was an occasion of great joy. Now it seems that three or four heads put together in a corner can decide in whispers on points which should be left to the massed voice of the plateau people.

"It is necessary, also, to raise a point which concerns me personally. Since the murder of my father and the illegal seizure of our lands, the chair of the Ildeburghs has been kept open, as I, a minor at the time of my father's death, had been sold into slavery to a Roman master. Today I find to my astonishment that the chair has been filled. I demand to know on what authority this has been done."

The voice of Ranno interrupted at this stage. He leaned forward with both elbows placed on the small table in front of him. One hand grasped the mace of office. His voice was hoarse with anger.

"This has gone far enough," he declared. "I propose to have these matters understood now and for all time."

Nicolan advanced a further step into the open square of space and the two protagonists faced each other for a moment in silence.

"This man," said Ranno, discarding the mace and pointing a forefinger at Nicolan, "this traitor to his own people, is charged with an offense so great that there can be no longer any delay in dealing with him. He is making an effort to obscure the issue by complaining about matters of procedure."

"I am claiming," said Nicolan, "that the Council which proposes to try me has not been legally elected and has no right to pass upon this, or any other, case."

"And I am claiming," cried Ranno, thumping the table with a hand which seemed fat and white for a man who lived in the saddle, "that no one, saving the defendant in this case, has any objection to the measures which have been necessary to assemble a court."

The clerks had been hurrying with great zeal to write down the questions and answers and to send the slips to the officials in the raised spaces. The voices of the latter came back faintly, as well as the murmuring of the listeners.

"I propose," continued Ranno, "to take a general vote. Are you content, my good friends, to have the Ferma as it stands today proceed with the hearing? All in favor will stand up."

There were a few moments when the issue of this direct appeal seemed to be in doubt. There was shaking of heads and much talking back and forth, as though the people realized the arbitrary course which Ranno was taking. It was not until a few of the more aggressive spirits got to their feet and thus set an example that any considerable number answered Ranno's suggestion. There is something contagious, however, about the mere act of rising; and gradually the slower members began to stand up also.

Ranno looked about him with a satisfied air. "The people of the plateau are with me," he declared. "Are you content to proceed now, Master Orator?"

"It is my duty," said Oslaw, after bowing in response to the question, "to call attention to the fact that the new head of the judges has laid this charge. It has been customary in the past for members of the Ferma to withdraw when cases are called in which they are to give evidence. May I ask if Ranno of the Finninalders proposes to vacate his chair until a decision is reached?"

Ranno indulged in a short and scornful laugh. "Master Orator," he said, "I have no such intention."

"There is no law to compel you. Save perhaps the sense of fairness which is strong in our race."

"Permit me to say that my sense of fairness compels me to retain my chair. To make certain that the bereaved families of the men who died on the field of Châlons will see full justice done!"

This expression of opinion drew an instant round of applause from the spectators, as, of course, it could not fail to do. Ranno nodded in the direction of Oslaw. "The people have spoken!" he said. "Now perhaps you will open the case."

The Orator was unhappy over the course events were taking. He remained silent for several moments before responding. When he did, it was in a voice which manifested his dissent.

"I am sure, my lord Ranno, that you know you are upsetting all the rules of procedure in this court. Any verdict obtained under these circumstances will be subject to appeal."

Ranno leaned as far over the table as he could. Raising an arm clothed in the white ermine of the court, he glowered at Oslaw. "Your duties end with the presentation of the evidence. The reaching of the verdict is the function of the Council. Is that clear?" A heavy scowl spread across his dark countenance. "Proceed, Master Orator! Proceed at once!"

There was no doubt in any mind that Ranno had won in the first clash.

3

When Ranno had taken the witness chair at the table beside the Orator, he plunged easily and confidently into his story. "An hour after dawn the mists began to clear. Roric, our commander, sent for me and said I was to take my men out on a scouting expedition. It was feared the enemy might attempt an encircling movement by sending horsemen around our left flank."

Oslaw nodded his head. "A wise precaution. But had not scouts been covering this open country to the left of our army during the night?"

"I do not know."

"Would you not consider it absolutely essential to keep watch on the flanks through the hours of darkness?"

Ranno gave his questioner a suspicious and unfriendly stare. "I was not in command. I was there to obey orders."

"Are we to assume that you were being sent out because this necessary, nay, this elementary, precaution had not been taken?"

Ranno demanded in surly tones, "Is it your intention to turn this into a military inquiry?"

"It is necessary," declared Oslaw, in a voice which had suddenly become high and even peremptory, "to probe into all phases of a case, so that the Council, and back of them the people, may be convinced that the truth has been obtained. May I point out to you, my lord Ranno, that this hearing is now in my hands and that my decisions on points of evidence are final?"

When Ranno made no response, the Orator continued: "What I am trying to establish is that there would have been no need to send you out on this scouting mission if the open land had been patrolled during the night. It may be that I shall have a witness later to prove that the usual precautions *had* been taken."

"As to that, I have nothing to say. I received the orders, as I have told you. I was to report to the three princes who were in command of the left army for any additional instructions."

"And you went to see them?"

"I did. I saw one of them only. The others had not recovered from their drinking debauch of the night."

"Which one did you see?"

"Prince Tallimundi. He told me he had just received an order to send the plateau troops under Roric in an attack up the northern slopes of the high ground held by the enemy."

"Did this order come from the Emperor Attila himself?"

"It was alleged to come from him. But it was Nicolan of the Ildeburghs who sent it."

"In sending it, was he obeying instructions from Attila?"

There was a pause. "I do not know."

"You used the word 'alleged.' Do you mean to imply that Tallimundi had any doubts that the order came from the emperor?"

"How could I tell what was in his mind?"

"But he ordered the attack. Is that not proof that he had no doubts?"

"It may be."

"In that case you must withdraw the word 'alleged' as improperly used."

"He said"—Ranno looked about him with a sly sense of anticipation of the effect his statement would have—"that he did not trust Nicolan. That he was sure Nicolan was anxious to see the troops under Roric assigned this dangerous duty."

"What reason did he have for making such a dangerous accusation?"

Ranno paused before answering this. "He, the prince, told me that Nicolan discussed the situation with him the evening before. He told the prince then that he believed the best place for the attack was on the northern slope."

"Did any of the plateau leaders share this belief?"

"None. We had discussed it together the evening before. We were all in favor of an attack on the east."

Oslaw placed before the witness a large map. "This," he explained, "shows the part of the battlefield of Châlons which was occupied by the army of the left. Will you look at it, please, and tell me if you think it is correct?"

Ranno studied the map and nodded finally. "It seems correct."

Oslaw drew a forefinger through the map. "This is the front of our line. Here is the raised ground held by the enemy and this dotted line is the course taken by the plateau horsemen in the attack led by Roric. Here, farther east, is the open country which you were under orders to patrol. When you returned from the tent of Tallimundi you must have ridden straight through the line."

"I did."

"You rode then within a very few yards of the position held by our troops."

"Yes."

"Did you see Roric?"

"No."

"But did it not occur to you that he was unaware of the order he would receive from Tallimundi? Surely it was clear to you that, if you *did* let him know, there might be time for him to protest and get the order changed."

"I had received my instructions. I was carrying them out."

The voice of the Orator was raised to a higher pitch as he asked the next question.

"Did it not occur to you that the situation would be changed when Roric did receive the order?"

"In what way?"

"Roric might decide under the circumstances that he could not afford to send you out with so large a force. He might think you would be needed for the attack on the hill."

"When you are acting on orders, it is your duty to proceed without any delay."

There was a long pause. Oslaw lifted the map again and studied it.

"You had a strip of land to cover which was roughly twelve miles in width and half of that in depth. At what hour did you set out?"

"About six. I am not sure of the exact time."

"When did you return?"

Ranno hesitated. "I am not sure."

"But it was in the afternoon?"

"Yes."

"Was it not close to four when you came back?"

"I have told you I am not sure."

Oslaw tossed the map to the table with a dramatic gesture. "You were away, roughly, nine hours. The battle was in its final stages when you returned. And most of your comrades lay dead on the slope of the hill."

Ranno placed both hands on the table and leaned forward toward his questioner. His features were contorted with anger.

"Master Oslaw!" he cried. "Is Nicolan on trial here or am I? I resent the suspicions you are trying to create. I refuse to answer any more questions."

This was one of the occasions when, as Nicolan had noticed in his first talk with Oslaw, the voice of the old man became vibrant and compelling.

"You are forgetting that my duty is to reach the truth for the guidance of the Ferma by questioning both parties to a case, as well as the witnesses. It is my duty, moreover, to sum up the evidence on each point as the case proceeds. I am compelled by the answers you have given me to say this: that no other captain of plateau horsemen would have ridden away to scout through country which probably was bare of the enemy without offering to serve with his comrades in the desperate duty assigned them.

"You have made the charge. Nicolan sits here in court to answer it. But over the years I have found that sometimes things come to light which are fully as revealing as the facts of a case.

It should be clear to you that the reasons and motives of the accuser must be probed as well as the actions of the accused. The role of the accuser is often one of unsuspected difficulties, even of peril. He must stand with the man he has accused under the strong white light of scrutiny.

"And so," he summed up, "it happens that, in a sense, you also are on trial. With this difference: your honor alone is at stake, with him it is his life."

Ranno had won in the first clash but he had been badly worsted in the second.

4

Ranno returned to his elevated chair and it became apparent at once that he had decided on a change of tactics. He had attempted the role of the bully in the court and had been so severely dealt with that his pride, for the moment, lay in shreds. No longer would he try to carry off things with a high hand. Instead he called his witnesses in a restrained voice and he neither offered comment nor allowed his feelings to show as the Orator of the Ferma questioned them.

The first one called was Rustrum, son of Illelac, son of Gorlaw, son of Telf. His full name was used in summoning him to the stand in order to establish his unquestioned plateau descent. He began by saying he had ridden beside Ranno all through the day of the battle and by confirming what the latter had told of his movements. Although he had been on hand when the visit was paid to the tent of Tallimundi, he had not heard the conversation which ensued between the two men.

"Did you know," asked Oslaw, "that the forces from the plateau country were to attack the hill?"

"Yes, master."

"Did your captain tell you?"

"No, master. But we heard about it soon."

"Did you think you should have turned back to have a part in the attack?"

The man's brow wrinkled in a bewildered frown. "Turn back? No orders were given to turn back, master."

The second witness was another of Ranno's troop. His name was Radgel, son of Sulmen, son of Rashgo, son of Culkan. The point of his testimony was that he had heard his captain receive the order from Roric earlier in the morning. He had accompanied Ranno to the well-screened spot where all that was left of the fire, before which Roric had slept during the night, was a pile of ashes, and had heard the conversation there.

When Oslaw began to question him in detail, he became a little vague about many things. Nothing shook him, however, on the main part of his testimony; he had heard the order delivered by Roric to take a party out and scout through the land to the east.

A more voluble witness was Vollena, son of no known father and, therefore, referred to always as Alph Vollena. He testified to having heard a conversation between Nicolan and Ivar on the day when they visited the Roymarck lands to complete the report for Attila on the man power and the horse supplies of the country. They had been standing apart when he, Alph Vollena, had been influenced by curiosity to hear what was being said. Nicolan, he declared, had told Ivar he must have back his lands which Ranno held, and that, in order to get them, he must contrive to get Ranno out of the way.

"Where were the two men when this talk went on?" asked Oslaw.

"At one side, of course, master."

"Did they speak in low tones?"

"Ay, indeed, master. They had their heads together and they whispered, one to other."

"How close were you to them?"

"As close as one dared." The witness measured the open square in the room with his eyes and then said, with a gesture as though dividing the distance in half, "About as close as that, master."

"Then you were about twenty feet away from them?"

Ranno tried to get his man's eye at this point but Alph Vollena was too busy to pay attention.

"Yes, master," he said. "Yes, twenty feet."

Oslaw paced off twenty feet from where the witness was standing. Then he summoned a guard and said something in his ear.

"Now," he said, turning back to the witness. "What did I say to him? And what answer did he make?"

The witness did not yet sense the pitfall. "Why, master," he answered, "I heard nothing. How could I? It was whispering you were."

"You heard nothing at all?"

"No, master."

The Orator turned to look up at the elevated chair of Ranno. "I am compelled to inform the Council that the word of this witness is not to be believed. He could not have heard what was said that day. His evidence must be set aside."

The spectators were now seen to be wearing smiles. Nicolan was to learn later that Alph Vollena had the reputation of being a great liar. Ranno had shown poor judgment in his selection of this particular witness.

It was not likely that anyone present believed that this illegitimate son of a maidservant had heard the statements he imputed to Nicolan. The latter, however, sensed that the witnesses called to corroborate Ranno's story had convinced most of the spectators of the truth of the story told by the head of the Finninalders. Their faith in Ranno may have been shaken by Oslaw's vigorous outburst but this had no effect on the main point at issue.

The appearance of the next witness created such surprise that all whispering stopped and all eyes were turned in his direction. It was clear that he was not recognized by any save Nicolan, who had seen him last shackled to the side of one of his trade wagons, a very sick and very frightened man. It was Micca the Mede.

The once great merchant from the East was attired in a plain robe of the cheapest material. The heavy gold chain he had always worn around his neck was missing. His fingers were bare of rings. His face was almost skull-like in its emaciation and he tottered as he stepped to the witness chair.

"Micca the Mede!" said Oslaw. "It is a long time since your face was seen among us."

The witness nodded with extreme gravity. "A long time," he said. "And now you are seeing me for the last time. I am returning to Damascus where I was born and where I shall close my eyes for the final sleep."

"Have you evidence to give us?"

"Yes, my lord Orator. I have something to tell of the relations between the emperor and the defendant."

"Proceed, then."

"The emperor had such opinion of his ability that he entrusted to him the preparation of marching orders. Often, also, he sought his advice. I saw Nicolan of the Ildeburghs when he paid a visit to the headquarters of the emperor above the mountain pass, when the army was marching through to the Lombardy Plain. He had not been entrusted with the preparation of the marching orders for the attack on Rome. Attila had found reasons for distrusting him."

"But how were you in a position to know this? It is my understanding that you were being held a prisoner."

"That is true. I had been wrongly accused of paying one Sartuk to kill the emperor and was being held under sentence of death. Nicolan had returned from a mission which proved the truth of certain information I had supplied. Because of that, my life was to be spared."

"There has been a persistent rumor that you acted as a spy for the emperor. What you have now told us would seem a proof of it."

"Why should I deny it? My days are numbered. Yes, I sold information to him."

"Why had Attila begun to distrust Nicolan?"

"He suspected, my lord, that Nicolan was not loyal. He had given the emperor bad advice on the night before the battle of Châlons."

"Can you speak plainer?"

"Yes, my lord. Nicolan had advised that the attack be made on the northern face of the hill. The emperor had followed his advice and the attack had been a failure."

Oslaw seemed disturbed by the unexpectedness of this evidence. He remained silent for several moments, his brow creased in thought, seeking perhaps for the weak link to attack.

"Do you expect us to believe," he said, finally, "that you learned this while you were held in chains and under sentence of death?"

"The emperor spoke with me at some length when he came to tell me that my life was to be spared. He was bitterly distrustful of Nicolan and did not hesitate to speak of it."

Nicolan's confidence was sinking lower with each word spoken by the old merchant. The way the latter was twisting the facts was diabolically clever and it might be impossible to wring the truth from him. But why should Micca come forward with such a story?

"What was the nature of the mission from which Nicolan was returning?" asked the questioner.

"He had been sent behind the Roman lines to find and speak with the Princess Honoria. He had been successful."

"Attila then sent him on a much more important mission. To deliver an open message of warning to Aetius. Why would he do this if he distrusted Nicolan?"

"It was more hazardous than the first. The emperor expected that the Romans would put him to death. It was, in a sense, a punishment."

"But is it not true that Nicolan was the means of saving your life?"

Micca gestured indifferently. "I was released from my chains, yes. But perhaps it would have been better if I had not been pardoned. All my property was confiscated and I am now no better than a beggar. I return to the home of my fathers with an empty purse."

"Knowing you, and understanding you thoroughly, I am wondering why you have come so far out of your way to give this evidence unless there is some advantage in it for you." Oslaw was silent for a moment. "Nicolan performed this mission successfully and at the risk of his life. In doing so, he saved your life. Why then do you come here? Why are you repaying him by swearing to evidence against him?"

Micca raised both hands in the air and displayed his teeth in the semblance of a smile. "Shall we say that I feel it my duty to put this court in possession of what I know about the case?"

"You are known to the world as a purveyor of lies, Micca the Mede. I find it hard to believe what you have told us."

But nothing, Nicolan realized, could disturb the fact that the merchant had succeeded in lending weight to the story previously told by Ranno.

There was a stir when Nicolan rose and took his position on

the opposite side of the witness table. Necks were craned to get a better view of him and there was much shoving and scuffling among the spectators.

"Nicolan of the Ildeburghs," said the Orator, "it has been charged that you were responsible for the order which sent the men of the plateau on a mounted charge up the northern slope. Is this true?"

"It is utterly untrue."

"Did you discuss the matter with Prince Tallimundi?"

"No. I have never set eyes on Prince Tallimundi in my life."

Oslaw looked somewhat surprised. "But in the post you held you must have been in contact with all the army leaders."

"My lord Oslaw, the army that Attila led to the battle of Châlons was half a million strong. There were scores of army commanders. There were many I did not see, and the prince was one of them."

"But communications were exchanged between you?"

"On the day of the battle, yes. The emperor had placed me in control of the dispatch riders."

"Did you have any part in reaching the decision?"

"Not the terrible decision to attack on the north slope. Allow me to tell you briefly what occurred."

"Take all the time you need. Tell us everything."

"When the staff reached the battle positions at Châlons the night before the battle, the emperor was enraged to find that the enemy had been allowed to secure possession of the high ground on the left. He sent three of the staff to look the situation over. I was one of them. I returned and reported that in my opinion it was extremely dangerous to leave them in possession. I was sure, however, that the position could be captured by an attack from the east where the ascent was gradual. I urged that an attack be launched at dawn before the Ostrogoths, who had taken the hillside, would be ready."

"What did the emperor say?"

"He said he would wait until the other reports reached him before making a decision. But he sent an order at once that the enemy must be dislodged before the main battle began."

"Did you suggest to him that the attack should be carried out by the plateau troops?"

"Most certainly not. That decision would rest with the three brothers who commanded the left."

"What happened then?"

"Early the next morning the emperor told me I was to direct the dispatch riders during the battle. He sent off a message at once to the three princes that the position of the Ostrogoths on the hill was to be challenged and that the attack was to be made on the eastern slope."

"Was the order conveyed in writing?"

Nicolan shook his head. "All of the orders during the battle were by word of mouth. There was no time to write them. The report reached us after the battle that this message was not delivered. The rider was thrown from his horse and badly injured. The first message, ordering the attack, had been received."

"Did Tallimundi take it on himself to make his own decisions about the attack?"

There was a pause before Nicolan made any answer. "My lord Orator, it is my belief," he said, "that he had the benefit of advice."

"Do you mean advice from someone other than you? Or the emperor?"

"Yes, my lord."

"Have you evidence to submit on the point?"

"One of the dispatch riders, who carried instructions later to the prince, heard how it came about that the plateau troops were selected and that the attack was launched in the north. He told me what he had heard."

"You understand, I am sure, that evidence based on hearsay is not well regarded in the courts of the Ferma. It is no better than gossip. Sometimes it carries even the stamp of slander. But if the rider in question could be brought into court, that would be a different matter."

"He is here, my lord."

This statement, when announced to the spectators, created a sensation. People turned to stare at their neighbors and to exchange opinions. A murmur of surprised comment came from all sides.

Ranno had been whispering to the Council member at his right. He stopped in the middle of a sentence and looked up, his

THE DARKNESS AND THE DAWN

face suddenly set and hard. After a moment of reflection, he snapped a finger to one of his personal servants who sat on the grass beneath his elevated post. The latter listened and then left.

"We will want to hear what your witness has to say," declared Oslaw. "In the meantime, you might continue with what happened after the battle began."

"The emperor led the center in person and made an early attack on the Alani forces which opposed him. I received all the reports brought by the riders and, when the information warranted it, I sent the message down into the zone of conflict to be delivered to the emperor. One of the first messages transmitted that way came from the left, with the report that Prince Tallimundi had ordered the plateau horsemen to attack the hill, using the northern slope. I—I found it impossible at first to believe this. What a disastrous mistake! Not only would the attack fail but the attacking force would be wiped out. An early report had reached us that the three princes had spent the night drinking and I was sure this was the result, that Tallimundi was not sober enough to know what he was doing. But Somutu, the rider, gave me some information which was—quite different."

"Is this man Somutu your witness?"

"Yes, my lord."

"What steps did you take?"

"I sent a rider down into the lines to inform Attila of the grave error which had been made and to beg that he countermand Tallimundi's instructions. Then I sent Somutu back to the prince to demand that the charge be delayed until the emperor's answer could be received."

"What answer did the emperor send?"

"A peremptory order to the prince to stop the charge and to attack from the east instead, using foot soldiers for the work. Before this order reached Tallimundi, the charge up the steep slope had been made. And had failed."

Oslaw began to question the defendant closely, eliciting from him all the information about the messages which had passed back and forth with Tallimundi. He did not ask anything further, however, about the advice to the prince of which Somutu had spoken; that, clearly, was being left for Somutu himself to tell.

"And now," said Oslaw, "let us go still further back into the past."

There was in his manner a hint of confidence which he had lacked earlier. Nicolan, who was watching and listening with the closest attention, detected it at once. He said to himself, "He is better satisfied, I think, with the way it is going."

"I consider it important," went on the Orator, "for the judges to hear your reasons for choosing to serve Attila. Our men of military age were forced to serve in the emperor's army but you chose to follow him of your own free will."

"My answer to that," said Nicolan, in a clear voice, "is that for many years I was a slave in Rome."

Oslaw commented quietly: "A good answer. But I hope you will now go on and explain your feelings more fully to us."

"Yes, my lord Oslaw. I don't suppose anyone here has shared this experience. How can I make you understand then what it means to exist under the feet of those cruel and degenerate people? Perhaps the best way would be to show you the marks I carry on my body."

He threw back his tunic so that he was naked from the waist up. He walked slowly about the open space, facing inward, so that everyone would have a chance to see the deep, red scars which covered his back in crisscross pattern.

"I am not proud of the mutilation to which I was subjected by order of the great Aetius," he said on returning to his place. "Because I always kept my back covered, they called me the Coated One in Attila's army. But today I thought I must let my judges and my countrymen see one reason why my soul sickened at the thought of a world ruled forever by Rome."

"Begin your story now," said Oslaw, "with the murder of your father and the rape of your lands. All of us know something of it but I am afraid we have been inclined to forget it, as something past and done. Take your time, if you please. Omit nothing that may serve to open our eyes to your reasonings."

So Nicolan told his story, with urgings from the questioner and shrewd promptings. It took the balance of the day and he could see that his audience was listening intently. They might still be against him but with their bitterness now there was a tincture of sympathy. At the finish he told briefly of his absence from the

Hun army in the fighting which had come to such a sudden ending and finally he drew a document from under his belt and handed it to the Orator.

"I submit this," he said, "as a proof of the truth of what I have been telling."

At his first glimpse of the paper, Oslaw's eyes showed the extent of his surprise, and perhaps some gratification that this weapon had been placed in his hands. He read it through twice and then held it up with a dramatic gesture.

"This," he announced, "is a legal order, issued by the Emperor Attila, conveying back to Nicolan the lands which belonged to his father and which are now held by the family of the Finninalders."

Nicolan's eyes were on Ranno when this statement was made and he believed he could see a hint of fear under the dark anger on the surface of his opponent's face. It disappeared in a moment, however, as the latter started up from his chair.

"You have gone too far!" cried Ranno. "I have tried to be patient under your goadings. But I refuse to have you exhibit in court this—this deliberate forgery!"

"It is not a forgery," declared Oslaw. "It is a proper and legal document, transferring the lands to Nicolan of the Ildeburghs, son of the previous owner. Still, this is no threat to your continued occupation; for, as you will see when you have the opportunity of examining it, the deed has been canceled." The questioner turned back to Nicolan. "What was the reason for the cancellation?"

"I refused to accept it."

"On what grounds did you refuse?"

"Because it was given me in the expectation that I would continue to act in the same capacity as in the campaign which ended with the battle of Châlons. Despite what Micca the Mede said, the emperor wanted me to continue."

"Why did you refuse to serve?"

"In the interval I had been converted to a belief in the teachings of the Lord Jesus Christ. I could no longer take an active part in another war as terrible as the first. I could not make out orders to turn armed forces loose on defenseless people."

"But you continued to serve the emperor?"

"I was given no option. He sent me on a mission into Italy as I have already testified. He was certain I would be back before the march began and that I would have changed my mind in the meantime. But almost immediately after I left, he learned that the Roman commander was making no army dispositions to defend the mountain passes and so he grasped the opportunity to move at once."

"But he found more work for you?"

"Yes, my lord. Again I had no option. It is the belief of the Emperor Attila that no man may voluntarily leave his service. He sent me to the Roman commander with the warning that he would destroy all the cities of northern Italy if Aetius laid waste the country to prevent the Hun armies from living off the land. It was a mission of great danger. I accepted it with no hope of emerging alive."

"Then the emperor had not lost confidence in you as Micca declared on the stand?"

"No, my lord."

"Did you see Micca when you returned from your first mission into Italy?"

"Yes, I had a talk with him. Attila was so convinced of his guilt that he was kept in chains and his life hung on a promise made to him because he had given certain information. It is inconceivable that the emperor, knowing him for a spy and a double traitor, would discuss with him any matters of a military nature. The statements he made here were completely false. They were inventions of his own."

"But why would he, an old and broken man, come far out of his way to testify? Was there bad blood between you?"

"No. When I saw him chained in one of his own trade wagons, he was most grateful because I had proven the truth of some of the information he had supplied to Attila."

"Is it true that all his property has been confiscated?"

"He has nothing left. Even the rich robes were stripped from his back."

"Have you any explanation to give for his presence here today?"

Nicolan hesitated. "He has already made it clear that he stops at nothing where money is concerned. He would have hesitated to show you the color of the coins in his purse. I suspect it would be largely plateau gold."

5

Nicolan was escorted back to his own chamber and found Ivar there. As no one of alien blood was allowed to attend hearings, he had been kept outside. It was clear from the gloom on his face that what he had been able to learn of the proceedings had disturbed him very much.

He had bad news of his own to impart. "Friend Nicolan," he said, "it may not be possible to produce Somutu in court. He has disappeared."

"Do you suppose," asked Nicolan, "that he has become impatient of the delay and has started for his home?"

The Briton shook his head. "His horse is still tethered in the lines. His belongings are in my tent. No, he has been carried off to prevent him from testifying. He may even have been killed."

Nicolan sat down and gave in to his bitter discouragement. "So far," he said, "I have been able to offer only my own unsupported evidence. It's true that Oslaw succeeded in casting doubt on the conduct of Ranno, even questioning his courage. But will that suffice? I'm afraid not." He was silent for several moments, keeping his face lowered in his hands. Then he looked up and seemed to have partially conquered his fears. "I knew the danger when I decided to come. But it had to be done, Ivar, my friend, it had to be done."

CHAPTER XI

1

IT RAINED during the night, neither heavily nor long, but too heavily and too long for the comfort of the thousands of plateau people who had decided to spend the night where they were rather than risk losing their places. Dawn broke on the unhappy people, sitting in the discomforts of the muddy slope. The supplies of food they had brought with them had been nearly exhausted and the cries of hungry children filled the air.

The first hint of ameliorating circumstances came from the northern bend of the amphitheater. Someone stood up and sniffed energetically. "Food!" he cried. "Hot food. I smell it roasting."

Confirmation came soon from those on the crest. They discovered that a trench had been dug during the night and that the carcasses of cattle and sheep were being roasted whole. In a brief space of time thereafter attendants were carrying platters, heaped high with thick cuts of beef and slabs of hot bread, through the closely packed spectators. The discomforts were quickly forgotten.

"Have we Ranno to thank for this?" asked the head of one family, whose face was already greasy because he had secured a rib bone for himself.

The attendant scoffed. "Ranno! Don't you know that Ranno starved his old father to death? Ranno was suckled on a brass du'pius."

"Then who pays?"

"This, my friend, is the gift of a lady. The widow of Ti'gest."

The word quickly permeated the packed circle of humanity that the widow of Tergeste, who was no longer a widow but the wife of the English Samson, who was in turn the friend of Nicolan, had provided the food. There was much speculation, as a result. Had she done it to win their favor or was it purely out of goodness of heart? Whatever the reason, the people were happy about it and the hum of cheerful voices rose from all directions.

By seven the seats of the judges were filled. A minute later Oslaw appeared, carrying a statement in one hand. He issued copies to the clerks and gave instructions to have them carried at once to the announcers on the platforms.

There was a solemnity about his manner and a tautness in the muscles of his face. He waited until the copies had been distributed.

"'Two hours ago,'" he began, reading from the statement, "'a herdsman, searching for stragglers, looked over the edge of the Scaur and saw among the rocks of the Lintgaw a touch of color which held his eye. It looked to him like a man, partly covered by a cloak. He made his way down and found that his guess had been correct. It was what was left of a man after the long fall. There was an arrow protruding from between the shoulder blades. He was identified later as Somutu, the dispatch rider who was to have been a witness in this court.

"'The man Somutu,'" he went on, "'had not been here long enough to make a mortal enemy for himself. He had not figured in any drinking bouts or quarrels. From all reports he was an amiable fellow with a wife and family awaiting him in Sarmatia. Only one conclusion is left to us and I would be a traitor to my oath of office if I did not say he had been put out of the way deliberately.'"

When the announcers had completed the reading of the first part of the statement a silence fell for a space of several moments over the thick ranks of the spectators. Then a hum of voices began and grew into a deafening roar. Most of the men sprang to their feet, waving their arms excitedly.

Oslaw waited for the noise to subside and then continued reading. "'Yesterday afternoon, Dalbo, a Roymarck groom, was seen in a pothouse well to the south, at least twenty miles away. He was drinking and he had a new feather in his hat. He was boasting loudly of the contents of his purse. Dalbo, who was missing yesterday, had evidence of some importance to give about things which happened the night before the battle. All of us know Dalbo as a witless fellow who could labor all his life

and not save enough to pay for that feather in his hat. Again
there is only one conclusion to be drawn. Dalbo had been bribed
to absent himself.' "

The spectators reacted in the same way, although the volume
of sound had become deeper and more sustained.

" 'Finally,' " read Oslaw, " 'it is necessary for me to report that
an order I gave yesterday for the witness Micca the Mede to be
held for further questioning has been overruled. He was instructed to leave yesterday afternoon.' "

No one was more astonished than Nicolan at Oslaw's an-
nouncements. He had received no word from the Orator following the conclusion of the session the previous day. He had slept
little, tossing on his narrow bed, his mind filled with doubts of
the outcome. He had glanced, on rising, at the sun. "Perhaps I am
seeing you for the last time," he thought. First among the bitter
regrets which filled his mind was the probability, if not certainty,
that he would never see Ildico again.

Since rising to face this fateful day he had been aware of activities in other parts of the building, the arrival and departure
of visitors, the rumble of voices. When a man stands in peril of
his life, his senses become unusually acute. He is able to hear
what is said at unusual distances, he draws correct conclusions
from many things: an expression, a gesture, a movement. He can
read meanings into the tread of a foot, the rustle of a gown. Instinct tells him if things are going well for him or badly. But
Nicolan had not been sure of the meaning of the activities going
on about him when he rose that morning. There was a briskness
about things and that, by itself, would have been reassuring. But
why had no one come to see him?

Oslaw paused before continuing with the balance of his announcement. The loud din, which indicated a high state of excitement among the spectators, took some time to die down.

" 'All this,' " he then went on, " 'is proof of a deliberate determination to conceal the truth from us. Fortunately our laws
cover the case. They make it incumbent on us to do one of two
things. We must dismiss the charges or postpone the hearing until a close inquiry can be conducted into this effort to thwart the
course of justice.' "

It seemed to Nicolan that the noisy demonstration in which

the spectators indulged was proof of a wide concurrence, though not a universal one, in the conclusions of Oslaw. And he had this to lean upon: Somutu murdered, and Dalbo and Micca spirited away, would prove in their enforced silence the best of witnesses for him.

Ranno had listened to Oslaw with a set and angry expression, his heavy brows drawn down, his mouth a grim straight line. He now got to his feet.

"I see no reason for taking either course," he declared. "Sufficient evidence has been introduced to prove the charges against the defendant. The case must go on."

It had been assumed by everyone that Ranno would have the people of the plateau with him. But when his statement had been read to them, there was an instant response. It consisted of one word, repeated loudly and in unison.

"No! No! No!"

"It is clear, my lord Ranno," said the Orator, "that the people do not agree with you."

"There are occasions," declared Ranno, glancing down from his elevated post, "when new circumstances must override old laws. The decision in this case rests with me. I repeat that the hearing must go on. Without further interruption or delay."

Oslaw left his table and advanced closer to the prominent row of seats where the judges sat in their costly white and red robes. He glanced steadily at Ranno. "It has been customary to refer decisions to the voice of the people when any changes in the laws are involved. If the Council of the Ferma does not decide to dismiss the charges or to postpone the hearings until an investigation has been conducted, I shall draw on the authority vested in my office to call for a general vote."

"Very well, Master Orator. A poll of the Ferma will be taken. The result will not suit you but I give no promises of any further action." He rose to his feet and gestured widely as though saying to those who favored him, Observe closely the stand I am taking and be prepared to follow my lead. Although the sun had broken through the clouds for the first time and was laying welcome warmth on their still damp backs, the spectators were too concerned with the drama being enacted beneath them to notice it.

"The point at stake," went on Ranno, "is whether we are to

continue the hearing of this case. I cast my own vote first. I say, yes."

It was not necessary at this point to send messengers to the platforms occupied by the announcers. Oslaw had raised his right arm to indicate that an affirmative vote had been cast.

"Cristus, what say you?" asked Ranno of the judge on his right.

Cristus was very young and he flushed at finding all faces turned his way. He cleared his throat nervously and said in a high-pitched voice, "I say, yes."

A believer, clearly, in the effect of an early trend, Ranno polled the two other young members and received a "Yes" from each. He then called on one of the older judges. Silence had followed each of the earlier votes but when Oslaw raised his left hand in the air to indicate the expression of a negative opinion, the spectators stirred and a wave of sound reached the ears of those below. Watching with a nervous intensity, Nicolan found relief in the clearness and lack of hesitation displayed by the three senior members who followed. After each of them spoke, the Orator raised his left arm, eliciting an immediate response from the hearers.

The vote now stood four to four.

Ranno's manner exuded complete confidence at this point. He glanced about him with an almost jaunty air as he declared: "The deciding vote will be cast by our most recent member, Hasca, who was selected at the last moment to occupy the chair once filled by the Ildeburghs. Hasca, how do you vote?"

Nicolan looked at the sheepherder in his chair at the end of the line of judges, and his heart sank. He was an uncouth figure with long, untrimmed hair and a nose of vulpine length. If there was a barely discernible trace of shrewdness in the man's face and even a glint of humor in the corners of his yellowish eyes, they were nothing to supply the defendant with any hope. Nicolan knew that Ranno had ridden into the north to see Hasca and to offer him a place on the Ferma. Without a doubt they had come to terms.

"It is well," thought Nicolan, "that Ildico hasn't succeeded in getting back in time. She will be spared the outcome of this."

Hasca stood up after a moment's hesitation and glanced slowly about him. His eyes rested on Ranno and then turned to stare at Nicolan.

"I did not know," he said, "that the seat I was to fill had belonged to the Ildeburghs. If I had been aware of that, I would have refused to sit here. My brother, my only brother, died at Châlons and if Nicolan issued the order which cost him his life, I want to see him pay the penalty."

Ranno nodded his head encouragingly at this point.

"Also I want to say I believe that justice should be administered by the people. Will we ever have such a chance again, with every inch of sod filled with sons of the plateau, to reach a verdict with the solid opinion of the people back of it?

"But"—his voice rising to an even shriller pitch as he proceeded —"I must confess to a doubt. Can we be sure of Nicolan's guilt without having heard the evidence he was prepared to offer? Perhaps it is presumptuous of me to express this opinion. Here I stand, a lowly son of a beggarly line of sheep men, surrounded by the proud and lordly horse breeders of the plateau. They draw away as though they detect a whiff of wool about me which even this fine cloak can't conceal. But this I want to say, my friends —if I have any—a herder of sheep spends all his waking hours in the open, under the warm rays of the sun or watching through the hours of the night with no company but the stars above him; and I believe a love of truth is one of the things he learns. I think my fellow tenders of sheep would like me to say this on their behalf: that they would not murder a soldier unheard who had come a long way to give his evidence, that they would not fill the pockets of a witless gabune so that he would run away, that they would not hire a triple traitor and spy to come here and swear to a pack of lies. The man who is guilty of these crimes might be the one who connived to send the men of the plateau up the bloody slope at Châlons. Certainly we can't fix the guilt elsewhere until these points have been cleared up."

He turned and scowled at Ranno, whose face had taken on the high color of outraged surprise.

"My vote is—no!"

And then unexpected things happened. Although many voices were raised in dissent, there was an outburst of laughter along the slope, accompanied by a vigorous clapping of hands and then a great shout which continued without a check for many moments.

2

Oslaw laid a hand on Nicolan's arm and led him back into the room he had been occupying. He closed the door after them.

"It will be safer," he said, "to remain here until this excitement is over. I think most of the people have been won to your support but there will be many who still believe you responsible for the deaths of fathers and husbands. One of them might plunge a dagger into your back." He went to the window and stood there for several moments, watching what was going on outside. "They are swarming down from the slopes. As I expected, there's much bitter argument among them. The guards will have their hands full."

"Where is Ranno?"

"He hasn't moved. I don't believe I have ever seen anyone so completely discomfited as our fine and honorable Ranno. Wait, he seems to have vanished. At least, I cannot see him."

"What of Hasca?"

"Our brave sheepherder remains in his chair. There's a smile on his face. It seems to me to be one of satisfaction, although it borders on the sly as well. The people below him are engaged in a bitter dispute. But this doesn't disturb him at all."

Oslaw walked to the table and seated himself beside Nicolan. "My son," he said, "you realize, I am sure, how lucky you have been."

Nicolan nodded gravely. "I had small hopes of a favorable vote from the Ferma. I owe you my life, for your forceful presentation of the case."

"It remains now to decide on a course of action. With the hearing postponed, I can do either one of two things. First, I can take the position that the killing of your chief witness makes it impossible for you to present a complete case and that the charges should be dropped. Second, I can begin a hearing at once into the circumstances of the murder of Somutu and the bribery of the other two. This would make it necessary to appoint a committee of investigation, to be chosen by the people at large."

"I returned voluntarily," said Nicolan. "My main purpose was to remove the stain cast on my name by the lies of Ranno. To close the case now would not give me the complete vindication I seek. I believe the hearings should be resumed. But," he added, after a moment's consideration, "two steps must be taken first. We must have a thorough investigation. And a meeting should be called of the people of the plateau to vote on the filling of the nine seats of the Ferma."

Oslaw's face, which had carried a hint of inner conflict, cleared at once. He nodded his head and smiled at the defendant.

"That is what I hoped you would say. You are taking an honest and courageous stand. I shall be happy to report what you have said at the meeting of the Ferma which will be held as soon as the excitement subsides. But you must recognize the unpredictable side of Ranno. There's no telling what violence he may attempt. So wait until a course of action has been decided on."

There was a knock on the door and Hasca put his head in. He winked at Nicolan and bowed to Oslaw. "Come in," said the latter.

Hasca entered with a trace of swagger. It was clear that he was quite pleased with himself.

"I seem to have spoiled the plans of this new Caesar," he said. "After I had given my vote, he sat and glared at me, and there was death in his eye. But I have no fears. His fangs will be drawn before we see the end of this."

"You took an honest and fearless stand," said Oslaw.

"I am deeply in your debt," declared Nicolan. "It may well be that your vote saved my life."

The sheep man gestured carelessly. "In spite of what I said out there, it was clear to me from the start they had nothing against you. Except the word of this land thief and perjurer and his own servants and toadies. Oh, I was against you until the trial started. I didn't speak for a week after I heard of my brother's death. He was a little bowlegged runt, and I loved him." He turned to stare intently into Nicolan's eyes. "I'm sure now it wasn't you who went to those three drunken princes."

"No. But I can tell you who it was."

Hasca gestured with both hands. "No need. I *know*. And, my lord Oslaw, there is a rumor stirring about in the crowd. That's why I came in to see you. Ranno doesn't give in easy and he was trying to get all his supporters gathered together at one end. He had not heard the rumor until I risked the lightning in his eyes to tell him Roric was alive and on his way here. His face went as white as a Hun's teeth. He snarled at me that I lied but he gave up the idea of starting an armed demonstration."

Oslaw asked eagerly, "What is the word about Roric?"

"It seems to be true. A neighbor of mine, a sheep man with the stench of the critters in every inch of his hide, told me that Roric's riding in with a party of friends. They are not far away. He told me that Roric is still weak. His memory"—Hasca waved one hand back and forth—"comes and goes."

"That is to be expected." The Orator nodded briskly. "But, with care, he can be brought back to health. And then we'll get the truth. This means my hands will be full today. I must leave you."

When they were alone, Hasca began to talk at great length and about a wide variety of subjects. Finally he said: "I may get to like you. Since I've had a taste of sitting up there in the chairs of the great, I think I would like to stay. You and I, now, we might do a lot together."

"And with Roric."

Hasca drew down the corners of his mouth as he considered this phase of the situation. "Roric too, of course. He'll be the head of the Roymarcks and he'll sit in the chair that Ranno has been trying so hard to steal. But he's not going to count for much. When an arrow touches the brain, it's luck if you stay alive at all. But you and I, we could step along together when the time arrives for"—he paused and looked with sober intentness into Nicolan's eyes—"for the great chance."

"This fellow is shrewd," thought Nicolan. "He is looking ahead."

It quickly became even more clear that the sheep man was a great talker and that, once launched, the ships of his conversation took a long time in reaching port. He seated himself beside Nicolan and crossed one heavy leg over the other. "When I was young, with skinny legs which bowed out like the antlers of an elk, one of our rams charged me from behind. He sent me head over heels and—Belokin bear me out!—it was near the finish of me. Ever since I've had a dislike for being butted around. Last night Ranno came to me and said, 'There's going to be trouble tomorrow. A regular earthquake. Keep an eye on me,' he said, 'and I'll signal how I want you to vote.' That left me in a rage. I said to myself, 'He's starting to butt you around, this fellow.' And then when I found it *was* an earthquake, I did my best to make sure it was Ranno himself who got swallowed up."

He burst into a loud laugh and reached out a fist suddenly to pound Nicolan on the knee. "We'll work together. And, if there's any butting around needs to be done, you and me, we'll do it between us."

Their talk was interrupted at this point by a din outside which outdid anything in the way of noise which the excited people of the plateau had yet achieved. Hasca ran to the window and stared out. Then he gave vent to a loud whistle and turned around to stare excitedly at Nicolan.

"They're arriving!" he said. "Must have been much closer than we thought. I can see the first of them. They've turned in and are going to ride down the center path."

Nicolan joined him at the window, his heart beating wildly. Ildico, his brave and wonderful love, had fulfilled her difficult mission. In a moment he would see her. In several more she would be in his arms. No, it would be too public for that. But she would be with him. He rose on his toes in an effort to glance over the massive shoulders of Hasca but was unable to see anything of the path.

"How many are there of them?" he asked, eagerly.

"Eight, I think."

"No, no!" cried Nicolan. "Not eight! There were eight in the party when they started out. Look again, Hasca, my friend. There must be nine."

Hasca watched carefully and then shook his head. "No, there's only eight."

"Then there is no truth in the story that Roric is alive," declared Nicolan, his hopes falling lower and lower. Another thought, an even more disturbing one, came into his mind. "Hasca! Is there a lady in the party?"

"If there is," declared the sheep man, "she's tall and she's broad and she's got shoulders on her like a bull."

3

Forgetting Oslaw's warning, Nicolan rushed out and forced his way through the mass of people who now filled the level space. He was recognized at once. Some glowered with hostility but most of them smiled and a few went to the extent of patting him on the back as he passed.

The horseman in the lead had been selected by Oslaw to command the party, a tall fellow who scorned to wear any kind of hat. He was coated with dust from head to foot. Nicolan stopped him as the party reached the end of the descending path.

"Sarsan! Where is she?" he cried.

The horseman seemed reluctant to speak. "They surprised us," he said, looking away with a shamefaced air.

Nicolan's first thought was that the surprise attack had been the work of Ranno. When he voiced this fear, the man Sarsan shook his head. "No, my lord Nicolan," he said. "It was a large troop. Twenty of them or more." He leaned over his horse's head, to speak in a lowered voice. "Huns. Mounted archers. We didn't have a chance to strike a blow."

Nicolan was left speechless. He knew that the possibility of this had been hanging over them but it had seemed to him a danger for the future. That Ildico's return had become known so quickly pointed to treachery within the close circle of the family. Someone had sent word immediately to Attila's headquarters.

He looked up at Sarsan with a stricken air and waited for more information. "It happened yesterday morning," explained the leader. "There was a sharp bend and when we turned it, there they were, sitting their horses right across the road. Each man had an arrow in his bow and any move on our part to engage them or to get away would have brought a volley down on us. Their captain was almost friendly. He said they wanted the lady and that was all. I asked him what was back of it, and he said, 'Orders from the Lord of the Land and the Sea.' My Lady Ildico behaved with the greatest courage. She whispered to me that any movement would get us all killed without being of any help to her. She said we must turn at once and take her brother safely back around the bend. She said to get word to you and then she called, 'Farewell, dear Roric'—and that was the end. The Huns closed in around her and rode off at a furious gallop." He seemed almost on the point of tears. "Ah, my lord, what a brave lady, and we couldn't save her!"

The shock, which had left Nicolan unable to speak, was beginning to give way to a feeling of black fury. Why had this been allowed to happen? What precaution had he failed to take? He realized it had been impossible for him to do anything once they had come to see Oslaw and he had been put under orders to remain, pending the trial. But before that there had been an opportunity to secure her safety. Macio's instructions should have been followed. If Ildico had been persuaded to accompany Eugenia on the road to safety north of the Alps she would now be well on her way to a lifetime of liberty. Why, why, had he not refused to let her have her own way? It was his fault, he realized now, that the worst had happened.

It could all be traced back to Ranno, who had laid the charges. He was convinced even that it had been the latter who had sent the information to Attila. In a few moments the blind fury which had taken possession of him cleared sufficiently for him to see that this could not be so, for Ranno had been determined to make Ildico his wife. Who then could be responsible? He became convinced almost at once that the word had been sent to the emperor by Laudio. She had always expected to marry Ranno and it had been a bitter blow when she had been compelled to see that he preferred her sister. The only way she could win him back was to remove Ildico from her path. That, almost certainly, was the explanation. How deep her hatred must be to have driven her to such a course!

Hearing Sarsan say, "My lord Roric is with us," he turned back, trying to clear his mind of the terror which was driving out all other emotions, the terror he felt for Ildico and the fate ahead of her.

Roric had a rider on each side of him and it was apparent that the fast pace they had maintained had worn him out. If it had not been for the black patch he wore over his blind eye, no one would have recognized him. He was thin and pale, with a deep shadow under his good eye and a hollowness of cheek which made him seem an old man.

"Roric!" said Nicolan, walking up beside his old friend.

The wounded man looked at him with an expression of hesitation and doubt. "Who are you?" he asked.

"Don't you recognize me? Look! Roric, I am Nicolan and we were once the closest of friends."

The injured man sighed with weariness as he studied Nicolan's face. "Nicolan?" he said. "It seems familiar. Nicolan. Nicolan." Then he paused. "I thought it was coming back. But now it is gone again."

Sarsan said, at Nicolan's shoulder, "That's the way he is. His memory seems to be returning. Then it fades out."

"Did he know his sister?"

"Not at first. He looked at her steadily and then he smiled. Very faintly. Her name didn't seem to mean anything to him, for he repeated it several times and then shook his head. It was not until she removed the wrap and he saw the color of her hair that his memory stirred. He cried, 'Ildico!' After that, there were times when he knew her but it was never for long."

"But isn't that proof of a bettering in his condition?"

Roric had been watching and listening, rubbing his hands across his forehead as though trying to brush the mental fog away. At this point he said, "Gather—into your hands the—the reins that I—I shall drop tomorrow."

Nicolan cried excitedly, "Roric, my friend, you are beginning to remember! Try, try harder!" He added to the leader of the troop, "That was the last thing he said to me on the night before the battle."

Roric gave a rather wan smile and then nodded his head. "Yes," he said, in a whisper, "I seem to see clearer. Perhaps—perhaps——"

But in response to Nicolan's questioning and prodding he failed to achieve any further light. All he seemed capable of saying, in dull tones, was, "No! No!"

Nicolan, his hopes dashed and his unhappiness returning in full measure, asked, "Did you find him at the Victorex lands?" and was surprised when Sarsan shook his head.

"We went there first," explained the latter, "but they had seen nothing of him nor heard anything. We cast around in all directions and searched the roads for miles. Then we found him, crumpled up under a tree and unable to move. He must have been without food for a long time. It was the barking of a dog which led us to him and the shouts of boys who were pelting him with stones. After he had been fed and rested, the Lady Ildico told him about the dream. He had no recollection of it at all."

Oslaw joined them at this point. He stared hard at the frail figure strapped on the horse's back ("Roric, the daredevil among all riders, in a saddle!" he thought) and shook his head despondently. He asked Nicolan, "Did he know you?"

"No. But I think his memory is showing some signs of coming back. He repeated the last words he said to me on the night before the battle."

"Roric!" said the old man, in a persuasive tone. "It is well that you have returned. Your father's post remains to be filled."

The weakened horseman looked down at him with a trace of a frown. A question seemed to hover on his lips. Then he sighed and his head sank lower between his shoulders.

The Orator continued to study the thin frame and the unhappy face. Finally he said to Nicolan in a low tone, "My lord Roric has come home in body but, alas, not in spirit. Still, while there can be hope of his recovery, his hereditary post must be kept open. The law leaves no doubt on that point. I shall make an announcement to the people, explaining the situation. Our poor young friend is in a very weak condition. I fear—well, see that he is taken to his home at once. It may be that a few weeks of rest and good food will restore him physically. Perhaps mentally to some extent as well."

"What of Ranno?" asked Nicolan.

"Ranno," said the Orator, "ceases to play any part, unless he can win enough support in the meeting of all the people which will be called as soon as a definite conclusion is reached about Roric's condition. I doubt very much if he will even be allowed to fill the seat of his family."

Nicolan told him then the sad news about Ildico. Oslaw listened in silence and the slight trace of ruddiness in his cheeks left him completely. For the first time he looked like an old man, sad and disillusioned and unhappy.

"All this can be laid at the door of Ranno!" he said, with sudden heat. "He has been selfish and false and cruel from his earliest years!" He added after a pause devoted to bitter reflection,

"There is nothing we can do about her. A protest to Attila, perhaps, for whatever small effect it might have. I would not expect any results from it, save perhaps an increase in the burdens laid on our people." Aware of a silence which had fallen about him, he looked back over his shoulder. His manner became taut although he displayed no signs of apprehension.

"He is coming," he said. "See to it, Nicolan, that Roric is removed at once. Give instructions that he is to be well guarded."

4

The men of the plateau had fallen back, opening a lane for the advance of the head of the Finninalders. Nicolan and the Orator stood shoulder to shoulder at the narrow end of the cleared space and waited for the self-appointed head of the Ferma to draw near. A silence had fallen over the crowded field, as the eyes of the beholders rested in turn on each of the principals in the drama.

"Leave this to me," said Oslaw, to his companion. "The law is on our side now."

Ranno halted a dozen or more paces away. "I stand among friends," he said. "I know that the people of the plateau have not changed their minds about the guilt of this man."

Oslaw raised his eloquent hand in the air. "There is nothing to be gained by further discussion here or at this time. Even if the judges had not voted to stop the hearing, the arrival of Roric, son of Macio of the Roymarcks, would have made a postponement necessary. No further steps can be taken until he has had a chance to regain his strength."

Perhaps Ranno read into the words a suggestion that Roric's condition was serious. He looked up quickly and there was a hint of relief in his eyes.

"Why isn't Roric here, so the people of the plateau may see him?" he demanded. "Why have you taken it on yourselves to conceal him so quickly?"

"He has not recovered fully from the effects of his wound. As he had ridden far and fast this morning, he was sorely in need of rest."

If Ranno had intended to press the point, he decided it would not suit his purpose to do so now. He advanced close to where Nicolan stood and began to speak in a low tone, employing the Latin tongue which few of the spectators understood.

"You proud and overconfident fool, putting yourself in my power!" he said. "They would be preparing the block and sharpening the edge of Expiation for you now if that rancid fool of a sheepherder had not broken faith!"

"*You* will be sent to the block," declared Nicolan, "when Roric has given his evidence."

Ranno stepped back several paces. "There is another issue which I find of more concern than the condition of the son of the Roymarcks. Is it true that his sister Ildico has been carried off by the troops of Attila?"

"It is true," answered Oslaw.

Ranno continued to address himself to Nicolan, reverting to the native tongue. "Are you aware," he cried, "that she was to have been my wife? The last time I saw Macio he confirmed the arrangement which we had made."

"I was not aware of such an arrangement," declared Nicolan.

Ranno glanced about him. "You will find," he cried, "that it was known from one end of the plateau to the other. In spite of this, you made no secret of your desire and intention to marry her yourself."

"It was so understood between us."

A wave of angry color took possession of Ranno's face. "You have tried to steal my promised bride from me. There is only one answer I can make. I challenge you to a Duel of the Whips."

Oslaw laid an urgent hand on Nicolan's arm. "Choose your words carefully," he warned. "You are not in physical condition to fight him yet. The law provides a delay of weeks for the challenged party to acquire sufficient skill. You will need all of it."

"There can be no delay," said Nicolan to his elderly adviser. "Do you think me cowardly enough to spend so much time practicing a trick with a whip while Ildico is a captive in Attila's hands?"

"But, my son, what can you do for her?"

"There may be nothing I can do. But I must be near her. I must be ready for any opportunity which may arise."

Nicolan raised his voice to a high pitch. "I hold you responsible,

Ranno of the Finninalders, for all the misfortunes which have fallen on the family of the Roymarcks. I accept the challenge."

"As the challenged party," Oslaw reminded him, "you have the right to set the date and select the place."

"The date?" cried Nicolan. "Today. As soon as the arrangements can be made."

"For the first time in memory," declared Ranno, "I find myself in agreement with you. There must be no delay, of an hour, of a minute."

CHAPTER XII

1

NICOLAN had the staked enclosure in the east, which meant that he, the challenged, would have the sun in his eyes for the first cast. This actually was a small matter. He would need to exercise care in the first few moments and be prepared to flatten himself across his horse's back if his antagonist showed immediate aggressiveness.

He had eaten nothing for so long that, as he thought on the best strategy to employ, he was hungrily devouring a bowl of chopped mutton and cabbage which Ivar had brought him.

The Briton was in an embittered mood. "Why must you act like this?" he demanded, glowering darkly. "The word reaches me that the case is over and you are free. I run like mad to tell my wife. She is overjoyed. There is no one else about, so we sing and caper like a pair of children. Then we hear that Ildico has been taken. My wife falls into despair. 'It is good that Nicolan is free,' she says, 'because now you, my great ox of a husband, can go with him to rescue her. If you don't bring her back, that sweet little golden lambkin of mine, I never want to set eyes on either of you again.'"

"It was well said," declared Nicolan.

"Then," went on the Briton, with a rising emphasis in his voice, "I come here and find that you have deliberately put yourself in peril of your life again. He may kill you out there. He has kept in training with the whips all his life. Do you think I can rescue Ildico alone?"

"Put yourself in my place," said Nicolan. "When you saw that all our efforts had been in vain, that Attila had found the beautiful blonde wife he had been searching for so long, and that the blame could be traced back to one man, what would you have done? You would have done exactly what I did." He looked toward the west and studied the signs of activity behind the stakes in the opposing enclosure. "I shall know no peace until his gross body is under the sod and his evil tongue has been stilled."

"But couldn't his punishment have been left to the Ferma? Couldn't you, at least, have waited a day, a week, a month? Long enough for Roric to recover his memory?"

"I am forestalling the executioner."

"Perhaps," declared Ivar, whose spirits refused to lift, "you will precede him into the shades. Will it be any consolation for us if Ranno is then put on trial and sent to join you?" He placed himself beside Nicolan, who was still scrutinizing the other enclosure. "Do you realize you won't have Harthager to ride? Since our poor Ildico has been carried off, Laudio has become the head of the Roymarcks. She won't let you have the black in a fight against the man she loves."

"I will have to do with my faithful roan. Jackopol is probably as good as anything Ranno can get."

"Has it entered your head that Laudio might give Harthager to Ranno?"

Nicolan turned a sober pair of eyes on his friend. "That possibility hadn't occurred to me. Still, riding the king for the first time is not easy; and it might be that the great black would refuse to carry that lying hound. He is a fine judge of men, and he knows the smell of treachery."

The mood of the plateau people had continued to veer around since the conclusion of the hearing. Many of them were standing outside Nicolan's enclosure as though hoping by their presence to lend him support. A few had ventured inside, including the three younger men who had been members of the Ferma and had voted first with Ranno. They were a shamefaced trio and seemed almost pathetically anxious to demonstrate their change of heart. Two of them had brought their favorite chargers and had offered them to him. Cristus, the third one, had brought his whip as a peace offering. Nicolan tested it and then gave his head a nod.

"I like it," he said. "It has fine weight and balance. Better than mine, I think."

"It is yours," declared Cristus, eagerly. "And I hope it brings you luck."

Hasca also put in an appearance. He gave a look at the available horses and shook his head. "I know sheep and I don't know horses. But I know enough to see that none of these will do. Is the roan yours?"

Nicolan nodded. Jackopol was standing in a corner of the enclosure. He knew what was ahead and he was too nervous to eat the measure of oats in front of him.

"He's steady and sure," said Nicolan. "And he understands me. Every pressure of my knee means something to him. We'll get along."

"No fire to him!" declared Hasca. It was apparent that he feared the outcome.

A servingman with the red collar of the Roymarcks entered the enclosure. He made a cautious gesture in Nicolan's direction.

"She wants to see you, master," he said, in a low voice.

"Who do you mean? The Lady Laudio?"

"Yes, master."

"I haven't much time. The herald will be sounding his trumpet in a few minutes. Where is your mistress?"

"Close at hand, master. A little distance back in the woods."

Laudio was standing in a clearing not more than two hundred yards from the enclosure. Harthager was behind her and it was taking the efforts of two grooms to restrain him. The older daughter of the Roymarcks did not raise her eyes as Nicolan approached her.

"I am here to make a confession," she said, in a low tone. "I betrayed my little sister."

"Do you mean you sent word to Attila?"

She nodded somberly. "Yes, I sent him a message. But I realized almost at once the wickedness of what I had done. It came to me suddenly that I didn't hate her after all." She raised a hand to her mouth as though to restrain her feelings before saying anything more. "I've always been jealous of her. I was the first daughter but my father preferred her. It was because of her yellow hair. He couldn't get over his pride in it. When we first expected Attila, and all men thought of keeping their wives and daughters out of sight, my father sent Ildico away. He did nothing to protect me. I have enough beauty, haven't I, for the emperor to want me? My father wouldn't have cared. And then when Ranno, who was to have married me—it had always been understood that he would—began to think he wanted Ildico instead, my father was willing to give in to him."

She looked up then and he saw that her eyes, which had been cold and withdrawn before, had suddenly become charged with stormy emotions. "I could see that Ranno wanted her and not me. She couldn't help it. She didn't want him. I know that now when it's too late. I don't hate her, even if I always was jealous. But I do hate him. He passed me over, he discarded me. Yes, I hate him so much that today, when one of you must die, I don't want it to be you. Nicolan, you must have every chance to win. I have brought Harthager for you to ride."

"Laudio, you are being very generous," he said.

"Generous?" She turned away. "I am not being generous. I am trying to make amends for the terrible thing I did. Perhaps, if you live, you can do something for my poor little Ildico."

Nicolan walked over to soothe the impatient black. Harthager let his forefeet come back to earth.

"O King," said Nicolan, "we had a wild ride up in the hills, you and I." He placed one hand on the silky skin of the regal muzzle. "What a ride we are to take now!"

Harthager gave his head a toss and snorted loudly.

"O King," said Nicolan, "you may know already that the mistress we both love, the little lady with the golden hair, is in great peril. Perhaps there is something we can do for her today. It is no more than a first step; but it must be done. We must go out there now and outride and outmaneuver an evil fellow who will be seated on a charger not fit to stand within eyesight of you. What do you say? Are you ready to issue forth with me and do battle with him on his ill-bred and puny horse?"

Harthager gave his head another toss, a high one, and snorted loudly. Nicolan sprang to his back, and they were off.

2

According to custom, the antagonists circled the field in opposite directions, which brought them together once. They should have passed with no more than the raising of their whips by way of salute. But Ranno, wearing a riding jacket of resplendent red with black and gold facings, saw fit to do more. He reined in abruptly and stared at Nicolan over the excited head of his rather small brindled mare.

"Things are going badly for me," he said. His eyes began to glow like coals under the bellows. "But that isn't going to stop me from killing you. I intend to drive my knife into your heart! And I'll have the sweet memory of your last agony to carry me through whatever may follow."

"We share this one thought at any rate," declared Nicolan. "My good knife has been thirsting for the taste of your blood, Ranno of the Finninalders."

The voice of the herald reached them from the side lines. "This is against the rules," he cried. "There must be no communication between you."

"He doesn't realize how easy it is to break rules," said Ranno, with a sly smile. "Must we heed the silly restrictions made by living men when we stand on the brink? I see that one has been broken already in your favor. You are supposed to ride your own horse but that madwoman has seen fit to let you have the great Harthager." The angry eyes looked at the glossy black stallion with a hint of envy. "The little idiot! She pretends to hate me but when neither of us is here to see it, she'll weep her eyes out at my bier. I wish you no luck at all with that heavy-footed monster. My Barta here will cut swift little circles around him."

"The king wouldn't let you sit on his back. See how he twitches to get out of range of the scent of your treachery."

"You stubborn fool!"

"You liar and thief!"

The trumpet of the herald had not sounded yet to summon them to their stations at opposite ends of the Field of the Fast Hoof. Nicolan turned a brief moment in the direction of that official and looked back when some inner sense warned him of danger. Perhaps he had remembered what Ranno had said about the futility of rules and his own right to break them. He fell flat on his horse's back. It was well that he had not delayed, for he felt the whip of Ranno cut through the air with such vicious force that it touched his shoulder in passing like the sharp edge of steel. A roar of disapproval and anger rose from the huge crowds around the field but this had no effect on Ranno. He had expressed his scorn for foolish rules when death in one form or another faced him. His heart pounded with desire to send his enemy into the shades ahead of him.

He had chosen a new method of attack which startled the spectators into a moment of awed silence. Instead of circling about in the traditional way and waiting for the opportunity to make the winning cast, he drove his nervous little mare straight in toward the black stallion and his rider. Twice his whip lashed out at close range and missed by no more than the width of a hand. Astonished at this method of fighting close in, and having no answer ready for it, Nicolan kept himself as flat as he could on his mount's back. It was Harthager who saved him in this crisis. The big horse wheeled and reared and side-stepped with the sure and graceful steps of a dancer, and never gave the viciously charging Ranno the chance for a steady cast.

Hanging on grimly, Nicolan caught a glimpse of the massed spectators and saw that they were jumping up and down and waving their arms and shouting in paroxysms of an uncontrollable madness. All this was wrong but they were impotent to do anything. The fury of the attack would bring things to an end before anyone could reach the center of the field.

The third cast from the lethal whip of the furiously attacking Ranno fell short by a wider margin and Nicolan saw his chance to escape. "Fast!" he cried, and the black responded with a burst of speed which took them quickly out of range of these hornet-like tactics.

Now the initiative had passed out of Ranno's hands. The lightning feet of Harthager forced him to guard himself in the traditional way of fighting: the bursts of speed, the sudden starts and stops, the circling about to attack from the rear.

"We have him, O King!" cried Nicolan, gripping the flanks of the straining black and dictating with the pressure of his knees the tactics they would now use.

But it was by no means certain that the victory would be theirs. Ranno was a crafty opponent and a skillful rider. He kept his quick-footed mount out of range of Nicolan's whip. They galloped up and down the field, they changed pace, they veered and circled and feinted. Neither seemed able to get into the position where a sure cast could be made.

And then the chance came, suddenly and unexpectedly. The

mare had not come about quickly enough and for a second the back of Ranno, in the gorgeous red jacket he had selected, was turned. Nicolan drove in closer and made a perfect cast. His whip lashed out like the forked tongue of a serpent and touched his opponent's neck. It fastened itself with the winding acceleration of a tethering rope and then tightened as he pulled.

Nicolan never did know how it came about that Ranno succeeded in some miraculous way in making a maddened backward cast. Aim and timing were perfect. As Nicolan tugged desperately on his own whip, he felt his throat constrict. There could not have been more than a second's interval between the completion of the two casts; and then both men were sprawling on the ground within easy reach of each other.

A silence fell on the spectators. Then a roar of excited comment was raised and of one accord they came pouring out on the field to be closer for the last act in this brief and mad drama. They sensed the danger in which Nicolan was placed before he did, for cries of warning reached his ears. He felt for the dagger he had worn in his belt. It was not there. It must have been torn away in his fall.

He had no time to look for it. Ranno had already seen the great advantage that chance had given him. His blade was out and he was stalking triumphantly on his disarmed opponent, ready for the kill.

Nicolan struggled to his feet. The fall had shaken him up and he believed that one of his ankles had been turned. In desperation he tore off his tunic and wrapped it about his left arm. If he could succeed in parrying the first thrust of his opponent's steel, he might be able to get his free hand on Ranno's neck. It was his only chance. The hate he felt for his opponent was still so deep and all-absorbing that he even found himself welcoming this chance of a struggle at close range. Ranno's advantage did not disturb him. All he needed was to get his fingers on that strong and swarthy neck!

The hand of Providence, which had been stretched out to him in the tense drama of the trial, was to do him a second service by bringing him assistance from an unexpected source. He became aware of a thudding sound behind him. Harthager had not stopped short on being relieved of his rider as the little mare

Barta had done. The great black did not consider his role to be at an end yet. He charged past Nicolan, feet flying, mane tossing, a screech of the fighting excitement, which sometimes rose from the front line of horses in a charge of cavalry, rising above the roar of the crowd. Ranno, seeing death approach him in this frightening guise, shrank back and raised his dagger. No such puny defense could be of any avail. One of the flying hoofs caught him squarely in the face. He crumpled up on the sward.

The days of Ranno of the Finninalders had come to an end.

CHAPTER XIII

1

THERE WERE flags fluttering over the entrance to Attila's city when Nicolan rode in a week later, with his injured leg strapped to a stirrup. Although the afternoon sun was already in decline, the open spaces were crowded with people in a festive mood, wearing (his eyes opened in wonder at this) garlands of flowers in their hair or around the brims of their hats.

"What is the reason for all this frivolity?" he asked the captain at the gate. He feared that he knew already but he wanted to be sure.

The captain grinned. "The emperor's orders. It's in honor of his bride. He was married an hour ago."

"The emperor has had a hundred brides in his day."

The captain indulged in a suggestive wink. "But never one like this! I saw her as close as I see you now. Ah, what a slender little chick! Her hair as bright as the sun."

Nicolan turned a tragic face to Ivar as they made their way down the street. "I don't know what I could have done but I hoped to get here before anything happened. I might have succeeded where Sartuk failed."

"You mean you would have tried to kill him?" Ivar's horror at such an idea showed in his face. "If you had succeeded, you head of mutton, Ildico would have been burned alive on the emperor's bier."

They observed at once a tendency to treat the occasion with scorn on the part of the Hun girls who were out in great numbers, and dressed in their gayest and best. One plump and button-eyed maiden planted herself in front of Nicolan's horse.

"My handsome captain," she said, "are you like all the rest of these blind donkeys? Do you want a wife with a face as dead white as the belly of a fish?" She slapped a well-rounded buttock. "Has she got anything to equal this?"

Giso was on the steps of the palace gate, and when he saw Nicolan, he came down to greet him. "He's been as giddy as a goat," he said. "And him with his face twisted this way and that by that last attack he had. He hasn't visited the Court of the Royal Wives since he returned and you should hear how the tongues wag! If they had their way, those others, they would hold burning tapers to the soles of the yellow-haired woman's feet. . . . He has been asking for you."

"The emperor?"

"Who else? Perhaps he will have time to see you before the great banquet begins. I will find out."

Nicolan realized it would be wise to leave at once. If any inkling of the truth about his relationship with Ildico had reached the ears of the emperor, the command issued for his presence was a death summons. But he could not bring himself to turn and ride away. Ildico was here, and already married to the emperor. There was nothing he could do for her, save to remain, even though it might cost him his life. Continued existence, after all, held nothing for him.

When Giso returned and confirmed the imperial desire with a nod, they made their way to a door at one side. Before they entered, Black Scyles came out from the kitchens with a fine mouthful of shining white teeth in his ebony face.

"Emperor's going to be proud as a peacock with three tails when he sees what I send in to him tonight," declared the head cook. "Roman feasts? Pah! I spew at them. There's been nothing to equal this since all the gods got down at one table and picked Nero's bones bare. I have fifteen cooks in there and every once in a while I walk down the line and kick their damp backsides as I go, to keep them busy."

Attila, sitting in his dark and narrow little cubicle, was already dressed for the great banquet in a tunic made entirely of golden thread. He had been powdered and pomaded and perfumed but there was no concealing the contortion of his face muscles which Giso had mentioned. He looked old and wizened and very sick.

"You killed that traitorous dog!" he said to Nicolan. "I am glad. It relieves me of the need of planning a public execution for him. I have had so many men killed that I am weary of it. I need a time of rest which I can devote to my children and my new wife.

I have decided to postpone the assembling of my armies again. The brave Romans need not begin trembling for a year at least."

Looking at this rapidly aging man, Nicolan said to himself: "It is all over. He will never assemble another army."

Attila nodded his head with a return of his former pride. "But I still keep spies at work. A few days ago the word reached me that the weak fool who calls himself emperor is plotting to put Aetius out of the way. He will summon his general to court and have him murdered in front of the throne. It is even said that the brave Valentinian will thrust the knife into his heart with his own white hands."

Attila's expression had hardened as he spoke. "Aetius must be warned. I want him kept alive. I have never said this before but I was fond of him when he first came to my uncle's court as a hostage. He made things very"—he paused for the right word and then pronounced the one that came into his head—"he made things very *gay*. It was not until he laughed at my short legs that I began to hate him." A trace of the old antagonism showed once more in his face. "He must not be killed before I have inflicted the crushing defeat I am planning for him.

"Togalatus, I have selected you for a special honor," he went on. "You are to set out for Rome and find a chance to whisper in his ear the news of this treacherous plan."

"Great Tanjou, am I permitted to make an explanation?"

"Proceed."

"When your victorious armies were destroying the cities of Italy and all Rome trembled with fear of you, the people clamored for retaliation. As I was being held prisoner, they demanded that I be put to death at once. My lord Aetius forestalled them by making it possible for me to escape. But I had to give him a promise before he let me go that I would not return to your service."

This information had a different effect on the Hun emperor than Nicolan had expected. Instead of asserting that no man could leave him, he beamed with a sly pride. "You see? He still fears me. He wants to weaken me in every way he can. Well, then, I shall have to send someone else." Then he winked at his visitor with an almost senile relish. "This will amuse you, as you have seen and talked with the Princess Honoria. She has returned.

The Eastern prince grew weary of her and so she was not allowed
to land. The ship was turned about and sent straight back to
Ravenna with her on board. As the old woman is dead, the
princess will become like an open door where anyone can enter
without knocking." He paused and then resumed his usual air of
great pride. "Did you return in time to witness my marriage to
the Lady Ildico, a daughter of your own race?"

"No, Great Tanjou."

"Then you must not miss the royal banquet tonight. My bride,
my lovely little golden-plumed bird, will sit on a golden chair beside me. The same chair in which she will be carried into Rome
when I have brought those proud people to my feet."

As he turned away Nicolan realized that the spies of Attila,
for once, had been at fault. They had failed to discover that he
had known Ildico since she was a small girl. Many of the excited
spectators at the trial had been aware that he, Nicolan, loved
her and that she preferred him to all other men. None of this
apparently had reached the ears of the emperor's emissaries, for
Attila had talked to him with no reservations whatever.

There could be only one explanation for this. The Huns knew
that the last act in this greatest play that mankind had lived and
suffered through was nearing an end. They must be certain that
he was a sick man, perhaps even that he was dying. The iron
discipline was no longer felt. Attila's men had ceased to fear him.
The party sent to lead Ildico back into captivity had accomplished
their mission but had not tried to do anything more. No whisper
of the love between the golden-haired daughter of the plateau
and the man who had once served the emperor so well had
reached Attila's ears.

How lucky for Nicolan that this was so! If Attila had possessed
the smallest part of the truth, he would have seen to it that
Nicolan's lifeless body was already swinging at the main city gate.

2

Nicolan and Ivar encountered Giso as the guests for the nuptial
feast were pouring into the banquet hall. They plied him with
questions and found him pleased to answer them.

No, the emperor's new wife had not been brought by force.

Attila had sent Onegesius to question her and to apply, if necessary, what might be termed moral persuasion. If she would accompany the imperial train back to headquarters and there become the last wife of the emperor (Attila promised definitely that he would never take another wife), she was to have a household of her own with every luxury that the world had to offer. No rules or traditions would bind her, save fidelity to the marriage vows. Her companions and servants would be of her own choosing. She would have an income of her own, large enough to maintain a court on an opulent scale.

There was a pause after these conditions had been explained and enlarged upon out of Giso's personal contacts with the actual conditions.

"She did not accept," declared Nicolan, with the deep conviction of a lover.

"No. She didn't lunge at this shining bait. Mind you, young sirs, there was no barbed hook concealed in the offer. The emperor's promises were made in all honesty. He wanted her and he was ready to pay any price. But when she made it clear that she could not be bribed into acceptance, then Onegesius applied pressure. He threatened reprisals on the people of the plateau if she persisted. They would be treated like a conquered race. The imperial troops would be quartered on all families. The strongest of the young men would be taken for the army and the best of the horses would be seized. The people would be bound to the land. It would not be their right to marry and have children." Giso shook his head with a suggestion of involuntary respect. "He knows no limits, this Lord of Earth and Sky. He meant it. She, and she alone, could save her people from slavery." He gestured with both hands. "So, of course, she gave in."

"Yes, she gave in then," declared Nicolan. In the low tone he employed there was a smoldering anger which was held in check only by his appreciation of Ildico's willingness to sacrifice herself. "There's nothing she wouldn't do for her people. Even this."

"She came here by slow stages," continued Giso, "like an empress of the East, in a great covered wagon. No eyes, other than those of the Greek servants he had provided, could rest upon her. When they camped for the night, sentries were placed in a circle about the wagons, allowing three hundred yards in all directions so she could enjoy the evening breeze without being seen. She had the softest couch, the choicest foods, the finest wines cooled with ice and snow from the mountains. If she expressed any desires, the world would have been ransacked to satisfy her. But she wanted nothing."

"Were they married in private?" asked Nicolan, who dreaded the answers he invited but could not refrain from seeking information.

"No, no! It was held on the largest square and all could come who were able to struggle for foot space. He wanted for once to savor his triumph. He wanted all his people to see her beauty with their own eyes. She came to the ceremony loaded with precious stones—he insisted on that—and she dazzled them all. You Christians tell stories about some race of godlike servants who fly between the earth and the skies. The name I haven't on my tongue."

"Angels?"

"That is the word. She looked like one of these angels. The most beautiful one that ever visited the earth. But without wings."

Nicolan motioned over his shoulder in the direction of the banqueting hall into which the guests were still pouring. "And she will be on display again in there?"

Giso nodded. "For the last time. After tonight she will retire into seclusion. It is the emperor's wish as well as her own. And I must point out, my friends, that you had better go in now, if you want to have seats. You will find yourselves in some close and dark corner as it is."

Nicolan hesitated. This might be his last chance to see Ildico before she retired behind the impenetrable curtain that Eastern custom drapes about the consorts of rulers. Would the pain of seeing her beside the emperor like a captive, a pampered one but a prisoner nonetheless, prove unbearable? He paused, torn between the two thoughts.

"Better come," said Ivar. "You'll never cease to regret it if you don't."

"I'll regret it all my life if I do."

"What would her wish be?" asked Ivar. "I'm sure her eyes will seek into all corners of the hall. She will be hurt if she fails to have a last look at the man she loves."

Nicolan shuddered as his eyes rested on a pair of Hun warriors who passed them on their belated way into the hall, both of them thickset, short of leg, with the lumbering gait of captive bears and a feral light in their eyes.

"This is my fault," he said. "I didn't take the proper precautions."

"You were on trial for your life," reminded Ivar. "Do you think she would have left?"

"I have brought her to this!" cried Nicolan. "She sits inside now with all these eyes devouring her. It's not a bearbaiting. The order of things has been reversed. It is a beautiful white woman, tied to a stake and baited by the bears!"

Nevertheless he went inside with his companion. As Giso had intimated, the only seats left were against the wall in the most secluded corner. The emperor and his latest, and last, wife were already in their places, high up above all the company, where all could see them. Attila had fulfilled one of his promises. The chair on which Ildico sat was of solid gold and studded with enormous precious stones.

She was in white, with a gold band in her hair and a girdle of purple silk. The jewelry she wore was not conspicuous; perhaps she had refused to come as heavily adorned as she had for her wedding. Nicolan, watching her intently over a shoulder which almost blocked his view, read a bewildered and despairing expression in her eyes. There were violet shadows under them; and yet she smiled and strove to appear easy and natural.

Attila was drinking much more than usual. His flagon was raised several times in the first few minutes and he swallowed deeply. Nicolan noticed that his hand shook.

The scene was indescribable; it was wild and bestial and unhuman. The faces of the guests were dark and hirsute, and under the heavy black fringe of their hair their eyes were reptilian. They were like wraiths come down from ghostly mists on mountaintops or like half-men issuing from the gloom of malarial jungles. Cramming themselves with food from the steaming platters that the helpers of Black Scyles carried about, they also drank with such abandon that the din of their flagons on the table tops, demanding replenishment, was like the beat of galloping horses.

They stared at the white goddess beside their master and gabbled about her, and mouthed obscenities.

The Briton was watching the Hun ruler with an intent eye. "His days are numbered," he said. "He thinks that it won't be noticed when he pours something from a bottle into his wine. I've seen him do it twice. Is he using stimulants? He's eating nothing. But have you noticed the wildness in his eye?" After further watching, he gave his head a shake. "Something is going to happen, and it will be soon. I'm going to leave you here. I want to have a look at the household set up for her. Giso tells me it is close at hand, and quite large, with stables behind it. I may be able to get some of the servants to talking."

For half an hour more Nicolan sat alone in his corner. It was clear that Ildico had given up any attempt to find him in that maze of faces and prying black eyes. She was keeping her head lowered and toying with her food.

The noise suddenly lessened and then, at a signal, fell to nothing. Attila rose to his feet. He stood in silence for several moments, his eyes studying his drunken followers with a curious intentness, as though he were assessing them properly for the first time. His manner had acquired a note of dignity and, when he spoke, there was no trace of intoxication in his voice.

"I always know what my people think," he began, with a hint of censure in his tone. "And so I am aware that now some harsh things are being said. The belief is in many of your minds that I have led you to battle for the last time. You listen to the voices of the Romans, who have gone back to their marble palaces, and their gluttony and their women and their hot baths, like the soft fools they are, content to think that the terrible shadow of danger has lifted from the northern skies. They dance and sing and say that their great pope frightened the ignorant emperor of the Hun people. Behind the crumbling walls of Byzantium, they are whispering with relief in their beautiful halls. How wrong they are! How wrong you are, who hear this foolish gabble and believe there is truth in it!

"I shall conquer Rome and set my foot on the neck of Constantinople before the priests light the sacred torches and prepare the burial fires for my body! It will not be next year. My warriors have been in the saddle too long. They need a rest, a chance to see their wives and sit with their sons at the family fires. I am granting the world, and all the people in it, a full twelve months of peace. Let them make the most of it. For when that year is over, let the cowards of Rome shiver on all of their seven hills and lift up their voices to the unhearing sky! Attila will ride against them again! He will go down over the mountains in all his might, and break their hollow squares, and strew the plains with their dead. He will ride across the Tiber with his new wife beside him, and then all the world will know but one master.

"It is being said also that I am too old to marry again." He threw back his great shocky head and released a peal of laughter that filled the hall. "Hear me, ye whisperers and nodders and tattlers of idle scandal. I give ye my answer. I shall raise a large family of sons and daughters. Fine children all of them, and with hair the color of the sun!"

Attila stood in silence for several moments. Then he glanced down at his new wife and his face twisted in a smile. "The nuptial couch awaits me, so I leave you, my brave men, to your drinking." He bowed once and then walked down the steps from the dais, his bride following him. He led the way with dignity and outward sobriety to the steps of the raised floor which served him as a sleeping chamber. He drew back the curtain to admit Ildico and then followed her in, the curtain dropping back into place behind him.

Nicolan remained where he was for a long time. There was no other place to go. He did not want to think, for thought would be full of horror and madness. He sat in the midst of the drunken turmoil and stared with unseeing eyes at the roistering figures about him. He refused all offers of food and drink with savage shakes of his head, and declined to be drawn into any of the loud talk. One phrase from Attila's speech kept going around in his head, repeating itself interminably: "And all of them with hair the color of the sun."

Finally he heard a familiar voice speak at his shoulder. He turned and saw that it was Giso. The emperor's servant was pale, if such a term could be applied to his leathery skin. His eyes were filled with panic.

"Come!" he whispered. "There is something wrong."

Outside the palace the noise was almost as great as inside. Tuns of wine had been set up in all the open squares for those who had not been summoned to the banquet. The soldiers were already blissfully drunk. "Rome! Rome!" they were shouting. "Give us another chance to ride over the bodies of the long-noses!"

Ivar was waiting for them in a dark corner of the palace court-yard. Apparently he already had the news from Giso, for his manner was grave and restrained.

"A few minutes back I was listening in the little room below, where I always wait in attendance on the emperor," said Giso. "I heard a sound. At first it seemed like the mewing of a small animal but then I strained to hear better and I knew it was a woman crying. Not loudly; but in the low tone of great sorrow. I knew it must be the new wife.

"I am going to tell you a secret that no one else shares," he went on. "There is a very small trap door in the floor of the sleeping chamber. I stay under it every night, so that I am within call. This is so I can get in quietly to make sure the lights are burning. You know how great a dread he has of the dark. But I have been taught that when Attila has a new wife in his couch he will not allow interruptions. It is my custom then to sit beneath the trap door but never, under pain of death, to open it unless he calls a command to me. So, I had settled myself down to a long night of waiting when this sound of weeping reached my ears. There was no other sound. Not a footstep had I heard on the floor and not a whisper from the master himself. I decided I must risk my neck to see if they needed me. I raised the door no more than an inch, very cautiously, I promise you. The candles still burned and I could see the little bride, crouched in a corner. Then I saw that Attila was stretched out on the bed. I watched him for many minutes and he did not move. I asked myself if it was the drinking. But I was sure it couldn't be that. When he is drunk, he twitches about and mutters and groans." The fear that possessed the imperial servant showed in the eyes he turned on his two auditors. "I am sure Attila is dead!"

Nicolan roused himself from the torpor of despair in which

he had been sunk. Attila dead! That put a decidedly new face on
the situation. Now there were steps to be taken, where formerly
their hands had been tied. There was a chance to rescue the
frightened bride. He nodded briskly to Ivar and then turned to
Giso.

"Someone must go into the chamber at once," he said. "We
must know the truth."

Giso hesitated. Long years of blind obedience could not be
broken easily. He did not dare intrude.

"I am not sure it can be risked," he whispered. "If he is sleeping and my going in wakens him, his anger will be beyond belief.
He will have my head on a pole in a matter of minutes. Or perhaps he will turn me over to these savages"—motioning toward
the nearest open square from which rose sounds of wild debauchery—"to kill me as they see fit."

"Will you let me go in?"

Giso was still overcome with doubts. "It is such a risk that I
dare not think of it." He remained in this painful dilemma, turning things over slowly in his mind. "You may be right, O
Togalatus. If he is dead, there is much to be done and little
enough time to do it."

3

Nicolan followed Attila's servant into a small corner room, directly under the royal bedchamber. It was airless, unfurnished,
and unkempt, but well lighted by a beautifully designed and or-
namented silver lamp, suspended by chains from the ceiling; a
sample, no doubt, of the looting which had accompanied the Hun
conquests in eastern Europe. A steep wooden stair led to the floor
above. Nicolan removed his shoes in preparation for his invasion
of the imperial sleeping quarters but kept possession of his sword
and the dagger in his belt.

"Lift the trap no more than an inch at first," cautioned Giso,
who looked pale and disturbed. "If my master has wakened, we
will pay for this with our lives."

Nicolan raised the trap door with his head, keeping his hands
on his weapons in case he had to defend himself.

The royal chamber above was brilliantly lighted by many

lamps. His eyes encountered the royal couch first, with the inert body of the emperor stretched across it. He then glanced quickly about the room and found Ildico in a corner. She was sitting on the floor with her head in her hands, and leaning against the side of a luxurious Byzantine couch. She had stopped weeping.

The sound he had made in raising the trap door attracted her attention and her eyes became distended with increased alarm. When his face could be recognized in the widening space, she looked first incredulous and then overjoyed. Rising to her feet and gathering her long skirts in one hand, she ran on silent feet toward him. Nicolan paused for a moment to hook the door back against the wall and then advanced to meet her.

"You! Here!" she said, in an excited whisper. "How did you succeed in getting in?" Then a sense of the terror which surrounded her came back. "They will kill you. If they find you here, you will share my fate. For me there is no escape. But you —you must not be involved."

"My brave child!" said Nicolan, taking her hands in his and studying her face with worshipful intensity. "You must come away with me. We haven't much time." He glanced in the direction of the still figure on the bed. "Is he dead?"

"I don't know," she whispered. "As soon as he reached the room he began to stagger. I tried to support him but he fell heavily on the bed. I looked at him—for a moment only. He was bleeding terribly." Her voice became so low that he could scarcely hear what she was saying. "They will think I did it! They will have me killed in some dreadful way!"

He pressed her hands reassuringly. "We may be able to get away. But I must be sure about him first."

Nicolan relinquished her hands and made his way to the side of the bed. One glance was enough. Attila was lying on his back, with an arm hanging over the side of the couch. His face and neck were covered with blood, and some of it had stained the cover of the bed. To make sure, Nicolan touched one hand which was clenched convulsively. The flesh was cold. The heart of the great conqueror had stopped beating.

Despite the need for haste, Nicolan lingered a moment longer to look down at the figure of the man who had wanted the whole world and had come so close to winning it. So this was the end of all the preparations, the arming of continents, the slaughter of innocent people in the hundreds of thousands! This was the final act in the grim drama which had involved all the nations in the civilized West. The fire which had burned in the brain of one amazing man had gone out.

Did this mean that Rome would move now to regain all the wide provinces which Attila had taken from her? Would the iron foot of the legions settle again on the necks of people who longed to be free? He did not think so. Aetius was a strong leader and a resourceful general but he was not a Caesar or a Scipio Africanus. No, the day of great empires was over, he said to himself. Soon the plateau people would again be able to assert their independence and live according to their own traditions and beliefs. He must be there to play a part.

While these thoughts occupied him, Nicolan was conscious of a sense of pity, stirred in him by the figure lying so still on the wide imperial bed. How much more fitting it would have been if this great warrior had died on the field of battle, at Châlons perhaps or on the Lombardy Plain, with his dreaded horsemen riding behind him and the enemy ahead!

He stepped back and gave Ildico some whispered instructions. "Don't stop to change your clothes but find a warm cloak. If all goes well, we will have a long and cold ride tonight. Take off the jewelry you are wearing and leave it on the table. You mustn't be accused of taking anything of value with you. And hurry, dear child, for we have little time."

She did as he had bid her and then followed him on tiptoe to the head of the stairs. "Can this really be true?" she asked. "My mind has been so filled with hideous dreams that I can't believe anything good can be happening to me! Nicolan, is it really you? You are not just a dream? And are you going to take me away? Away from this place and these dreadful people?"

"We are going to try," he whispered back. "The martyrdom you were willing to face is at an end. We may be killed in getting away but that will be better than staying here for them to find you."

Ivar and Giso were waiting for them at the foot of the stairs, both filled with a desperate anxiety.

After telling them that Attila was dead, Nicolan addressed the emperor's servant. "Where is the oldest son?" he asked.

"The emperor did not want any reminders tonight of his other marriages. Ellac was ordered to stay at his house. He will be there still. And in a sulky rage, without any doubt. He was bitterly opposed to his father's determination to marry again."

"How far is it?"

"Two minutes' walk."

"We must see him at once." Nicolan turned then to Ivar. "Did you see any of the servants?"

The Briton gave a nod. "Fortunately they had allowed two of the Roymarck maids to come in the party. They recognized me and were glad of a chance to talk."

"Can they be depended upon?"

"I believe so. All the servants are loyal to their mistress. Even the two strange ones from Greece."

"God grant they are brave as well as loyal. Everything will depend on that. Take our dear lady back at once and I will join you in a quarter of an hour, if all goes well. Tell her servants to clothe her warmly and see that she has something to eat. Have the horses saddled and ready."

As they set out for the house of Prince Ellac, Nicolan asked the servant, "Do you know the password for the night?"

"I heard it when they gave it to the emperor. 'Sun goddess.'"

"Will it get us through one of the gates?"

Giso considered the point. "I think old One-Eye is on the eastern gate. Do you remember him? He's one of the emperor's oldest veterans. He's getting a little careless. If he had his share of the wine ration issued tonight—and knowing old One-Eye, I'm sure he did—he will be seeing double by this time. He's our best chance."

Nicolan asked other questions as they picked their way through the narrow streets. "Did Ellac love his father?"

"Ellac has no love for anyone. He was frightened of the emperor."

"How did he feel about his brothers? Is it true they are all by different mothers?"

"Yes. If Ellac had his way, they would all be tied up in sacks and thrown into the great river."

"Is he ambitious?"

Giso snorted. "He is sure he will be a greater man than his father when the power is in his hands. If it ever is. The truth is that Ellac is as vain as a peacock and as stupid."

"For the well-being and peace of the world," said Nicolan, solemnly, "as well as for the safety of our beautiful lady, and for our own skins, we must convince him that the shoes of the emperor are waiting for him."

4

Ellac dismissed his servants when he saw who his visitors were. "Well?" he said, in an unfriendly tone. "What brings you here? What has happened?"

"Illustrious Prince," said Nicolan, "we have your best interests at heart and we have come to give you some advice."

Ellac cut a very good figure with his straight back and legs and the features he had inherited from his mother; but on close inspection, it could be seen that his eyes were small and close-set and that his mouth was both avaricious and cruel. He looked at them with open suspicion.

"You come to give me advice? You," to Giso, "my father's servant. And you," to Nicolan, "a member of a conquered race."

"The time may be near at hand when you will need friends, Prince Ellac. If you value your rights as the first-born son."

"I need no one to tell me what my rights are." The prince addressed himself to his father's servant. "Giso, I suspect the Coated One fears I will punish him when I take my father's place on the throne. He is trying to win favor with me in advance."

"My motives are of no importance and we haven't time to discuss them now," declared Nicolan. "I came to point out to you that, when your father dies, you will have to move fast if you want a full inheritance. You have brothers, illustrious Prince, all of whom want a share of the power. And all of them, moreover, have uncles and other supporters among your father's leaders."

Ellac took a step nearer Nicolan and stared into his eyes at close range. "I think," he said, slowly, "that you have come here to tell me something. Speak up. What is it?"

"Great Prince, your father is dead."

An excited flush spread over the face of the young prince and his eyes took fire. "Dead!" he exclaimed. Then he seized Nicolan by the shoulders. "Was it a plot? Was he murdered? Were you in it?"

"There was no plot. The emperor was not killed. He has been desperately ill for some time, as you must have known. He died tonight of this disease."

"When did he die?"

"We found him a few minutes ago. But he died as soon as he left the banquet."

"How did you find out?"

"Giso heard a sound of weeping in the bedchamber. He has been under such strict orders that he feared to go in. I went in his place and I found the emperor dead on his bed."

"Was she there? The yellow-haired woman?"

"She was in a corner of the room, too frightened to move. She was afraid they would think she had killed him."

Ellac's face now showed a trace of triumph. "She killed him!" he exclaimed. "I'm sure of it. And she will have to die."

"Illustrious Prince, you have a chance to make yourself emperor if you do what we say. But first of all, you must remain calm. You mustn't let personal considerations sway you. The new wife did not kill the emperor and you won't have her killed. You must accept that first of all."

"Is she still there?"

Nicolan shook his head. "No. She is out of reach of all danger."

"Now I am sure!" cried Ellac. "It is a plot. You are in it. Perhaps you want the yellow-haired woman for yourself. Well, I will see to that, my ex-slave and traitor. You will die with her."

Nicolan did not allow himself to lose any of his coolness. He even smiled at this evidence of mounting hysteria in the first-born of Attila's sons. "You might have me killed," he conceded, "but in doing so you would lose the throne. Be calm for a moment while I explain what the situation is." He walked to the door and opened it, thus allowing the sounds of the wild debauchery in the streets to fill the room. "Prince, all I have to do is to step outside and shout at the top of my voice, 'Attila is dead!' What will happen then? Within a matter of minutes every man in the place will know—and the mad scramble for power will be under way. It's not only your brothers who will oppose you. Some of the emperor's generals and advisers hope to succeed him. How much chance will you have in such a race?

"Now," he went on, "let me present the other side. When your father left the banqueting hall, he gave orders that he was not to be disturbed until noon tomorrow. Giso promised him that no one would be allowed to enter the room. If you place sentries at each of the doors to make sure, you will have fifteen hours clear to get the power into your hands unopposed. In fifteen hours you can get your personal party together. You can bring in troops favorable to you and take command of the city. You can seize the treasury and the horse lines. You can do all this before any of the others know that the emperor is dead."

Ellac's hand fell to the sword in his belt. "Then I am emperor now. I can do what I please. First of all, I can order your death."

He tugged the sword from its scabbard but Nicolan had anticipated the move and had drawn his sword a second sooner. Ellac felt a twist on his wrist and saw the weapon fly out of his hand.

"I could kill you now," said Nicolan, "and go to another candidate who would welcome me warmly. One sound out of you and that is what I shall do." He kicked the sword to a greater distance, so Ellac had no way of retrieving it. "Now make your decision. I have told you the only way in which you can become emperor. If you want the chance, say so at once. Every moment that you hesitate is a moment lost."

Anger still seethed under Ellac's skin. "What do you want?" he demanded. "What reward? How do I know you haven't some treacherous plan to get the power yourself?"

"I want nothing. Once I am sure you intend to act as your father would, I shall leave here. And you will never see me again."

"Are you taking the yellow-haired woman with you?"

"She is already in safety. You will never see her again either."

Silence fell on the room. The prince had succeeded in putting his passion sufficiently to one side to enable him to give careful thought to the situation. Watching his face, Nicolan could see some degree of reason dawning under the scowl.

"What of Giso?" asked the prince.

"Always remember," said Nicolan, "that Giso was your father's best friend. He will be faithful to you if you become emperor."

As he left the house alone, for Giso was remaining to advise the prince on his first moves, Nicolan said to himself: "That stubborn and vicious fool will fail. He will bungle things and get himself killed. But this was the only way to make sure of the time we need. Fifteen hours of hard riding will take us beyond the danger of pursuit."

5

Old One-Eye came out of the gatehouse with unsteady steps. He looked up at Nicolan, sitting his horse in advance of his party.

"Ha, Coated One," said the captain. "Where are you going— at this time of night?"

"I am married and I am taking my wife away with me."

"Married?" The captain brushed a hand across his eyes as though he found it necessary to clear his vision. "The Great Tanjou was married today. You also? Is it catching, like a disease?"

"Can a loyal subject do better than follow such an example?"

"Is it this one?" Old One-Eye shuffled closer to the party and stared up at Ildico, who was enveloped in a warm cloak and had a woolen bonnet drawn down tightly over her head. "She's young, this one. And kind of small."

"Of course she's young and small. Do you think I would choose a fat widow with hips as broad as a saddle?"

"They say wife of emperor is—is beautiful—like a bird."

"My wife, One-Eye, is just as beautiful as the new wife of the emperor."

The captain cackled drunkenly. "I have spent whole day in— in company of mistress—more beautiful still. A fine round barrel of wine. That's right kind—of company—for a man." He teetered across the stand beside Nicolan's stirrup. "Something wrong here. Don't know what it is."

"There's nothing wrong, my brave captain."

"Yes. Something wrong. I've forgotten—something—AH!—have it. Password. You haven't—haven't given it."

"The word is 'Sun goddess.'"

"Sun goddess," mumbled the inebriated officer. "I—I think that —may be it. On your way, Coated One."

IN CONCLUSION

I WISH to make it clear that in telling the story of *The Darkness and the Dawn* I have adhered quite closely to such facts as history supplies of that spectacular conqueror, Attila the Hun. Readers may now desire to know what happened after the death of the man who became known as the Scourge of God.

Attila was buried with barbaric state, and the anticipated struggle for power among his sons and generals began at once. Ellac was defeated and killed on the banks of the Netad in Pannonia. Another son named Dengisich managed to hold together a section of the empire along the Danube for a number of years. But gradually the territories which had acknowledged the sway of the great Hun were overrun and submerged.

A year after the retreat of the savage armies from Italy, the Emperor Valentinian murdered Aetius when the latter appeared before him for an audience. The jeweled sword, which had never been drawn in defense of the Roman empire, was plunged into the breast of the victor of Châlons. The following year the cowering Valentinian was himself cut to pieces by an avenging group. The dissensions thus created paved the way for the sack of Rome by the Vandals under their king, Genseric.

The Princess Honoria returned to Italy, and it is believed that a husband of obscure rank was found for this unfortunate but not entirely worthy member of the imperial family. At any rate, she disappeared from the pages of history.

As for the fictitious characters who played their parts in the story, there is little left to be told. It may be taken for granted that Micca the Mede died in abject want, that the wealthy and amiable lady of Tergeste remained content with her fourth husband, that Harthager sired many sons with shiny black coats but that none of them could match him for speed. Finally, it is the author's belief that Roric's powers would never be fully restored and that, in consequence, Nicolan and Ildico would find it necessary to devote themselves to the leadership of their people on the Plateau; and that they lived in accord for the most part and with as much happiness as is possible between two reasonable people.

THOMAS B. COSTAIN